THE RIDDLE

Alison Croggon is an award-winning poet whose work has been published extensively in anthologies and magazines internationally. She has written widely for theatre, and her plays and opera libretti have been produced all round Australia. She is also an editor and a critic. *The Gift* was the first of the Books of Pellinor and her first fantasy novel, and *The Riddle* is the much anticipated second book in the sequence. Alison lives in Melbourne with her husband Daniel Keene, the playwright, and their three children.

For more information about the author, visit:
www.alisoncroggon.com

Books by the same author

The Gift
The Crow
The Singing

ALISON
CROGGON

**WALKER
BOOKS**

First published in Great Britain 2005 by Walker Books Ltd
87 Vauxhall Walk, London SE11 5HJ

This edition published 2012

2 4 6 8 10 9 7 5 3 1

Text © 2004 Alison Croggon
Introduction © 2012 Alison Croggon
Cover illustration © 2012 Toby Lewin
Maps drawn by Niroot Puttapipat

Published by arrangement with Penguin Books Australia Ltd.

The c...h

Th...rel

Pr...plc

All rights...nsmitted
or stored...ny means,
graphic...ing and
reco...sher.

ISBN 978-1-4063-3875-1

www.walker.co.uk

FOR ZOË

A NOTE ON THE TEXT

T*he Riddle* is the second instalment of my translation of the classic Annaren romance, the *Naraudh Lar-Chanë* (*The Riddle of the Treesong*). In *The Gift*, the first part of this epic, we are introduced to Maerad of Pellinor and Cadvan of Lirigon, and follow Maerad's adventures and travails as she comes into her Gift as a Bard. *The Riddle* picks up from the events at the end of *The Gift* and takes us on the second stage of Maerad's quest, as she seeks the Riddle of the Treesong itself.

Here the narrative moves out of Annar to encounter some of the diverse cultures and environments of Edil-Amarandh, from the communal society of the nomadic Pilanel and the warlike Jussacks to the Inaruskosani of the Arctic north. Perhaps most significantly, we begin to learn something about the profound mysteries of the Speech and the Treesong, the abiding themes of this epic.

Much recent speculation on the *Naraudh Lar-Chanë* has focused on the tensions between written and oral cultures, and some scholars – notably Dr Jean Joras in her 2010 monograph, *Written Speech: The Battle of the Pen* – argue that its unknown writer dramatizes the revolutionary impact of writing at a time when, very like Classical Athens, both oral and written cultures existed side by side. She also makes an intriguing link to the medieval Welsh poem *Cad Goddeu* (*The Battle of the Trees*), which has striking resonances with the *Naraudh Lar-Chanë*. In particular, she convincingly reanimates the long-discredited theory that the *Cad Goddeu* encodes the Ogham alphabet and esoteric Druidic secrets that were suppressed in Christianized society.

There are many aspects to such a multifarious story, but it's unarguable that the natures of orality and literacy are important themes in *The Riddle*: Maerad's conversations with the illiterate sage Ankil, and her riddling arguments with the seer Inka-Reb and the Elemental Winterking, Arkan, suggest that the introduction of written language means losses as well as gains, raising questions about how our notions of reality have changed from unmediated experience to the heavily mediated world in which we now live.

The Riddle consists of Books III and V of the *Naraudh Lar-Chanë*. I have preserved the general structure of the narrative, although I have found it necessary, in transposing this text from Annaren to modern English, to take some liberties. In particular, the division of books in the translation does not correspond with the division in the original text, and some sections have been rearranged or slightly extended. In my defence I will say that I have excised nothing and added little, making only such changes as I deemed necessary, within my limited judgement, to give the narrative the immediacy it would have possessed in its own time. I hope the result does not displease. For those who are curious about the complex structures and tropes of the original story, Mexico's University of Querétaro Press has published a fully annotated Annaren text of the *Naraudh Lar-Chanë*, a milestone in Annaren studies, for which I was honoured to write the introduction.

As a convention, throughout *The Riddle* I have used the Speech word *Dhillarearën* to refer to Named Bards with the Gift who have not been trained in the Schools of Annar, retaining the word "Bard" to specifically refer to Bards of the Schools. As those familiar with Annaren mores will be aware, people born with the Speech who did not gain their true or secret Bardic Name were unable to come into their full Gift and were considered unfortunate and, in some cases, dangerous individuals. However, there were many *Dhillarearën* in cultures outside Annar who did gain their true Names by other means and were therefore able to access their full powers. Their mores and cultural assumptions were often very different from those taught in the Annaren Bardic traditions of the Balance and the Three Arts, and so it seemed useful to make a distinction between the different *Dhillarearën* in this way.

As before, I have included appendices with further information on the cultures of Edil-Amarandh, drawn from the ongoing translation of the Annaren Scripts after their spectacular discovery in Morocco in 1991. For the amateur reader, however, the definitive studies for those interested in the background of the *Naraudh Lar-Chanë* remain *Uncategorical Knowledge: The Three Arts of the Starpeople* by Claudia J. Armstrong and Christiane Armongath's authoritative *L'Histoire de l'Arbre-chant de Annar* as well as, more recently, Clark Jackson's popular history, *The Bards*.

As always, a work such as this translation owes much to the contributions of others, many of whom I am unable to name here. Above all, I need to thank my husband, Daniel Keene, who contributed his proofreading skills yet again and bore with patient good humour the myriad inconveniences of living with a translator obsessed with such a long-term project. My children – Joshua, Zoë and Ben – demonstrated a similar grace. I also owe thanks to Richard, Jan, Nicholas and Veryan Croggon, who read the rough drafts with attention and enthusiasm and whose encouragement has meant a great deal. My thanks are also due to Chris Kloet for her excellent counsel on all aspects of the text. Lastly, I wish to record my gratitude to Professor Patrick Insole of the Department of Ancient Languages at the University of Leeds, who was unfailingly generous with his expertise on the Treesong and kindly permitted me to publish parts of his monograph subject in the appendices.

A

Melbourne,

A NOTE ON
PRONUNCIATION

MOST Annaren proper nouns derive from the Speech, and generally share its pronunciation. In words of three or more syllables, the stress is usually laid on the second syllable: in words of two syllables, (eg, *lembel*, invisible) stress is always on the first. There are some exceptions in proper names; the names *Pellinor* and *Annar*, for example, are pronounced with the stress on the first syllable.

Spellings are mainly phonetic.

a – as in *flat*. *Ar* rhymes with *bar*.

ae – a long sound, as in *ice*. *Maerad* is pronounced My–rad.

aë – two syllables pronounced separately, to sound *eye–ee*. *Maninaë* is pronounced Man–in–eye–ee.

ai – rhymes with hay. *Innail* rhymes with *nail*.

au – ow. *Raur* rhymes with *sour*.

e – as in *get*. Always pronounced at the end of a word: for example, *remane*, to walk, has three syllables. Sometimes this is indicated with ë, which indicates also that the stress of the word lies on the vowel (for example, *ilë*, we, is sometimes pronounced almost to lose the *i* sound).

ea – the two vowel sounds are pronounced separately, to make the sound ay–uh. *Inasfrea*, to walk, thus sounds: in–ass–fray–uh.

eu – *oi* sound, as in *boy*.

i – as in *hit*.

ia – two vowels pronounced separately, as in the name *Ian*.

– *uh* sound, as in *much*.

– always a hard *c*, as in *crust*, not *ice*.

– soft, as in the German *ach* or *loch*, not *church*.

dh – a consonantal sound halfway between a hard *d* and a hard *th*, as in *the*, not *thought*. There is no equivalent in English; it is best approximated by hard *th*. *Medhyl* can be said Meth'l.

s – always soft, as in *soft*, not *noise*.

Note: *Dén Raven* does not derive from the Speech, but from the southern tongues. It is pronounced Don Rah–ven.

CONTENTS

THOROLD

I	Pursuit	3
II	Busk	21
III	The Broken Promise	38
IV	Midsummer	56
V	Goats and Cheese	77
VI	The Lion of Stone	98

ANNAR

VII	The Idoiravis	115
VIII	The Stormdog	132
IX	Ossin	147
X	The White Sickness	168
XI	Encounter with Bards	183
XII	The Gwalhain Pass	197

ZMARKAN

XIII	The Pipes of the Elidhu	219
XIV	Mirka	226
XV	Alone	242
XVI	Murask	259
XVII	The Pilanel	271
XVIII	White	290

XIX	The North Glacier	308
XX	Inka-Reb	314
XXI	The Jussacks	331

ARKAN-DA

XXII	Delirium	341
XXIII	The Ice Palace	361
XXIV	The Game	374
XXV	The Song	397
XXVI	Wolfskin	424
XXVII	Pellinor	445

APPENDICES

The Peoples of Edil-Amarandh	467
The Elidhu	477
The Treesong	483
Notes	487

One is the singer, hidden from sunlight
Two is the seeker, fleeing from shadows
Three is the journey, taken in danger
Four are the riddles, answered in treesong:
Earth, fire, water, air
Spells you OUT!

Traditional Annaren nursery rhyme
Annaren Scrolls, Library of Busk

THOROLD

Do not twine garlands of myrtle for my forehead
Nor pluck sweet roses to adorn me
Make me a crown of sombre violets
    For I am dying

The sweet lips of the maidens of Busk
And the flashing feet of dancing goatherds
Will never again quicken my desire
    For I am dying

Come to me merciful Meripon
In your ebony chariot drawn by swallows
From the dim halls beyond the Gates
    For I am dying

I kiss the peaks of Lamedon with my eyes
And the white arms of the passionate sea
Which loves this beautiful island that I love
    For I am dying

The Song of Theokas, Library of Busk

I

PURSUIT

MAERAD was a being of the upper regions of air, bodiless and free, without self or memory or name. She gazed at the landscape beneath her, fascinated. For a long time she didn't even recognize it as a landscape; it looked like a strange and awesome painting. For as far as she could see there stretched a huge red expanse covered with ripples, like sand under water; but these ripples, she began to understand, must be enormous. She was very high up and she could see very far, and there were no clouds at all, only a tiny shadow moving over the earth, which she realized after a while was her own. She seemed to be flying with some purpose in a particular direction, although she couldn't remember what the purpose was.

After a while, the land changed: the red ripples ran up against a ridge of purple rock and stopped, and she was passing over mountains whose shadows stretched long and sharp behind them. On the other side of the range ran tracks like rivers, lighter veins spreading in delicate fans, but she could see no water in them. The colours of the earth changed to subtle purples and dull greens that signalled vegetation. In the far distance she could see a whiteness that seemed to gather light to itself: it looked like a lake. But a lake of salt, she thought with surprise, not water…

Then everything shifted. She was no longer in the sky, but standing on what seemed to be the spine of a high ridge of bare rock that dropped sheer before her. She looked over a wide plain that stretched to the horizon. The soil was still a strange red orange, but this land was nothing like the one she had flown over: it seemed blasted, poisoned, although she could not say how. As far as she could see there were rows and rows of tents, interspersed with large open spaces where masses of figures performed some kind of drill. A red sun sent low, level rays over the plain, casting black shadows back from the tents. Somehow the figures didn't seem human: they marched with a strange unchanging rhythm that cast a chill over her heart.

Maerad had never seen an army before, and the sight shocked her: so many thousands, uncountable thousands, anonymous as ants, gathered together for the sole aim of injury and death. She turned away, suddenly sickened with dread, and saw behind her, on the other side of the ridge, a white, bare expanse. The sun struck up from it, hurting her eyes as savagely as if someone had stabbed her. She cried out, clutching her face, and stumbled and fell. Her body, now heavy and corporeal, fell with the ominous slowness of dream: down, down, down, towards the cruel rocks below.

Maerad woke, gasping for breath, and sat bolt upright. This was an unwise thing to do, as she was sleeping in a hammock slung below the deck of a small fishing smack called the *White Owl*. The hammock swung dangerously and then, as she flailed for balance in the pitch dark, tipped her out onto the floor. Still trapped in her dream, Maerad screamed, putting out her hands to break her fall, and hit the wooden floorboards.

She lay still, breathing hard, as above her a trapdoor was flung open and someone came stumbling down the steps. Maerad could see his form silhouetted against a patch of stars, and then a soft light bloomed in the darkness, illuminating a tall, dark-haired man who moved easily with the motion of the boat.

"Maerad? Are you all right?"

Maerad sat up, rubbing her head. "Cadvan," she said with relief. "Oh, I had a terrible dream. I'm sorry, did I cry out?"

"Cry out? It sounded as if a Hull were in here, at least."

Maerad managed a wan smile. "No Hulls," she said. "Not yet."

Cadvan helped her up, and Maerad groped her way to a bench along the walls of the tiny cabin and sat down. Her hands were trembling.

"Bad dreams?" said Cadvan, looking at her intently. "It is little wonder you should have nightmares, after what we've been through."

Maerad felt his unasked question. "I think it was a foredream," she said, brushing her hair out of her eyes. "But I don't understand what it was about. It was horrible." Foredreams, in Maerad's experience, were always horrible.

"Tell me, then." Cadvan sat next to her on the bench.

Maerad haltingly told him of the dream. Put into words, it didn't sound so awful: the worst thing about it was the feeling of despair and horror it had inspired within her. Cadvan listened gravely, without interrupting, and when she finished there was a short pause.

"What you describe sounds to me like the deserts south of Dén Raven," he said. "And perhaps your dreaming semblance stood on the peaks of the Kulkilhirien, the Cruel Mountains above the Plains of Dust, where the Nameless One was said to have marshalled his forces in the days before the Great Silence."

"Was it a vision, maybe, of the past?" Maerad looked earnestly at Cadvan, and he met her eyes.

"It is possible that you might dream of the past," he said. "Foredreams come from beyond the Gates, where time is not as it seems on this earth. But I think it more likely you saw the armies of the Dark as they are now, massing in the south for an attack on Turbansk."

Maerad drew in her breath sharply, and thought of her brother Hem, now riding to Turbansk with their friend Saliman.

"I hope that I dreamed of something else," she said. "It was an evil thing I saw. The soldiers looked – they didn't seem to be human beings."

"They sound like dogsoldiers to me," said Cadvan. "They are not creatures born as others are; they are forged of metal and flesh by some ill art in the mighty armories of Dén Raven. They are invested with a strange parody of life, so they seem to have will and intelligence."

Maerad's heart constricted with fear for her brother: so young, so damaged, so lately found and lost again. For an instant, she saw his face vividly before her, with its mixture of arrogance and mischief and vulnerability and, behind that, a bitter desolation she did not quite understand, but which pierced her heart with pity.

She had, by the strangest of chances – although Cadvan said it was not chance at all – discovered Hem in the middle of the wilderness. She had long thought him dead, slaughtered as a baby during the sack of Pellinor. He was now a gangly twelve-year-old boy, dark skinned like their father, and unlike Maerad, whose skin was very white; but they both shared the same dark hair and intense blue eyes.

She had felt bonded to Hem even before she knew who he was. For most of her sixteen years Maerad had been unbearably lonely, and when she had found Hem – silent, terror-stricken and even more destitute than she had been – her starved soul had flowered towards him: she loved him fiercely, protectively, with all her passion. The thought of the army she had seen in her dream marching on Turbansk, marching on her brother, filled her with black dismay.

* * *

Cadvan broke her gloomy reverie by offering her a brown stoppered bottle and a glass from a cupboard nearby. "Have some of this," he said.

It was a strong spirit designed to ward off chills on cold nights at sea, and Maerad gulped it gratefully, feeling the liquor sear a path down her gullet. She coughed and then sat up straightly, feeling more substantial.

"If my dream is true, it is a very great army," she said, at last. "Turbansk will be hard pressed."

"It is ill news, and not only for Turbansk," said Cadvan. "But even that vast force is only one piece in the great stratagem the Nameless One is now unleashing. And you, Maerad, are as significant to him as that huge army. Maybe more so. Everything turns on you."

Maerad bowed her head, oppressed beyond measure by Cadvan's words. On me? she thought bitterly. And yet she knew it was true.

She pressed her hands together to stop their trembling, and glanced at Cadvan as he sat down again beside her, his face sombre and abstracted with thought.

Their first meeting came vividly into her mind. It had been a mere three months before, but to Maerad it felt like a lifetime. She had been milking a cow in Gilman's Cot, the grim northern settlement where, for most of her short life, she had been a slave. He had stood silently before her, amazed and disconcerted that she could see through his charm of invisibility.

It had been a morning like any other, notable only for being the Springturn when winter, in theory at least, began to retreat from the mountains. Then, as now, his face had been shadowed with exhaustion and anxiety and – Maerad thought – an indefinable sadness. Despite everything – despite his being a stranger, despite her fear of men, learned from the violence of life in the cot – she had trusted him at once. She still didn't really know why; it went too deep for words.

It was Cadvan who had revealed to her who she was, and he had helped to unravel some of the history of her family. With her mother Milana, Maerad had been captured and sold as a very small child after the sack of Pellinor, the School where she had been born. It was Cadvan who helped her escape from the misery of slavery, who had told her of her Gift and opened up to her the world of Bards. He had taken her to the School of Innail, and for the first time in her conscious life she had found a place where she felt at home. A sudden sharp ache constricted Maerad's throat as she thought of Silvia, who had become like a mother to her in the short time they had known each other; and then of Dernhil, who had loved her. Despite that love she had spurned him, and when Dernhil had been killed by Hulls – the Black Bards who were servants of the Nameless One – she had mourned both his absence and a vanished possibility that she would always regret.

She wished fiercely that she had been able to stay in Innail – *loved as you should be*, Dernhil had said to her – and that she could have spent a quiet life learning the Bardic Arts of Reading, Tending and Making. She would have liked nothing better in the world than to learn the scripts of Annar and decipher its immense riches of poetry and history and thought, or to study herblore and healing and the ways of animals, to observe the rites of the seasons and keep the Knowing of the Light, as Bards had done for centuries before her. Instead, she was on a tiny boat in the middle of a dark sea, hundreds of leagues from the gentle haven of Innail, fleeing from darkness into darkness, her future more uncertain than it had ever been.

It wasn't fair. The tale of her life since leaving Gilman's Cot had been of finding what she loved, and almost at once losing it. Closely pursued by the Dark, she and Cadvan had fled Innail, heading for Norloch, the chief centre of the Light in Annar. During their journey across Annar, Maerad had at last come into the Speech, the inborn language of the Bards, and had found her full powers. Her abilities were much greater and stranger than those of a normal Bard: she had vanquished a wight, the malign spirit of a dead king from the days of the Great Silence, which was beyond the magery of even the most powerful Bards. She had discovered that part of her strangeness was her Elemental blood, her Elidhu ancestry that led back to Ardina, Queen of the golden realm of Rachida, which lay hidden in the centre of the Great Forest. But she was still nowhere near able to control the powers of her Gift.

When they had at last reached Norloch...

Maerad flinched, thinking of the burning citadel they had left behind them only two days earlier. It was in Norloch that she had met Nelac, Cadvan's old teacher, a wise and gentle man who had instated her as a full Bard of the White Flame. The simple ceremony had revealed her Bardic Name, the secret name that was an aspect of her deepest self. It had confirmed that she was, as Cadvan had suspected, the Fated One, prophesied to bring about the downfall of the Nameless One in his darkest rising. *Elednor Edil-Amarandh na*: the starspeech echoed in her mind, with its cold, inhumanly beautiful music. Yet, for all her innate potencies, Maerad was but a young girl, unschooled and vulnerable: it was a mystery to her how she was to defeat the Nameless One, and it seemed more likely to her than not that she would fail. Prophecies, as Cadvan had once told her, often went awry; her birth was foreseen, but not her choices, and it was through her choices that her destiny would unfold.

And it was in Norloch that she had last seen her brother. The loss of Hem seemed the cruellest of all. She had found, in Hem, a missing part of herself, and losing him was the old grief all over again, multiplied by new anxieties. When they had fled Norloch, it had been safer to split their paths: Cadvan and Maerad's path lay north, and Saliman took Hem south to his home in Turbansk, there to learn the ways of Barding. But even if Turbansk did not fall, even if Hem survived the coming war, there was no certainty that she would live to see him again. She was pursued by the Dark, and now perhaps by the Light as well: the Bards of Norloch had no doubt put a price on both their heads. Enkir, the First Bard, might have been killed in the battle that raged as they fled Norloch: Maerad hoped with all her heart that he was dead.

Involuntarily, Maerad's lip curled. A decade ago, Enkir had sold Maerad and her mother, Milana, into slavery. He had betrayed the School of Pellinor, and because of him it had been burned to the ground, its people slain without mercy, its learning and music smashed beyond recall, its beauty quenched for ever. Because of Enkir, Maerad had seen her father murdered, and had watched her mother wither away in Gilman's Cot, her power broken. But Enkir was cunning, and very few people knew or suspected his treachery. He was the First Bard in Norloch, the most important in all Annar. Who, not knowing what Maerad knew, would believe that such a man was a traitor? And who would trust the word of a young untutored girl against the word of a First Bard?

It had been two days since they had fled Norloch, rescued by Owan d'Aroki in his humble fishing smack. They had slipped unseen out of the harbour, even as the citadel's high towers collapsed in flames and a terrible battle was fought on the quays. Now they ran north-west on a charmed wind, scudding swiftly over the swell. The sea's deep solitude had done much to clear Maerad's mind, although she found it hard to sleep on the boat and suffered recurring bouts of seasickness. But now the weather was fair, and Owan said they should reach Busk, the main town of the Isle of Thorold, within another two days.

Perhaps, at the end of this brief, uncomfortable voyage, they would be able to rest. She longed for rest as a thirsty man longs for water; every fibre of her being cried out for it. But underneath, Maerad knew that even if they found a haven it would be temporary at best: nowhere was safe.

And, overriding everything, was the need to find the Treesong, although no one really knew what it was.

The Treesong is an ancient word for the Speech, Nelac had told her in Norloch. *It signifies that which is beyond words. And it is also a song, supposedly written down when the Bards first appeared in Annar, in which the mystery of the Speech is held. It is long lost. Even in the first days after the Silence, when Bards began to find again much that had vanished, many said that it never existed.* Maerad felt it was like being on a quest for moonbeams.

All this passed through Maerad's mind quicker than it would take to tell, and she sighed heavily, prompting Cadvan to turn and look at her, his eyes suddenly clear and present. Around his left cheek and eyesocket curled the marks of three cruel whiplashes, injuries from their battle with a wight. The wounds were still criss-crossed with tiny herringbone stitches, and when Cadvan smiled, as he did now, he winced slightly.

"Well, Maerad," he said gently. "I suppose you should try to go back to sleep. It's deep night yet, and we still have some hard sailing to do."

"As if I know anything about sailing," said Maerad. "You know I just get in the way. But maybe I could do some watching for you."

"We need a lookout," said Cadvan, nodding. "It is wearing, I tell you, sailing so hard with just me and Owan. The sooner we reach Busk, the sooner we can rest."

* * *

The sun rose the following day in a perfectly blue sky. Owan gravely professed himself satisfied with the weather, and said they were well on track for the Isle of Thòrold.

With his olive skin, lively face and grey eyes, Owan looked typically Thoroldian, but he was uncharacteristically taciturn for those loquacious islanders, although it could have been exhaustion. Both he and Cadvan were grey with tiredness. The *White Owl* was Owan's pride; she might only have been a small fishing vessel, but she was a beauty of her kind, every spar and plank lovingly laid. In her making each part of her had been embedded with charms, to keep her from upset or to ward away hostile creatures of the deep; and she had also a steering spell placed on her so she could, in a limited way, sail herself. Unfortunately, under the stiff wind Cadvan summoned to the sails this was too risky, and Owan and Cadvan took turns day and night on the tiller. When Cadvan was too tired to keep the wind, the *White Owl* sailed on the sea's weather; but he never slept for more than a couple of hours at a time. Maerad had already witnessed Cadvan's powers of endurance, but his stubborn will impressed her anew: his face was haggard and his mouth grim, but he moved with the alertness of a well-rested man.

Maerad sat in the bows, trying to stay out of the way. She was still disconcerted by how tiny the boat was, a mote in the vastness of the ocean. And she was miserable with seasickness. Cadvan managed to stay it a little, but he was so busy she felt hesitant to bother him and had decided to suffer it, unless it became unbearable. She hadn't been able to eat for the past day and night, and her emptiness made her feel light-headed.

There was, Maerad thought, nothing to see except water: water, water and more water, and on the northern horizon a darkish blur that might be land, or might be a bank of cloud. It frightened her a little: she had spent her childhood among mountains, and had never imagined that space could seem so limitless. The *White Owl* was pitching strangely with the wind, bumping across the tops of the swell, which probably accounted for her nausea, and she gazed with an empty mind across the endless blue-green backs of the waves.

By mid-morning she had entered an almost trance-like state, but towards mid-afternoon something captured her attention. At first she followed it idly with her eyes: a darker current rippling cross-ways through the larger patterns of the waves, beyond where the path of their wake spread and dispersed over the surface of the sea. As she watched, it seemed to draw a little nearer. She sat up straighter and leaned forward, squinting, and stared. It was hard to be sure, but it did seem to her that it was a definite trail, and she had an uneasy feeling that it was following their boat. It had something about it, even at that distance, of a hunting dog on a scent.

She called Cadvan, and nodding towards Owan he came over to Maerad. Wordlessly, she pointed down the *White Owl*'s wake, and he leaned forward, shading his eyes.

"Can you see something?" she asked.

He shook his head.

"There's a sort of … trail, in the water," said Maerad. "I think it's following us. Just there, by the wake."

Cadvan finally saw what she was pointing at, and studied it briefly. "Have you been watching it long?" he asked.

"A while. It's hard to tell at this distance, but I think it's drawing closer."

Cadvan called Owan over. He lashed the tiller and came back to them, and when he saw the dark line in the water his face tightened.

"Do you know what it is?" asked Cadvan.

"No," said Owan. "But I can guess." He looked at Cadvan. "And if it is what I'm thinking, then it would be best to outrun it. Can you whistle any stronger wind, do you think?"

Cadvan grimaced up at the sails. "Perhaps," he said. "How strong is the *Owl*, Owan? I fear her breaking if the wind blows too hard."

"Strong enough," said Owan shortly, and went back to the tiller. Cadvan's shoulders sagged, and he sighed, as if he were mentally preparing himself for an effort beyond his strength. He went back to his post near the prow of the boat and lifted his arms, speaking words that were tossed away by the wind so Maerad could not hear them. She knew he was using the Speech, and she felt a prickle in her skin, a resonance of magery. At once, the sails bulged with a new, stiff blast of wind, and the *White Owl* sprang willingly forward, like a horse urged to a gallop, which it had, until that moment, restrained within itself. Maerad's neck snapped back with the speed, and she put out her hand to steady herself and looked down the wake towards the ominous track in the sea behind them.

For a little while it seemed to vanish, and she relaxed; but with the new motion of the craft her sickness came back, worse than before. She battled with herself, trying to find a stillness within her body that could counterbalance the nausea, and it seemed to work for a moment. But when she looked out over the bows again, her nausea returned threefold. Whatever it was had more than matched their new speed; it was now cutting through the *White Owl*'s wake, gaining on them, and two white waves like wings fanned out behind a dark form she could now see breaking the surface of the water.

She cried out, and Cadvan and Owan looked back. Owan shrugged his shoulders.

"You can't whistle up more?" he asked Cadvan flatly.

Cadvan shook his head.

"Well, then..." Owan stared over the bows, scratching his head. "I'm pretty sure we're right. I've never seen one so fast, though. And it's behaving strange, for an ondril."

"What's an ondril?" asked Maerad, trying to sound as casual as Cadvan and Owan. They could have been discussing a slight problem with that evening's meal.

"A kind of snake, a serpent of the sea," said Cadvan. "I mislike this."

"It's a mighty big one, if it is," said Owan. "They usually leave fishing craft well alone, unless you're unlucky enough to venture into their territory. But we're going so fast now, we'd have long gone past its borders. Normally an ondril would have just turned round by now and gone back to its place."

"It has the stink of Enkir about it," said Cadvan.

"So he lives," said Owan. "I'd believe anything, after what I saw in Norloch. Didn't know Enkir was a sea mage, all the same."

"He is many things, alas, and few of them good," said Cadvan. "And he draws on powers far beyond his own native abilities. I think he has summoned some creature of the Abyss out of the shadows. I did not think that he was dead; I think this monster proves that he yet moves against us."

"Well, what can we do?" Maerad stood up, suddenly impatient.

"We'll have to fight it," said Cadvan. "It's obviously following us. And we're not going to outrun it."

Maerad looked back. The creature, whatever it was, was gaining fast. Its head, the only part of it that was visible, was a massive black wedge that drove through the water like a spear; even at that distance it looked unimaginably huge. At the thought of being attacked in their flimsy boat in the middle of a great desert of water, Maerad's stomach lurched with fright.

"I'd let the wind drop, if I were you, Cadvan," said Owan, breaking the heavy silence. "No point in using up that energy now."

"Yes, it's no use having it snapping at our tail," answered Cadvan.

Instantly the sails slackened, and the *White Owl* slowed and then almost halted completely. Without the charmed wind, only the lightest of breezes ruffled the waves. Owan spun the boat around, and they looked towards the creature driving inexorably towards them.

"Do you think you could sail towards it?" Cadvan asked suddenly.

Owan cocked his head and thought briefly. "Aye, easily enough, if you put a breeze in the sails," he said. "Think you that's a good idea?"

"I don't," said Maerad violently. "I think it's mad."

"We may be able to wrest the initiative," said Cadvan. He looked at Maerad and smiled with a sudden sweetness that illuminated and transformed his sombre face. "Come, Maerad. It is better far to put away fear, than to be driven by it. You know that."

Yes, I know that, Maerad thought sardonically. But I'm tired of having to be brave when really I'm so terrified I scarce know what to do. She swallowed hard, and then stood and drew her sword.

Cadvan nodded, lifted his arms and spoke. "*Il sammachel Estarë de* ... I summon you, Wind of the West..." Hearing the Speech used in its full power always sent a thrill down Maerad's spine, as if she had stepped into a fresh mountain spring from the morning of the world. For a moment she forgot their peril, feeling only the irresistible tug of Cadvan's command, and turned to face him. He glimmered faintly with a silvery light. The sails bulged and the *White Owl* creaked as she leaned into the wind, and Owan guided the boat back down her wake, towards the black thing that now made its own huge wake as it swept towards them. The speed with which they rushed towards each other was dizzying.

Cadvan turned to Maerad, his hair whipping his face.

"I think this creature does not expect us to rush it," he said. He drew his sword, Arnost, and it glimmered with a pale fire. "Perhaps we will catch it unawares. Look to your Gift, Maerad."

Maerad held up Irigan, her own sword, and an answering light blazed up from its hilt.

"Owan, I'll make a fastening charm so you are not thrown out if the monster hits the *Owl*," Cadvan said. "Stay your course until the last moment, then turn north – sharp as you are able. Maerad and I will attempt the rest."

Owan nodded, his face unreadable.

"You do the fastening, too, Maerad," Cadvan continued. "Be alert. I have not encountered one of these creatures before. The eyes are vulnerable; hit there first. And it is said that under the carapace of the head there is a soft spot, just where the skull meets the neck. Watch for it! And may the Light protect us!"

Maerad nodded fiercely, clutching her blade. There was no time for fear: the monster was so close that she could see its head scything through the waves, a fearsome wedge-shaped thing, bigger than their boat, greenish-black and spotted with yellow-and-green weeds and parasites, with two huge pale unblinking eyes and a wide lipless mouth. It stank like brackish, stagnant water. As their tiny craft neared it, the mouth opened to reveal a nightmare of fangs, rows behind rows of snaggled yellowish teeth, like a cave of knives.

Maerad thought they were going to plunge into that dark gullet, to be shredded and crushed. For a crucial moment she was too terrified to move. Beside her, Cadvan lashed forward with his sword, and a bolt of white light sprang from the blade and hit the fearsome head. Maerad saw one eye go out like a quenched lamp, suddenly clouded with black blood, and then, just as Maerad thought they would surely be swallowed, the sail swung around and the *White Owl* darted past the horrific mouth, which snapped shut on nothing with a crash, drenching them with seawater.

The boat was bobbing wildly, but Cadvan leant forward, his sword raised, and Maerad scanned the side of the monster with furious concentration. Suddenly she saw it, where the carapace of the skull left a gap, revealing darker, unscaled skin. She was filled suddenly with a passionate hatred: she remembered Enkir's pitiless eyes, his cold voice that had condemned her to slavery. She struck out with her blade, crying aloud words that seemed to come into her mind without volition: *Takarmernë, nachadam kul de!* Be cursed, monster of the Dark!

Two bolts of fire arced from the boat: one bounced off the hard scales of the creature's long body and vanished sizzling into the waves, but the other clove deep into the unmailed skin. The sea boiled as the ondril thrashed violently and roared, a deafening noise that raised all the hairs on Maerad's skin. For a while she saw nothing but a white chaos of spray. She heard Cadvan shouting "Back!", fearing they would be swamped, and felt the boat move under Owan's sure handling.

When she could see again, they were a safe distance from the ondril. For the first time, Maerad could see how big it really was: it had a thick, scaled body that stretched back for hundreds of spans, coiling and uncoiling in spasms of fury and agony that sent up geysers of spray. A black cloud of blood boiled out into the sea, reaching even to their boat, and Cadvan called Owan to draw back still further.

"Have we killed it?" Maerad asked.

"I doubt it," said Cadvan. "It may give up and go to lick its wounds. But I think we dare not count on that. I think it more likely that it will come for us now in a fury of revenge, and we will be most imperilled if it dives and comes up from beneath. I think we will need to blind it, at least."

He turned to Owan, and Owan simply nodded. "Best be quick, I reckon," he said. "Before it works out where we are."

"I fear the *Owl* might be swamped," said Cadvan.

"My beauty won't sink," said Owan with certainty. "Not unless she's broken to bits." He began to steer steadily back into the eye of the maelstrom, where the ondril was beating the ocean into a tumult.

Maerad shared none of Owan's confidence, but said nothing. She drew a long breath and then took her place by Cadvan on the prow of the boat, her sword raised in readiness.

They were tossed wildly as they neared it, and but for the fastening charms would surely have been thrown into the ocean. It was much more difficult now to see where to strike; all was a seething chaos of scales and water. Maerad did not understand how they could avoid being smashed to pieces, but for the moment fear had left her, to be replaced with a steely resolve. She squinted fiercely, scanning her side of the boat.

Suddenly, no more than ten paces from the rail, the head broke the surface of the water, rearing up before them, the mouth opening wider and wider and wider. Time seemed to slow almost to a halt as the ondril reared high, towering monstrously above them. Maerad cried out, and she and Cadvan struck for its one remaining eye. Both bolts hit their mark, and a black torrent of blood burst out and splattered onto the deck. The monster roared and fell back, drenching them all with a huge rush of seawater that washed over the deck and fell in streaming torrents down the sides, and Owan was guiding the tiny *Owl* so it darted away, slipping as nimbly as a minnow evading the rush of a pike.

This time they kept running. Cadvan put a swift wind in the sails, and they scudded westward over the waves. Owan lashed the tiller and silently disappeared below decks, and Cadvan and Maerad both sat down heavily, looking behind them at the sea still boiling with the ondril's fury, which now dwindled fast behind them.

Owan shortly reappeared with the small brown bottle of liquor, and they all took a swig. Maerad studied the deck; there was no sign of their ordeal anywhere. The ondril's blood had all been swept away by the water, and around them was a calm, blue sea, in which it seemed impossible such monsters should exist.

Cadvan toasted Owan and Maerad tiredly. "A brave bit of sailing, Owan," he said. "And well marked, Maerad. That was a great stroke, behind the head; I missed that one. I should not have liked to have gone down that gullet."

"By the Light, I think not!" said Owan.

Maerad looked away over the sea, feeling nothing but a vast emptiness. She had no sense of triumph, nor even relief. All she felt was a returning wisp of nausea. The only good thing about being frightened half to death, she thought, was that it made her forget all about being seasick.

I I

BUSK

FROM the sea, the town of Busk seemed to have been scattered along the cliffs of the Isle of Thorold by some idle giant. Its roads and alleys scrambled around the steep hills in a crazy but picturesque disorder, and its whitewashed buildings gleamed like blocks of salt amid the dark greens of cypresses and laurels and olives. Busk was a busy trading port, its harbour well protected against both storm and attack by a maze of reefs and currents, and by the arms of its encircling cliffs. These had been extended by tall crenellated breakwaters that ended in two harbour towers.

As the *White Owl* neared the towers, Maerad began to feel apprehensive. The entrance was very narrow, and the tower walls loomed over their small craft and cast a chilly shadow over the water. The echoes of the waves slapping on stone seemed unnaturally loud, even threatening. The ancient stone, green with slime and encrusted with barnacles and limpets, was uncomfortably close. She wondered if anyone watched their approach through the slits she saw high up in the walls.

She breathed out heavily when they sailed through into the sunlight again and entered the bustling haven of Busk. The buildings on the harbourside were plain and whitewashed, casting back the bright summer sunshine with a blinding glare, but any sense of austerity was offset by the activity going on around. The quay was crowded with rough woven baskets full of blue-and-silver fish packed in salt, giant coils of rope, piles of round cheeses coated in blue-and-red wax, lobster pots, barrels of wine and oil and huge bolts of raw silk, and dozens of people.

As she stepped onto the stone quay, it seemed to Maerad's startled perception that everyone was arguing. Many traders were bargaining, scoffing in disbelief at the prices offered, talking up the inimitable value of their wares. Elsewhere fishers were bringing in their catch, shouting orders at each other, and sailors were working on their boats or greeting friends, laughing and swearing. The teeming, noisy harbourside was a shock after the silence and solitude of their days at sea, and she glanced back at her two companions, momentarily discomfited.

Cadvan and Maerad fondly took their leave of Owan, promising to meet him soon, and headed up the steep streets to the School of Busk. Cadvan picked his way through the tangle of tiny streets and alleys and Maerad looked around eagerly, her tiredness forgotten.

The people of Busk seemed to live outside on their vine-shaded balconies; it afforded them the pleasures of chaffing passing friends, minding each other's business and exchanging gossip. She saw them washing, eating, dressing children and cooking, all in the open air. Cadvan noticed her staring.

"Thoroldians are a people apart," he said, smiling. "They think Annarens are cold and snobbish. Annarens, on the other hand, think Thoroldians are impertinent and have no sense of privacy."

"I think I like it," said Maerad. "It seems very ... lively. But I don't know that I'd like to live like that all the time."

"Perhaps not," said Cadvan. "But, of course, it's different in winter: everybody moves inside."

The School of Busk was set above the main town, surrounded by a low wall that served as a demarcation rather than a barrier. Here the ubiquitous whitewashed houses and twisting alleys gave way to wide streets lined with stately cypresses and olive trees. The road, like the roads in the town, was flagged with stone and threw back the sunlight blindingly. Behind the trees were Bard houses built of marble and the local pink granite, fronted by wide porticos with columns ornately decorated in bright colours and leafed with gold; many were entwined with ancient vines, their fat fruit purpling in the sun. Maerad glimpsed the dark tops of conifers behind high walls, and thought longingly of cool private gardens.

Unlike Innail and Norloch, the only Schools Maerad knew, Busk was not planned in concentric circles – the geography of the island, steep and irregular, made this impossible. And, as Cadvan said, the Thoroldians liked to do things their own way in any case. The streets were laid in terraces, with flights of broad steps to connect the different levels, and it was very easy to get lost until you knew your way about, because they seemed to follow no rational order. There were no towers in Busk, apart from the small ones guarding the harbour; the grander buildings were simply broader and wider, and built with higher roofs.

For all its impressive architecture, the School was as lively as the lower town. It was now mid-afternoon, when, as Maerad would discover later, Thoroldians put the business of the day aside for pleasanter pursuits. The streets themselves were deserted; the sun was really too hot for going out. As they walked through the School, Maerad saw that some of the wide, shady porticos were populated with Bards. Like everyone else in Busk, they all seemed to be involved in lively conversations and disputes. They looked up curiously when Cadvan and Maerad passed, and some waved a greeting. Cadvan smiled back.

Maerad stopped shyly, lingering outside one of the houses, burning with curiosity. The Bards lounged in comfortable wicker chairs arranged around low wooden tables, most of which were laden with platters of fruit and carafes of wine and water. She watched a woman, who was sprawled in a chair, declaiming a poem to a small group of Bards. They listened intently until she finished and then broke into a furious argument. The woman, who was tall and heavy boned, with a bright scarf wound about her head and long green earrings, stood up and argued back fiercely, finally throwing her arms up in the air in frustration and cuffing her most vocal critic, to the cheers of half the table.

The Bards alarmed Maerad more than the townsfolk; she was not, after all, a Thoroldian, and could be expected to be different. But in the School she was a Bard: one of them. She could not imagine being comfortable among such people.

Maerad looked sideways at Cadvan. "Are the Bards of Busk always so loud?" she asked.

Cadvan gave her an amused glance. "Pretty much, Maerad. But it's more lively than Norloch, don't you think?"

"Well, yes," she answered feelingly, thinking of the stern Bards she had met there. "But, you know, they seem just as frightening, in a different way."

"You'll get used to it," he said. "In a way, you're a Thoroldian yourself."

"I am?" Maerad turned to him open-mouthed.

"Of course you are. I told you," he said, with the edge of impatience he always had when he had to repeat himself, even if it was something he had only mentioned in passing two months before. "The House of Karn fled to Thorold during the Great Silence. Thorold was always one of the most independent of the Seven Kingdoms, and was a chief point of resistance to the Nameless One. I suppose it's eight hundred years or so since last your family was here, so you can be excused for feeling a little strange. But the Thoroldians are true bastions of the Light. The only real problem will be keeping up with their consumption of wine. I don't know how they do it."

As they were speaking, they stopped in front of a house and turned in to the porch. Maerad was blinded in the sudden shade, and Cadvan led her blinking through two large bronze double doors into a huge atrium flagged with marble. Orange and lemon trees and flowers were planted in big glazed pots, giving off a delicious perfume, and jasmine climbed around the slim columns. In its centre, in the middle of an intricate mosaic of birds and flowers, played a fountain. Maerad relaxed in the coolness and looked around. The atrium seemed to be deserted.

Cadvan rang a brass handbell that stood on a small plinth, and then sat down on a wooden bench and stretched out his legs.

"Someone will come in a moment," he said. "Sit down."

"It's lovely," said Maerad. She sat next to him, content to do nothing. She felt again how tired and grimy she was, and how much she longed to wear clean clothes and to sleep in a proper bed. Was it only yesterday they had driven off the ondril? It seemed like last year.

"Do you think we could stay here a while?" she asked.

"That is my plan," said Cadvan. "I'm tired of travel myself. And Busk has a very good library, one of the oldest in all Edil-Amarandh; I am hoping there might be some ancient writings there that refer to the Treesong. It would help if we knew what it was we're searching for."

Maerad turned to look at the fountain. The sunlight struck off the droplets in little prisms, and its murmurous music sank into her hypnotically, as if it were a song of which she almost understood the words. She didn't notice the old man who stepped out of the shade at the other end of the atrium until he was only a few paces away.

Cadvan stood up, extending his hand in greeting. "Elenxi," he said. "Greetings."

"*Samandalamë*, Cadvan," said the old Bard, smiling widely. He had strong, white teeth. "Welcome."

Maerad looked at him wonderingly; he must have been a giant in his youth, and still towered over Cadvan. His hair and beard were utterly white, and his dark eyes were sharp, the eyes of a much younger man. Like Cadvan, he used the Speech, the inborn language of Bards, and not the common tongue of the Thoroldians. It was much more than a courtesy to strangers: to use it was an offering of trust as much as a practicality. It was said to be impossible to lie when using the Speech.

"My companion is Maerad of Pellinor," said Cadvan. Maerad bowed her head, and Elenxi, bowing his head in return, gave her a swift, piercing glance, but made no comment. "We are here seeking refuge, fleeing peril on land and sea, and bring news of great import."

"You are always welcome, Cadvan," said Elenxi. "And I have heard somewhat of Maerad of Pellinor." Again he directed that sharp, disconcerting gaze at her. "Nerili will no doubt wish you to join her for dinner; she is detained at present. In the meantime, I will arrange rooms, and I expect you will want to refresh yourselves and rest."

So almost as quickly as she had desired, Maerad found herself in a graceful room with cool stone walls decorated with embroidered silk hangings, and a huge bed draped with a white net, which Cadvan told her later was for keeping out stinging insects at night. On one side were wide, windowed doors, with white shutters both inside and out. These were now open and led out, past a verandah, to a shady garden. Fresh clothes – a long crimson dress in the Thoroldian style, with a low neck, well-fitted sleeves and a wide brocaded belt – were laid out for her, and Maerad earnestly requested to be shown the bathing room. The chatty Bard who Elenxi had assigned to show her around finally left her to her own devices.

Maerad was addicted to baths. For most of her life, the years of drudgery in Gilman's Cot when she had been a low slave, she had never even heard of bathing. But since her introduction to Bardic ideas about cleanliness in the School of Innail, Maerad couldn't get enough of them. This bathroom was especially pleasant: it was painted a cool blue, and opened out on a tiny courtyard where finches hopped in the potted trees. The bath itself was tiled with a mosaic of dolphins and other sea creatures, and the water was hot and plentiful. When it was deep enough to come up to her neck, Maerad dropped a bunch of lavender and rosemary into the water and stepped down into the fragrant bath with a sigh. She emerged much later, dressed herself leisurely, wandered to her room, and unpacked.

Unpacking had become a ritual, a kind of reckoning of her life. First she took out her wooden lyre, freeing it from the leather carrying case, stamped with the lily sign of the School of Pellinor, which had been a gift from Cadvan. The lyre had been her mother's, and of everything she owned it was the most precious to her. But she knew that, despite its humble appearance, the lyre was precious in other ways: it was an ancient instrument of Dhyllic ware, made by a master craftsman, and was engraved with runes that even the wisest Bards could not decipher. She brushed her fingers gently over its ten strings, simply to hear its pure tone, before she leant it carefully in the corner. She put all her clothes aside for washing, unpinning the silver brooch from her cloak and laying it on the table. She unpacked the light chain mail and helm that she had been given in Innail, and put them, alongside her sword, Irigan, in the cabinet. She put various other items in one of the drawers: a small leather kit containing a hoofpick and brushes for horses, a pen and a small pad of paper, a leather water bag, a clasp knife, and a blue bottle of the Bard drink medhyl, brewed to combat tiredness, which was almost empty.

Lastly she took out a number of objects, which she placed carefully about the room, for they too were precious to her. She unpacked a reed flute, given her by an Elidhu in the Weywood, who Maerad alone knew was also the Queen Ardina of Rachida, and who had, in her other incarnation, given Maerad the exquisitely wrought golden ring that she wore on her little finger; and a black wooden cat that might have been carved as a toy for a child, retrieved from the sacked caravan the day they had found her brother Hem. Lastly, she unwrapped from bound oilskin a small but beautifully illuminated book of poems given to her by Dernhil of Gent. She looked at it sadly. She had not had much time to read it, and reading was, in any case, a slow business for her; but she knew most of the poems in it by heart. Dernhil's death still weighed on her heavily, a regret and a grief.

She shook her head, clearing her thoughts, and picking a golden pear out of the bowl on the table, she stepped outside. All the rooms on this side of the house had doors that opened on to the garden. The shadows were now beginning to lengthen and a fresh breeze had sprung up, smelling faintly of brine. Maerad walked barefoot onto the cool grass and sat on the ground in the shade of a trellis overgrown with pale-yellow roses. She ate the pear slowly, letting its sweet juice fill her mouth, her head entirely empty of thought, utterly content. Somewhere a bird burbled unseen in the bushes, but otherwise all was quiet.

As night fell and the lamps were lit, Cadvan knocked on Maerad's door and they wended their way through the Bardhouse to the private quarters of Nerili, First Bard of Busk. Nerili's rooms were on the other side of the Bardhouse, and they had to pass through the atrium again on their way there. Maerad dawdled through it, feeling that she would rather sit there all evening than meet any Thoroldian Bard, let alone the most important Bard in the School. The fountain bubbled peacefully in the twilight, murmuring its endless song, as the white stars opened above it in a deep-blue sky.

They left the atrium and entered a labyrinth of corridors, turning again and again until Maerad had completely lost her sense of direction. The Bardhouse was enormous. But Cadvan led her unerringly, and at last they stood outside a tall door, faced with bronze like the front door of the house, and knocked. It opened, and a slim woman stood in the doorway and greeted them, smiling.

"Cadvan of Lirigon! It is long since your path has led this way."

"Too long," said Cadvan. "But, alas, such has been my fate."

"I regret that the charms of Busk could not draw you here more often," said Nerili. There was a sharpness in her tone that made Maerad look again, but now the woman was smiling and stretching her hand towards Maerad. Cadvan cleared his throat and introduced her.

Nerili of Busk was not quite what Maerad had expected. She seemed too young to be a First Bard, although among Bards age was always difficult to guess. Maerad thought she looked about thirty-five years old, which given the triple life-span of Bards meant she was perhaps seventy or eighty. She was not much taller than Maerad, but her authority and grace, and the challenging glance she gave Cadvan as they entered, gave her an illusory stature. She was strikingly beautiful, with the grey eyes, black hair and olive skin of a Thoroldian, and her grey silk dress fell softly about her, shimmering like a waterfall. Her hair was piled up on her head and held in place by silver combs and a length of silk, in a style worn by many Busk women, and she wore no jewellery apart from long silver earrings. Maerad was a little dazzled, and stammered as Cadvan introduced her. It seemed to her that even Cadvan was uncharacteristically awkward. She glanced at him curiously; surely he wasn't shy?

Her rooms, like Nerili herself, were elegant: she eschewed the usual silk hangings, ubiquitous in Busk, and instead the stone walls were painted a pale blue, with a faint stencilling of birds in a deeper shade. The only other decoration was a series of exquisite glazed blue-and-white tiles around the doors and windows and fireplace, each painted with a different scene from Thoroldian life: fishermen, silkweavers, goatherds, children playing. It was a calm, beautiful room. Through a half-open door Maerad could see what she supposed must be Nerili's study, from the chaos of manuscripts, scrolls and books she glimpsed piled on a table, and on the far side of the main room she could see a dining table set with candles in glass holders and a generous meal – flat rounds of unleavened bread, little bowls of pickled vegetables and sauces, cold meats and cheeses. There was a plate of round black spiky things that looked like strange fruit, and a large bowl of shells with orange lips. Her mouth started to water: she was very hungry.

Nerili invited them to sit down and poured out a light red wine. "So," she said, glancing at Cadvan with an unusual directness. "Elenxi tells me you have news? Serious, important news. And he said you were seeking refuge. Refuge from what? Though I see you have suffered some battles." She was looking at the whip scars on Cadvan's cheek.

Maerad suddenly thought: she's a Truthteller, like Cadvan. She couldn't have said how she understood this; she simply knew. It was a gift some Bards possessed: as Silvia had told her, Truthtellers could bring the truth out of a person, even if they didn't know it was there. It was impossible to lie to them. She examined Nerili with new interest.

Cadvan raised his glass. "Good wine, Neri. It's been a while since I tasted Thoroldian grapes; I had forgotten how excellent they are." Nerili smiled briefly, and Cadvan leant back in his chair and let out a long breath.

"I will tell you the worst news first." His voice hardened. "Maerad and I are seeking refuge from Enkir of Norloch, who has betrayed the Light. We fled the citadel only four days ago; it was then in flames. I fear civil war in Annar and I know that the Nameless One returns, the Dark moves on Annar; and even as it rises, the White Flame collapses from within. The First Circle of Annar is broken."

Nerili swallowed hard and was silent for a few moments as she studied Cadvan's face.

"I see that you say no untruth," she said quietly. "But I can scarce credit it. Norloch burns? The First Bard betrays the Light?"

"It's true," said Maerad. A sudden image flashed into her mind of Enkir's face, cold and vicious with rage, and she felt a bitter anger rising within her. "He has long been a traitor. The First Bard Enkir sent my mother to be enslaved, and betrayed Pellinor to the Dark. I was only a little girl when it happened, but I recognized his face. He knew he was discovered, and he tried to imprison half of the First Circle for treachery. He sent soldiers for us, and we only just escaped, with Owan d'Aroki's help."

"He sent an ondril to pursue us," added Cadvan. "And no ordinary ondril either."

Nerili shook her head in bewilderment, and put up her hand. "Let's go back to the beginning," she said. "You are saying that Enkir caused Pellinor to be sacked? That is a grim accusation."

"He did. He wanted me." Maerad looked up at Nerili, her jaw jutting out. She was tired of having to explain her story. "He knew the Fated One would be born to my parents. We don't know how he knew. But he took my brother Hem instead of me; he thought only a boy could be the Fated One."

Nerili gave a small, barely audible gasp.

"My father was killed with everyone else. My mother died

later, in slavery." Maerad stopped suddenly, twisting her fingers around the glass. This stark narration caused all her old sadnesses to rise up inside her, choking her throat.

"The One? You are sure?" asked Nerili softly, looking across at Cadvan.

Cadvan nodded. Nerili leaned forward and took Maerad's chin in her hand, looking at her intently. Maerad stared back into her eyes without fear or surprise; a few Bards had searched her this way before, not quite scrying her, but feeling her out. She felt a delicate touch in her mind, a light like music. Then Nerili sat back and passed her hand over her face.

"I shall need some time to absorb this." She picked up her glass and drained it. "Maerad, I do not know what you are."

"Neither do I," Maerad answered, a little forlornly.

"You have great power. But it is a strange power, a wild power, unlike anything I have felt before."

"There are many riddles in this tale," said Cadvan. "But I have no doubt that Maerad is the greatest of them all. None of us knows what she might be capable of."

Both Bards stared gravely at Maerad until she shifted under their gaze, suddenly glowering. Seeing her discomfort, Nerili refilled her glass and turned urgently to Cadvan.

"And what of Nelac?" she asked. "Is he still in Norloch? Or did he flee as well?"

"Nelac." At the mention of his old teacher, Nelac of Lirigon, Cadvan's voice thickened with sadness. "Nelac wouldn't come. I asked him. He said he was too old, and that he was needed in Norloch. I … I have no doubt he is in great danger, and I don't know what has happened in Norloch since we left. I fear for him greatly."

"He is a powerful Bard," said Nerili. "He is not easily endangered."

"Yes. But you do not know what Enkir has become. He

draws on powers other than his own. How else could he summon a creature like that ondril? And Nelac is old, even by the count of Bards. He is not afraid of death. Perhaps..." Cadvan sighed, and stared out into the garden. "Perhaps I won't see him again."

"Your news is all ill," said Nerili. There was a short silence. "Well, there is much to discuss. I'm sure you are both hungry; we can talk and eat." She gave Cadvan a strange private look, and Cadvan looked away, his face troubled. Maerad realized suddenly that Cadvan and Nerili knew each other, and that Cadvan's awkwardness had nothing to do with unfamiliarity. Cadvan called her Neri, not Nerili. Quite unexpectedly she felt a flash of jealousy, and awkwardly stood up to follow the older Bards to the dining table, almost knocking her glass over.

Over dinner, Cadvan and Maerad told of how Cadvan had helped Maerad escape from slavery in Gilman's Cot at the beginning of that spring, how he had come to suspect she was the Fated One, prophesied to bring about the downfall of the Nameless, and how her instatement as a full Bard in Norloch had confirmed his suspicions.

"And what now?" said Nerili, looking at him again with that strange directness. "For I do not imagine that Cadvan of Lirigon will stay long in Busk."

"The signs, if I read them aright, say that we must go north," said Cadvan. "Maerad and I, it seems, must find the Treesong."

Nerili lifted her eyebrows. "And what is the Treesong?"

"Nobody knows exactly," said Maerad. "Not even Nelac. But we have to find it anyway. We know we have to go north, because of my foredream and the prophecy."

"The prophecy?" said Nerili.

"Maerad speaks of a prophecy of the Seer Lanorgil's, found this spring in Innail," said Cadvan. "It foretells our need to seek the Treesong. The Song lies at the roots of the Speech, and somehow holds the very secret of our powers. Your powers, Neri, and mine, and those of every Bard in Annar. And something is wrong at the heart of Barding. Badly wrong. Even here, in the haven of Thorold, you must know that."

Cadvan spoke with such conviction that the scepticism vanished from Nerili's face, and for a moment she looked simply afraid, although she covered it swiftly.

Maerad and Cadvan then began to tell her the full story of their journey. It was a tangled telling: Nerili constantly interrupted with questions and speculations, and led the conversation in different directions. The atmosphere relaxed, and Maerad decided she liked Nerili very much; she spoke as someone sure of her authority, and there was a quick warmth behind her apparent austerity. Cadvan's face was inscrutable, and Maerad could not guess what he felt.

To distract herself, she experimented with the food. She discovered that she liked olives, although she found their bitter, oily taste a little unpleasant at first. The bread, crusty and tough, was delicious, and she enjoyed the pickled vegetables, most of which she didn't recognize, and the meats, which were flavoured with lemon and garlic and herbs.

She fared less well with the shellfish, which she had not eaten before, as she had never lived by the sea. Cadvan told her the orange-lipped shells were mussels, so she picked one up and, as Cadvan instructed her, split open the bivalve shell and picked out the flesh. Even that made her feel a little sick, but she persevered and put a small piece in her mouth. Only politeness prevented her from spitting it out on the table and she put the rest of it aside, uneaten. The black spiky things were sea urchins, boiled and split in half so their rosy insides were exposed, like exotic, poisonous flowers. Nerili ate them with enthusiasm, spooning out the flesh from the shell, but Maerad thought they smelt like rotting boots. She noticed that Cadvan, who was monopolizing the mussels, wasn't touching the sea urchins.

Nerili and Cadvan began a complicated conversation about the politics of Norloch, which bored Maerad slightly, and the wine conspired with her tiredness to make her drowsy. Her mind began to wander. She hadn't thought of Cadvan having a lover, apart from Ceredin, who had died when he was a young man; but now she did think of it, there was no reason to suppose that he hadn't. She guessed he and Nerili were not lovers now, and it wasn't as if she and Cadvan were, well, were ... she had no reason to feel jealous. But she did, all the same. She had so few friends.

She thought again of Dernhil, who had loved her, and whom she had turned away in panic and confusion, so long ago it seemed, in Innail. Dernhil had spoken to her of the Way of the Heart, and Silvia had, too ... even the Queen Ardina had talked to her of love. *You have a great heart*, the Queen had told her, *but will only find it to be so through great pain. This is the wisdom of love, and its doubtful gift.*

But Maerad hadn't understood. She still didn't understand. Was it love that had given Nerili's smile its ironic edge? But maybe she was imagining it all. Cadvan and Nerili were simply two Bards, debating questions of high policy, and these subterranean feelings, which so disturbed Maerad, were but flutterings of her tired mind.

She stared abstractedly out of the window, where the garden was now wrapped in purple shadows, with flowers glimmering palely in the darkness. Whenever Bards had mentioned the Way of the Heart to her, it had filled her with an unreasoning fear. She had spent her childhood protecting herself from the violent men of Gilman's Cot, and that was certainly part of it; but at a deeper level was some kind of foreboding, a sense of darkness that wrapped itself around the part of her that might love, as if to love might extinguish her. It seemed too full of risk, and she already risked too much, simply by being who she was.

"Are you weary, Maerad?" Nerili broke in on her thoughts, startling her. "You seem a little tired."

"I am," she answered. "I haven't slept much these past nights. I wouldn't mind going to bed."

"Maerad is no sailor," Cadvan said. "She was a very interesting green for most of our voyage here."

"And you didn't spell her? I thought you were a rare healer." Nerili gave him a mocking glance, and Maerad found herself bridling on Cadvan's behalf, although she said nothing.

"Will you be able to find your chamber, Maerad?" asked Cadvan. "It's still quite early, and I'm not ready for sleep. Nerili and I have much to speak of."

"I'll manage," said Maerad lightly, although she wished that Cadvan didn't want to stay and talk with Nerili, and would come with her instead. "I'll see you tomorrow." She bowed her head in farewell, and left the room.

She made her way back to her room, only turning the wrong way once, noticing with pleasure the familiar noises of a Bardhouse – the murmur of conversation in distant rooms, people laughing outside, musicians playing a duet somewhere, some young Bards arguing. A hunger she had been barely aware of flowered painfully inside her. Music! When had she last played? She couldn't remember.

Back in her room, Maerad picked up her lyre and started plucking it, randomly at first and then more seriously. She was out of practice. She ran through a few scales, and then picked out a tune she had once heard some minstrels play in Ettinor – she didn't feel like playing Bardic music tonight. It was a plaintive song about a man who had fallen in love with a water sprite. She couldn't quite remember the words, so she made up some of her own once she had the melody down to her satisfaction. She sang it through twice, feeling her anxieties subside in the absorption of playing. Then, yawning violently, she put her lyre carefully aside and prepared herself for bed.

III

THE BROKEN PROMISE

THE golden light of a late summer morning played over the garden outside Maerad's room. She sat alone in the shade, enjoying the breeze on her face. Birds argued in the trees and Maerad, using her Gift, idly eavesdropped. Birds, she thought, are so brainless. All they say is *Mine! Mine! Mine! Go away! Go away!*

She let the birdspeech return to pretty burbling, which was much more pleasant to listen to, and breathed in the balm of the garden. She ached: oh, how she ached. Her soul was like one big bruise.

It was so pleasant to sit alone in a beautiful garden, and not to feel filthy or exhausted or cold or frightened, not to feel hunted by the Dark. But now she had a little peace, all these disturbing thoughts bubbled up inside her. Was she any closer to knowing who she was? She had all these new names – once she had only been Maerad, then she was Maerad of Pellinor, and now she was Elednor of Edil-Amarandh, the Fire Lily come to resist the Dark – but what did they really mean? And now she was on a quest, charged to find the Treesong. From the voice in her foredreams she and Cadvan had decided that they must head north; but here, in this pretty garden, it seemed like the flimsiest of reasons. And what were they looking for? Even Nelac didn't know.

What are you? she asked herself, echoing Nerili's question of the night before. A freak?

She had been ruminating for some time when a door further

along the portico opened and Cadvan peered out. "Maerad! Good morning!" He came up to her table. "I see you've been spending your time well," he said, looking at the empty plates. "Is that coffee still hot?"

"Coffee?"

"The drink. Coffee."

"No."

"A pity. I'm rather partial to it. It's a drink from the Suderain: it's rare to find it anywhere in Annar except here. They trade with the south."

"I like it," said Maerad. "But it's strong."

"A bit like the Thoroldians, yes?" Cadvan said, smiling. He pulled one of the chairs up to the table and sat down.

Cadvan and Maerad sat in companionable silence for a while, looking out over the garden. Maerad toyed with the idea of asking him about Nerili, and then decided against it. She doubted he would tell her anything; and another part of her didn't want to know.

"It's lovely here," she said at last. "I wish we could stay for ever."

"We can't," said Cadvan. "You know that. But we can certainly stay for a few weeks. We both need a rest. And before we head north to seek the Treesong, we have to have some idea of what we're looking for. I'm going to have a good look through the Busk Library – it's the most ancient in Edil-Amarandh, except perhaps for the one in Turbansk – and try and find some clue. If we know what we might be looking for, then it might not be such a goose chase."

"It might be a goose chase anyway," said Maerad, thinking of the argumentative geese she had herded as a slave child, and then of the wise, gentle Bard Nelac, as she had last seen him in Norloch, solemnly charging them to find the Treesong. They were such incongruous images she almost laughed.

"Well, while you hunt about in the library, I'll just sit in the garden," she said. "I like it here."

"No, you won't," said Cadvan. "You can use the time to study. There's so much that you should know, and there are things that it's dangerous not to know. You really need years to catch up, but we'll have to make do. I've spoken to Nerili about it – she's agreed to let you have private teaching, so you don't have to sit in classes with children half your age. You have particular needs, anyway."

"But I want a rest," she said mulishly. "I'm tired."

"And a rest you shall have. For two days. It will take me that long to arrange your lessons. You'll need some beginner's instruction in High Magery, which is a bit peculiar, because you have all the abilities, and more, of a full Bard, but you've never done the basic lessons. I'll have to think about who is best to teach you. Me, probably, but I'll be busy. And, of course, there's swordcraft, and reading and writing. You're quick; you'll use your time well."

Maerad pouted, but made no other protest. The prospect of resuming study excited her, but she wasn't going to tell Cadvan that. For all her powers, she was painfully aware that she had very little skill.

In Busk, for the first time, Maerad began to live the life of a normal Bard. She slipped as easily into it as a fish into a stream. The days settled into a steady pattern: rising at dawn for breakfast, and lessons until the middle of the afternoon, with a short break for a light midday meal. After that, if she didn't have further study to do, her time was her own; she was free to go back to her room and rest, or to sit in the garden, or to wander down to the town and the markets of Busk, or, as she began to do more and more often after her first week, to join the noisy Bards in their colloquia. She usually ate dinner with Cadvan, either in the Common Hall or in one or other of their rooms, where they would swap news about their day: what Maerad had learnt (a voracious amount) or what Cadvan had found (nothing). Or they would wander down to the lower town to meet Owan. They would eat either in one of the many taverns, or at his house, which was surprisingly big for a humble fisherman, cementing what had become a fast friendship.

As Cadvan had predicted, Maerad used her time well, and within a week all her mentors were telling her that they were astonished by her progress. Years of brusque tutelage from the Bard Mirlad in Gilman's Cot, being taught musicianship by ear, meant her memory was excellent; she had only to be told something once to remember it. But more than that, she seemed to have an innate knowledge of Barding, which her teachers merely had to reawaken. They all commented privately on this to Cadvan; they found her aptitude a little unnerving.

Her teachers were all senior Bards in the School of Busk. Elenxi of Busk taught her swordcraft, Intatha of Gent taught her reading and writing and, to Maerad's initial abashment, Nerili herself had taken on the task of introducing her to High Magery. Partly, Cadvan explained, the senior Bards were teaching her because Maerad was such an unusual case and because she needed swift teaching; but another reason was secrecy. Maerad was known within the School as Maerad of Innail, travelling with Cadvan, who was too well known to conceal his identity.

"I don't doubt that some will guess that you are Maerad of Pellinor," said Cadvan, the first night after her lessons commenced. "Bards are the worst gossips, and your arrival and acceptance as a Minor Bard at Innail caused a lot of comment: a survivor of the sack of Pellinor was big news. As was the scandal when I applied to be your sole mentor. But even so, it's better for us to lie low and be discreet, even here. We are just travelling Bards, visiting the School at Nerili's invitation. There is nothing unusual about that."

Maerad shrugged. "Do you think there are spies here?"

"For the Dark, you mean?" said Cadvan. "I do not think there are spies in the School, but nowhere is safe for us and I would be surprised if there weren't any in the town. Busk is a trading port, remember, and strangers go unmarked. News has not reached here yet from Norloch. I don't doubt that it will soon. And then things will become more dangerous."

Maerad pondered what "dangerous", meant and then her thoughts turned, as they so often did, to Hem. The day before, Cadvan had sent a message by bird to Turbansk, to tell Saliman of their safe arrival in Thorold. Hem and Saliman would be riding there now; Maerad wondered where they were, and if they were safe.

The lessons were interesting. Her sessions with Intatha of Gent gave her a pang at first; they could not but recall Dernhil, who was the first to open for her the world of reading and writing. For Maerad, reading itself was imbued with memories of him. And Intatha was of the same School as Dernhil, although Maerad never dared to ask her if she had known him.

Intatha was an imposing-looking Bard: tall, with high cheekbones, a formidable eagle nose and hair that was silvering from black. She was a stern teacher, but gentle. Maerad worked hard for her, not because she feared her dispraise, but because Intatha expected much of her, and Maerad wished not to disappoint. She found herself mastering the alphabetic script of Nelsor very quickly, building on the basics Dernhil had taught her, and even found that her handwriting began to look pleasing, instead of scratchy and ill-formed. Intatha also started teaching her the Ladhen runes, coded symbols that Bards used when travelling to leave signs for each other, and some of the

Dhyllic pictograms. It was intense work, and Maerad left their long sessions feeling both stimulated and drained, with her arms full of work to do on her own.

Classes with Elenxi of Busk were surprisingly fun. For all his age and his giant frame he was quick and agile, and Maerad was not surprised to find he had been a famous warrior in his youth: she imagined that he would have been fearsome. Unlike Indik, the master swordsman who had taught Maerad at Innail, Elenxi was a patient and encouraging teacher. She was also no longer a raw beginner: holding a sword no longer felt strange. She had quick reactions and good natural balance, and was strong for someone of her size. Elenxi coached her in advanced swordcraft and unarmed combat, and Maerad began to feel for the first time that perhaps she might be able to hold her own against attack.

"Don't get over-confident," Elenxi warned, after praising her efforts in her first lesson. "You are still only a beginner. It's the stroke you don't see that kills you." He looked at her, wiping the sweat out of his eyes. "I think we deserve a wine, yes, young Bard? We have worked hard today."

"A wine?" said Maerad shyly, thinking of the vociferous Bards. Elenxi looked at her and laughed.

"Don't tell me you are frightened! Well, we'll have to cure that."

"But I'm filthy!" Maerad objected, blushing.

Elenxi lifted an eyebrow. "So? Does one have to be clean to drink? I should like to know when that was made a rule. No, young Bard, I will hear no excuses. We'll go to Oreston's house, he has the best wines."

They stowed their fighting gear, and only permitting her a quick wash, Elenxi led a reluctant Maerad down the road to one of the houses nearer the town. He strode among the tables confidently, expecting Maerad to be right behind him; and when he saw her still hesitating in the road, he went back and took hold of her, almost dragging her to a table where about six Bards, men and women, were engaged in lively conversation. At one end of the table, a young man was idly plucking arpeggios, which ran like a quick river of music underneath the talk, on a beautiful big-bellied stringed instrument.

Maerad felt paralysed by shyness, and sat down quietly, hoping nobody would notice her. Elenxi exchanged cheerful greetings with all the Bards, and then introduced Maerad as a guest from Innail. She was immediately swamped with questions in both the Speech and Thoroldian: Innail? It is long since someone came all the way from the east – how goes it there? How is Oron? They had heard of the death of Dernhil of Gent – how could that have happened? Hulls murdering Bards in a School?

Elenxi put up his hand to stem the tide. "Now, be fair," he said in the Speech. "Maerad is clever, but she can't speak Thoroldian. How can she answer all of you? Anyway, what does she know about the high policies of Innail? She is only a young Bard, and she hasn't been there for months. We have been working hard at improving her swordcraft this afternoon, and she is tired and needs some wine. She came all this way to be taught by me, which shows remarkable good taste."

He winked at her slyly, and Maerad, grateful for his intervention, gave him a small smile; she hadn't understood much, but she knew they had asked about Dernhil, and the mention distressed her. Suddenly a glass full of a dark red wine was in front of her, and she was being plied with delicacies instead of questions. She clutched her glass and gulped the wine. The conversation resumed, in the Speech so she could understand it, and she sat quietly listening. After a while, emboldened by her second glass of wine, she asked the young man with the instrument, a Bard called Honas, what it was.

"It's a makilon," he said. "My father made this one especially for me: he's a master crafter of instruments, famous in
Thorold. It's beautiful, yes?" He handed it to her, and she
stroked the smooth, mellow wood, admiring the mother-of-
pearl inlay around the soundhole and the delicate carving of
its neck.

"Oh, yes, it's lovely," said Maerad. She let her fingers trickle
over the strings, listening to its resonance. "So beautifully made.
I've never seen one before. How do you play it?"

Honas, his face alight with obvious passion, took the instrument back and started to show her the complicated fingerings
and plucking styles for the makilon. Maerad's fingers itched
to try them, and before long Honas gave it to her, placing her
hands correctly on the neck and the strings. She ventured an
arpeggio, marvelling at the sound. Honas was beginning
to be more interested in Maerad than the music, but only
Elenxi, keeping discreet watch from the other side of the table,
noticed this. He smiled into his beard. Maerad was completely
absorbed, and had now forgotten her shyness altogether.

Maybe they weren't so frightening, these Bards.

The most demanding studies were those in High Magery. This
was something Maerad had never studied formally, although
Cadvan had taught her much on their travels together. She
went to Nerili's rooms for her first lesson with a strange reluctance; she hadn't spoken to the First Bard since the night she
had arrived in Busk, and she felt apprehensive, as if she would
not know what to say. Nerili took care to put her at her ease.

"Well, Maerad," she said, smiling, when Maerad entered.
"Cadvan has told me of your feats, striking down both a kulag
and a wight. It seems passing strange to be teaching you, when
you have already done more than most Bards."

That day Nerili was dressed plainly, but Maerad still found

her beauty dazzling and she felt stiff and awkward. "There's still a lot I don't know," she mumbled, embarrassed. "I didn't think about anything when those things happened. It just – burst out of me."

"So I understand. Well, we will just have to feel strange about it, no? I'm sure that will disappear once we start working."

And so, Maerad found, it did.

They worked in a room that was clearly set aside for teaching: there were few pieces of furniture, only a big table and a bench by the wall where they could both sit, if need be. A broad window stood open in the south wall, and through it blew a wind that carried the distant soughing of the sea.

A large part of what Maerad learned over the ensuing weeks was the theoretical study of what the Bards called the Knowing, which was roughly divided into the Three Arts: Reading, Making and Tending, each of which was intricately related to the others. She was also taught various traditions about the Speech, some of which contradicted each other. "There is no single truth," Nerili explained. "But all these truths, woven together, might give us a picture of what is true. That is why it's important to know all the different stories. We can never see all the sky at once."

Maerad was also introduced to the complex system of Bardic ethics. It had evolved over many centuries, and was centred on the idea of the Balance. The more she learnt about these things, the more Maerad wondered that Bards did magic at all: it seemed that drawing on her powers was fraught with responsibilities and implications, and that in most cases Bards practised their powers in order not to use them. Often, in those days, she thought uneasily of the times when her powers had exploded out of her, uncontrollable and terrifying, and of the wild exhilaration she had felt when she had finally come into the Speech. Serious magery, she learned, was something practised seldom and only in great need. The Balance was a delicate thing, and the smallest action could have unexpected and unintended consequences. Bards who had turned to the Dark, the Hulls, were those who desired power above all else, and eschewed the responsibilities of the Balance.

"The difficulty is, of course," said Nerili thoughtfully, during their first session, "that because they have not the same inhibitions on their powers, they can access forces and take actions that Bards will not. And this can make it difficult to fight them: they laugh at us, because they say our hands are tied and we are weak. Despite their mockery, we are well able to defend ourselves, but we remember that if we did not try to adhere to the Balance, even in our extremity, we would become like them. And that would be the greater defeat."

Maerad wondered at this, but for the moment did not argue. She thought of the brutality of her childhood in Gilman's Cot and the malice of the Dark. She remembered the times when she had had to kill, in order to save her own life. She had always felt, with a deep discomfort, that the killing wounded her somehow, even though it had been necessary, even if she felt it completely justified. Yet, she thought, there might come a time when the Light couldn't afford such niceties.

Nerili looked at her steadily and then added, as if she caught the tenor of her thoughts: "There's a great force in the renunciation of power that those who are blinded by the lust for domination cannot understand, because those who love truly do not desire power. Among Bards, it is often known as the Way of the Heart. The Dark understands nothing of this: it is its greatest weakness."

Maerad started – this chimed a little too uncomfortably with her thoughts of the earlier night – but Nerili was staring out of the window, as if Maerad were not there.

"Love is never easy," said Nerili. "We begin by loving the things we can, according to our stature. But it is not long before we find that what we love is other than ourselves, and that our love is no protection against being wounded. Do we then seek to dominate what we love, to make it bend to our will, to stop it hurting us, even though to do so is to betray love? And that is only where the difficulty begins."

She turned to Maerad, smiling a little sadly, but Maerad didn't respond: she felt too surprised. For a moment she was sure that Nerili was speaking of her own feelings for Cadvan, and was aware, too, of the tangle of Maerad's emotions and sought, obscurely, to comfort her. To her relief, Nerili dropped the subject, and moved onto the more practical aspects of High Magery.

In these lessons, Maerad began to learn properly how to use her Bardic powers: how to control and shape the Speech, and how to make enchantments and spells. Nerili started with glimmerspells, the least part, she explained, of Bardic magic: a magic of illusion, not of substance. "You can already do glimmerspells, simply by willing them," Nerili said. "You are aware of that?"

"Yes," said Maerad. It was easy to make herself unseen, or to change her appearance.

"There's more to them, nevertheless, than those instinctive powers. Glimmerspells can be quite useful. Not against Bards, of course; Bard eyes can always see through them. But if we do this" – and Nerili made a strange pass with her hands – "we can persuade Bard eyes to collude with us, though it won't work against a Bard's will. Then we can share our imaginations."

Suddenly, in the middle of the room, there appeared a silver sapling. As Maerad watched, enchanted, it grew to the height of the ceiling, putting out branches and broad silver leaves. When it was fully grown, there burst out all over it little golden buds, which opened wide to luminous flowers that seemed to be made of pure light. The petals withered and vanished, releasing a delicate fragrance, and where the flowers had been there swelled marvellous fruits: golden apples so bright they threw shadows over the walls. There was a music in the room, the same clear inhuman voices Maerad had heard during her instatement, which seemed to her like the sound of stars singing. She gasped in pure delight.

"The Tree of Light, as I see it each year at Midsummer," said Nerili, looking at it with her head cocked to one side. "It is beautiful, yes? Each First Bard sees it in her own way. This is how it appears to me. If ever you do the Rite of Renewing, you will see a different one. But it will be just as beautiful." She clapped her hands, and the tree vanished. "Now you try."

Maerad's mind went blank. "What?" she asked.

Nerili shrugged. "Show me something," she said. "Something you remember. Did you catch the passes?" She showed Maerad the hand gestures again, and Maerad copied them slowly, fixing them in her memory. Into her mind leapt an image of the wight she had destroyed at the Broken Teeth, just before Norloch. She bent her imagination to visualizing it, and Nerili gasped.

"Not that!" she said quickly. "Not a creature of the Dark. No, show me something else."

My memories are full of horror, Maerad thought to herself. I can't help it. Obediently she pushed the wight out of her mind, and cast about for another image. Gradually, shimmering a little, the figure of a woman appeared in the room, facing away from them. She was dressed in white robes and her long dark hair fell unbound down her back. Slowly she turned to look at the two Bards. Her face was full of sadness.

"Your mother, Milana of Pellinor," said Nerili softly. "I never met her. She looks very much like you. Thank you, Maerad."

The figure faded and vanished, and there was a short silence. Maerad looked away. She didn't know why she had shown Nerili her mother, and she now wished she hadn't. Nerili took her hand, and Maerad jumped. If she had said anything to her, Maerad might have started crying, but they just sat wordlessly for a while, until Maerad collected herself.

"Magery, even the slightest, calls on the deepest parts of ourselves," Nerili said at last, releasing her hand. "And often that is painful. It is the pain of being in the world, where so much that is fair passes into death and forgetfulness. But if we are to know joy, we must embrace that pain. You cannot have one without the other."

Maerad nodded, her face downcast. Sometimes, it seemed to her, the pain far outweighed the joy.

An emissary arrived from Norloch very quickly, five days after Maerad and Cadvan. They made council with Busk's First Circle and left early the next day for Gent. After they had gone, Nerili called another council of the First and Second Circles, all the senior Bards of the School of Busk, and this time Maerad and Cadvan were summoned.

When they arrived in the Council Room, Maerad was surprised to see half a dozen people who were clearly not Bards. They were the Steward of Busk, a tall, burly man called Arnamil, and the members of his Chamber, three women and two men, one of whom, Maerad saw, was Owan d'Aroki. In tandem with the six Bards of the First Circle of the School, the Chamber governed the Isle of Thorold. With the sixteen Bards, it made a sizeable gathering around the large round table that dominated the room. When everyone was seated, Nerili stood and began without preamble.

"Welcome, Chamber and Bards. Thank you for answering my call. I realize this meeting is not at the usual time." She paused, and looked slowly around the table, meeting the eyes of each person present. "Bards of the First Circle, you know why I have called you here. You were present yesterday, when Igan of Norloch issued the edict of Norloch to the School of Busk. What he told me deeply concerns all of Thorold, and this is why I asked you, Lord Steward, and your Chamber to be present."

She drew a deep breath, as if she were nervous; but Maerad realized quickly that Nerili was, with difficulty, restraining fury.

"Igan of Norloch informed me yesterday that there have been certain changes within the School of Norloch, and within Annar." Here Maerad sat up more straightly. "There has been revealed, he said, a plot within the First Circle itself, a faction of rebels who are in league with the Dark. The rebellion has been put down, and its leaders imprisoned. The imprisoned traitors are Nelac of Lirigon, Tared of Desor and Caragal of Norloch."

There was an audible gasp of dismay from around the table, and Maerad met Cadvan's eyes. He looked saddened, not shocked; she suspected he knew this already.

Nerili continued. "Norloch is under the military rule of the White Guard, commanded by the First Bard, Enkir of Norloch, to combat the emergency caused by the rebels. He has invoked the triple sceptre, the emblem of the lost Kings of Annar, and claims the authority of High King over all the Seven Kingdoms."

Again there was a collective gasp of shock. Arnamil leapt out of his chair, his mouth open ready to say something, but Nerili held up her hand to indicate she wasn't finished, and he slowly sat down.

"Moreover, he spoke of news that the kingdom of Dén Raven is moving in the south. He said that Norloch expects that Turbansk will be attacked within the next three months by the Sorcerer Imank."

Maerad thought of the implacable army she had seen in her foredream. She bit her lip and looked at her hands, trying to keep down a surge of despair; even if Turbansk were attacked, it didn't mean that Hem would be killed.

Nerili kept speaking. "In this climate of danger, Igan tells me, the First Bard of Norloch and the King of Annar, Enkir of Norloch, seeks the loyalty of all Schools and all Kingdoms. We are to give our undivided fealty, without question, to the triple sceptre, or we are to be regarded as rebels. And he gave me to understand, in not so many words, that to be rebels, and thus to earn the enmity of Norloch, would be to risk the full wrath of Norloch's might and power."

The final statement nearly caused a riot. Almost everyone in the room stood up and started shouting. Nerili again held up her hand for silence, and her voice rang out over the room.

"My friends," she said. "My dear fellow Thoroldians. I know as well as you that never, even in the times of the Kings of Annar, were we or any of the Seven Kingdoms under the authority of Annar. And you can be sure that I said this to Igan, emissary of Enkir of Norloch. And he said to me, 'Nerili of Busk, things change. We have entered dangerous times, and if we are to survive them we must change our free ways. Thoroldians must obey the new laws, or be the victims of them.' Such is the edict of Enkir of Norloch." Nerili bowed her head. "I am ashamed to be the bearer of this news. It casts a shadow over all Bards."

There was a wrathful murmur around the table, and Arnamil stood up again, his eyes flashing. "What did you say to this insult, Lady of Busk?" he asked. "Did you throw him out of the School, with his tail between his cowardly legs, as he deserved?"

"I did not." Nerili looked him steadily in the eye. "Arnamil, to do so would be tantamount to severing all connection with Norloch, and would risk open war. Such a thing has not happened since the Kings ruled in Annar, and I am not prepared to risk warfare solely on my own authority." She again looked around the table where everyone now sat in tense silence.

"I received him politely. I listened politely. I told him that I was aware that we live in dangerous times, and that we must take heed of such that threatens us. I said I would consult with the Bards and Chamber, and then would let Norloch know of our response." She paused. "He gave us a week. And he said again that if our fealty was withheld, we would suffer grave consequences."

"I say, then," said Arnamil, thumping the table with his huge fist, "that in a week we send back his damned edict, torn into little pieces." Most of the table cheered. "We don't need Norloch." He sat down truculently.

Now Elenxi stood. "I suggest, for the meantime, another way," he said. "If we can avoid a war with Norloch, I think we should. Let them force the issue. If Norloch seeks to betray the covenant between Annar and the Seven Kingdoms in this way, then let Norloch break it. Not us."

"What do you suggest, then?" Owan, who had hitherto sat silently throughout the noisy meeting, twisted around to look up at the old warrior.

"I suggest we offer Norloch our fealty." There was an angry rumble. "We offer them our fealty, I say, under our unwavering allegiance to the Light. That covenant guarantees our freedom and our independence. If Norloch doesn't like it, Norloch has to say on what terms our fealty is unsatisfactory. This will take a little time, since we have broken no promises. Meanwhile, we send emissaries to other Schools in the Seven Kingdoms, and seek to know their own answers to this outrage. I think their minds will be like to ours. Will Annar seriously declare war on all of the Seven Kingdoms? And, in the meantime, we look to our fortifications." Elenxi glared around the table from under his bushy eyebrows, and sat down.

After a short silence, Arnamil started chuckling. "They always said you were a fox, Elenxi. I like it."

"This is the course I and the full First Circle advise," said Nerili, standing again. "Are we all agreed?" Everyone in the room, even Cadvan and Maerad, who were not really supposed to vote, put up their hands. Nerili nodded. "Good, then. We will pursue this policy until we find out whether Norloch's words have real steel, or are only empty threats. Norloch would be a dire enemy, doubt it not; but it would be no small thing to invade Thorold. We will all keep in close consultation. Elenxi and Arnamil can confer on the strength of our defences, and improve them, if need be."

"They'd have to kill every man, woman and child to defeat Thorold," growled one of the Chamber.

"Now, there is one more thing. I need to introduce to you Cadvan of Lirigon and Maerad of Pellinor." Cadvan stood up, and Maerad, taken by surprise, scrambled up after him. "Most of you know Cadvan well. He has spent much time here. Maerad only some of you will know; she has been Cadvan's student, and is now a full Bard. They are, Igan told me, dangerous members of this rebellion in Norloch, and they are outlawed. They are now sought over all Annar."

The council turned to look at them with lively curiosity.

"I want you all to know that I cannot and do not believe that either of these Bards have any truck with the Dark. Igan tells me that anyone who hands these criminals to Norloch will earn great favour with the citadel, but those who harbour them from justice will feel the full force of its displeasure. He is unaware as yet, of course, that they are here in Thorold. I warned my people to keep silent when the emissary came, and I know also that they were asked after, both within the town and the School. To my knowledge, they can prove nothing; but we cannot be sure of that. They may already know that these Bards have sought refuge here.

"I ask you now whether we, as Thoroldians, will hand them over to Norloch, as is ordered. Or do we suffer this risk – to grant haven to Cadvan of Lirigon and Maerad of Pellinor, and risk its punishment?"

The table erupted again. The mood against Norloch was so ugly that Nerili had no need of persuasive argument: to be declared rebels by Enkir was itself enough to ensure their protection.

"I need not tell you, then," said Nerili, "that their presence must be kept secret within the School, and must not be made known within the town of Busk, aside from those here, who already know. We cannot tell what spies are abroad, and the arm of Norloch is long. A loose word could forfeit their lives, and would cause Norloch to declare us rebels." She stared around the table, to underline her seriousness. "Well, that is the end of our business."

She lifted up her arms, as if in blessing, and said with a sudden wild joy that sent goosebumps down Maerad's spine: "My friends – you make me so glad. I expected no less from you. No tyrant will crush the heart of Thorold!"

The council ended in cheers.

IV

MIDSUMMER

NERILI acted on the decision with despatch: the Thoroldian emissaries left the following day. As one was to go to Turbansk, Maerad took the chance to write to Saliman and Hem. She closeted herself in her room and carefully laid paper, ink and a pen out on the table. She sat for a long time looking at them, without doing anything. She had never written a proper letter before.

At last, with a determined expression, she picked up the pen and began to write. She blotted the first sheet, and tore it up and threw it on the floor. Her second try was more successful. She wrote laboriously, with many hesitations.

To Hem and Saliman, greetings!

Cadvan and I arrived in Thorold safely, as you may know if the bird reached you. We are both much better than when we last saw you.

I was very seasick on my way here, Cadvan and I had to fight an ondril, which was very big, but we got here safely. Nerili has given us haven, and you will have heard the rest of the news from the emissary.

I hope you have arrived in Turbansk with no harm, and that Hem finds the fruits are as big as the birds said they were. I think of you all the time and miss you sorely.

With all the love in my heart,
Maerad

Writing this note took her a long time. She looked at it critically; her writing was still very wobbly, with none of the sure beauty of a Bard's hand, and it said nothing that she really wanted to say. She would have liked to tell Hem what Busk was like, to describe its low stone buildings and cool gardens, and its cheerful, generous people. Hem would have been amused by the sea urchins that smelt like old boots. She imagined him laughing, and then imagined him tasting them in his greed. But no good manners would have prevented Hem spitting them out onto the table, no matter who was present.

A terrible ache opened inside her. She longed to be able to tell Hem all these things face to face. A letter was no substitute; it made him seem even further away.

She wondered whether to try writing her letter again, but couldn't face it. With a deep sigh, she folded and sealed it, and took it to Elenxi to give to the emissary.

After the council meeting, Maerad felt completely safe in the School of Busk. Everyone in the School now knew of the threat from Norloch, but if it cast a shadow over their enjoyment of life, Maerad couldn't see it. She discovered the truth of Cadvan's comment, that the only real problem with Thoroldians was keeping up with their consumption of wine; if it hadn't been for how hard she was working, she would have thought that living in Busk was like being at a permanent festival. After one particularly bad morning, she learnt a few survival techniques: thereafter she sipped her wine very slowly and drank lots of water whenever she was out with the Bards.

On feast days, when she didn't have to do any lessons, Elenxi and his friends would sometimes take her into the town, where they would drink and dance all night in the gardens of the waterfront taverns under the glittering summer stars. Bards were always welcome in the taverns because

Bards meant good music, and Thoroldians loved music with a passion.

The people she met in town were just like the Bards: fiery, passionate, argumentative, generous. The Thoroldians' intensity was not always benign: to Maerad's alarm, she witnessed a couple of brawls, once between two drunken Bards who were literally lifted up by the scruffs of their necks by Elenxi and thrown into the road, and once in a tavern between a number of fishers.

It was all very different from anything she had encountered before, but she found that she liked it very much. It wasn't long before she was as argumentative and noisy as the best of them.

"Wild girl," Cadvan teased her one night when she sat down, flushed and out of breath, after dancing. "I said you were part Thoroldian."

"Well, if I am, maybe you are too," said Maerad, laughing.

"Not as far as I know," he answered. "But anything is possible." It was true that Cadvan, usually so solitary and often so ill at ease when he stayed for any length of time in a School, was unusually relaxed in Busk.

Apart from Norloch's ultimatum, the major topic of discussion among both Bards and townfolk was the Midsummer Festival, one of the high celebrations of the Bardic year: it was when the new year was welcomed in and the old farewelled. Maerad and Cadvan had arrived just under three weeks before the summer solstice, when the festival occurred, and this year's was especially auspicious because it coincided with the full moon.

"There will be a procession," said Kabeka, the tall Bard Maerad had seen declaiming a poem that first day. "Everyone comes to the procession – every man, woman, child, dog and chicken in Thorold; and half of Thorold is in it."

"It must be total chaos," said Maerad, trying to imagine how such a crowd could fit in the narrow streets of Busk.

"It is!" Kabeka answered, grinning. "But it's great fun. We look forward to it all year. The children wear masks and are allowed to steal sweetmeats from the stalls and to cheek their elders and get into all sorts of mischief, for they can't be punished on that day.

"But the real event is the Rite of Renewal, which is always made by the First Bard. It is one of the most beautiful of the Bardic Rites; I have seen it so many times, and I never tire of it. The First Bard takes the Mirror of Maras, which holds the old year, and she smashes it; and then she remakes it, and from the Mirror grows the Tree of Light."

Maerad remembered the glimmerspell Nerili had made in their first lesson, and her heart quickened.

"And afterwards there is dancing and eating and drinking. And kissing," Kabeka added wickedly, making Maerad blush. "You shall have to find someone to kiss."

"I don't want to kiss anyone," said Maerad hotly, thinking suddenly of Dernhil.

"There are plenty who want to kiss you," Kabeka answered, and Maerad's blush deepened. "You'll just have to work out how to stop them, then."

One day, Maerad finished her lessons early and decided to go to the library to find Cadvan, who she knew would be searching through its archives for any mention of the Treesong. The Busk Library, off the central square, was a labyrinthine building that stretched back deep into the rocky hill behind it. It had been added to in a chaotic fashion in the centuries since it had been built and it was now a bewildering honeycomb of rooms. Some were huge halls lit by long windows, others were tiny, dark chambers; but they were all lined from floor to ceiling with shelves, each of which was piled with scrolls or huge, leather-bound volumes or strange objects whose purpose she could not guess.

Maerad was quite happy to wander through the rooms, nodding to the Bards who sat reading at tables or stood on step-ladders rummaging through the shelves. She wondered how anyone found anything, and after a while began to feel awed by the sheer weight of the knowledge she was walking past so lightly. Even if she spent her whole life doing nothing but reading, she would never get through it all. As she worked her way to the back of the library – she supposed Cadvan would be in the older rooms that were delved into the rock – she found more and more chambers that looked as if no one ever went there: the shelves were covered with thick dust, and they had a forlorn air. She picked up a lamp, for many of these rooms were dark, and continued her wandering.

At last she entered a long, narrow hall hung with intricately fashioned silver lamps that let down clear pools of light over a table that ran the entire length of the room. Underneath the light furthest from Maerad sat Cadvan, his head bent over a scroll spread open on the table. Opposite him, Nerili leafed steadily through a heavy book.

Maerad paused irresolutely at the threshold, wondering whether to enter and greet them. Neither Bard had noticed her presence; they were deeply absorbed in their work. There was a self sufficiency in their silent companionship that she was too shy to disturb. In the end, she retraced her steps, trying to quell a small bitterness that had risen in her throat. In all their even-ings of discussion, Cadvan had never mentioned that Nerili was helping him in his search of the library.

On Midsummer Day, the sun rose into a sky as perfectly blue as a robin's egg. The winding alleys and small streets of Busk were packed with people, with the rest of the town seemingly out on their balconies, drinking and eating and waving and gossiping. Everyone had put on their best clothes, and the streets were a carnival of colour, shimmering with the blazing silks woven and dyed in Busk: emerald green and crimson and gold and azure and turquoise.

The crowds made Maerad feel breathless; she'd never seen so many people squeezed into such tiny spaces. As they pressed through the narrow streets she drew close to Cadvan, who was shouldering his way steadily towards the waterfront, where the procession was to take place later that day. The further they pushed into town, the more crowded and noisy and hot it became. Children who wanted to get through simply wiggled their way between people's legs. Some wore astounding masks made of dyed feathers and silk, others simply had their faces painted, and were little foxes and cats and owls and flowers. Most of them clutched be-ribboned treasures: silk bags of sweets or toffee apples, especially made to be "stolen", from the market stalls.

Nobody was in a hurry, and Maerad and Cadvan were often stopped for conversation, or waved over to balconies to share a drink. They smilingly refused and pressed on. Eventually they reached their destination, the Copper Mermaid, the Bards' favourite tavern, where they were meeting some friends who had sworn they would keep places for them. You could hear the Bards even over the noise of the crowd: a makilon player and a drummer were playing in the garden, and revellers spilt out, talking and laughing, over the garden and down to the waterfront.

Maerad looked with relief out onto the sea, which was the only place not packed with people. A breeze played over the waves and cooled the sweat on her forehead.

"I didn't realize there were so many people in the world," she said, wiping her hair out of her eyes, once they had sat down.

"They're not usually so close together," said Cadvan. He poured her some minted lemon water. "Well, now we're here, we need not move until it's time for the Rite of Renewal. We can just eat and watch the pageant."

And it was some spectacle. They had prime seats, high on the balcony of the Copper Mermaid. Maerad and Cadvan both agreed it was much better than jostling at the front, getting poked by old women with parasols and being trodden on. The gardens stretched before them in a series of terraces crowded with tables and chairs, down to the Elakmirathon, the harbourside road bounded on one side by the long quay and on the other by rows of taverns and workshops and, further on, by the open markets.

As the afternoon wore on, more and more people swelled the crowds along the Elakmirathon. Lamos, the proprietor of the Copper Mermaid, shut his gates so no one else could get in, and still people climbed over the walls. All the balconies and roofs along the waterfront, every available wall and window, were festooned with people, all talking and laughing. Despite a cool breeze coming in off the sea, the press of people made it uncomfortably hot. Looking at the crowd, Maerad wondered aloud why nobody was crushed.

"We're really quite orderly at this time of day, despite appearances," Honas answered, grinning. "The real drinking starts later. During the day, it's all eating. And by then all the crowds will have gone to their own celebrations. We've seldom had any trouble at Midsummer. A few brawls maybe, later. But shhh, it's starting."

Maerad craned her neck to see. She could hear a huge drum being hit in a solemn, commanding rhythm. Suddenly she saw an enormously fat man with a gilt-and-crimson drum hung around his neck. Where he walked the crowd parted miraculously, although it seemed impossible among those hundreds of people that any space should be available at all, and behind him came the procession.

First there were tumblers and jugglers, all dressed in bright primary colours. Some of the jugglers were throwing charmed balls that looked like fish or birds with wings of jewels and gold that flashed in the sun, or real stars, or blue and green and red flames. Maerad watched the acrobats with her mouth open: they leapt in impossible tumbling arcs onto each other's shoulders, or walked on their hands or on stilts, or built themselves into human towers made of a dozen people. She clapped her hands with delight.

After them came a cavalcade of dozens of children – some riding stocky mountain ponies with saddles and bridles decorated with feathers and flowers. Maerad thought the ponies, which often walked backwards or sideways instead of where they were supposed to go, looked less than enthusiastic about all the fuss. One dumped a tiny girl to the ground. Instead of bursting into tears she scrambled up, her high headdress of dyed pink feathers sadly broken, whacked the pony on its rump, and swung herself up again to a cheer. All the children were dressed as fantastically as the Thoroldians could manage: dresses with several layers of flounces and lace, shirts and trousers with brilliant brocades and masks made of feathers, glass, silk and mirrors. They wore wonderful headdresses nodding with feathers, many of which looked rather unstable. Some had met the same sad fate as the little girl's.

After the children came a series of floats representing the different guilds of Busk, drawn by gorgeously harnessed horses. There was clearly great competition between the guilds to see who could make the most spectacular float, and each one seemed more extravagant than the last. And last of all came the float for the School of Busk, with a dozen Bards working glimmerspells so it appeared to be floating in the air on its own. They had created an enchanted summer garden with colourful blooms six times their usual size, and a chorus of exotic birds singing *The Song of Making* in Thoroldian in unearthly voices. Maerad had known this song since she was a child, when she had been taught it by Mirlad, although he had told her nothing of what it meant. She recognized the melody, and her heart lifted.

In the middle of the garden grew the Tree of Light, just as Nerili had shown it to Maerad on her first lesson, but much bigger. It was in full flower. Above the Tree appeared to float a huge unhewn crystal, which Cadvan explained was an image of the Mirror of Maras, the stone used in the Rite of Renewal. As the float passed, a sweet perfume drifted up to the applauding Bards.

"Nerili has surpassed herself this year," said Kabeka, clapping enthusiastically. "That was very well done."

After the Bards' float there were a few more musicians and tumblers, and then the parade was over. People whistled and cheered for a while, reluctant to leave, and then everyone began to wander off on their own business. In a surprisingly short time the huge crowd had dispersed, and Lamos reopened the gates. The makilon player and drummer began their music again and a few people started to dance.

Maerad sighed with sheer happiness. "That was the best thing I have ever seen," she said, her eyes shining. "Oh, it was wonderful!"

"You just want to be an illusioner," said Cadvan, laughing at her.

"I can think of worse things," she said. "Look how much people enjoy it. And it must be so exciting to be able to make things like that, and to let people see them."

"Yes, indeed," said Cadvan. "Though there are not many places where they love the arts of illusion as much as they do here, and have brought it to such perfections. In most other

Schools they are scorned as a minor part of Barding. Perhaps, one day, you will be the finest illusioner of them all. But now, alas, you walk a darker path."

Maerad felt as if he had poured cold water over her. She wanted to kick Cadvan for reminding her of the shadows that pursued her, even here, and for popping her bubble of delight. She scowled at him, and turned to talk to Honas, and Cadvan looked reflectively into his glass and said nothing. Something was troubling him.

As the sun slipped lower in the sky, the Bards left the tavern and started to make their way back to the School. The Rite of Renewal took place at moonrise in the centre of the School, where the music house, the library, the meeting hall and Nerili's Bardhouse surrounded a large square. It was paved with pink and white granite in a chequerboard pattern, but otherwise was without decoration. In its exact centre was a round white dais.

The square was full of people, both townsfolk and Bards, but there was a solemnity in this gathering that had been entirely absent from the procession. Maerad sensed the presence of the Bards' collective power as she and Cadvan wove their way through the crowd towards the dais. It was like a music or a light in her head, but she could never quite find the words to describe it; another sense woke within her and stirred in recognition. These are my people, she thought to herself, and I am glad to be with them.

Cadvan led Maerad right up to the dais, so they were standing with the Bards of the First and Second Circles and the members of the Chamber of Busk, who nodded gravely in greeting. Maerad couldn't see Nerili anywhere.

She looked up into the sky, where the full moon was just swinging clear of the horizon, casting a still, white light over the gathering.

Before long she began to hear strains of music, flutes and a lyre, and a hush fell. This was not wild Thoroldian dancing music, but the pure music of Bards. Its complex clarity rang over the crowd, and a listening silence rippled out from the musicians as they came closer. Then Maerad saw Nerili, robed in white, with the white diadem of her status hung from a silver fillet on her forehead, slowly pacing towards the middle of the square. Behind her were three musicians, all Bards of the First Circle, and before her walked Elenxi, with the Mirror of Maras floating before him, guided by his hands. Maerad sensed with a deep thrill that this was no mere glimmerspell, no deception of the eye, but a real magic: a magery of transformation that released the Mirror from the laws of the natural world.

The small procession stepped solemnly onto the dais, and the three musicians arranged themselves so they faced out: north, south and east. Elenxi placed the Mirror in the centre of the dais, where it remained as if he had put it on an invisible plinth. He stood so he was facing west. Then the music stopped.

In the sudden silence, Nerili circled the dais with her arms uplifted, her face turned out to the crowd.

"Welcome, and thrice welcome," she said, her voice reaching effortlessly to those at the back of the crowd. "We are come to the Rite of Renewal."

Everyone in the square held up their arms in reply and spoke with one voice. "May the Light bless us!"

"May the Light bless us all, and make true our tongues, and truer our hearts, and truest of all our deeds."

"May the Light bless us!"

Now Nerili was standing next to the Mirror, her arms still upraised. She began to glimmer with a silver light, which grew until she was almost as bright as the moon itself. Then, with a startling suddenness, she picked up the Mirror and cast it to the ground. Even though Maerad had been told of what happened during the rite, she gasped; the stone smashed into a rainbow of shards, with a flash like lightning. It seemed an act of terrible violence against so beautiful a thing.

"The old year has passed, and is now a thing of memory and dream: of regret and loss and joy, of birth and death, of hope realized and hope disappointed," she said.

"The old year has gone," came the response.

"And now the new year is to come, returning to us everything that is ours: our dreams and memories, our regrets and losses and joys, our births and deaths, and our hope."

"And the new year is to come."

Nerili began to sing *The Song of Making*. Maerad had always thought this most Bardic of songs was beautiful, but this was the first time she had heard it in the Speech, invested with its full power, and for the first time she realized what the song really was. The hair stirred on her neck. No instrument supported Nerili's voice; it rang, a full, rich contralto, into the absolute silence of the square.

She turned to Cadvan, wanting to share her wonder, and was brought up short. Cadvan's face was tight with anxiety. She looked back at Nerili. She couldn't see anything wrong; but now she watched with closer attention. Perhaps, although Maerad had never seen the Rite before, she could sense something that ought not to be there: a heaviness, a prickling shadow that was not at first perceptible.

Nerili continued to sing *The Song of Making*, and with each stanza she grew brighter until the power she was exerting began to make Maerad's head buzz. Very gradually the shards of the broken Mirror began to lift from the ground and floated in the air. Maerad drew in her breath. Slowly, slowly, every fragment of the Mirror began to come to the centre of the dais, and, as Nerili reached the final stanza of the song, all the broken pieces joined together, each fitting into its original place. But it was still not whole, it was still only a cracked stone.

Nerili put her hands over the Mirror and her power increased yet again. Light blazed from her hands and her face, making her seem insubstantial, no longer human. Suddenly, so quickly Maerad couldn't see when it happened, the Mirror was whole again: not mended, but remade as if it had never been shattered. There was no sound: it was as if hundreds of people held their breath.

Nerili drooped, as if she were suddenly weary, and most of the light went out of her. But now the crystal was blazing with radiance, the brightest thing in the square, throwing strange black shadows back over the crowd. She straightened herself with a visible effort, and placing her hands on the crystal she looked within it. Maerad couldn't see her face, but after a short time she saw her shoulders tense, and her hands clench, so the knuckles went white. Then it was as if somebody had cut all the strings in her body, and she slipped to the ground in a faint.

Before Maerad knew what had happened, Cadvan had bounded onto the dais next to the Mirror of Maras, and was looking within it himself. No one else had moved; each person present was frozen, as if possessed by sudden dread. Maerad glanced swiftly behind her and saw hundreds of faces all weirdly stamped with the same shock. She looked back at Cadvan: he was now brilliant with magery, his incandescent hands holding the blazing Mirror. She felt the force of his power with amazement; she had never before seen Cadvan like this, unleashed, undimmed by injury. And gradually an image began to form in the air above him, a luminous semblance of the Tree of Light. It was the same Tree and yet it looked different from the one Nerili had shown Maerad: the light it shed was a rich gold rather than silver, its blossoms subtly ruddier, the fruit a deeper gold.

A gasp came from the square, as hundreds of people let out their breath.

"Behold the new year, renewed and given back to you!" cried Cadvan.

"Behold the new year!"

The response came back, and the ceremony was over, but from the crowd came only a few ragged cheers. Cadvan took the Mirror of Maras and gave it to Elenxi, and the musicians began to play. Solemnly, in the reverse order to which they had come, they stepped off the dais and through the crowd. As soon as they had left the dais, and the music started to fade into the distance, Cadvan stooped to Nerili, who was beginning to stir, and Maerad and several other Bards rushed to help him.

Nerili opened her eyes and looked up at Cadvan. Her face was white as paper, and a single tear rolled down her cheek. "I failed to make the Tree," she whispered. "I have failed you all. The Rite has failed."

"No, the Tree has been made," Cadvan said, stroking her hair back from her face. "The year has been renewed. The Rite did not fail."

"No, no, you don't understand." Nerili seemed on the verge of bursting into tears, which was grievous to see in one so self-controlled. "I saw … the Tree…"

"Don't say now," said Cadvan in an urgent whisper. "Later. The Tree has been made. All is as it should be."

Nerili grasped Cadvan's hand hard, examining his face with a desperate intensity. "It has been made? How?"

"I made it," he said.

She let go his hand, bowed her head, and said nothing more. Cadvan helped her up and led her through the square, the crowd silently parting to make way for them. The Bards of the First Circle and Maerad followed them to the Bardhouse, unspeaking; and, as they left, Maerad heard people beginning to emerge from their shocked silence, to murmur, and then to talk.

Elenxi and the three other Bards of the First Circle who had participated in the Rite of Renewal were already in Nerili's sitting room when the rest of them entered. They looked almost as ashen as Nerili herself. Cadvan poured the First Bard a glass of the golden liquor laradhel, which she gulped down, her hands trembling on the glass. Her head was still bowed, as if she were unable to look anyone in the eye. All in the room watched her with silent concern. At last, she gave herself a little shake and sat up, looking straightly at Elenxi, her eyes dark with grief and shame. She looked utterly exhausted.

"I am undone," she said. "I have failed my place as First Bard. You must elect another."

"No!" said Elenxi, and several others. "No," he continued. "I was there. I felt it. It was not that you failed."

"If Cadvan of Lirigon had not been there, the Tree of Light would not have been renewed," she said, a flat deadness in her voice. "I had not the strength."

"Not to remake the Mirror and the Tree as well," said Cadvan. "There were other forces at work." He shook his head. "I felt it, too, Neri. It took everything I had to make the Tree, and I doubt that I could have made the Mirror as well."

There was a long silence.

"I saw ... I saw something terrible," said Nerili. "In the Mirror."

"Please say," said Kabeka gently. "Please tell us what you saw."

Nerili drew a long, shuddering breath. "I was so tired. I have never had such a struggle to renew the Mirror; it was as if all the fragments were pushing apart, resisting me, as if it wanted to remain broken. So when it was remade, I looked into it, and

I felt I had spent all my power. I was weak." She said this with a kind of contempt. "So … I looked. And at first it seemed to be as it should be. The sapling sprouted and grew as it always does, brightly and with joy, and my heart lifted. It grew to its full height and began to put forth buds. But then…" She shut her eyes, and began to speak in a whisper. "Then I felt a terrible sense of wrong, it was like a dagger slipped between my ribs. I cannot explain it. As I watched, a sickness began to spread from the roots of the Tree. A terrible poison, it seemed, that ran up the trunk. About the whole Tree was a stench of corruption. I watched the leaves and blossoms wither and fall, and leave the naked trunk bleached and lightless; and then even that rotted before my eyes, and nothing remained, nothing, except a vile smoke, a vapour of darkness…"

She began to shake all over, and Cadvan wordlessly poured her another glass of laradhel. Maerad looked around the half dozen Bards in the room. They were all pale, and some also reached for the laradhel. She realized that, unlike them, she was not shocked, that what Nerili described was already somehow familiar to her, and she felt suddenly appalled at herself. She met Cadvan's eye, and knew that he was not shocked either. Both of them were more familiar with the Dark than any of the Bards here.

"How did you know, Cadvan?" Maerad asked, breaking the silence. "You knew, before it happened. How did you know?"

"I didn't know what was going to happen," he said. "But I knew something was wrong. I could feel it. I have felt it all day, as if the wind were blighted, as if the moon were out of her course. When Nerili began *The Song of Making* it grew stronger and stronger, a sense of ill working against the song."

"I felt it, too," said Elenxi grimly. The three musicians nodded. "When I added my strength to Nerili's, it was like a poison seeped into me."

"The worst thing was…" Nerili said, even more quietly, as if her voice would fade altogether. "The worst thing was, that the poison seemed to come from within *me*. All the blackness from within my own soul." And now she did begin to weep.

The Bards seemed helpless in their consternation, but Maerad felt a sudden wash of empathy. She knew too well what it felt like to suspect a darkness within herself. Nerili took a deep breath, steeling herself, and then sat up, dashing the tears from her eyes impatiently.

"Oh, I am like a child," she said. "It is such a shock, such a terrible thing. But the Tree was made, after all, and so it is not a disaster. Not yet. But I fear the next Rite. I fear that I will not be able to do it on my own." She looked about the room with a restoration of her normal authority. "I think that perhaps you ought to consider instating a new First Bard. We cannot risk this again."

"Nerili," said Kabeka softly. "None of us is as powerful as you are. How would another Bard fare any better? And perhaps we would fare worse. Perhaps we would be unable to make the Mirror, let alone the Tree."

Nerili nodded. "That is a just thought," she said.

"We trust you as our First Bard," said Elenxi firmly. "And will have no other. But next year, perhaps another Bard should help with the Renewal, in case the same thing happens. I too can make the Tree."

Nerili nodded again.

"That's sensible," said Kabeka firmly. "We have no lack of trust in you, Nerili." The other Bards nodded. "We need you more now than ever before."

"The Dark rises," said Cadvan, his face haunted. "And this rising is more insidious than the last. I wonder how other Schools have fared this Midsummer? Do they enter a broken year, unrenewed, unblessed by the Tree of Light?"

Every Bard in the room shuddered at the thought.

"Leave me now," said Nerili. "We will speak further tomorrow, when we have all recovered somewhat. No, you stay, Maerad and Cadvan. I want to talk with you."

The Bards of Busk filed out of Nerili's room. Each, as they left, kissed her on her forehead and pressed her hand, and Maerad, watching them, realized how deeply Nerili was loved by the Bards she led. She felt suddenly a little forlorn, and sat down on a chair on the far side of the room. She doubted that she would ever be loved like that.

Nerili poured herself some wine, offering the decanter to Maerad and Cadvan. Maerad already felt light headed, since she hadn't eaten since midday, but had a glass anyway.

"Well, Cadvan, maybe at last I begin to understand." Nerili looked at him, smiling crookedly. "Maybe at last, after all this time ... I confess, I didn't know what you meant, all those years ago."

Cadvan looked up, a deep sadness in his eyes, but he said nothing, and a long, deep look passed between the two Bards. Maerad, still perched on her chair on the other side of the room, felt as if she were intruding on a private conversation. She remembered Cadvan's revelation in Norloch that he had been drawn to the Dark Arts as a young man, and had suffered greatly as a result; and she thought of his drivenness, his solitariness. No, she could see that he could not have stayed with Nerili, if that was what she had wanted. There was a sharpness in Nerili, a will not so much of steel as of adamant, Maerad thought; she had a feeling that, once crossed, Nerili would not forgive easily, nor forget. Maerad shifted uncomfortably in her chair, wishing she didn't think these things.

"A coup in Norloch: that is bad, yes, even very bad, but it does not pierce the centre," Nerili said. "But this ... this goes to the centre of things, in a way I do not understand, nor did I expect. To feel that I was poisoning the Tree of Light – ah, that is a torment as bad as anything I have experienced."

"Darkness lives in each of us," said Cadvan. "But we are all creatures of choice. We can turn to embrace it, as Enkir has, as the Nameless One himself did all those centuries ago; or we can resist, even if that resistance seems futile. Neri, you resisted with all your strength; no one can do more."

Nerili's face relaxed, as if she were absolved, and then hardened. "I shall be more wary from now on," she said. "It is true that here in Thorold, we are a wild and free people and we perhaps let the darkness in us play more than other Bards. But—"

"I do not think that a weakness," said Cadvan, interrupting her. "Rather a strength."

"Indeed," said Nerili. "Nevertheless, today has shown me that it needs but a small doorway to let corruption in."

"Do not shut it, nevertheless." Cadvan spoke urgently. "That is the greatest mistake. It is the mistake Enkir made, I believe: to wall himself up, until he saw in himself everything that was right, and he thought all else was wrong. It was but a small step from there to believing that power alone is truth and rightness, and a small step from that to what he now is. And, after all, joy bubbles on a fountain of doubt."

Nerili sighed, and then laughed. "Oh, this is stuff for minor Bards," she exclaimed. She glanced at Maerad, and sat a little straighter, as if she had suddenly remembered that she and Cadvan were not alone. "It is the way of the Balance. After all."

"Aye," Cadvan answered. "It is all in the Balance. Perhaps we should all do beginner's lessons again with Maerad."

Maerad had been toying with her glass, wishing fiercely she was elsewhere. She was plagued by the same irritating jealousy as before, only made worse now, being full of conflicting emotions. She looked up when Cadvan mentioned her name.

"Perhaps," said Nerili. "It does no harm to go back to

beginnings now and again. But yes, I understand better, after tonight. And I think now that it is not such a good idea that you and Maerad remain in Busk."

"Where will we go?" Maerad felt suddenly very tired. Not travelling again? She had hoped they might have more time here.

"We cannot stay," said Cadvan. "But I have still found nothing about the Treesong in the Library of Busk. I have been searching as hard as I can, and I have found nothing. And how are Maerad and I to find the Treesong, as we must, if we have no idea what it is?"

"And I haven't finished my lessons," said Maerad quickly.

Nerili looked between them. "These are not minor matters," she said. "Nevertheless, I feel a quickening sense of danger in your being here. Do you think that the hundreds of people in the square tonight will not wonder who made the Tree, and will not ask, and will not be told? I cannot see how your presence here can be concealed any more: word will spread. I think perhaps you might stay in Thorold for a while, but not in the School."

Cadvan bowed his head, accepting her argument. "I think Maerad is reluctant as I am to leave here; but of course we cannot stay if it endangers both you and us. Am I right in thinking you know of a place where we could go?"

"Yes, I do know a place, in the mountains." Nerili placed her empty glass on the table. "I will send a messenger tomorrow. It will be impossible for anyone to find you there." She smiled at Maerad. "It is not as comfortable as Busk, perhaps, but it is as beautiful, in its own way. I will continue to search the library, Cadvan. I will make it my first priority. I cannot believe there is nothing there that tells of the Treesong. And Cadvan is quite capable of continuing your lessons, Maerad." She stood up. "I will advise you when I hear if it is possible; it will take a few days. In the meantime, I think it is time to eat. And Midsummer is supposed to be a time of celebration, after all."

She smiled, dismissing them, standing straight and digni-fied: every inch a First Bard, Maerad thought, as they bowed and took their leave. There was no sign of the distressed and broken woman Nerili had been. As they left, Maerad stole a glance at Cadvan's face; he looked both relieved and desolate, as if he had found something important, and at once had lost it. She didn't want to think about what it meant; it gave her an ache somewhere in her middle.

V

GOATS AND CHEESE

BEHIND the School of Busk the mountainous interior of Thorold drew upwards, peak after purple peak, until it reached the rocky pinnacles of the Lamedon, the highest mountain in Thorold. Even in summer, the crown of the Lamedon was white with snow.

From the mountains shelved down a wild country, with harsh ridges and peaks hiding green, sheltered valleys. Now it drowsed in the summer heat. On the slopes of the peaks clustered groves of myrtle, acacias and olive trees, and there were clumps of scented mimosa and wild roses; bees murmured in the fragrant grasses where the goatherds and shepherds grazed their flocks. Through the haze of distance, Maerad could see dark forests of pine and firs growing on the higher lands, and the snow-capped peaks, bereft of all trees, towered behind them.

The landscape was beautiful to look at, Maerad thought, but it was a different matter altogether to ride through it. She pulled up her horse and wiped her brow, taking a swig from her water bottle. She was wearing silk trousers and a light tunic, and Cadvan had plonked a wide-brimmed straw hat on her head to prevent, he said, her going even sillier with the heat; but even so, the sweat ran down her back in runnels, and she was sure her face was puce.

Still, the view was spectacular. She, Cadvan and Elenxi had been toiling up one of the hundreds of narrow roads, most of them barely more than goat tracks, which wound through the

interior of Thorold. From here she could see over the knees of
Thorold, right out to sea, although the town of Busk was hidden behind a ridge. Way off in the distance she could hear, on
a flock of goats, the clinking of bells that floated down a distant
hillside like a languid cloud, and otherwise the only sound was
the buzzing of bees and the shrill music of cicadas. It was still
morning, not yet the hottest part of the day, but the sun beat
down fiercely.

"The village of Iralion is not far," said Elenxi, turning on
his horse, his eyes creased against the light. "And we will stop
there until it cools. It has a famous tavern." His teeth flashed in
a smile, and Maerad dredged up a smile in return. She didn't
like the heat; or, at least, she liked it well enough from a shady
balcony, with nothing to do and plenty of minted lemon water
by her elbow. But Elenxi, who seemed as tough and unkillable
as an ancient olive, appeared to be completely unbothered by
it. She sighed, putting her water bottle back in her pack, and
urged her horse onwards. Any tavern Elenxi recommended was
bound to be excellent; and, really, what was she complaining
about? She had endured far worse. But she was still smarting at
the necessity of leaving Busk.

They had trotted out of the School of Busk in the cool of
that morning. Maerad had packed wearily before having a last
bathe in the glorious bathroom the night before, wondering, as
always, when she would next enjoy this luxury. She was well
tired of her fugitive life.

The week since the Midsummer Festival had been a blur.
Nerili had been correct: it was all over Busk by the next morning that Cadvan of Lirigon had saved the Rite of Renewal from
disaster. Although the Bards put it about that it was someone
else, confusing the rumours, it was only a matter of time now
before that news reached unfriendly ears. Maerad and Cadvan
stayed hidden within the School, continuing with their routine

as before, and when they ventured into town, they disguised themselves. Maerad began to feel hunted again, a feeling that had disappeared altogether those few weeks in Busk; and with it returned her dreams of Hulls, reaching out their bony hands towards her from the darkness.

The delegation from Norloch had returned from Gent and been given the answer decided on by the council. Igan was not, by all accounts, well pleased, and had left frostily for Norloch; Nerili expected a response within a month or so. Bards from Thorold had been sent secretly by swift ways to all the Schools of the Seven Kingdoms for counsel, and Elenxi had been busy travelling the isle, consulting with the village mayors on possible resistance to an invasion from Norloch. He had a double purpose in guiding Maerad and Cadvan, for he was also planning to visit several isolated villages in the very middle of Thorold.

Nerili advised Maerad and Cadvan that they should stay until the travelling Bards returned from the Seven Kingdoms, in order to get fresh information on what was happening elsewhere. She calculated it would be a month at most. "Then," she said, "I think you ought to leave, and swiftly. It would make sense to go to Ileadh first, and then north up the coast to Zmarkan. Annar is too dangerous to cross, I judge; the Light seeks you now, as well as the Dark. I think that the only safety is in movement. But, for the moment, I think you will be protected enough in the mountains."

Cadvan had spent long hours in the library before they left, but had still found nothing. And Maerad had continued her lessons, gloomily wondering what good her snatched knowledge would be, once they were on the road and in danger again.

And then had come the necessity of farewell. My whole life is just one long farewell, Maerad thought. I begin to make friends and then I must leave, probably never to see them again.

At a dinner held at the School to drink the parting cup, Honas, who had indeed tried to kiss her on Midsummer's Night, had been downcast. Although Maerad had pushed him away that night, laughing, it was a wrench saying goodbye; she had become fond of him, and in the short time they had known each other he had taught her to play the makilon, an instrument she liked very much. It was the same with all her new friends in Thorold – Owan, Kabeka, Nerili, Intatha, Oreston, and the many others. As she climbed the rocky slopes on her sure-footed Thoroldian mount, she felt that everything she had found in Busk, the merriment, the joyous defiance, was all dropping away, and now she was returning to her usual dour self; that the wild dancing girl she had been was nothing but a dream, and now she was waking up again, in a dark room full of foreboding shadows.

After a while, the path they were following took a sudden dip, leading them down into one of the unexpected valleys folded into the deep creases of Thorold. The silk makers lived in these valleys, near the bitterly cold mountain streams of Thorold, and tended the orderly orchards of mulberry trees that fed the silkworms. It was the waters of Thorold, the silk makers said, that was the special secret of their skill, and gave the dyes their famous brilliance and purity.

Shade fell over the riders, and the vegetation became more lush as they moved downhill, until it seemed they were moving through a dappling canopy of green, humidly hot and hushed, but with the promise of cool water burbling in the distance. They trotted through groves of mulberries, the fruits red and dark purple among the green leaves, or fallen on the ground, staining it like wine. The air grew steadily cooler and the sweat dried gently on Maerad's skin. At last, they reached a small village of stone buildings, rather like the buildings in the School of Busk, only smaller; each was entwined in vines and flowering plants. There was only a single road through its centre, and a river of clear water ran singing beside it.

"This is Iralion," said Elenxi. "And there is the tavern. I shall leave you two there while I see Mirak, the mayor, and speak with him."

They tethered their horses outside the tavern by a water trough, and with relief Maerad followed Cadvan into the cool interior. It was crowded with people taking their ease after a day's work, and all of them turned to look. They greeted the Bards cheerily, some obviously hoping there was going to be music; but when the Bards just ordered drinks and something to eat, they turned back to their own conversations.

Elenxi turned up later, obviously well pleased. "It's the same story over the whole isle," he said, rubbing his hands. "Outrage at Norloch, and vows of resistance. There are caves all through these mountains, which I've advised them to stock well with provisions and supplies against an invasion. In a week, all Thorold will be ready." He took a deep draught of wine, and then looked down at the table. "By the Light, I hope it doesn't come to that," he said soberly. "School against School – and Norloch, the centre of the Light, the aggressor – such a thing has never happened. Kings have always fought, alas, to make their kingdoms greater, but Bards have never made war against each other. But if it does come to that, Thorold will not fall."

Looking at the fierce old man, now pouring himself another drink, Maerad thought that she understood why Thorold had held out against the Nameless One during the Great Silence. Thoroldians would make bitter and ruthless enemies, she had no doubt, and in defence of their own she suspected they would never concede defeat.

The three Bards continued their trek, riding from village to village across the mountainous terrain of Thorold, for three days.

The weather cooled on the third day, and Elenxi sniffed the air suspiciously, wondering if there was to be a storm. That night they stopped at a tiny village called Velissos, huddled in the lee of a high ridge. Elenxi was obviously well known there, and they were greeted warmly. They stabled the horses at the tiny tavern, which was really little more than the front room of a house. They planned to leave the horses in the village; from here they would go on foot.

The storm broke with a sudden violent downpour almost as soon as they reached shelter, and Maerad looked with wonder out onto the wall of rain, a solid grey curtain that hammered down on the tiled roof of the tavern.

"We're deep in Thorold now," said Cadvan. "This is mountain country. You can feel the bones of the earth."

"Well, as long as it doesn't break my bones," said Maerad.

"It won't, if you're careful," Elenxi answered. "Which you should be. We're near the Lamedon now, and it's tough country. These are my people."

Maerad looked around her at the Velissos villagers. They did seem tough; these were the shepherds and goatherds who made the delicious white cheeses Maerad had eaten in Busk, and most of them looked as craggy as the mountains their holdings clung to. Some of the men were almost as big-boned as Elenxi, and the women looked strong and capable.

"They breed special goats here, because the mountains are so steep," said Cadvan. "On one side their legs are shorter than the other, so they can graze more comfortably."

"How strange," said Maerad. "Poor things! What happens when they have to turn around? Wouldn't that be a bit difficult for them?"

"Well, they breed different goats for different hills – right-legged goats to move one way, and left-legged—"

Elenxi snorted with laughter, and Maerad realized she'd

been taken in.

"Oh, that's not fair! It might have been true," she said. "And there I was believing you."

That night they brought out their instruments, and there was dancing. Maerad was amazed by how the taciturn villagers became as high spirited and noisy as the Bards of Busk; she was picked up and whirled around by big men with huge black moustaches and muscles as gnarled and brown as old trees. After the dancing there was singing, and the whole tavern joined in, their hands clasped to their breasts, their voices trembling with emotion. They retired late, after finishing with an old favourite of the Thoroldians, *The Song of Theokas*, a lament that throbbed with sorrowful desire:

I kiss the peaks of Lamedon with my eyes
And the white arms of the passionate sea
Which loves this beautiful island that I love
    For I am dying...

When she went to bed Maerad snuggled into the sheepskins against the surprisingly sharp cold, the lament still ringing in her head, and its meld of love and sorrow echoed all night through her dreams.

The following morning they picked up their packs and left Velissos with many warm farewells. Elenxi led them up a path even more vertiginous than those they had already travelled, winding its way around tumuli of granite and along sharp ridges. They were so high up now that it was cool, although the sky was clear and blue, and the air held a special freshness, as if they were the first to breathe it. Very often, little mountain streams leapt down the slopes, some no wider than a step, pouring in miniature waterfalls into pools full of shiny pebbles.

Maerad tasted the water: it was so cold it numbed her lips.

"It's fresh from the snowline of the Lamedon," said Cadvan, nodding upwards to the bare stony pinnacles that stretched above them.

Maerad watched a pair of eagles circling so high up they could hardly be seen. She didn't look down for very long or very often, because the height made her feel a little dizzy.

"It must be harsh here in winter," she said.

"It is," Elenxi said. "Winter is when the herders come in, the goats and sheep are shut up in their sheds, and we eat the sweet stored apples and grain and tell long stories by the fires. And then the storms howl about our heads! The weather here is like the people: fierce and unpredictable." He grinned.

It was very tiring, climbing these slopes. No wonder the Velissos people were so strong, Maerad thought. You needed muscles of iron just to walk around. After three hours they paused for a meal, and then pressed on. Maerad's thighs were beginning to ache badly, and she was glad of the walking stick Elenxi had cut for her from a thorn tree. At last, they reached one of the meadows that were scattered over the mountains, like emerald liquor in cups of stone. This one was much bigger than most of them and at its end was a stone house surrounded by three wooden huts and a small garden. Goats wandered the grass, their bells clinking lazily as they cropped, but otherwise there was no one to be seen.

Maerad flopped down and lay on her back, squinting at the blue sky through the nodding grasses and wildflowers. "Leave me here," she said. "Oh, my poor legs!"

"What, complaining so after a mere leisurely stroll?" said Elenxi, lifting his eyebrows. "If you're to be an honorary Thoroldian, you'll have to do better than that."

"Mercy!" said Maerad. "I'm not sure I have the strength to be Thoroldian. You're all made of wire."

Elenxi dragged her up, and they made their way across the meadow to the stone house. Goats came up to them and butted them curiously, their tails wagging comically. Maerad looked into their strange yellow eyes, but didn't try to talk to them. She was sure she'd have plenty of time later.

As they neared the house, a man as big as Elenxi came out, his arms spread wide. "Welcome, my brother!" he said, enfolding Elenxi in an embrace and kissing him on both cheeks and then turning to the other two. "I am Ankil. And you are Cadvan and Maerad? I am glad to meet you at last, Cadvan; welcome, Maerad. Nerili has told me much about both of you. Come in, come in. I have wine, I have water, I have food. Come in and rest yourselves."

Maerad studied Ankil with an intensifying curiosity. He was very like Elenxi, but what puzzled her more was her conviction that he was a Bard. He had about him something of the subtle glow by which Bards could recognize each other, although in his case it had an evanescence that made her feel unsure; it was strangely different in him. And, in any case, what was a Bard doing up in the mountains herding goats?

The house was surrounded by a small version of the wide porticos obligatory in Thorold, and there was set a table and a single chair. Ankil went into the house and returned with three stools. "Guests are not frequent here," he said cheerfully. "So you must forgive the cobwebs on these." He gave them a perfunctory brush and disappeared inside.

Maerad dropped her pack on the porch and sat down gratefully, rubbing her legs. Before long, Ankil was back with a tray on which was set a carafe of rich Thoroldian wine, another of cool water, four cups, and fresh bread and cheese. They sat and ate, their appetites sharpened by the mountain air and their long walk.

By herder standards, Ankil's house was luxurious; it was

smaller than most houses Maerad had passed in the villages on
their way, but much more substantial than the plain wooden
huts she had seen dotted around the mountain pastures. She
found out later that unlike other herders, who only moved to
the mountain pastures in summer, Ankil lived there all year
round. The house was clearly very old, and had been built with
thick granite walls through which were punched small, shuttered windows. The roof, made of clay tiles, was steeply raked
to prevent a build-up of snow, and the whole was built on high
foundations, so the porch was several steps up.

Unusually for a Thoroldian house, it was built on three levels: there was a cellar, used for storage and work, above that
a kitchen and living area, and on the top, above the stove,
two bedrooms, with sloping ceilings and shuttered dormer
windows that poked out through the tiles. In the rooms were
fragrant mattresses stuffed with dried mountain grasses and
covered with soft sheepskins. During their stay, Ankil moved
out to one of the ancillary huts, where he slept on a mattress in
the empty stalls, for the goats slept in the meadows during the
summertime. Maerad felt guilty when she saw this, but Ankil
just laughed and said it was no punishment for him to sleep like
a proper goatherd.

She soon found out why Ankil had the puzzling Bardic
glow. He and Elenxi were, indeed, brothers.

"I went down to the School, like Elenxi, when I was a boy,"
he told them over the midday meal. "But, you know, I just
didn't want to be a Bard. Not like Elenxi here," and he poked
him with affection. "He is the clever one. But me, I got bored
with all that."

"He was in love," said Elenxi, smiling.

"Well, that too," Ankil said. "My Kiranta was the most beautiful woman I have ever seen. Her eyes were as grey and stormy
as the sea and her hair was black as olives, and her skin was like

the pale golden silk they make in the valleys. Yes, I was in love. But it was more than that: I could never learn how to read and write. No matter what they tried, I couldn't make any sense of those squiggles they call letters."

"So what happened?" asked Maerad, fascinated.

"Well, when my teachers had all thrown their arms into the air and declared that there was nothing they could do, I came back to Velissos and married my Kiranta. I didn't want to be a Bard, I just wanted to tend my goats and trees and garden and grow my children. I was very happy for a long time. But then," he shrugged, "as is the way of things, my children grew up and my Kiranta grew old. And that's when Barding caught up with me, you see, because I did not grow old. I was little different from the way I had been when I had come back from the School, and Kiranta's hair grew grey, and then white. But my Kiranta looked no different to me, because I loved her; for me she was always the same beautiful girl who looked for me in the pass, with her eyes shining."

Ankil sighed heavily, and Maerad felt tears start in her eyes. Cadvan was looking at Ankil with a quick empathy. "That is hard," he said.

"Yes, it was hard when she died," said Ankil. "It is always difficult to have Bards in a family, and we have so many in ours... Well, I buried my Kiranta, and wept for her, and I still miss her, every day I miss her. So I made sure my children had what they needed, and I came up here. And here I've been ever since."

In the silence that followed his story, Maerad wondered how long Ankil had lived here, in this beautiful, isolated meadow. One hundred years? Two hundred?

"Did you not want to go back to the School?" she asked.

"Ah, no, young Bard," he said. "It was too late for me, and there was still that little matter of the reading and writing.

I am more useful here; I breed fat goats and I make a famous cheese."

"He is too modest," said Elenxi. "Ankil is a famous healer, and many send all this way for his help."

"Pffft, that is nothing," he said. "I am content."

"Were any of your children Bards?" asked Maerad curiously.

"Yes, two," said Ankil. "One is in Gent, another in Turbansk. And my granddaughter is First Bard in Busk."

"Nerili?" exclaimed Maerad in surprise.

"Yes, my little Neri. She is the image of my Kiranta, and when I see her I am both proud and sad; she calls up in me so many happy memories, and so many sorrowful reflections. So you see, although I was no good as a Bard, I have made my contribution."

Elenxi stayed the night before heading down the mountain to confer with more villagers. They had a merry time – merry enough for Maerad to feel very unwell the following morning. She was fascinated by the two brothers, at once so similar and so different, and looked from one to the other in wonder all night: one a Bard of the First Circle, the other a goatherd. The respect between them was palpable; there was no sense that Elenxi felt in any way superior to Ankil; in fact, she felt that he deferred to his brother in a way she hadn't seen him defer to anybody, not even Nerili. Elenxi, she found, was the older brother, by four years, so seniority did not explain it.

Over the coming days, she began to understand Elenxi's respect. Ankil was, for all his unletteredness, as wise as Nelac, Cadvan's teacher in Norloch, and beneath his gentleness and apparent simplicity was a rare strength of spirit. His memory was prodigious, and his life had left him plenty of time for reflection. He was a vast storehouse of songs and tales, and his

knowledge of herblore was, Cadvan told her, reputedly unri-
valled in Thorold.

He lived a life of comfortable austerity. Inside his house
was tidy and clean, and everything in it had the beauty of func-
tional things well made. There was little decoration, and no
books at all. The kitchen was dominated by a black-iron wood
stove with a huge, smoke-blackened chimney. It was furnished
only with a broad table and stools, and was surrounded by
shelves, which were well stocked with bottles of dried herbs
and pulses and grains and salt. Yet more herbs hung in bunches
from the ceiling, interspersed with bunches of onions and garlic, infusing the room with a pungent fragrance. The cellars
were carefully sealed against damp and were stacked with jars
of pickles and jams and preserves and honey, bags of nuts and
grains and flours and pulses, and shelves of fruits and vegetables gathered from the previous year – wrinkled golden apples
and pears, turnips and potatoes and carrots. And barrels and
barrels of wine. There was no meat, because Ankil would not
eat animals. Some food and all the wine came up from the village, but the bulk of what he ate was grown and preserved by
Ankil himself.

Maerad was to find that visitors were not so infrequent as
Ankil had intimated; at least once a week a Velissos villager
would struggle up to the meadow, leading a pony that carried
supplies on its back – wood or grain or wine – and leading it
back down laden with cheeses or combs of honey or some especially requested healing potion.

It all bespoke a life of hard physical labour, and, indeed,
Ankil was busy from dawn to dusk. At night he sat with them
in the fragrant kitchen or, if it was not too cold, outside on the
porch, and they told many tales and sang many songs, their
music echoing out over the mountains of Thorold.

Maerad and Cadvan had their own routines, although they

helped Ankil in his tasks whenever they could. Cadvan was now intensively drilling Maerad in High Magery, practical and theoretical, and she continued to learn the Ladhen runes and Nelsor scripts, although they hadn't many books with them. In the afternoons, mentally tired by the work, it was a relief to practise swordcraft and unarmed combat. It also provided much entertainment for the goats, who after a couple of days would gather around them in a circle, their jaws constantly chewing, following the strokes with interested expressions, skittering off in mixed alarm and hilarity when the sparring became too violent. One, a huge billy goat, constantly made rude remarks. Occasionally he was so obnoxious that Maerad would purposely let a loose slash go his way, and then, his dignity affronted by having to skip backwards, he would butt the other goats so they scattered in alarm.

Maerad found a tranquillity in this simple life, very different from the busy intensity of Busk, and her nightmares again subsided. The longer she stayed with Ankil, the more the peace of the mountains began to enter her. Sometimes, when her day's work was done and Cadvan was off with Ankil helping him with the garden or the goats, she would climb to another tiny meadow nearby and just sit, letting the deep quiet fill her up slowly, an unhurried accretion of light. From this meadow she could look over the whole south of the Isle of Thorold, right down to where the sea vanished into blue mists of distance. At these times, the things that troubled her seemed far away and unimportant: all that mattered was the hum of the bees and the chirp of birdsong, the way the sun gleamed on the edge of a blue wildflower, the distant bleat and clink of grazing goats.

In these moments she usually didn't think about anything. But when she did, her thoughts most often turned to Hem. He would rise vividly in her mind, his gangly limbs, which had, nevertheless, a surprising grace, his dark, haunted face with its mischievous smile, the intense blue eyes that alone hinted that he was her brother. She remembered the terrible day that she and Cadvan had found him, stinking of urine and terror, concealed in a Pilanel caravan. Maerad still dreamed sometimes of the slaughtered bodies of the family who had hidden him. It had been the first time Maerad had really understood the horror of Hulls – the "Black Bards", as Hem called them. It had opened up a shocking vista of emptiness that appalled her. Hulls enjoy the suffering of others, Cadvan had said to her at the time; it answers some lack within themselves...

Maerad sometimes felt she was all lack. It frightened her. Hem had filled an emptiness within her that she had not been aware of. She smiled, thinking of how he refused to call himself Cai, his birth name; he was, he insisted, Hem. But she also wondered what was behind that refusal, what it was about himself that he sought to deny. She had thought it was because Hem was not comfortable as a Bard. But perhaps it was something else. Hem, after all, was not an Annaren name; it came from the wandering people of Zmarkan. Maybe, without realizing it, Hem was cleaving to the distant memory of their Pilanel father.

There was about her brother something irrepressible, a spark that even his abused childhood had not extinguished; and yet she feared for him, feared the blackness stamped in him was a damage that would never be healed. But, Maerad thought fiercely, it must be healed; she could heal it, if they only had time.

At least she knew her brother was alive, and that mere fact made her feel a little less alone in the world. No matter how many friends she made, Maerad still felt deeply alone. Part of it was her fate as the One, but it was more than that. She had been alone for as long as she could remember.

* * *

It was inevitable that their evening conversations would turn at some point to Maerad and Cadvan's quest, and to the riddle of the Treesong. Ankil hadn't expressed any curiosity about their reasons for concealment in the mountains, although he was clearly well informed about the recent events in Busk.

One night, they were speaking of Maerad's Elemental ancestry, which interested Ankil keenly. Maerad showed him the gold ring that the Elidhu Ardina had given her, and then ran upstairs to get the pipes that she had been given when they met in the Weywood in Annar. Ankil inspected the pipes closely; like all Bards, he was a musician. He forebore to blow through them, handling them gingerly, as if they might be dangerous.

"I used to make pipes like that when I was a child," Cadvan commented.

"As did I," said Ankil. "Out of the river reeds. They're the kind only children make. It's like those rhymes that children sing. They are never taught them by adults; but they sing the same nonsense from Zmarkan to Turbansk."

Ardina's face sprang vividly to Maerad's mind: her wild, fey face, with its yellow eyes, cleft by an iris like a cat's. Maerad had seen her both as the grave Queen of Rachida and as the wild Elidhu. There was, she reflected now, something childlike in her different guises; perhaps it was why the Elementals were so distrusted by Bards.

"The Elementals do not read books, as I do not," said Ankil. "They have their own Knowings, and their memories are deep. I have spoken myself with the Elidhu Lamedon."

"Indeed?" said Cadvan, his interest quickening. "I did not know he still spoke with humans."

Ankil laughed. "He does not. But I, it seems, am half goat and half eagle, and so he deigns to speak to me. It is like talking to a storm! But he has told me many interesting things, and sometimes, when I am troubled, I will visit him."

"How does he appear to you?" Maerad asked eagerly.

"Sometimes he won't appear at all. I climb all the way up there, and come all the way back. But when he wills, he appears to me as a form of mist; or sometimes he will speak as an eagle, but bigger by far than even the Thoroldian mountain eagles."

"I am quite certain that Bards have not taken enough account of the Elementals over the centuries," said Cadvan. "To all our peril."

"I too think that," said Ankil. "But not many Bards agree. Here in Thorold it's a little different, perhaps: I believe Elidhu blood runs in the veins of many Thoroldians. There are many tales here of love between water sprites and men, or of women who have gone into the mountains and come back ten years later leading a little child with strange eyes."

"I wonder if the Lamedon would know anything about the Treesong," Maerad said.

"Well, there is nothing in the library in Busk." Cadvan made a gesture of disgust. "I have been inhaling ancient dust for weeks, to no avail."

"The Treesong?" said Ankil.

"We're supposed to find it," said Maerad.

She felt no doubts about trusting Ankil, and she plunged without hesitation into the tale of their quest. Ankil listened with close attention, his bushy eyebrows drawn together. Cadvan sat in silence, his face clouded with thought.

"Hmmm," Ankil said, when she had finished talking. "Well, I do not know if the Lamedon can help us. He is not overfond of Bards, as he has told me on many occasions, and he has no interest at all in the struggles of the Light and the Dark, and never has had. He is not like the Elidhu of Annar, who remember the Dhyllin and the days of Afinil, when Bard and Elidhu sang together."

"Do you think he might talk to me?" asked Maerad doubt-fully. "I can speak their language."

Ankil gave her a look of such candour that she almost blushed. "I don't know," he said. "But I think it more likely that he would not. And could you climb to the peaks of the Lamedon?"

Maerad thought of how the heights even here made her dizzy, and shuddered.

"No," she said.

"I don't think so either," said Ankil frankly. "It is a challenge even for a skilled climber, and even in summer. And you are so slight – the wind would pick you up and throw you into a crevasse, or send you sailing towards Busk."

"A shame," Cadvan said restlessly. "Though it might be as fruitless as my search through the documents of Old Thorold. How do you find something, if you do not know what it is?"

"I don't know," said Ankil. He was frowning in thought. "But I am thinking that it reminds me of something. Do they tell in Annar of the Split Song?"

"No," said Cadvan. "The Split Song?"

"It is a very old story, and not a well known one." Ankil picked up a boot he had been mending, and spat on the leather. "I will tell you, if you like. It was told me by an old man when I was a little boy, and I thought it such a strange tale it has stuck with me all these long years." He began to polish the boot care-fully, pausing every now and then to admire its sheen; when Ankil told a story, he always started doing something with his hands. Maerad settled herself comfortably. She liked Ankil's stories.

"Once, long ago, when time was an egg, before there was above and below, or before and behind, or deep or through or wide, there was a Song. There was no voice to sing it, and there was no ear to hear it, and the Song was lonely in the nowhere and nothing that everything was. For what is a Song without a voice and an ear?

"Now it happened, as you know, that the world was made, and the sky spilt over the nowhere like a bolt of blue silk, and then the stars tumbled over it as if someone had dropped countless gems, and the earth was solid beneath it, rock and iron and fire. And the earth loved the sky, and the sky loved the earth, but they could not touch each other, no matter how they tried. And how they tried! And both began to weep from sorrow, and from the sky came the first rain, and the earth filled up with rivers and seas, and where the rain touched its fire great steams went up and made the clouds and mists, and out of the clouds and mists were born the Elidhu, the oldest children of time, and then the trees and the silent and still plants of the earth, with their flowers like trumpets and their leaves like lyres. But the Elidhu had neither voices nor ears.

"Now, the Song said to itself, at last there may be a voice to speak and an ear to hear. So it came out of the nowhere into the now, and slipped into the veins of the Elidhu, as if it were a shoal of minnows slipping into a stream, and each Elidhu felt the Song within it like a shudder of life, and all the sounds of the world burst in on them: the fall of the rain, and the sough of the sea, and endless sighing of the wind through the green trees. And they opened their mouths in wonder, and so it was the Song leapt out of their mouths, and at last became itself. And the Song was happy, for a very long time."

Ankil put down the boot and picked up another.

"Well, it happened after a long age that a shadow fell upon the world, and there was a great war and so death entered the world. And there was much suffering for all creatures: the plants and the beasts and the humans and the Elidhu. But the shadow was beaten back, and then there was a long peace. All this time the Song lived in the Elidhu, and was happy, although it found that the world was more complex and more sad than it had thought. And so the Song changed, and became more beautiful as it changed, for the shadow and death entered into the Song and made it bright and dark and high and deep. And the voices of the Elidhu lifted in joy, for they loved the beauty of the Song.

"But it happened that a king arose, and he heard the Song, and he was overborne by longing for its loveliness. He could not sleep and he could not eat for thinking of the Song, and each day that he could not have the Song for himself was to him an eternity of dust. And one day he stole the Song from the Elidhu.

"But the Elidhu would not let it go, and the Song split in two, with a terrible noise, like the sound of the whole world cracking, and one half went south and one half went north. And when it split, the bright went one way, and the dark went another. And ever since the world has been twain, and the Song has been unhappy."

There was a long silence, apart from Ankil's brushing.

"Is that it?" asked Maerad.

"Yes," said Ankil, nodding. "That is it."

Cadvan was sitting up straight and alert, his face eager. "Ankil, I've never heard that story before," he said. "But the Song – the Song of the Elementals – surely it's the Treesong?"

"Well, it still doesn't tell us what it is," said Maerad.

"No, maybe not … but the story obviously refers to the Wars of the Elementals, and then to a king … it has to be the Nameless One. Sharma, the king from the south." His brows knotted. "And I think it is talking about the Spell of Binding he made, to banish death and to cast out his Name. Maybe he split the Treesong…"

"Well, you've said for a while that you thought the spell was to do with the Knowing of the Elidhu," said Maerad. "Maybe you're right. But how do you find a song? Was it written down?"

"I don't know. It could be that's what the story means by the Song being stolen, that it was written down instead of living in the Elidhu. It's all so vague." Cadvan thumped the table in frustration.

The three fell into a reflective silence, watching the old moon swinging above the mountain pastures, and Maerad became aware of the sounds of the crickets singing in the grass, and the sleepy night-time coughs of the goats.

"Do you know what they call the Nameless One in some places in Thorold?" asked Ankil thoughtfully, breaking the silence.

"What?" Cadvan turned to him.

"The Half Made."

"The Half Made. The Split Song." Cadvan looked down at his hands. "It has to be connected, surely?"

"Perhaps." Ankil had finished polishing his boots, and placed them neatly side by side next to his chair. "Well, for what it's worth, from an old goatherd, I think it as likely as not."

VI

THE LION OF STONE

OVER the following weeks, life continued its slow routine. Maerad woke early every morning, refreshed, and walked to the window to look out over the highlands of Thorold. She loved her simple bedroom, devoid of the luxuries of Innail or Busk, but with other beauties those chambers could not match. Every morning, the early air came fresh and unbreathed through her casement, smelling faintly of grass and carrying the gentle chimes of the goats' bells as they grazed; and no mural could match her view. She felt the deep weariness, which had lingered since she left Norloch, dissipate and finally disappear. The shadows vanished from beneath her eyes, and her skin glowed with health.

The view was different every morning: sometimes the valleys were wreathed in mist, so that it seemed she were looking out over a huge white sea with green islands of high ground rising abruptly through it, bathed in golden sunlight; sometimes the whole countryside, all the way to the sea, possessed a preternatural clarity, so colours seemed saturated and every edge was hard and unmistakable; sometimes it was wrapped in a mauve haze, so you couldn't see the sea at all, and the landscape was soft and blurred, muted and almost ghostly.

After a light breakfast, Maerad plunged into her work with Cadvan. They started her studies in Ankil's kitchen, working intensely until mid-morning, when Cadvan would call a break. At these times, Maerad would usually go for a solitary walk towards the mountains that soared above Ankil's meadow, grim rocky peaks draped with snow. Highest of all was the Lamedon, its sheer precipices, even in midsummer, often shrouded with mist; then, falling away in the range, were the triple peaks of the Okinlos, the harsh naked walls of the Indserek, so steep no snow could cling there, and the sharp summit of the Kyrnos, that looked as narrow as a blade. The shoulders of many other mountains slouched behind these high peaks, forming the central range of the Thoroldian mountains. Some mornings it was hazy and, to Maerad's astonishment, the mountains would disappear altogether, as if nothing was there at all; or they hung like ghosts in the sky, visible only in faint outlines, and you could see them only if you peered carefully, knowing they were there.

It was a peaceful time, despite the worries that beset both Maerad and Cadvan. Maerad felt as if she were gathering strength for a struggle to come, although she didn't know what that struggle would be. She bent her concentration fiercely to learning: by now she had mastered the alphabetic Nelsor script, and was able to write and read quite creditably, and was making inroads into learning the Ladhen runes. These were numerous, a complex system of thousands of signs that changed meaning by subtle additions and deletions from a vocabulary of a few hundred images. They were written as strokes that could be just as easily carved as written in ink. It was a little like learning a code and had all a code's fascination. Bards used it to communicate secret knowledge to each other, scratching the runes on trees or stones when other communications were not possible.

Cadvan was very pleased with her progress in magery; she was beginning to have the skill to control her Bardic powers, although he warned her that he could not teach her how to use powers of which he knew nothing. He called them her Elemental powers, to distinguish them from her innate Bardic Gift, although Maerad argued that the two were intertwined.

"And why," she asked him one morning, "are they not more commonly understood? Ankil himself said there are many tales of Elemental blood here in Thorold – why does no one know about these things?"

Cadvan looked at her thoughtfully. "Maerad, quite frankly, I do not know. I have never heard of such powers as you have. And you are probably quite right that they are deeply linked with Bardic potencies. But you must remember that you are the Fated One, and perhaps in you these different gifts have fused in a new way."

Maerad thought about it for a while. "Well, it feels to me that the more I can use the Bardic powers, the better I can access the others."

"I don't know how you destroyed the kulag or the wight in Annar," Cadvan said. "That is something outside the abilities of Bards. And I don't know how to teach you – that's something you'll have to learn by trial and error. But we should at least attempt to see if they are controllable. It would be perilous to test you only when your life is in danger."

They started with some cautious exercises, outside in a neighbouring meadow so that Maerad could not unintentionally damage Ankil's house. At first, Maerad could not focus her powers at all, although she had now enough sensitivity to tell whether or not she was using them. It was fiddly, delicate work, and sometimes intensely frustrating. She thought it was a little like trying to work out how to wiggle her ears: first she had to identify these unused muscles with her conscious mind, and then learn how to command them.

Bardic powers were rational, aided by visualization and will and guided by the Speech, but the Elemental powers were altogether different; they were quicker than thought, and seemed primarily intuitive. They flowed out of Maerad's emotional state, although they, too, could be guided by strength of will.

They found out early that her powers were of no use in the arts of illusion; after a few unsuccessful experiments, Cadvan speculated that maybe when the Elidhu created illusions, they worked with substance rather than tricks of the eye.

"You mean that Ardina was changing herself completely?" asked Maerad curiously. "I mean, when she vanished in the meeting hall, say."

"Yes, I think so," said Cadvan thoughtfully. "Look, let's try," He made the glimmerspell passes and then glanced around, settling on a rock jutting out of the ground nearby. "Now, I can make this look like a lion." The rock suddenly stirred, and there was a mountain lion, blinking sleepily in the sun. It yawned, showing its long, yellowing fangs, and then vanished into rock again. "But it changes nothing about the rock, only how you see it. Now, just see if you can change the rock yourself, without using a glimmerspell."

Maerad shut her eyes in order to help her concentrate, sought the place in her mind where the Elemental powers slept and willed the rock to become a lion.

After a while she opened her eyes, but nothing had happened.

"Try again," said Cadvan encouragingly.

"I don't think it's going to work," she said. "Maybe you can't do this sort of thing."

Cadvan shrugged. "Probably not," he said. "But try anyway."

Maerad sighed and shut her eyes again. Irritated by her failure, this time she made her feeling of command more insistent. She thought of the mountain lion she had once seen in Annar, its heat, its shaggy coat, its feline stink, its hugeness. She concentrated until her mind began to buzz.

Suddenly there was a deafening crack of rock splitting. She opened her eyes in alarm. A huge lion stood where the rock had been, its mouth opened to roar, its tail thrashing. Its eyes were red with anger, as if it had absorbed and magnified the irritation Maerad had been feeling when she had accessed her powers.

"By the Light!" Cadvan jumped up and moved cautiously backwards, his hands outstretched before him. "*Ilader, and-haseä*," he said soothingly, and the red light dimmed in the lion's eyes, and it yawned. "*Ilader. Ilader.*" The beast gradually drooped, as it was overborne with a great weariness, and then quite suddenly curled itself up like a domestic cat, nose to tail, and went to sleep.

Maerad was sitting with her mouth open.

"Well, that proved something, I suppose," said Cadvan, glancing at Maerad and running his hands through his hair. "Though why I suggested a lion I'll never know. Next time, make a rabbit. I think you had better turn it back into a rock."

"I don't know how," said Maerad.

"What do you mean? You just turned a rock into a lion, you must be able to turn it back."

Maerad struggled to articulate what she meant. "I think it's a different thing, returning something to what it was. I have to do something else," she said. "It's not just the same thing backwards."

"Well, we have to do something," said Cadvan. "I don't think Ankil will appreciate having a mountain lion preying on his flocks."

Maerad took a deep breath, cleared her thoughts, and sought inside her mind for the right thing to do. The first transformation had completely drained her. She focused on the lion and thought of the rock as it had originally been. She flexed her mind, but it hurt this time, as if she were pressing too hard, and when she stopped she was trembling with effort. The lion was still there, fast asleep.

Cadvan swore, and, walking up to the lion, stooped down and rubbed it behind its ears.

"Well, it's definitely a real lion," he said, returning to Maerad. "Not some trick. I've bound it with a sleep spell, so it will not wake for some hours. We can try again later." He shook his head. "I didn't really think you could do something like that. More fool me: I should know better by now than to underestimate you. I wonder if you really turned the rock into a lion, or if you've called a lion from somewhere and now, where the lion was, is a rock. And maybe a very surprised deer. But you'd better work out how to reverse this one."

"Easier said than done," said Maerad, looking up at him sardonically from underneath her hair. "I really don't know how to do it. I almost felt how, just before, but I'm so tired. Maybe I can try again later."

Maerad had a nap, and after a few attempts later on that afternoon she did succeed in restoring the rock to its proper rockness. But they didn't try transformation again after that; it was rather unnerving. And every time she passed by the rock, Maerad gave it a wide berth, as if it might suddenly turn into a lion again.

They had been at Ankil's for almost a month when, one afternoon after lessons, idling in front of her favourite view, Maerad saw two small figures making their way up the steep path towards the meadow. She was almost sure one of them was Elenxi: he towered over his companion. She squinted, trying to see more clearly, and went to the cheese shed to warn Ankil of the imminent visitors.

Ankil looked up from the board, where he was wrapping curds in muslin. "Elenxi? Then he is a little earlier than I expected," he said. "Well, I am almost finished here. Ask Cadvan to put out a table and chairs on the porch. I shall not be long."

As the visitors climbed into the meadow, it became clear that the tall figure was indeed Elenxi, and that the other was Nerili. Maerad ran forward to greet them, and they walked towards the welcoming shade of Ankil's porch, wiping the sweat from their brows.

"Good morrow, granddaughter," said Ankil, kissing Nerili's cheek. "It is long since I saw you here."

"All too long, grandfather," said Nerili, smiling. "I have missed you." Maerad had a sudden incongruous vision of Nerili as a five-year-old child, sitting on Ankil's knee.

They sat down around his table, which was already laden with pickles and bread and cheese, and carafes of wine and water.

"Water first!" said Elenxi, his eyes sparkling. "It is thirsty work to visit you, brother. And, then, when my thirst is slaked, we will have your fine red wine."

"You have no shame," Ankil said solemnly. "Surely you don't visit me only for the wine?"

"I can't imagine why else I would bother to climb this path," Elenxi answered. "It's a sore trial for an old man."

The talk bubbled along cordially until the visitors had recovered from their climb. Then Nerili looked soberly around the table, and a silence fell over the company. To Maerad, Nerili seemed sterner than when they had last met, as if she had been through some inner struggle.

"You will know, friends, that despite the excellence of the wine, we have come here to speak of other things," Nerili said. "I decided to come personally because I wished to speak to Cadvan and Maerad before they left."

"Left?" said Maerad involuntarily. Cadvan's face was in shadow, so she did not see his expression.

"Yes, it is time you two left this isle." Nerili paused, and cleared her throat. "Firstly, I have arranged passage for you from Thorold to Gent, with Owan d'Aroki." Maerad's face brightened at the mention of Owan, and then clouded as she remembered her seasickness. "He is willing to take you, and you know he is brave and trustworthy. He will pick you up from Nisa harbour four days hence."

"That is excellent, Neri," said Cadvan. "I thank you for your help. But I assume you have other news. The emissaries to the Seven Kingdoms have returned?"

"They have. And it is much as we guessed: all the Schools of the Seven Kingdoms have been given the same edict from Norloch. And none of them are happy about it. Like us, they have decided to bypass the challenge and wait for Norloch to break the covenant, if that is indeed what Enkir plans to do. But I am sure now that they will be allies, should the worst happen. I have not dared to send similar emissaries to Annar."

"Innail would be of like mind," said Cadvan. "And I think more than a few others – Til Amon, Elevé, Il Arundeh, Arnocen…"

"Yes," said Elenxi. "But we cannot be so sure of Annar. The ties between Annaren Schools and Norloch are much closer than with those in the Seven Kingdoms; Enkir is still, after all, First Bard of Annar. And as times darken, with ill news from both north and south, I do not feel we can depend on their seeing rightly that Norloch betrays the covenant of Barding. Circumspection is the wisest path, I judge."

"If word of these talks got out, we would be considered open rebels," added Nerili. "Which, unless it is forced to the point, I would rather avoid. We are certain now that there are spies in Thorold, we know of at least one within the School. We have been openly warned by Norloch that they have information that we have assisted you, and that this will be considered a provocation to war. Unless we hand you over, of course. We have naturally denied all knowledge of you. But the noose draws close."

Cadvan drew his lips tightly together. "I see. I suppose it is not surprising that word should have got out."

"There has been a very certain sighting of both of you in Amdridh," said Elenxi dryly. "And I believe there are rumours that you have been seen in the Suderain as well. They have no proof of your whereabouts. And they will get none." He grinned wolfishly, baring his teeth, and Maerad felt a chill.

"Why?" she asked, with a sudden anxiety.

Elenxi turned to her, and for the first time Maerad perceived in him the implacable ruthlessness of a warrior. Involuntarily, she shivered. "I dealt with the spy," he said.

"How did you know that he was a spy?" she said.

"Come, Maerad, you are not so simple," he answered. "There are ways to see into a man's mind. He shall not betray us again."

"Did you kill him?" Maerad felt distressed; she didn't want anyone killed on her account. Elenxi met her eyes, and his stern face suddenly gentled.

"Maerad, I would have thought you would be less queasy, knowing what it is that we face. But no, I did not kill him. He has been punished, nevertheless. And it will be a time before he is forgiven. You, above anyone, should not waste pity on him."

Maerad didn't feel like pursuing the question any further and did not ask who the spy was. She didn't want to know. It disturbed her; she understood Elenxi's harsh logic, but at the same time part of her resisted the absolute judgement she saw in his face. It was too easy, after all, to make mistakes, even for the best of reasons. Who was to know what was right?

"Pity is never wasted," said Cadvan softly. "Even the worst deserve pity. Even the Nameless One himself is a pitiable being." Elenxi gave him a piercing glance.

"Perhaps," he said gruffly. "I will not argue with the wisdom of the Balance. For all that, this man was betraying you, and us, for gold. There is not much to pity in that."

"Whatever the argument, it is true there are spies, and that Norloch strongly suspects that you are here," said Nerili. "So you must leave as soon as you can. Elenxi will guide you to Nisa, and then you must head for Gent. Gahal is expecting you, and will advise you on how to proceed north. Myself, I advise that you go by sea, along the coast, despite the perils. I think crossing Annar is more dangerous still."

There was a reflective silence.

"Have you been looking in the Library?" asked Cadvan, changing the subject.

"I have," said Nerili. "I have ransacked it from top to bottom and consulted all the most learned librarians. There is nothing I could find that could help you."

"Nothing will be written down," said Ankil, who hitherto had sat in silence, following the conversation alertly.

"Probably not," said Nerili, giving him a curious look. "I would be surprised, Cadvan, if you found anything in any of the other Libraries."

"Nelac had read something of the Treesong," said Maerad. "So there must be something written somewhere."

"The reference he found was very vague," Cadvan answered. "But I think Ankil is correct." He told Nerili and Elenxi of the Split Song, and they listened with deep interest. "That is the nearest we have come to any clue," he finished.

"Do not look for nuts in a mulberry tree," said Ankil. "I think you must move wholly from the realm of the written to the realm of the remembered."

Maerad felt her heart quicken within her. She was sure, in a deep part of herself, that there was a profound truth in what Ankil said. Maerad too had come to writing late; until that spring she had known nothing of written language, and like Ankil she felt closer to oral lore than most Bards.

"Perhaps the knowing is kept in the north," she said. "And that's why we have to go there. To talk to someone."

"Yes," said Cadvan. "But who?"

No one had any answer to this, and Nerili changed the subject. "The emissaries did not bring only bad news," she said. "One carried something for you two." She reached into her bosom and pulled out a sealed letter. "This comes from Saliman of Turbansk."

Maerad cried out gladly, and reached out for the letter, forestalling Cadvan, who had also put out his hand. He checked himself and sat back, although he was clearly as impatient as Maerad to see what the letter said. Maerad looked curiously at the seal, which bore the emblem of the School of Turbansk – a sun surrounded by flames – and then broke it with her fingernail, unfolding the parchment. The letter was written in Saliman's clear, sure hand.

"Read it out to us, Maerad," said Cadvan.

Maerad hesitated, and then slowly began to read, Saliman's mobile, laughing face rising vividly in her mind as she spoke.

"It says, 'Maerad, Cadvan – greetings, my friends! I write in haste, as the emissary from Thorold seeks to leave this hour. But I was never so glad as to hear that you are safe in Thorold. My thoughts have turned your way each day since last we saw each other, and to hear no news is hard: it breeds phantoms.' Oh, Cadvan," she said, turning to him impulsively, "They never got our news!"

"Birdnews oft goes astray," said Cadvan. "Sometimes they are apt to forget their messages. What else does it say?"

"'I hope that you received our note, and are not so anxious as we have been'," Maerad continued. "Well, we didn't; aren't there better ways than birdnews? Anyway. 'Hem and I arrived safely within three weeks of fleeing Norloch, and Hem has been accepted into the School here. He is, I fear, having trouble settling in; he is the only Annaren student in his level, and I fear he is not making friends. Despite this, he is well, and still eating pro—' Hold on, I can't quite read this, oh, it's 'prodigiously, and I think he has grown two hand spans since our arrival. He has good teachers, and despite the initial difficulties, which are only to be expected, I am optimistic about his progress.

"'Cadvan, I have heard of Nelac's imprisonment, which grieves me deeply, and of the ultimatum from Norloch. Indeed, we have had a similar demand here. It did not take our Circle quite by surprise, since I had already told them of Enkir and we had already formulated our response. I also hear that you and Maerad are declared outlaw. I cannot tell you how this saddens me. I wish I could say I was shocked, but I was less sanguine about Norloch than perhaps you were. I have long been troubled by the dimming of the Light there. But we have spoken of this.

"'I am kept very busy here, since there is talk (and more than talk) of an invasion imminent from the east. Our scouts tell us of armies of dogsoldiers massing along the borders of Dén Raven, and worse rumours I won't burden you with. The days are darkening, my friends. But no one – neither Norloch nor the Iron Tower – will take Turbansk with ease. Amdridh, too, stands firm. But I fear we are alone here, in the coming storm, and we know we can expect swords rather than help from the north, and perhaps will be squeezed between the pincers of a vice. We are in the midst of some vast plan, and soon all the pieces will be moving across the game board. We will fight, as we have always done, to protect our own, and to safeguard the Light, but I fear it will be a bitter fight, and I do not know that we shall prevail.'" Maerad faltered, and she stopped for a little while. Her audience waited patiently until she started again, her voice rough with emotion.

"'But these are gloomy words, and while such great hearts as beat around me do not quail, I shall refuse to despair. Our plight is desperate, I believe, and will become more desperate still; yet there is still much beauty in this world, and much love. And so it is my thoughts turn to both of you, houseless in this torn world, and wish for you all blessings and all help along your dark road; and I pledge we will meet and drink the friendship cup again together in this world. To that day, and from my heart, Saliman. Before I finish, Hem begs me to say, Maerad, that the fruits here in Turbansk are as marvellous as the birds told him, and that he is getting fat. And he too sends his love, and wishes you were here. S.'"

Maerad folded up the letter, and sat silently, with her face downcast. She missed Hem so fiercely it felt like a physical ache. No one said anything for a while, and then Ankil stood up. "I have to attend to the goats," he said. "Pray, make yourselves at home, Bards. Do you seek to stay the night? Or will you be departing today?"

"We should leave today, before the light begins to fail," said Elenxi. "We can get down to Velissos by dusk, and start for Nisa tomorrow."

"Yes, we can no longer tarry." Cadvan stood up, his tall figure suddenly impatient, as if he intended to leave that moment. "My heart tells me that time grows short."

Maerad shook herself, pushing back her tears, and stood up as well. There was work to be done.

Soon they were packed and ready to leave Ankil's house. Ankil embraced them both fondly as they stood on his porch, looking for the last time over the magnificent vista from his home.

"I shall miss you both," he said. "It has been good, having your company. May you fare well."

"And you also," said Cadvan, smiling. "Your hospitality has

been of the very best."

"You are welcome any time," said Ankil. "I like your touch with the goats. And you too, Maerad. Though next time, do not summon any lions!"

Maerad laughed, and kissed Ankil's cheeks, sniffing his fresh, almost astringent smell, clean and neutral as mountain grass. She looked around the flower-starred meadow, mentally farewelling each goat by name, and then she sighed and picked up her pack and stepped down to join Elenxi and Nerili, who awaited them at the foot of the steps.

The previous weeks had been a holiday, a blessed restoration, a chance to rectify some of Maerad's worst areas of ignorance. She was no longer the naive girl who had left Gilman's Cot only that spring: she knew enough now to be much more than a passive passenger of fate. She and Cadvan were outcasts, fleeing both Light and Dark, seeking a mysterious goal of which they knew almost nothing. But now, instead of quailing before her future, a part of Maerad leapt to meet it with exhilaration, a bittersweet gladness that they were beginning at last.

ANNAR

I have seen the darkness frail with unending stars
Through the twining beeches of Calicider
When daybirds settled to their roosts and the red deer slept in the bracken
And I have smelt the cedars of Malinan at moonset

I have heard the chorus of frogs in the Caln Marish
Lighting blue candles among the bog mahoganies
And the sphagnums whose pale flowers shimmer in the green night
I have heard the plovers piping among the mangroves of the Aleph
And it made me glad

I have walked the fields of Carmallachen when the kine are sleeping
And also in the wide meads of Lauchomon and Lukernil
And I laughed when I caught the moon bathing in the Lake of Til Amon
As if no one saw her silver tresses spreading in the waters

O Annar that I love, once darkness was your comely other face
O Annar that I love, now night's refuge is broken
And all creatures hide from your terror

From *Songs of Annar*, Dormisian of Til Amon

VII

THE IDOIRAVIS

THEY spent that night at Velissos, planning to set off for the coast early the following day. Elenxi was to guide them to Nisa, a tiny harbour in the north of Thorold where they would meet up with Owan and thence sail to the peninsula of Gent. Their way led them through the Thorold mountains, but to Maerad's relief, Elenxi said they did not need to cross over them: a deep winding valley, known as the Snake's Belly or the Idoiravis, would take them to the northern plateau without any rock climbing. From there it was a relatively simple ride to Nisa, which would take them three or four days at most. Snuggling into her bed, Maerad pondered the difference she saw in Nerili. The subterranean shifts of feeling between the older Bards that Maerad had found so disturbing seemed to have vanished altogether. They now spoke together as old friends will, easily and fondly.

Perhaps as a result, Cadvan seemed less constrained with Nerili. Maybe Nerili understands something she didn't before now, Maerad thought. About what the Dark is, inside as well as outside. Maybe she's forgiven Cadvan something… But it felt impertinent to speculate any further, and that was her last conscious thought before she drifted into a dreamless sleep.

They rose before the sun, when fog wreathed itself between the pines and larches that straggled up the hills, and they saddled and loaded up the horses they had left at Velissos nearly a month before. After they packed, they had a quick breakfast. Nerili farewelled Maerad and Cadvan in the tavern's front room, booted and cloaked for her own journey to Busk, her long dark hair streaming down her shoulders.

"I will not keep you," she said sombrely, kissing Cadvan and Maerad formally on their foreheads. "I send you with all our blessings and all our hopes. Only you, I feel it in my heart, have any hope of unriddling this strange quest. You will find help on your road, perhaps when you least expect it, as much as you find danger. May the Light protect you!"

"And you, also," said Cadvan. He smiled, his rare brilliant smile, and kissed Nerili's hands. "All is not dark, Neri, not yet. And though we walk through perils unnumbered, we will carry with us the blessings of those who have given us their friendship and love. And that is a shield from the worst despair, in all places: even in the dungeons of the Nameless One himself."

Maerad thought she saw a faint flush rise in Nerili's cheeks, though she held herself as proudly as before. "That seems a little grandiose for my humble blessings," she said. "But if you say it is so, then it is so, since you have been in such dungeons, and I have not."

Nerili turned then to Maerad. "I give you no gifts but the blessings of Thorold," she said. "I do not wish to burden you. Go well!"

"The gifts you have already given are more than enough," Maerad answered. "May the Light shine on your path." A catch in her throat took her by surprise and she turned hastily and walked swiftly to the door where Elenxi was standing impatiently, tapping his foot. They swung onto their waiting horses, and soon the village of Velissos was hidden behind them in the folds of the hills.

They rode steadily all day, following the westward track out of the village. The shadows grew shorter and shorter before them until they shrank to black pools beneath the bellies of their horses, and then slowly stretched behind them as they blinked in the long, level shafts of the sinking sun. Their way led them steadily higher and higher into countryside that was almost completely uninhabited. They passed only a few solitary huts. Their path was a vertiginous track through a scrubby landscape littered with huge lichened boulders and tumbles of smaller rocks. It was unusually desolate for that fertile island.

"We call this place the Bones, *I Lanik* in the tongue of the Isle," said Elenxi as he lit a fire for their camp that night. "Have you seen a stream today?"

Maerad thought, and realized she hadn't.

"By some trick of the hills, all streams fall on the other face of the ridges. And there are no springs. The only water that comes here falls out of the sky. It is said that long ago the spirit of the place offended the Lamedon, and was punished by the banishment of the waters."

Despite this, Maerad thought the next day, this hungry land had a curious beauty; the naked rocks were rich in colours, mauves and pinks and deep purples and white, and they caught the light in curious and interesting ways. Towards afternoon they entered a broad valley, the snowbound peaks of the central range of Thorold rising sheer on either side of them. Now, for the first time in more than a day, she could hear running water; streamlets dashed down the sides of the valley, meeting further on to make a wide, shallow river that ran over a bed of smooth pebbles towards the northern coast of Thorold. Their path met the river and ran alongside it.

"Soon we enter the belly of the snake," said Elenxi, looking over his shoulder. "The Idoiravis."

Maerad felt an obscure shiver run through her at his words. "Are there bandits here?" she asked. It reminded her a little of the Broken Lands near Milhol, a notorious haunt for such thieves.

"There are no bandits in Thorold, my friend," said Elenxi, grinning over his shoulder. Nevertheless, they instinctively drew closer together as they passed under the ominous shadows cast by the towering cliffs on either side.

Like the Bones, this was unforgiving country; as they pressed into the valley, the slopes on either side grew more sheer and ever higher, until they were riding through a gorge that sliced through the very heart of the mountains, as if they had cracked open in some primordial tumult. It was very cold: even in midsummer the floor of the Idoiravis stayed in shadow for most of the day, only a few direct shafts of sunlight finding their way past the precipitous walls. Sometimes they saw grey piles of snow from the previous winter hidden in crevices in the rocky walls. Maerad called a halt to put on her woollen cloak, which she had not worn since they had arrived in Thorold, and rode on through the chilly gloom. Along the narrow floor of the gorge were low tangled yews and bog myrtles growing above thick carpets of moss, and stands of some fern she hadn't seen before, with dark fronds. She didn't like this place so well. It seemed the horses were in agreement; they quickened their pace to a swift trot, their hoofbeats multiplying disconcertingly in the echoes off the stone walls, as if a cavalry were clattering through the gorge behind them.

Perhaps the clamour of the echoes was why they were taken by surprise. Cadvan pulled up his horse and called out a warning. Instantly he raised a defence, just before Elenxi, who was still leading them, threw up his arms and slithered off his own mount. His horse reared in dismay, and then swung around and bolted off. Maerad stopped in shock, trying to work out what was happening even as she drew her sword, an automatic reaction now, and shielded her mind against attack. Her mare shied beneath her, and Maerad fought to keep control as she felt another attack, sensing a dark presence nearby. Both she and Cadvan were aglow with magelight.

"It's a Hull," hissed Cadvan. "At least, I hope it's only one."

"I can't see anyone," said Maerad, searching the bracken nearby. They were tall enough to conceal a man. Maerad reached out with her mind to touch Cadvan's, uniting their strengths, and together they searched the valley, tracking down the source of the evil they both felt. It was hidden in a thicket of the low trees. Even as they found it, another attack came, this one directed at Cadvan.

This time, Maerad could see it: a bolt of energy as swift as an arrow. As always when her life was in peril, time seemed to have slowed down. They instinctively parried the blow, using both their swords and their Bardic powers, and it ricocheted up the gorge wall, hitting it with a huge crack and splitting off splinters of rock. One hit Maerad's face, cutting her on the cheek, but she didn't notice the pain.

It wasn't, she thought, a particularly powerful blow; dangerous for a Bard caught unawares, but unlikely to hurt anyone with their defences up. She and Cadvan both dismounted, silently commanding their quivering horses to remain where they were, and moved warily towards the thicket of trees. Elenxi lay very still on the ground, his arms outflung, and for a moment Maerad wondered how badly he had been hurt. There was no time to think about that yet.

"Not too close," murmured Cadvan. "It could be trying to draw us closer, and spring a trap."

They steadied themselves and then sent a blast of light towards the trees. It was white fire, the most powerful of Bardic weapons against the Dark, but it seemed to have no effect; it was as if a pebble had been thrown into a swamp. The energy simply vanished. They still could not see anyone.

The answer was swift in coming: an assault that shocked

Maerad with its strength, and which almost knocked the two of them flat. Her sword rang as she swung it against the Hull's bolt of black light, driving it into the ground in front of her, and her shoulder jarred with the effort. There was a black notch on the blade afterwards, as if it had struck fiery iron. The blow singed her hair and filled her mouth with a taste like burned iron, bitter and foul. She reflexively lashed out with another strike, this more powerful than the previous one made by both of them, and it was answered at once with a bolt of dark energy that nearly broke her defences, shivering her mind as if she were a thin blade of steel. She reeled with pain; she hadn't been struck in this way before, with magery. It was if a black, hideous void exploded in the midst of her being.

"Stop!" said Cadvan sharply, as she readied another bolt. "It's using us. I don't know how, but that had white fire in it."

"What?"

"We can't attack it. Not with the white flame. It's having no effect on it. And that was your flame."

Maerad turned to Cadvan in disbelief. "Then what do we do?"

"Are you certain of your shield?"

Maerad mentally tested her defences. Despite the jarring shock, they seemed whole. "As certain as I can be," she said.

"Good. Keep it whole. We shall have to fight hand to hand."

"But what if it's a trap, like you said?"

"I feel there is only one. And I do not know what else we can do."

Maerad took a deep breath. Then she and Cadvan continued their slow pacing towards the trees, buffeted by attacks from the Hull that were not serious enough to get past their shielding. As they neared the trees, she saw at last a single figure among them; it was hard to see, since some sorcery entwined it with shadows so it tricked the sight, and it seemed to be part of the tangle of branches. It did not come forward to meet them.

When they were only ten paces away, Cadvan called out in the Speech.

"Who attacks travellers in this peaceful land? Name yourself!"

There was a long silence, and they were about to take another step forward, when a thickset man moved into the lesser shadow of the gorge.

"It is none of your business who I am, Cadvan of Lirigon," said the Hull. He, too, used the Speech, but it seemed strangely glottal, and his voice raised the hair on Maerad's neck. "I am but a servant of greater laws."

No hooded cloak hid the horror of the bony, unliving face that turned its depthless eyes upon them. Despite herself, Maerad shuddered.

"As for you, outlaws, I seek to bring you to a larger justice. It is well broadcast through all these lands that you are wanted for treason against the Light."

Cadvan spat on the ground. "It ill behoves a Hull to speak of treason against the Light," he said.

"I am no traitor," said the Hull. "I am a loyal Bard of Norloch. And it would be well if you came with me. You cannot fight me." The Hull was idly fiddling with an object it held in its hands. "I have a blackstone; your magery is useless. Even such powers as yours, Maerad of Pellinor. And I am a greater swordsman than you might guess."

"You're a liar," said Maerad hotly. "Like all Hulls."

Casually and contemptuously, the Hull lifted the blackstone and spoke, and Maerad gasped; it felt as if serpents were biting her innards. She clutched herself in sudden agony, almost falling.

Cadvan grasped her hand, and the agony vanished.

"It has your pattern," he said inscrutably. "And he is right, we cannot attack him. Not with magery. It will only be turned against us."

"I don't believe you can fight us and prevail, even so." Maerad lifted her sword, and the Hull laughed.

"Oh, I have heard of your prowess," it said deliberately. "A promising beginner, I'm told. But no more than a beginner. And do you think the great Cadvan can defend you? Not with his magery useless, surely. He is not so great."

"I will not bandy words with traitors," said Cadvan grimly. Come, Maerad, he said in her mind, and moving together as one, they attacked the Hull.

The Hull moved blindingly fast, sending a blast of black lightning and attacking Cadvan with his sword. Maerad doubled in agony again, and a darkness came over her vision, as if it was suddenly the deepest night. She collapsed to the ground, writhing and struggling to breathe.

For a few moments, she was conscious of nothing except pain. Then she remembered the urgency of their situation, and wrestled with herself. She still couldn't see anything, but she could hear the sound of weapons clashing, as if from very far away. With all her willpower, she forced herself to ignore the pain. She opened her eyes, staring sightlessly ahead of her; after a short time she could almost see, but it was as if a black mist flooded her sight. She took a deep breath and tried again.

Cadvan and the Hull were in vicious combat, but neither had as yet gained the upper hand. The Hull had not been lying about its swordskills; Maerad could see, even through the dimness that afflicted her sight, that they were formidable. What if Cadvan couldn't defeat him?

Maerad bit her lip so hard it bled. It helped to clear her mind. She struggled to her knees, and tried to see more. She saw Cadvan knocked head over heels by the force of a sword stroke, but he sprang back onto his feet like an acrobat. His right arm was bleeding, and the Hull was yet unscathed. The Hull was now fighting him back, step by step, towards the gorge wall.

Maerad pushed her agony down into the back of her mind. It's only pain, she said to herself. It's only pain. Shaking with the effort, she reached deep inside her mind, and, as she did so, the pain lessened slightly. She took a deep breath, and began to visualize the first thing that came to her mind. The Hull was paying no attention to her, believing she was disabled, and Cadvan was fighting back fiercely, demanding the Hull's full concentration. He almost disarmed the Hull, who righted itself, springing back, but Cadvan was breathing heavily, and Maerad thought the arm wound was perhaps a serious one. She focused fiercely on the figure of the Hull and shut her eyes. *Now.*

She heard a clatter of stones as Cadvan fell over, slashing wide with his sword against blank air, and she opened her eyes again. Her first thought was overwhelming relief; the pain in her belly was gone. She looked up.

Cadvan had rolled as he fell, twisting like a snake to avoid any sword thrust aimed his way, and had scrambled to his feet, his sword upraised. There he had halted, his face a mask of astonishment, looking this way and that. His opponent was nowhere to be seen.

Then something small hit his boots, making him step backwards, and he looked down. On the ground was a furious, mangy brown rabbit with black ears. It hopped forward and sank its teeth into the ankle of his boot and tried to slash the toe with its back claws.

It seemed that the Hull hadn't quite realized that it had become a rabbit, and it still attacked with single-minded ferocity. Cadvan sheathed his sword and bent down, grabbing the struggling rabbit by its ears. He held it up and looked sardonically at Maerad, who was stumbling towards him, and then back at the rabbit. Maerad started to giggle.

"It was the first thing I thought of," she said. She sat down heavily on the ground, exhausted suddenly by the shock of the fight and her relief that it was over, and feeling laughter bubble hysterically inside her. There was a short silence.

"Well, that resolves one conundrum about your wild magic," Cadvan said at last. The rabbit was kicking viciously, making growling noises in its throat. "I think this rabbit was definitely a Hull. Well, what should we do with it? I wouldn't eat any stew this rabbit was part of."

"Let it go, maybe," said Maerad.

"I don't think so." Cadvan looked at the creature, which was frothing at the mouth with rage. "It is a vicious thing, but somehow it is still hard to kill it in cold blood, much as it deserves death. Do you think the transformation might wear off, Maerad?"

"I don't know," said Maerad. "But turning it back would be hard." She hiccupped; despite all her efforts, giggles kept rising inside her in giddy waves.

Cadvan made a sharp chop with the edge of his hand at the rabbit's neck, breaking its spine, and suddenly it hung limp from his hand, its eyes glazed. "We dare not take the risk," he said. He cast the pathetic corpse to the ground with a gesture of disgust.

Maerad stared at the dead rabbit, suddenly sobered, and Cadvan pulled her to her feet. "That was well done," he said, searching her face. "Are you all right? Your cheek is bleeding."

Maerad nodded, and brushed away the blood. It was only a small cut. "But what about your arm?" she asked.

Cadvan looked ruefully at his right arm, pulling up his torn and bloodied sleeve. "Not so good, I suspect," he said. "But nothing really serious." He held his hand over a nasty slash to stem the bleeding. "I'll attend to that later. But now we must see to Elenxi."

Elenxi! In the heat of the battle, Maerad had completely forgotten about him. They walked hastily back to where the old Bard lay, his arms flung out before him.

He had been knocked out and seemed to have suffered nothing worse than a bad bruising. Cadvan laid his hands on the Bard's forehead briefly and he stirred, groaning, and then sat bolt upright and looked around, sniffing.

"What happened?" he growled. "I smell sorcery."

"We were attacked by a Hull," said Maerad, and told him what had happened.

Elenxi was outraged that he had missed the battle, and when Cadvan told him of what had happened to the Hull, he looked at Maerad with amazement. "Is this true? You can do this?" he asked, his eyebrows almost hidden in his hair. Maerad nodded, but Elenxi refused to believe it until they showed him the corpse.

His face froze with incredulity, and then began to shake with laughter. "A rabbit, eh?" he said, when he had recovered from his mirth. "I begin to see what Cadvan means about your powers. Perhaps you can do that to all the Hulls, and give the Nameless One an army of rabbits."

"Mangy rabbits," said Cadvan dryly. He began to attend to the wound on his arm. Elenxi grunted, and leant forward to help, cleaning the wound with water, smearing it with a sweet-smelling balm and binding it with clean cloth. "It bothers me that the Hull should have ambushed us here," Cadvan said, as Elenxi worked. "It knew we were coming this way."

"I told you there was a spy." Elenxi's eyes hardened. "And, alas, we did not find him until too late. But no news will come back from this one. The Idoiravis is the obvious place for an ambush: it is the only land route from north to south. I should have been more careful. I am angry with myself that I did not see this coming."

"The Hull was well concealed," Cadvan said. "It was hidden by some ensorcellment."

Elenxi, who was tying off the bandage on Cadvan's wound, snorted. "Even so," he said, "it was an elementary ambush. What disturbs me more is that he had a blackstone."

"What's a blackstone?" Maerad asked curiously.

"They are very rare," said Cadvan. "But, as you saw, they are very difficult to fight. They will absorb all the energy from a strike and then direct it back at the assailant. A blackstone is made from a mineral mined in the south, called albarac; it is worth much more than gold, because it is so difficult to find, and even more difficult to work. Most often it's used in shields, as very thin plating, because it will deflect and absorb attack. You need a lot of albarac to make a blackstone."

"And was he using the blackstone to attack me?" Maerad thought of the terrible pains that had afflicted her. "You said something about him having my pattern – what did you mean?"

"That is more difficult to explain." Cadvan drew his sword and began to examine the blade as he spoke; it bore some new notches, and he frowned. "Well, as you know, every Bard's magery has an individual flavour, a signature. This is sometimes called a pattern. If another Bard can trace that pattern, it is almost like knowing your Truename; fortunately for all of us, it is very difficult, nay, almost impossible to do. But if you have a blackstone, and can control it – which is not easy to do either – it is possible to see a Bard's pattern from a strike."

"I don't quite understand," said Maerad, frowning.

"I am concerned that the Hull had a blackstone at all," said Elenxi. "And he claimed to be of Norloch. Perhaps there is a secret store of them there, being handed out to Hulls. We have to hope that the Dark is not making them. Did you find the stone?"

"We didn't look," said Maerad. "Perhaps it was changed with the Hull."

"Maybe, but we should look anyway," said Elenxi.

Cadvan sheathed his sword. "The blackstone explains why a single Hull would attack three Bards such as us."

"If we find it, it will be a great prize," said Elenxi.

The Bards returned to the thicket of trees, and searched the ground painstakingly. It wasn't long before Maerad let out a cry and lifted a strange object in her hands, waving to the others. They came over to her, and examined it curiously.

The blackstone was large enough to fill her palm. It was ringed with a band of silver, wrought in an intricate design of flames wreathing around each other, and was attached to a silver chain. The stone itself was blank of all carving, and very strange; looking at it was not like looking at an object at all, but rather as if it was a hole, an absence of light. It was curious to touch; Maerad felt as if her fingers slipped over it, unable quite to register whether it was cool or hot, or rough or smooth. Cadvan took it and looked at it closely, and let out his breath in relief.

"Well, it is certainly a blackstone of Norloch, and not fashioned by the Dark," he said. "No stone of the Dark would use the White Flame. But why would a Hull have such a thing?"

"My guess," said Elenxi grimly, "is that Enkir strongly suspects that you are in Thorold. And, if so, any fool would know that you had a good chance of travelling this way, if you wished to leave; you could not leave Busk unwitnessed."

Maerad shivered; it meant pursuit was at their very heels.

"I think you ought to keep this, Maerad," said Cadvan unexpectedly, handing the blackstone back to her. "It would be of use, I think. And it was won in fair fight. I'll teach you how to use it."

Maerad smiled, and put the blackstone in her pack. Cadvan squinted up at the sky; the sun was now well past its zenith. "It's time we moved on, if we wish to be out of here by nightfall. But first we have to find Elenxi's horse; I don't think mine can bear both of us."

The horse hadn't run far after its initial panic, and they soon found it, calmly munching on some sour grass. They then pressed swiftly on their way, all of them alert in case of further attacks. As they cantered through the gorge, the silence between them was broken by occasional deep chuckles from Elenxi. "A rabbit! Brilliant, Maerad. Brilliant!"

They reached Nisa without further incident three days later. Once they came out of the Idoiravis, the countryside before them was flat for many leagues, stretching over the high northern plateau of Thorold before it plunged steeply down towards the coast. This was rich farming country, with many thick forests of larch, beech and pine interspersed with a patchwork of fields sown with wheat or rye, the heads beginning to turn golden in the sun, or meadows where grazed herds of sheep or goats, or the dark greens of vineyards and olive groves.

Impelled by an increasing sense of urgency they pushed their horses hard, reaching the edge of the plateau by the end of the second day. Here the land tipped precipitously down towards the sea. From then on the going was slower; they had to pick their way carefully along steep, narrow tracks winding through the tangles of myrtles and acacias that grew luxuriantly around tumuli of pink granite boulders and mazes of small, noisy streams.

Nisa was a fishing village that hugged a tiny harbour carved into the rose-coloured cliffs. To reach it, they had to leave their horses at a nearby village and descend on foot by a path cut into the rock. From there they looked down on the red-tiled roofs of about three dozen houses clustered in a single row against the cliff walls. Maerad, contemplating the blue expanse of the sea, reflected that she was getting better at dealing with heights; she didn't feel nearly so dizzy.

"You wouldn't want to climb up here after a few glasses of wine," she said, as they negotiated one particularly sharp bend.

"I believe many do exactly that," said Elenxi. "And some have even lived to tell the tale."

"You'd fall right on someone's house!" Maerad risked another glance downwards. No, it was not so bad; though it was better if she didn't look at all.

Compared to the hive of activity in Busk, Nisa appeared deserted. They arrived when all the boats were out on the sea and everyone else was having their mid-afternoon break. Apart from rows of seagulls perched on the rooftops, the only visible living thing was a grey tabby cat curled up in a coil of rope. Maerad looked along the stone quay and spotted the familiar red sail of the *White Owl* bobbing in the water. But there was no sign of Owan, either above or below decks.

"I suppose Owan would be at the tavern," said Maerad, stooping to scratch the cat's head as they walked back towards the main road.

"That would be right," said Elenxi. "I was just thinking it was time for some wine myself."

They found Owan stretching out his long legs under a wooden table in the back garden of the tavern; he had a palpable air of well-being. When the travellers entered, he gave a cry of welcome and came forward to embrace them. They called for wine and food and joined him at his table.

Owan had been sailing around the island on the same errand as Elenxi, bringing the news of Norloch's ultimatum to the coastal villages and warning them to ready their defences in case of war. "They watch for the signal, and are vigilant," he said. "And each has messenger birds to send to Busk if they are attacked. All is well."

"But you don't have an army." Maerad suddenly realized this fact, and involuntarily said it out loud.

"No, not as such," said Elenxi. "We don't need one. All our people know how to fight; and it is hard to defeat an entire population. In this land there is no place for open battle, and Thoroldians fight by other means. When the Nameless One attacked Thorold before the Silence, a great fog came down from the mountains. The entire army was lost."

"What happened to them?" asked Maerad, fascinated.

"No one knows. Our people hid in the places they know, and when the fog lifted there was no sign of the army. Some said they had wandered, lost and misled by phantoms, until they fell off a cliff into the sea, others that they were led into a great ravine in the mountains, which closed over them. But it is certainly true that they vanished without trace."

Maerad shuddered as an image passed over her inner vision of terrified soldiers running raggedly through a merciless, impenetrable whiteness. "Was it the Lamedon?" she asked. "Or was it the Bards?"

"It was not the Bards," said Elenxi. "But it is said that Limod, the leader of Thorold at that time, went and begged the Lamedon himself for help when he heard that a great army was on its way. The Lamedon might not be interested in human wars; but perhaps the thought of invasion offended him. In some tales, although not all, it is said that the Lamedon was Limod's father."

Maerad fell silent as the talk moved on to other topics. Elenxi's story disturbed her, although she could not say why. The question of her Elidhu heritage always filled her with discomfort. Ankil had baulked at the suggestion she speak to the Lamedon, despite his unquestioning acceptance that she had

Elemental blood, and she thought again of the curious look he had given her when the plan was suggested, and wondered what he had seen that made him doubt her. Was it weakness? Or something else, that was beyond her knowledge? A vague foreboding weighed upon her spirits; there was so much about herself that she didn't understand. She was glad of the distraction when Owan said they would leave on that evening's tide.

VIII

THE STORMDOG

I T was a beautiful summer evening, the final light lingering in faint streaks of pink and purple on the rippling surface of the dark sea, as they slipped out of Nisa harbour. Elenxi stood on the quay, his hand raised in farewell and blessing, and Maerad, who had little to do with the sailing of the boat, stood in the stern facing him as Owan's craft surged on the outgoing tide. Elenxi glimmered faintly in the shadows, a blur of light that steadily grew smaller and smaller. Above him stretched the dark cliffs that surrounded Nisa, and above them the white stars opened in a clear sky.

It wasn't long before they reached the head of the harbour. Maerad looked uneasily at the cliffs, which loomed uncomfortably close as Cadvan and Owan negotiated the reef that lurked under the water, ready to scrape or hole any unwary boat. Soon, as if the *White Owl* leapt gladly out of harbour, they passed into the open sea.

Instantly a strong wind bellied out the sail, and they began to scud across the waves as a full moon climbed above the dark line of the land. Maerad breathed in the cold salt air with delight, seeking out Ilion, the star of dawn and eventide, which burned low and very bright over the western horizon. Hello, my friend, she said in her mind, and then laughed at herself; who did she think she was, talking to a star?

Now the waves were bigger: they weren't the waves of the deep ocean, as they were still sheltered by the island, but they were large enough to make the boat climb and fall as it rode forward. It wasn't long before Maerad felt the first stirrings of seasickness, and her spirits instantly dampened. Although Elenxi had given her a remedy he said was guaranteed to work even in the worst of storms, she felt nausea roiling through her guts. But it seemed the remedy did work; once she had adjusted to the new movements of the ship, the sickness vanished. Her relief was beyond words.

Cadvan stepped over to the bow and sat next to her. "No need of mage winds tonight," he said. "The Isle of Thorold sends its last blessing."

"I am glad of it," said Maerad. She turned to him, her face outlined by moonlight, and, for a brief moment, she saw an expression on his face that she hadn't seen before, and something in him seemed to flinch. Maerad looked up at him questioningly; they knew each other well enough by now not to need to speak. Cadvan looked out over the sea for a moment and then back towards her.

"You looked exactly like the Queen Ardina," he said. "It took me by surprise."

The unexpectedness of his comment made Maerad laugh. "But she has silver hair," she said.

"Your hair looked silver in the moonlight," said Cadvan, smiling in return. "So it is not as ridiculous as it might sound."

"And she is beautiful," said Maerad, more softly.

"Yes," said Cadvan. "She is."

There was a short pause; Maerad felt strangely abashed. "Well, then, I suppose I ought to thank you."

A silence fell between them that was not quite comfortable. Maerad didn't know how to respond to Cadvan's mood. He seemed sombre and weighed down by some preoccupation, and it caught an underlying mood within her, bringing shadows into the present. But it was more than that; Cadvan had often given her compliments, but they had always been in play.

This time there had been an emotion in his voice that Maerad didn't understand, a complex adult emotion, and it quickened some deep sense of alarm. She did not think he meant that she reminded him of Ardina; someone else, perhaps. The thought gave her a small, cold feeling in the pit of her stomach.

Cadvan broke the silence, asking after Elenxi's seasickness remedy. Maerad replied lightly, and the strange moment passed. Maerad fell gratefully into the easy, casual trust between them, a trust that had already been tempered by several conflicts; but the cold feeling persisted for a while longer. Maerad had a deep distrust of men which stemmed from her brutal childhood and, in that unguarded moment, Cadvan had unintentionally woken her old fears.

The next day, the fair sailing continued. The sea was blue and calm, and a sou'-westerly carried them steadily towards Gent on the southern coast of the peninsula of Ileadh. Now Maerad was not crippled by seasickness, she realized sailing was exhilarating: the fresh, biting wind blew all the darkness out of her heart.

Cadvan and Owan began to teach her the basics of handling a craft. It was, she discovered to her chagrin, something she did not have a natural talent for; she couldn't feel instinctively how a boat might respond to the currents of wind and wave, or predict how it would move. At one point, while Owan was attempting to teach her the art of tacking, she accidentally sent the *White Owl* into a violent spin, almost knocking Owan into the sea. Although the other two thought it was funny (after the vessel had been righted), Maerad felt it as a humiliation, and worked the harder to gain some basic skill.

"You'll make a decent sailor one day," Owan said comfortingly that evening. He had lashed the tiller, letting the *White Owl* follow her own course as they had dinner. "If you work at it."

"If I don't sink myself first," answered Maerad ruefully. "But thank you."

"It's perfect teaching weather, anyway. There was no real danger." Owan settled himself on the bench that ran along each side of the deck, and began to eat with relish. He had set out fishing lines that day, and dinner was grilled bream, flavoured with his carefully hoarded dried herbs. Eating in the open air, as the sun spilt a path of flames along the darkening sea, gave the meal an extra piquancy. At last they sighed and pushed away their plates, watching the sun send out its last pale gleams into the sky. The moon had not yet risen, and the stars were especially brilliant, letting fall a light strong enough to throw shadows. No one moved to light a lamp.

"I can't see Thorold any more," said Maerad, gazing southwards over the heaving waves.

"It must be concealed in a haze," Owan answered. "Sometimes you can see the Lamedon from two days out."

"It's a beautiful place," said Maerad dreamily. "I'm sad to leave it."

"Aye, it is that," answered Owan. "Have I told you of the Lamedon and the Sea?"

"No," said Maerad, sitting up straighter. "Is it a story?"

"Ah, yes, it is an old story," said Cadvan, smiling. "I'd like to hear it again, Owan, if you're in the mood."

Owan lit a pipe, and gazed over the water in silence for a few moments. "Well then," he said. "It goes like this." His voice modulated into a new register, as if he were almost singing, and Maerad had a sudden image of herself as a small child sitting at Owan's feet, wound into the spell of the story. Owan had clearly told it many times.

"The sea around Thorold has many moods," he began. "Sometimes it is blue, sometimes green, sometimes yellow, sometimes grey, sometimes a blinding silver dazzle; but it is always beautiful, and always dangerous. One day it will tickle the toes of small children playing on the beaches and the next it'll erupt in a tempest of water and spume, dragging down trees and houses and goats from the lowlands.

"You see," Owan continued, "the sea once loved the mountains. And she confessed her love to the mountain king, showing him her corals and her pearls and her beautiful foaming hair. The king laughed and said to her: why should I come down to your dark, wet, weedy bed, when I love the sky, and the wind, and the cold nests of eagles? And the sea was humiliated and furious, and she returned to her palace beneath the waves.

"And ever since she has hated Thorold. She eats up the cliffs, until they collapse; and she calls up her tides, until the feet of the king are flooded with fish and weed; and she summons wild storms to pull the drowned sailors down to her dark bed. But still, underneath her hatred, remains her love; and when she remembers that, she forgives the king his insult, and is calm. And then there are the still days, when fishermen set their nets far out and take of her bounty of fish, and the landsfolk look out on her beauty and marvel."

Owan knocked his pipe out against the railing and all was silent for a moment, apart from the clink and creak of the sails against the wind. "Today," he said, "she remembered her love."

"I guess the moral is, never refuse the love of a powerful woman," said Cadvan. "Eh, Maerad?" He stretched lazily and grinned at Maerad through the shadows. She thought involuntarily of Nerili, and flinched at his sally. She did not want to think about those inscrutable emotions.

"Maybe, the moral is that it's best not to love at all," she answered stiffly, without looking at him. "It just causes trouble."

Cadvan raised his eyebrows at Owan, but said nothing.

Shortly afterwards, Maerad retired to her hammock, and Owan unlashed the rudder, whistling. The wind was beginning to shift to the east. Cadvan, who was sleeping in the tiny cabin on deck, retired not much later; the two men were sharing the labour of sailing and Owan was taking the first shift. The little boat rode on through the night, a frail shell bearing its human cargo between the twin darknesses of the sea and the sky.

The following day, the wind continued to shift and strengthen, and a bank of dark clouds began to build on the northern horizon. The sea was now a dull, yellowish grey with choppy waves, and the wind had a bitter edge. Maerad's sailing lessons were postponed; she sat, cold and bored, in the prow, as out of the way as she could get without going below decks, with her cloak wrapped tightly around her. They were still making decent time north towards Gent, Owan said, but he feared being driven off course and asked Cadvan for assistance. Maerad watched as Cadvan raised a wind into the red sail, pushing the *White Owl* face on into the rising squalls.

Now Maerad was very glad of Elenxi's seasickness remedy because the boat had a most uncomfortable action, rising to the top of each foam-tipped wave and dropping with a thump into the trough. She felt nothing worse than a slight queasiness, whereas without it she knew she would have reached an abyss of misery. But even so, sailing today did not seem quite as much fun as it had the day before.

The weather steadily worsened all day until they were pushing through a driving rain, and the wind was almost gale force. Towards evening, Maerad retreated to the tiny galley in the cabin and prepared a meal that was within her limited cooking skills: a thick soup made from dried peas. It made her feel less useless, since she was no help with the sailing. She couldn't work out how to fix the utensils so they didn't slide on the stove or the table, so she cheated a little and used a charm, and after that most things behaved. The stove, however, was moody and she was a little vague on which herbs to use. In the end, she tried a pinch of each of them, and the result was rather strange; but, she reflected, if the soup was no masterpiece, it was at least hot and thick.

There was no leisurely meal on deck that night; Cadvan and Maerad ate in the cabin at the little table, their knees touching, as Owan managed the boat. The lamp that hung from the ceiling swung to and fro as they ate, throwing strange shadows across their faces. Cadvan went out to relieve Owan at the helm, and Owan came in with a blast of spray, his hair dripping. Maerad ladled out his meal. He tasted it and paused, looked up at her expressionlessly, and then steadily finished the meal without comment.

"Was it that bad?" Maerad asked mournfully, when he handed her the bowl.

"It was hot," he said kindly. "And that was right welcome. And, no, it was not that bad – I've tasted far worse. But next time, I'd leave out the allheal, because it's really for poultices; and it has a bitter taste."

Maerad's mouth twitched. "I'm sorry," she said. "I'm about as good at cooking as I am at sailing."

"Ah, young Bard, you can't be good at everything," he said. "And it is folly to think you should be. But practice is a good aid." He yawned. "And it's made me tired; it's heavy work out there."

"Is it going to be like this all night?"

"My nose tells me it's going to get worse; I think we're in for a storm."

Maerad almost said, "you mean, this isn't a storm?" but stopped herself in time.

"It's not the season for it," said Owan. "But these are strange times. Do not fear, Maerad; the *Owl* has seen me through a lot of bad weather. She's a beautiful vessel, and what's more, she's knit together with the strongest charms Bards can make. We should be entering Gent by dawn of the day after tomorrow, even with this heavy weather."

Maerad felt slightly reassured. The *White Owl* was creaking and groaning in the swell, and the noise had begun to make her nervous.

"You should sleep, too," said Owan, gently reminding her that the cabin was his bedroom. "I'll clean up, you go below."

Maerad opened the cabin door. It slammed back on its hinges, and a blast of spray-laden wind sent the lamp swinging in circles before she was able to wrestle the door shut. She stood, breathing hard, on the deck; the wind was howling and the sail was rattling against the wind. Cadvan stood a mere three paces away, in a pool of magelight, but he was clearly busy and she didn't hail him as she stumbled unsteadily to the gangway. It was shut, and she had another battle to open the trapdoor, climb down the ladder and close it above her. When she pulled the trapdoor to, the roaring of the wind and waves suddenly dimmed, and she became aware of water sliding coldly down the back of her neck; but the creaking of the ship below decks was much louder than in the cabin.

She remembered Owan's words about the *White Owl*, and stroked the wooden panels almost superstitiously, feeling how the boat vibrated like a living thing. Then she took another dose of her seasickness medicine and strung up her hammock. It was icy cold and her hands fumbled. It's no good, she thought, I'm just afraid. If the boat sinks, what will we do? Who will know? It's not like I can swim back to Thorold. And what if an ondril comes? We're out here, all on our own, and no one can help us.

She pushed her gloomy thoughts away and pulled out two blankets and wrapped herself in them. It was too cold to undress, so she tipped herself into the hammock, hunching as small as she could and rubbing her hands together to generate some warmth. The hammock swayed to and fro, and her stomach tightened. Maybe the allheal will help my sickness too, she thought, as at last she began to feel a bit warm. She smiled as she remembered Owan's stoic politeness at the taste of her soup. Despite the heaving of her hammock and the noise, which she was sure would keep her awake all night, Maerad was asleep in moments.

She woke up suddenly. She had no idea how long she'd been asleep. It was pitch black, and she sat up in sudden alarm, knocking her head on the wooden panels. Something had woken her, but she couldn't, in the first moments of consciousness, work out what it was. Then she realized: everything had gone quiet. The storm must have blown out, she thought; but her heart was hammering with anxiety, and she did not lie down again.

She set a floating magelight near her ear and looked around the small, neat cabin. All seemed to be as it should be, but a mounting tension sent the blood thrumming through her body. She felt all the hairs on her neck standing on end. Her breath hung in front of her face; even down here, it was freezing. She swung herself out of the hammock, dragging on her boots, and reached for one of Owan's oilskins, which hung near the table. She had to get outside, to see what was happening.

Just as she shrugged the oilskin over her cloak there was a massive crash, like a huge crack of thunder, and the whole boat lurched violently as if it were tipping over, and then just as violently righted itself. Maerad was flung over to the table, narrowly missing the edge of it with her head, and her magelight went out. She scrambled to her feet, breathing hard, and relit the light. Now the strange silence that had woken her was broken: the boat was creaking and groaning again, but in such a way that it sounded as if its timbers might fly to pieces at any moment, and the wind suddenly increased to an ear-piercing howl. Not howling, Maerad thought: it's screaming. It sounded as if a thousand dogs were being roasted alive. She covered her ears, shuddering, until the scream died back to storm.

Had they hit a reef? Maerad panicked at the thought of being trapped in this tiny space as the *White Owl* spiralled down into the chill depths of the sea. She staggered to the gangway, and had just reached it when there came another crash, just as loud, and the boat lurched again. This time, she was holding on to the ladder and wasn't flung down. She waited until the craft righted itself, and then scrambled up the ladder as fast as she could, flinging up the trapdoor just as a huge wave broke over the deck, drenching her instantly and pouring down the gangway behind her. She gasped, stunned by the cold, and swallowed a mouthful of seawater.

The wave had the effect, at least, of shocking her out of panic. When she had recovered from the dousing, she crawled through the gangway and, clinging to the railings, kicked the trapdoor shut behind her. She squinted through the chaotic darkness, trying to see what was happening.

It was a black, starless night, and the *White Owl* pitched on a huge sea. As her eyes adjusted, Maerad almost lost courage: maybe it would feel safer in the cabin, where she could not see anything at all. But at the thought of crouching alone in that suffocating darkness she steeled her nerves. The boat was now hurtling down into what seemed like a bottomless abyss, and Maerad's stomach lurched. When at last they reached the trough, the boat twirled sideways until frantically corrected by Owan; then they were lifted with a heart-stopping suddenness to the top of the next wave, where they paused for a brief dizzying moment before tipping down again, the deck as steep as the side of a mountain, into the boiling blackness.

The noise was almost deafening, and the sky was a strange colour, the clouds infused with a greenish-blue glow. The sails were furled to the mizzen mast, the ropes that lashed them standing out horizontally in the gale, and Owan was at the tiller. Maerad looked around wildly for Cadvan, fearing that he had been swept overboard, and saw him at the prow of the boat. Around him was a strange stillness; it seemed as if the wind did not affect him. Maerad clutched the railing, her heart in her mouth, and then remembered a charm of fastening that would stop her being swept off the deck. She muttered it frantically, and felt a little safer.

She put her head down and fought her way, step by step, towards Cadvan. Her mouth was full of salt and her hair whipped into her eyes, stinging them. Although she was wet through, she was glad she had put on the oilskin; at least it kept out the worst of the gale. Another wave broke over the deck, and she stopped, clinging to the rail and gasping again with the cold, until it had rolled off the boat. She looked up; Cadvan was only five paces away, but it could have been five leagues, the rate she was going. She took one more step, and then stopped, a chill, which had nothing to do with cold, gripping her heart.

It was difficult to tell the difference between sea and sky; both were a boiling chaos. But what appeared in front of Cadvan now was neither; it was some monstrous being, almost too big to look at, which seemed to be made out of stormlight and cloud. Maerad shut her eyes, staving off her terror, and then forced herself to look again.

What she saw looked like a giant dog, a heavy hunting dog, like a mastiff, snarling and slavering, crouched for attack. The monster seemed to boil out of the very clouds, and was as difficult as vapour or air to fix in the vision; its jaws were etched with the same weird green-blue light Maerad had noticed earlier in the sky and its eyes were points of emerald fire. Its form shimmered eerily with little lightnings that continually flashed and vanished, so it was not quite substantial, despite the impression it gave of massive bulk. It was, Maerad realized, reaching back to tales of fear she had heard as a child, a storm-dog. She was frightened of ordinary dogs, from a childhood memory of seeing a man torn apart by them, but this was much worse than the dogs of Gilman's Cot. It opened its huge mouth, baring long fangs, and howled, and Maerad cowered. The sound she had heard below decks had been its baying; on the open deck of the ship it was completely terrifying.

Cadvan stood unmoving on the ship's prow, his sword drawn, his form blazing with power. He was only a little bigger than the stormdog's fangs; its size was staggering. It seemed inconceivable that it would not simply bend forward and snap up the *White Owl* as a lion would a mouse. As she watched, it reared up and crashed its huge paw against the ship, hitting it with a crash of thunder. Cadvan slashed down with his sword, bringing behind it a blinding arc of white light. Even through the stormdog's baying and the chaos of the storm, Maerad could feel his words of power echoing through her bones.

The *White Owl* spun dizzily into the face of a wave and Maerad feared that they were sinking; cataracts of water broke violently over the deck, so that it seemed that they were already all but drowned. Miraculously the *Owl* righted herself, bobbing upright as the water streamed off the deck. Maerad, clinging to her railing, dashed the water from her eyes and looked desperately to the prow: Cadvan was still there, balancing easily, as if he were a part of the boat, a figurehead rather than a man who merely stood on the deck. He was so bright now it was difficult to look at him and, from an answering shiver deep in her mind, Maerad could feel the power he was invoking. She looked down at her hands and with a thrill of wonder saw that a silver-gold light was breaking between her fingers: Cadvan was investing the entire craft with his power. Before long every timber, every rope and spar of the boat was shining, as if it were made of light, and the glow kept increasing until it was so bright that tears of dazzlement ran down Maerad's cheeks, mingling with the cold spray that lashed her face. As the *White Owl* glowed in the tumultuous darkness, suddenly transformed from a humble fishing smack into an airy thing of light, beautiful and strange, the stormdog howled with rage.

Even in the midst of peril, Maerad felt a deep awe: this was a different power from that which Cadvan had revealed during the Rite of Renewal. He was unleashing capacities that Maerad didn't know Bards possessed. In the full strength of his power, he was almost as terrifying as the stormdog itself.

She pulled herself straighter, collecting her mind into some semblance of thought. There had to be some way she could use her own powers to assist Cadvan.

The stormdog lashed out again, but this time the boat barely shuddered. Maerad was relieved; she wondered how many blows the *White Owl*, for all its sturdiness and Bardic charms, could take from such a monster. She wiped the hair and water from her eyes, and sent out her mind to join Cadvan's, gently, lest she jolt his will and disturb his magery. There was a slight answering surprise, and then relief as he let her join her power to his.

To join Cadvan's mind was to share with him the full force of the stormdog's fury, and Maerad staggered under its sudden onslaught. At the same time, her fear of the monster suddenly vanished altogether, and was replaced by a strange exhilaration. It was almost as if she could understand the stormdog, although it spoke no language that she knew. She looked into its eyes and, for the first time it noticed her presence. It snapped at her, letting out a volley of yells, and into Maerad's mind sprang the most incongruous memory possible: her mother stroking her hair, when she was a very little girl.

Maerad took a deep breath. Then, keeping her eyes fixed on the dog, she began to sing. She sang both in her mind and with her physical voice, although any sound she made was instantly torn away by the gale. It was the smallest of whispers in the tumult, but she thought the stormdog heard her. She felt Cadvan falter in surprise, and the boat briefly dimmed as he momentarily lost concentration.

> Sleep, my pretty one, the day is over
> Sleep, my darling one, night is falling
> The sun bends down to her star-crowned lover
> The hare sleeps now in her scented clover
> And the brindled owl is calling

The old melody – how long since she had heard it? – rose in her throat and her voice grew stronger. Was she mad? Singing a lullaby to a stormdog? But she thought she saw a change in the stormdog's eyes. She took another breath, and sang the next verse, filling her mind with tenderness: remembering the way her mother had stroked her brow as she lay near sleep, the soft burr of her voice, her kiss as she fell into slumber.

> Sleep, my pretty one, the night is coming
> Sleep, my darling one, night is here
> Soon you will ride a ship of gleaming
> Silver light, with your soft hair streaming
> Bright on the darkling air

Now Maerad was sure her mad idea was working; the wind was abating, and the stormdog had stopped its baying and seemed to be looking at her enquiringly, its ears cocked. Its lightnings were flickering less violently and its terrible shrieks

muted to a strange low thunder. She kept on singing, starting
again when she reached the end of the lullaby, keeping her eyes
fixed on the stormdog; and as she sang the force of sea gradually lessened, until the waves were only a little larger than the
height of their boat. She sang and sang, her voice loud enough
now to be heard over the gentling wind; and the stormdog
dimmed, and then began to vanish, almost imperceptibly, as a
cloud vanishes in a clear sky if you keep staring at it. At last it
was gone.

As the stormdog faded, the boat slowly returned to its ordinary colours of dark varnished wood and white paint and
furled red sail. It was only as Maerad blinked at the colours that
she realized it was morning.

IX

OSSIN

OWAN lashed the tiller and stumbled up to Cadvan and Maerad. He was not his usual neat self: his face was grey with exhaustion, his eyes rimmed red, his hair and clothes stiff with salt, his knuckles skinned raw from his battle to keep the *White Owl* upright. He fiercely embraced both Bards.

"By the Light," he said hoarsely. "I thought we were for the Gates, and my *Owl* was going down to join the fishes."

Maerad looked up into his eyes, and saw reflected there her own emotions: simple relief at being alive, a dazed exhaustion, and the warm fellowship of those who have survived peril together. She could feel tremors running through Owan's body, in long waves. She smiled back shakily, and unexpected tears filled her eyes.

Owan let them go, and Maerad stepped back and looked around with a sense of disbelief. The night's terror was like a dream that had vanished without trace; the sun was shining mildly in a pale blue sky, and all she could hear was the faint mewling of seagulls and the peaceful lapping of the waves against the boat. Only the *White Owl* showed any evidence of the night's travail; the deck, which was usually spotless, was covered in a mess of ropes and detritus all rimed with salt, her sail was still furled to the mast, and her starboard rail was snapped and splintered where the stormdog had landed a blow.

Cadvan surveyed the damage. "We got off lightly," he said. "Not many survive such a meeting on the open sea." Maerad smiled tiredly, and Cadvan took her hands and kissed her cheek. "It was well done, Maerad," he said quietly. "Very well done. I do not know if we would have survived, else."

"It was certainly the strangest audience I've had," said Maerad, and Cadvan smiled gently and let go of her hands.

"I confess, I'm dying of curiosity," he said. "Why did you *sing* to the monster? What on earth or under it made you think of that?"

"I couldn't believe it, when I worked out what you were doing," put in Owan, grinning. "There I was, in the teeth of a tornado, battling to keep the *Owl* upright, and there you are, singing lullabies. I know Bards are peculiar, but..." He shook his head.

Maerad studied her hands, searching for words. "I don't know when I've been more frightened," she said at last. "Even when we saw the wight, I don't think I was more terrified than when I saw the stormdog. And when I joined my mind with yours, I could feel all its fury. The funny thing was, as soon as I could *feel* it, I wasn't frightened any more."

She looked up at Cadvan, who was listening gravely. "As soon as I looked it in the eye and it looked at me, I felt different. I knew it was a monster, and that it wanted to break us all into little pieces and drown us. But it was *innocent*, a wild thing. It wasn't like the wight, or the Hulls, or even the kulag or the ondril. When you're near them, all you feel is—" She paused, shuddering, as she remembered these encounters. "All you feel is their malice. They are full of the malevolent will to destroy life, I mean, all that is beautiful and loving about life. But the stormdog wasn't like that."

"It bloody wanted to destroy *us*," said Owan.

"Yes, I know, but it wasn't deliberate. We were just in its way, and it could just as easily have gone on to destroy something else, or not destroy anything at all. Like a storm would."

Cadvan nodded thoughtfully.

"And as soon as I realized that it was innocent, I remembered my mother singing me to sleep, when I was little, oh, such a long time ago. And the song was the first thing in my head. So I started to sing it."

"It's a lovely song," said Owan reflectively. "I haven't heard that one."

"It certainly worked." Cadvan gave Maerad an inscrutable glance. "I would never have thought of stormdogs as innocent before, I must say. I shall have to contemplate this new wisdom."

"Well," Maerad returned, slightly annoyed. "You didn't think Enkir could be of the Dark, either."

"No, that's true," he said, and then he laughed, and the sombreness vanished completely from his face. "It seems that all my certainties are doomed to crumble to dust." There was a short pause. "Well, I for one need some breakfast," said Cadvan. He pulled up the trapdoor and disappeared down the gangway.

Maerad sat down on the deck, suddenly too exhausted to move. Owan, with the discipline of long habit, began to coil up the littered ropes.

Soon Cadvan returned with a flask, some plates, a cloth, a loaf of bread and some cheese. "It's a mite wet down there," he said. "But these escaped the general drenching." He spread the cloth out on the deck and laid out their meal. "Leave that, Owan. I'll help you later. Have some of this."

He passed him the flask. Owan took a long swig, wiped the neck of the bottle and passed it to Maerad before he sat down to join them. She took a large gulp, blinking: it was laradhel, a liquor Bards used as a restorative. It went down into her belly like fire, and its warmth spread instantly through her body, driving out the chill that lay deep in her bones.

They ate for a while without speaking, all of them realizing suddenly how hungry they were. The cheese was good Thoroldian goat's cheese, but it had an extra edge this morning, Maerad thought; or perhaps it was simply that she paid more attention to its taste. Despite her weariness, all her senses seemed sharpened.

Maerad scanned the sea as she chewed, and saw a long, low smudge on the horizon. "Is that Ileadh?" she asked, pointing with her bread.

Owan squinted. "Yes, it is. And that's the west coast of Annar there, to the east. We weren't blown off course as much as we might have been. We'll be there by eventide, I guess."

There was a short silence, only interrupted by munching.

"I was right glad you Bards were here last night," he added.

"Well, if you hadn't had us Bards on board, you might not have met such a peril," said Cadvan dryly. "So we're a mixed blessing. Have you ever heard of stormdogs this far south?"

Owan paused for thought before he answered. "There was tell of stormdogs during the Great Silence," he said. "But never since. And I hear that further north, up around the coast of Zmarkan, they do appear, at least recently. But this far south, no."

"It seems like a bad sign to me," Maerad said. "As if it was pursuing us."

"That's how I read it," Cadvan answered. "They will have guessed we are heading for Ileadh. I think, Owan, we should not put in at Genthaven."

"I was not planning to, at any rate," said Owan. "For that reason. There is a hamlet not far from Gent, up the Argent River, called Ossin. We are expected there."

Cadvan nodded, pleased with the arrangement, and turned to Maerad.

"Stormdogs are elemental spirits. I suppose that's why you had that idea of singing to it, Maerad." He smiled at her tiredly.

"Only an Elidhu would be crazy enough to think of something like that. The stormdog could only have been sent by Arkan, the Winterking. They are his creatures, he used them in the Elemental Wars, and also during the Great Silence. I have long suspected there is league between the Nameless One and the Winterking, and that Arkan wakes from his long sleep: but this is close indeed."

"It means that they know where we are," said Maerad, shivering. "And they're not far behind."

They reached Ossin at nightfall, after Cadvan agreed to Owan's entreaty for a charmed wind. They had sailed up the long bay of the Nathe of Gent, and Maerad gazed at the green-purple hills sloping gently up on either side in the distance. In a hollow at the far end of the Nathe she caught a glimpse of Gent itself: white walls overtopped by a cluster of onion-domed towers gleaming silver and gold and copper in the lowering sun. She inwardly sighed that she should not be visiting the School; even from a distance it looked beautiful.

Instead, they sailed a league or so west, and turned into the wide mouth of the Argent River. A deep channel ran through its middle, but otherwise it sprawled its shallow waters, which flashed dazzlingly silver, over gravelly shoals. A blustery, cold wind sprang up, blowing inland, and under sail they pushed upstream past steep, deeply forested banks, the treetops gilded with the last rays of the sun, their shadows falling on the surface of the water. The gentle scents of leaf and grass and flower floated over them and they could hear the hubbub of birds settling to their roosts, and the occasional quarrels of ducks. When the sun had set and a waning moon swung high in the sky, they pulled in to a stone jetty that jutted out into the river, enclosing a tiny stone harbour built around a kind of natural lagoon. It was big enough to hold half a dozen boats at most.

All three left the *White Owl*, Maerad giving the railing a farewell pat as she stepped over the gangplank. She would never be, she knew, any sort of seawoman, but she felt a warm obligation to the boat nevertheless; it had held together despite the worst that sea and wind and monster could do and had carried them safely back to shore.

They walked in silence along a small leaf-strewn track, which led up the banks and then broke out of the trees into open fields. Maerad saw a cluster of lights glowing through the darkness. Shortly afterwards they arrived at a hamlet of about a dozen buildings; Owan paused in the street, looking up and down, and led them at last to the biggest. It was a double-storey house made of wood and daub and painted all over with intricate murals of Bards and townsfolk at work.

"This is the First Bard's country house," said Owan, smiling, as they reached the front door and banged the silver knocker. "I've only been here a couple of times, but I warn you, he is famous for his hospitality."

The door opened, revealing a big, dark-haired man. He flung out his arms in welcome and ushered them inside. "Cadvan! Owan! Come in, my friends. It is overlong since last we met. And you are Maerad of Pellinor? My name is Gahal, Gahal of Gent. Come in, come in. Dump your packs here, look, let me take that cloak. First, some food and drink, yes? Nothing makes you as hungry as sailing, I believe. No, don't worry about that, I'll show you your rooms soon. Now, here we are."

He hadn't stopped talking all the way up the hallway, Maerad thought in wonder.

She gasped as she entered the sitting room; she had become used to fine rooms, but this was especially beautiful. The long casements were shaded with floor-length curtains, made of embroidered silk from Thorold, which glowed with a rich sheen of gold, and the low couches were covered in the same fabric.

But it was the walls and ceiling that made her stop in wonder. The walls were panelled with pale cedar, each panel delicately carved and framing a painting of a different bird. The ceiling itself was painted with a riot of birds in flight, all flying in a spiral towards the centre of the room.

Maerad was momentarily struck speechless, and automatically accepted the glass of wine thrust into her hand. She felt far too filthy to sit down in such a room, but Gahal almost pushed her onto a couch and then, still chatting amiably, handed around sweetmeats and drinks. Maerad contented herself with examining the room, craning her neck to see the painting on the ceiling. The birds were of dozens of different kinds, all meticulously rendered in every detail on an azure sky with rose clouds scudding across it. It darkened to evening colours towards the casement, and there between the clouds twinkled a single star. Maerad was sure it was Ilion.

"You like my birds?" said Gahal, startling her out of her reverie.

"Oh, yes," said Maerad. "I don't think I've ever seen such a beautiful room."

Gahal looked pleased. "It took me six years," he said. "Gent keeps me so busy, you see. But every chance I got, I came down here until all the panels were completed. And now I can sit among the creatures I love, even when they fly south."

Maerad glanced at the Bard with new respect. His loquaciousness, which was not what she had expected from the First Bard of Gent, had at first made her wonder privately if he were not a little foolish; but the loveliness of the paintings, and a certain sharpness in Gahal's regard, dispelled her suspicion. He was clearly not a man to underestimate. "You obviously know a lot about birds," she said.

"Birds are my passion," said Gahal. "They are the most beautiful creatures on earth; the sky is their element, and they live in it with such grace. All my life I have watched them, and loved them, and learned from them."

"If you need to know anything about birdlore," said Cadvan, "Gahal is the first authority." He lifted his glass. "And this room is one of the masterpieces of Edil-Amarandh. We are lucky to be able to see it."

"But it's comfortable as well," said Maerad. "In Norloch there were lots of beautiful rooms, but somehow they felt too grand, like you couldn't just sit down and enjoy them."

"I thank you for that," said Gahal. "Well, I am happy that you are here."

"So are we," said Owan. "We almost didn't get here. We were attacked by a stormdog on our voyage."

Gahal looked at him in astonishment. "A stormdog? They haven't been seen around here since the Great Silence." He shook his head. "It is not even winter. How did you survive it?"

"Maerad sang it a lullaby," said Cadvan dryly. "And it went away."

Gahal was sipping his wine, and at this he spluttered. "You are joking, of course," he said, when he had recovered himself. "I mean, really."

"No, I'm not joking. Maerad has – ah – some original solutions to such things. I must tell you of how she turned a Hull into a rabbit. But that is, in fact, what happened, and it is why we are here, and not dashed to the bottom of the Ileadh Strait."

Gahal grunted, and gave Maerad a very sharp glance indeed. "You are pursued, then, and by the Winterking himself, it seems."

"I believe so," said Cadvan. "I also think we daren't go further north by sea, as we had planned."

"Annar is dangerous for you, as well," said Gahal. "There is a price on both your heads, orders from Norloch, and many eyes will be seeking you. I wonder, which is the worst risk?"

No one responded, and he sighed and poured them all another wine. "Well, we will talk more seriously over dinner, when you have refreshed yourselves. Meanwhile, I have heard from Thorold, of course; and I assume you know of the situation here?"

"We know of the ultimatum from Norloch, and what your response has been, if that is what you mean," said Cadvan.

"It is the worst news for a long time. I have been disturbed these last fifty years, as you know, Cadvan. Something is deeply wrong. But it is no satisfaction to be proved right."

"No, none at all."

"Nerili tells me you are going north, on a quest I don't fully apprehend. And I am given to understand that Maerad of Pellinor is the Fated One?"

"So we believe."

Gahal looked her over with a cool curiosity that belied his former manner altogether. Maerad bore his examination with patience, wishing she were cleaner.

"I see." Gahal put his glass on the table, linked his hands behind his neck and leaned back into the couch, contemplating his ceiling. "That is news of greater significance than the happenings at Norloch. The Light stirs at need, it is said." He leant forward suddenly and to Maerad's surprise took her hand in his. "You are very young. Over-young, I would say. Much rests on your shoulders, young Bard. I had heard of your extraordinary powers before tonight, but I do not doubt you will need any help you can get."

"There is much I do not understand," said Maerad. "But I am learning."

"Gent you can count on. But Annar is split." Gahal let go of her hand and glanced at Cadvan. "There are those who remain loyal to Enkir – allies of the Dark or those who believe that as First Bard he must be acting against the Dark – and there are those who are deeply troubled or in deep disagreement, yet fear to be called rebels by Norloch. Even in Gent, I cannot be sure there are no spies. And the Dark is on your very heels. It will not be easy to pass through Annar."

"Still, I think it would be less perilous than stormdogs," said Owan. "There was only one, and it nearly sank us."

"As always, we have to choose between bad and worse," said Cadvan. "There are no safe paths."

"No," said Gahal. "Well, I have warned you of the perils of Annar, so I must consider my duty done. You must make your own choices."

"Everything tells me that time runs short for us," said Cadvan. "You have heard of the Rite of Renewal in Busk?"

Gahal sighed heavily. "Yes," he said. "It will not surprise you to hear that in Gent it almost failed. Almost. But I do not doubt that across Annar there will be Schools where the Rite has failed completely. Something draws out the Dark within us all. This is not just a war of arms and martial strategies, Cadvan."

"No," said Cadvan. "That has been clear for a while."

Maerad shuddered. "I had an evil foredream in Norloch," she said. "And also in Innail. And there was a voice that said, *I am again, but none shall find my dwelling, for I live in every human heart.*"

Gahal looked at her in surprise. "You are a seer as well?"

Maerad didn't answer, and Cadvan stirred and said, "Yes, she is. Well, it was always a gift of the House of Karn. There is much to tell you, Gahal; and not just about Maerad. But I am glad to know that we can count on Gent. Not that I would have expected anything else."

There was a short silence, and then Gahal drained his glass and rose. "Alas, my curiosity makes me discourteous. You will want to refresh yourselves," he said. "Your rooms are waiting for you; I'll show you to them. And then we will eat a dinner worthy of your exploits."

Maerad woke the next morning with a feeling of complete luxury. Her skin felt soft and clean, instead of itchy and rough with brine, and all the aches of tiredness had vanished. After the discomforts of a hammock, a real bed felt wonderful. She stretched lazily, listening to the sounds coming through the casement: the cluck of chickens scratching in the road, a couple of men chatting in the rich dialect of Ileadh, the low of cattle drifting in from the distance, the *cark cark* of crows. A warm late-morning light shafted through the casement and tempted her out of bed. She wriggled her toes in the soft carpet, and looked out of the window.

From Gahal's house she could see over the roofs of the hamlet all the way down to the river, which glimmered silver as it twisted between the hills. Close to the hamlet was a patchwork of fields with a white road winding through them that dived into the birch forests that stretched up to hills purpling in the distance.

Maerad had slept long and deeply, after a dinner as convivial as Gahal had forecast. At dinner, they had been joined by Gahal's household, which counted about twenty people. There was his direct family: his wife Rena, his two adult sons, Nik and Beljan, and his daughter Lyla, who was about Maerad's age. But there were also other Bards and laypeople who were not related to Gahal at all, but bore some other profound relationship of work or inclination. Lyla, for instance, seemed to regard the other adults as intimately as if they were second fathers or mothers. Maerad, whose family had been fragmented by disaster and who had, up until now, mainly stayed at Schools, did not remember the broader patterns of responsibilities and kinship that operated in Barding households, and it struck her for the first time.

Lyla had sat next to Maerad, and the two liked each other on sight. It was the first time that Maerad had met anyone her own age who wasn't awed by her reputation or her association with Cadvan.

The conversation remained general, and Maerad had eaten her way through several courses of beautifully prepared food: a dish of fat yellow asparagus cooked to absolute tenderness, a salad of herbs and nasturtiums, fresh trout baked with almonds and honey, wood mushrooms seethed in milk and butter. Then Gahal had insisted she try his limonel, an apple spirit he made himself, which was more delicious (and stronger) than laradhel. It was no wonder she had slept so well.

She lazily watched a horseman trot up the road towards the house, dismount and knock on the door.

Rena had lent her some of Lyla's clothes, as her own were being laundered, and she had just decided she had better dress and see what was happening with the day when there was a knock on the chamber door.

"Yes?" said Maerad.

Lyla popped her head around the door. "Morning, Maerad! Papa wanted to know if you'd like breakfast."

Maerad indicated her nightgown. "I've been a bit slow this morning," she said. "I'm not even dressed."

"Oh, he said to tell you there's no hurry." Lyla came shyly into the room. Like Gahal, she was dark-haired and dark-eyed, and her hair was tied in a long plait down her back. "He just wanted to know whether to put it all away yet. Cadvan and Owan aren't up, either."

"Well, I'm glad to know it's not just me being so lazy," said Maerad, laughing.

"Besides, Anhil's arrived, and he wants to meet you."

"Who's Anhil?" asked Maerad, unselfconsciously pulling

off her nightgown and dragging on some underclothes.

"He's a Bard at Gent. I like him, he's always lovely. And he's *very* good looking." Lyla sat down on the bed. "Is this your lyre? It's not very grand, is it? Papa's has gold inlay and golden strings. But I suppose you can only get old ones when you're young like us. Anhil is Dernhil's brother, you know, the Bard who was killed at Innail. I didn't know him so well, I only met him once, when I was three, but it was just awful. I was so sad for Anhil."

Maerad was grateful that her dress was over her head, and Lyla couldn't see her expression. Dernhil's brother! She had known that Dernhil was from Gent, and it was, in fact, one of the reasons that she had wanted to go there, but the thought of meeting his brother keenly brought back her sorrow at his death. But the moment passed and she shrugged the dress over her shoulders.

Lyla looked at her critically, her head on one side. "I like that dress," she said. "But I think it looks nicer on me than on you."

"I should wash first," Maerad answered. "I'll be downstairs after that."

"I shall see you then," said Lyla. "I'll tell Papa."

By the time she appeared downstairs, washed and brushed, Maerad had composed herself enough to greet Anhil. He was sitting in the dining room talking to Gahal, leaning back in his chair, one foot on the other knee. When Maerad entered, he stood up and Gahal introduced them. She felt a start of painful recognition: Anhil was both like and unlike Dernhil; his hair was light brown, and he was not quite so tall. But his eyes held the same mobile expressiveness as Dernhil's, and she found it hard to look at him straightly.

"I am glad to meet you," Anhil said courteously, taking her hand. "My brother wrote to me about you, shortly before he died. You impressed him very much."

A lump gathered in Maerad's throat and she nodded, unable for a moment to answer.

"His death was a great grief," she said. "I am very sorry. It must have been hard for you."

"Yes," answered Anhil. "He is a great loss to all of us; but most of all to those who loved him."

Maerad had no idea how to respond, and simply nodded again, biting her lip, and at that moment, to her relief, Cadvan entered the room. Anhil turned to greet him, and Cadvan embraced him wordlessly. Maerad sat at the table, her heart thumping, feeling graceless and awkward.

Lyla leant over to her and whispered, "See, I told you he was good looking." Maerad blushed scarlet. "I didn't know you knew Dernhil."

"Yes," Maerad said. "For too short a time."

"It was sad, what happened to him," said Lyla. "His ashes are at Gent, you know." Maerad mumbled something inaudible in reply, and Lyla at last worked out that Maerad was uncomfortable talking about Dernhil and changed the subject. "Anyway, have some of this honey; it's very nice. Mama keeps the hives and she gives the bees plenty of sweet clovers to work with."

Gratefully Maerad buried herself in the business of eating, and gradually her emotions settled enough for her to start listening to the conversation between Cadvan, Anhil and Gahal. Anhil was one of the First Circle of Gent, and his visit was not prompted solely by Cadvan and Maerad's presence. Another emissary had arrived from Norloch, demanding men at arms from Ileadh for Norloch's campaign against the Dark.

"Naturally," Anhil said to Gahal, "we have told them that we can make no decisions in your absence from the School, and that they will have to await your return from Damaroch."

"Damaroch?" said Cadvan.

"We know how dangerous it is for you," said Anhil, turning

to face him. "And for us, if it is known that we are helping you. Only the First Circle knows where Gahal is, and why. Gahal sent a semblance of himself to Damaroch; it is actually Rhyd. Gahal rode here by circuitous means, and in disguise himself, as I have done. I doubt that either of us have been followed, though I fear Ossin is watched. It is as well you arrived under cover of night."

Cadvan nodded, and Maerad felt her fear, which had retreated for a few precious hours, returning.

"I have put a ward about Ossin," said Gahal. "We are all safe enough, for the meantime; no one can observe us here. But this is ill news, Anhil. I will not contemplate sending men at arms to Norloch. And it means that perhaps the fears of invasion in Busk are not ill-founded, if Enkir is gathering forces." He knitted his brows. "My fears about you and Maerad travelling through Annar also increase fourfold."

"I agree," said Cadvan. "Nevertheless, I fear that three storm-dogs at sea would be a certain death sentence. One came close to killing us. Even with armies pursuing us, Annar is the lesser risk."

"I should tell you that two horses, Darsor and Imi, arrived at Gent a week ago," said Anhil. "Darsor said you told them to meet you there."

Maerad gave an exclamation of pleasure. Their horses had taken Saliman and Hem to Turbansk, and she missed her mare Imi almost as much as she missed Hem.

They stayed in Ossin another two days. Maerad spent most of her time with Lyla, with whom she struck up an easy friendship. In Lyla's company, she could forget that she was the Fire Lily of Edil-Amarandh, the Fated One pursued by both Light and Dark, or that she was a Bard at all. She could pretend that she was just a young girl of sixteen, with not much more to worry about than the day's lessons or tasks or gossip.

Although Lyla was not a Bard, her father had taught her many Barding skills: she was formidably well read – especially when compared to Maerad, who had hardly read any books at all – and had most of the great lays by heart. She could play several instruments and even knew some basics of the Speech, although on her tongue it had no power. She was going to be, she told Maerad, a healer.

"I can't do the Bard healing," she said ruefully. "I wish I was a Bard. But I can help women in childbirth and cure many things, even without that, as long as I have the knowing, and Papa says the more healers the better. And I like it." She glanced at Maerad, as if daring her to disagree, but Maerad was privately too impressed to say anything; the fact was, Lyla was much better educated than she was.

"I've never thought about what I might do," she answered reflectively. "It's not as if I've ever had much choice. First I was a slave, and then Cadvan got me out of there, and now I'm a Bard and I have to – well, I have things to do. And that's not a choice, either."

Lyla looked at her with sympathy. "I wouldn't like that much," she said. "Mama always says I am far too wilful, and she wishes I had been a boy, because they are much more biddable, and do what they're told. Whereas girls, she says, are stubborn as mules and as hard to train as magpies."

Maerad laughed, a little enviously. The kind of freedom Lyla was talking of was completely alien to her; and her comments made Maerad acutely aware of her lack of family. She barely remembered her father at all, and her mother little better; and those memories were themselves riven by horror and grief. It made her wonder what she would do with her life, if she survived the quest that she and Cadvan had now begun; she realized she had no idea at all.

Maerad didn't see much of Gahal, except at mealtimes,

but although he was always friendly she thought she detected a slight wariness in his manner. Once the Bard had taken her to see his tame blue wrens, which lived uncaged in a gnarled apple tree in the gardens. Maerad was enchanted by the tiny birds that flashed amid the green leaves like live jewels, and Gahal called one to come and sit on her finger, where it chirped and ate some seed from Gahal's hand.

"Featherheads, they are," said Gahal fondly, as the bird fixed him with a bright eye and asked for more seed, and then flicked back into the tree. "There is not much space for brains in those little skulls. But I love them."

"I can see why," said Maerad. "They're so beautiful."

"Beautiful and fragile. Like much that is threatened by the Dark," said Gahal, suddenly sober. Maerad glanced at him enquiringly, and to her surprise saw that he seemed to be embarrassed. They watched the tiny birds in silence for a little while, and then Gahal cleared his throat. "Maerad," he said, and then stopped.

"What is it?" she asked.

Gahal scratched his head and stared at the apple tree. "I wanted to say that much hangs on this quest of yours," he said at last. "And I wish to warn you, also. But I find that words fail me."

"Warn me of what?"

Gahal looked her in the eye with a strange earnestness. "That is what I have no words for, young Bard. There is somewhat in you that I do not understand, and I fear it."

Maerad stared back, unable to think of any response because of a strange dread that rose inside her. Gahal sighed, and then laughed and patted her arm. "It is hard to say, beware of yourself! But I do say it. Take care, my young girl. I think of Lyla, and I think of you, no older than she is, and I would not countenance my daughter facing the perils you must survive."

They walked back to the house, and Gahal seemed then his normal voluble self, but the conversation had troubled Maerad. She felt that she both did and did not understand what he meant. Was he speaking of the Elemental part of her? She knew that Bards distrusted the Elidhu.

Afterwards she had felt disturbed, and she wandered down to the river to spend some time in the undemanding company of Owan. She had scarcely seen Owan since that first night; he had been busy at the river harbour. He had drawn the *White Owl* out of the water and painstakingly examined her, mending the broken rail, which was the main hurt she had sustained in their battle with the stormdog, and checking each plank for cracks or weaknesses.

Owan left for Thorold shortly afterwards, and their parting had been warm and full of sadness. In their time together, Maerad had learnt to perceive the deep feeling that lay beneath his taciturn nature, and to respect his solidity, which held true and strong even in the most perilous circumstances, and she counted him among her closest friends. She wondered if she would ever see him again.

Darsor and Imi arrived that afternoon. A young Bard from Gent had ridden Darsor, leading Imi; she was about Hem's age and clearly delighted to be given such an errand. She was really guided by Darsor, rather than the other way round. Darsor was a magnificent black animal of about seventeen hands, with a proudly arched neck and a form made for both endurance and speed. He was out of the line of Lanorgil, the heroic mount of Maninaë whose ancestors were said to have had winged fetlocks, and his mettle was such that no one could ride him if he did not permit it. Maerad's steel-grey mare, Imi, was smaller than Darsor, but brave and hardy.

Maerad, who was outside with Lyla when the horses arrived,

rushed up to greet them. The young Bard slid off Darsor, shyly handing the reins to Maerad with a nod, and ran inside to look for Gahal. Maerad took the liberty of kissing Darsor on the nose and flung her arms around Imi's neck.

How are you, my friend? asked Imi, nuzzling her hair.

All the better for seeing you, Maerad answered in the Speech. *It has been a long road for you!*

Oh, yes, said Imi. *But it was fun. I liked Turbansk, they have golden mangers.*

Darsor snorted. *Brass mangers*, he said. *But good oats. Where is my friend?*

Inside, said Maerad.

At that moment, Cadvan flung open the door and came out, greeting Imi affectionately and embracing Darsor.

Always you are here at need, he said. *Now for our next journey.*

Darsor put up his head and neighed. The chickens scratching by his hooves squawked and fluttered away in alarm, and Maerad covered her ears. It sounded like a war cry.

That night, their last in Ossin, Maerad had another foredream. Like her previous dreams, it possessed an unreal, almost bitter clarity. It seemed she was lifted to a great height above the mists and fumes of a landscape scarred with battle; she saw towns thrown down in smoking ruins, fire set in forest and village, fields littered with bodies crumpled in odd poses and ominously still. The grass of the gentle meadows beneath her was drenched in a red dew.

She hung poised above it, as if she were an eagle, looking over destruction in every direction as far as the eye could see. All about her was an absolute silence. A great lake stood in the far distance, glinting red, with rivers running towards it like crimson threads, and behind her stood a range of mountains. Although she could not have said how, she realized, with a great heaviness in her heart, that she was looking at the Suderain, the rich, fertile region between the Osidh Am and the Lamarsan Sea.

Without warning, it seemed she was suddenly rushed at great speed to the east, towards the great lake of the Lamarsan. Beneath her she saw the white line of a Bard road, and more devastated villages and fields. As she neared the shore, she could see a high red tower topped with a golden dome that caught the dying rays of the sun. It was higher than any tower she had seen, save the Machelinor in Norloch, and it stood in the middle of a great city enclosed by high walls. She knew it must be the city of Turbansk, and her heart rose into her mouth. A black, evil-smelling smoke rose from it, and even at a distance she could see that in places its high walls were breached and scarred by fire.

Then suddenly, without transition, Maerad was within the city, looking down from a height just higher than the walls. Some terrible force had been at work there: some of the buildings were collapsed into utter ruin, with not a single wall left standing. Surely even war, she thought, could not cause such utter devastation.

Only the red tower and the buildings around it, which she guessed belonged to the School of Turbansk, remained whole; and they were teeming with the dogsoldiers Maerad had seen from a distance in her previous foredream. Seen close up, they made her gorge rise with fear: she saw long brutal snouts fanged with steel, eyes illuminated by dull red flames, limbs that were edged with weapons of metal or that expelled jets of fire, all animated by a malign intelligence.

Maerad realized the dogsoldiers were working in teams, sniffing through the ruins of Turbansk for survivors: she saw some hundred prisoners, bound and gagged, lined up by a wall, their heads bowed. She strained desperately to see, but she couldn't tell if Hem or Saliman were among them.

A scream gathered in her throat, but she could make no sound.

She woke drenched in sweat, the cry still on her lips, the dread and grief of her dream filling her mind to the exclusion of all else. Gradually she became aware of the outlines of her chamber, limned in a pale pre-dawn light, and her possessions, carefully placed about the room. She counted them over slowly to bring herself back to the present, as she always did when dreams afflicted her. Was Turbansk doomed to be a charnel house? Did Hem even now, lie cold in the ruins, while crows flapped down to pluck out his eyes? Maerad covered her face with her hands, struggling to drive out her dreadful visions. I could not bear it if Hem died, she thought. I would go mad.

Desperately, as she began to calm down, Maerad tried to recall what Cadvan had told her about foredreams. *Foredreams are perilous riddles to unravel*, he had said. *There are many stories of those who seek to avoid their prophecies, only to bring about what they most fear*. Perhaps I have seen only what *might* happen, she thought to herself. If all goes wrong. If our quest fails. If we do not find the Treesong… But she knew already of the forces ranged against Turbansk, and her arguments seemed futile, the empty words given to calm a child's terror, when the speaker knows there is no hope against the darkness drawing in around them.

X

THE WHITE SICKNESS

I
T was a morning of hard frost, presaging an early autumn,
when they rode out of Ossin. The horses snorted misty
plumes from their nostrils and skittered over the hard
ground, their newly shod hooves shattering the frozen puddles
and churning them into mud. Maerad had put on some extra
layers of clothes that morning, and, for the first time in weeks,
drew on the mailcoat she had been given in Innail. It was a marvellous thing, each tempered steel link forged so finely that it
was as light and flexible as a heavy cloak; but it was like putting
on a skin of ice, and she felt its weight with a shiver of dread.
Over all she wore her blue woollen cloak, the hood drawn
almost over her eyes. Cadvan was in black, his cloak bearing
only the smallest insignia of silver. She reflected, not for the first
time, that from a distance Cadvan could easily be mistaken for
a Hull.

Like Cadvan, Maerad wore her pack, with all her personal
belongings and travelling food, on her back. The horses were
burdened with other supplies: mainly oats, to see the animals
through the Pass where there would be no grazing, and rolled-
up sheepskin coats and jerkins for the colder weather Cadvan
and Maerad would encounter in the mountains and Zmarkan.
They were travelling as lightly as they could, but it still made
a heavy load. Darsor, who was strong as a warhorse, looked
unbothered by his burdens, but Maerad worried for Imi. She
was of a sturdy mountain breed renowned for its endurance,
but she was not as strong as Darsor. And if they were going to

be as swift as Cadvan planned, it would be a punishing journey for her.

Gahal and his household stood by the door, huddled against the cold, to farewell them. All Gahal's bonhomie was quenched as he soberly farewelled them.

"I cannot see far along your path," he said, "but we all know you are flying from shadow into shadow, and that no matter where you tread, perils will pursue you. All our blessings and grace go with you."

"Nevertheless, we will be safer moving than staying still," said Maerad.

"You are right, of course." Gahal gave her an unsettling look, and she remembered their conversation in the garden. "You have yet to know your heart, young Bard. Be vigilant! There are perils that have nothing to do with arms and weapons."

Maerad blushed slightly, and turned away.

"Peace be on your house, and all who live there," said Cadvan, and they both embraced each member of Gahal's family.

"And may the Light bring your journey to a safe end," said Rena. The customary farewell had an added weight. Maerad hugged Lyla hard without saying anything, kissing her on both cheeks. Lyla burst into tears, and ran back into the house.

Sombrely they mounted their horses and trotted out of Ossin, heading away from the river on the white-gravelled track. Maerad didn't look back, although she knew with another sense that Gahal stood looking after them until they turned the corner and were out of sight.

Around them the fields and trees were white with frost, only now beginning its slow melt under the pale heat of the early sun. All the dells and lowlands were thick with fog, wisping in curlicues as it drew up into the sky and disappeared. They followed the path as it ran into the birch woods, the shadows falling chill over them. The horses quickened their pace into a canter, and the air hit Maerad's cheeks like a cold river, tingling them into life as the blood began to move through her body and the cold receded from her bones.

Cadvan and Maerad had talked through their plans with Gahal the previous evening. Both of them felt that time was pressing, a sense that grew more urgent with every passing day.

"You are outlawed now," said Gahal. "I have contacted Carfedis, and you will be helped there; but you will need to enter that School in other guise in case you are sighted. You can expect no assistance from anyone, no farm nor inn nor School, once you leave Ileadh: anyone could betray you, to the Light or the Dark. And I do not doubt the Dark will be seeking you, Hulls sent by Enkir and perhaps the Nameless One himself, since the Dark, it seems, now has free movement through Annar."

"No road is without risk," said Cadvan grimly. "And I have taken thought of those you speak of. We can have hope in the fact that Enkir does not know where we are going, or why, and will not expect us to re-enter Annar, even if he has tracked us as far as Gent. He will expect us to be fleeing him, and I think he will believe that we are seeking refuge in the Seven Kingdoms; perhaps that we would go next to Culain, or even south to Lanorial or Amdridh."

Gahal nodded thoughtfully. "Perhaps we could take some precautions to draw the pursuit off your trail. I will give thought to making some semblances, perhaps they could head south to Lanorial."

Cadvan looked up quickly, shaking his head. "I do not want to think of Bards of Gent risking their lives for us. Are there any among you who could face a stormdog?"

"Nay, I wasn't thinking of sending any Bard," said Gahal.

"I have magery enough to trick the sight of any who watch, and to send a ghost ship south. It would work from a distance, perhaps long enough to muddy the scent."

"Well, if there is no risk," said Maerad. She didn't like the thought of more Bards dying to protect her, either. Dernhil's death still weighed on her heavily.

"I still think this is our best gamble," said Cadvan. "We have no choice but to brave the Dark; even if we hid in a burrow, it would find us. At the same time, we need swiftness; it is already almost autumn, and the north will grow daily less hospitable to travellers. We will have to use the Bard Roads, at least until we cross the River Lir. There will be few on the road at this time of year."

Gahal shook his head, but argued no further. He spread maps out on the table, holding down the curling parchment with his hands, and the three Bards pored over them. Cadvan wanted to ride as quickly as possible to the Gwalhain Pass, which pierced the Osidh Elanor, the great range that bounded the north of Annar, and would bring them out in Zmarkan. After that, he planned to go to the Pilanel settlement of Murask, a little north of the Pass, to gather news and to seek advice and help.

"It's three hundred leagues and more before we even get to the Pass," said Maerad, brushing the hair out of her eyes as she looked over the route. "It will be a hard journey."

"Aye, and we will have to go like the very wind," Cadvan answered. "It will try us. But I do not think we have a choice."

And now they were on the first leg of their ride. It was not so bad, Maerad reflected; she would feel stiff for a few days until her muscles adjusted to the riding, but now the sun had risen fully and drawn off the mists, it was a beautiful clear autumn day. The horses were fresh and eager, and the birch woods were beautiful, their motley white trunks stretching off up gentle grassy slopes starred with masses of small white flowers, the shadow of their branches dappling the ground with sunlight and shadow. Some leaves were just beginning to lose their green. Soon they would fade to yellow and spiral down to the forest floor; then their branches would be naked and the flowers would die, and the sere colours of winter would creep into the forest: browns and greys, and the peaceful white of snow.

It was the first time she and Cadvan had travelled alone together since they had arrived in Norloch, almost six weeks before. She fell into the rhythm of their being together; it was easy, a companionship born both of their shared dangers and long hours of uneventful journeying. But as they cantered through the woods, she found herself meditating on how their friendship had shifted since she was instated as full Bard in Norloch. While they had been in Thorold, their relationship had been mediated by many other people. But now it was just the two of them again, she felt as if it were suddenly thrown into relief, and it seemed to her less knowable than even she had thought.

For all their relaxed intimacy, there were depths and passions within Cadvan that she didn't understand. She had seldom seen him angry, but the glimpses she had had were frightening, and she had only recently witnessed the power that was the source of his fame throughout Annar. Once, for a mere moment, he had permitted her to enter his mind, to feel his private perplexities and shames as if she were inside his skin. She had found it very hard to bear; and even that concession, so difficult for him, had revealed only a small part of himself.

He was one of the most private people she had ever met: something within him drew away from human contact. In Thorold he had been more relaxed than she had ever seen him, and even there she had felt his abiding solitariness. And yet he was, paradoxically, capable of profound friendship, and was loved deeply and loyally by those he befriended. He was not an easy man to know. She remembered what Nelac had said of him: *If he seeks to keep something hidden, it is near impossible to find it out.* She thought of the moment on the boat when he had looked at her so unsettlingly. She flinched away from the memory, thinking confusedly of Gahal's warning: *Beware of yourself.* There was something within her that Gahal did not trust. It made her feel uneasy, because she knew her knowledge of herself was uncertain. Involuntarily she glanced over at Cadvan's dark profile, seemingly abstracted in thought as he rode beside her.

It was all too complex to unravel, and too disturbing. To divert her mind she decided to run through the alphabets and runes she had learnt in the past weeks. It passed the time, and the soft rhythm of the horses cantering over dead leaves melded with the rhythm of the letters: *onna, inla, tref, chan, edlan, cuif, va, a, ricla, pa, dha...*

There followed days of hard riding through the woods and farmlands of Ileadh. On their left the purple shoulders of the Ileadh Fells reared above the woodlands, and to their right ran a wide plain, the fertile downlands of Osirian, well stocked with grazing cattle and sheep, and run through by many small streams. The weather continued clear, but there was a chill in the air each night that told them summer was over: the moon, waning now to a nail paring, had a blue halo about it, and the stars blazed coldly in a frosty sky.

When they neared Gent they charmed themselves and the horses with a glamour that could even deceive Bard eyes. They had decided to disguise themselves as messengers, which would both explain their haste and the fact that they were strangers. Darsor and Imi became handsome bays ridden by two young men dressed in moss green, with a messenger's red feather pinned to each of their cloaks.

The charm was a speciality of Cadvan's and, to her chagrin, Maerad found it almost impossible. It took four attempts before she managed her own transformation, and in the end Cadvan had to help her with Imi, which considerably piqued her pride. It was also exhausting; she was dizzy for some time afterwards.

They joined the Bard Road at Gent, and on the well made course their pace picked up. It was sixty leagues to Carfedis, Gent's sister School, which stood at the border between Ileadh and Annar, and then a further eighty along the Bard Road to Edinur, where they would turn north and cross the Aldern River. The North Road ran with the Valverras Waste to the east, and the Caln Marish, a maze of fens and marshes, on its other side. By Cadvan's reckoning, they would reach Edinur in ten days.

They arrived at Carfedis late on the fourth day, and passed into the School, handing the First Bard, Melchis, a letter from Gahal. Maerad was too exhausted to take in more than a confused impression of halls painted with bright murals and a stone-lipped pond outside the Bardhouse, where many white swans swam like ghosts in the dusk. For one wonderful night they ate well, bathed, and slept in comfortable beds. And then they were on the road again, before the sun peeped above the horizon, pursuing their punishing journey north.

Maerad had bad memories of both Edinur and the Valverras Waste, and her heart sank as they neared them. It was in the Valverras that she and Cadvan had found Hem shaking with terror in a ransacked caravan, and the Pilanel family, who had taken him in, brutally murdered by Hulls. The image of their pathetic bodies haunted her, and they began to appear again in her dreams. After they left Carfedis and entered Annar, she began to feel more keenly that she and Cadvan were on their own; it made her edgy and irritable, and once or twice they found themselves on the verge of an argument.

Her mood wasn't helped by the dramatic change in the

countryside. As soon as they left Ileadh, the fertile garths of the Osirian gave way to uninhabited plains stretching flat as far as the eye could see, inhabited by shaggy wild ponies and goats whose white bones littered the tough tussocks of grass. The soil was thin and sour, supporting only the rankest vegetation, and everywhere were shallow pools and bogs where grew stands of black reeds that rattled constantly in the wind. Maerad's spirits drooped further with every day they continued through this unvarying landscape.

On the fifth day, as Cadvan had predicted, they entered Edinur, once a rich farming community like the Osirian. But Edinur was no more cheering than the wastelands they left behind them. The last time they had passed through Edinur at night. Now they rode through in daytime, and the blank, pitiless light exposed its full despair.

It hit Maerad as they entered the first hamlet. It was a collection of maybe two dozen houses, once a thriving community, but now it looked more like a battlefield. At least three houses had been burned down, and nobody had bothered to tidy their melancholy remains. They stood, shells of blackened timber and rubble, with bindweed and wild ivies already groping over them. Other houses just seemed to have been abandoned, their shutters swinging in the breeze, their doors, once painted brightly in reds and blues and oranges, hanging drunkenly off their hinges, their orchards and gardens grown wild with neglect.

A group of grubby, barefoot children were playing in the road. When they heard the clatter of the horses they looked up, frightened, and scrambled off into one of the houses. They were pitifully thin and their clothes were rags and scraps, barely enough to keep them warm in summertime, thought Maerad, let alone the coming winter. A child, little more than two years old, was left behind in the road bawling for his playmates, his upper lip encrusted with snot. Maerad pulled up Imi and stopped, bending down to speak to him.

"Where is your mother?" she said. The child leapt back in terror and fell over in a puddle, and began to scream more loudly. At this, Maerad dismounted and picked him up. He was a mess of tears, his ragged clothes wet through. She tried to soothe him, but his crying simply got louder, and he struggled in her arms until she was forced to put him down again.

Suddenly a door shot open and a big woman ran out, holding a frying pan, screaming. "Leave him alone, you scum! Get your filthy hands off him!"

Maerad, completely taken aback, moved away from the child, her hands in the air. The child kicked her shins and ran for the woman, clinging to her dirty skirts. Her face was grey with tiredness and her hair was a matted mess of knots and filth.

"I'm sorry," said Maerad. "He–he just fell over. I wanted to find his mother. I didn't mean—"

"He's got no mother, as you well know. You're all the same, all of you." The woman stood square, the frying pan raised above her head.

"Lady," said Cadvan. "I assure you, we meant no harm. We are but messengers passing through, and we thought to help the child."

The woman looked at him steadily, a glimmer of doubt in her face, and then slowly lowered the pan. She glanced furtively at Maerad, and something like shame entered her expression; Maerad had a sudden glimpse of the woman she might have been, had despair not nearly destroyed her. "Well, then. You speak kindly." She paused, as if searching for unfamiliar words. "I am sorry. His mother died of the sickness and it makes me fret, looking after all these kittens, and their parents under the ground, and no help. But I'll not let them be taken." She lifted the pan again, and Maerad cautiously backed away.

"Taken?" she said.

"It's always men who come. Men in cloaks. And they take the children who still live, they say to go into orphanages. With nary a question of those who care for them and love them." She wiped her nose with the back of her hand. "They've taken eight from here. But they'll not take any more. Not while I'm here." She lifted the pan again, and shook it, spitting. "Orphanages! It's not orphanages they're taken to, I'll warrant you that."

Maerad thought of Hem and his tales of the Edinur orphanages where he had been dumped as a small child, and shuddered.

"Where would they take them, then?" asked Cadvan gently.

The woman spat again. "It's for their armies, if you ask me," she said. "I've seen them marching through here, with all their rabble, and some of those soldiers are no higher than your breast."

"Armies?" began Maerad anxiously, but Cadvan silenced her with a look.

"Excuse us, goodwife," he said. "We did not mean to alarm you." He dismounted and walked towards her. She backed away nervously, but didn't resist when he took her hand. "Be of good cheer. What is your name?"

"My name?" She spoke as if her name was a thing long forgotten. "My name is … Ikabil."

Cadvan leaned forward and kissed her on both cheeks, murmuring something Maerad could not hear. "Farewell, Ikabil. Go well, with the Light in your heart." He returned to Darsor and remounted.

A look of amazement came into Ikabil's eyes, and she stood very still. Then she smiled, and Maerad saw, instead of a harridan exhausted and brutalized by long suffering, the gentle and strong woman she had been. A new peace had flooded into her face. She bowed wordlessly, stroking the toddler's head. He still clung to her skirts, hiding his face, but he had stopped grizzling.

"We should go now," said Cadvan to Maerad, and she swung onto Imi. The woman raised her hand.

"May the Light shine on your path," she said, shyly.

The Bards lifted their hands in reply and trotted through the hamlet. They rode on for some time in silence.

"What did you say to that woman?" Maerad asked at last.

"Say? Oh, I just said some words of healing," said Cadvan, jerking out of a deep reverie. "She was a good woman, in great pain. It is not true, that suffering is good for the soul. Too much, and even the strongest will break."

"What happened there? Was it the White Sickness?"

"Yes. It is a terrible thing, Maerad, and it is all through Edinur. There are few healers who can deal with it."

Maerad had heard people speak of the White Sickness in Busk; Cadvan had not spoken of it to her when they had ridden through Edinur two months beforehand, though even then, through the shadows of night, she had seen its scars.

"It only appeared in Annar two decades ago," Cadvan said. "Myself, I think it was brewed in Dén Raven by the Nameless One, to kill the strong and to break the spirits of those who survive. You've seen the results. Those who are most likely to die from it are the young and strong. If you catch it, you first go blind, and then you go mad. Those houses were probably burned by those dying of it. Either that, or their neighbours, in terror of catching the illness."

Maerad listened, her heart contracting. "Why is it called the White Sickness?"

"It's because of the silver cloud that covers the eyes of those who suffer it." Cadvan shook his head. "It is a terrible thing, Maerad, to see one who has this disease. Their eyeballs are white and sightless, and their bodies burn with a wasting fever that devours their very flesh. Unless they are lucky enough to be tended by a great healer – a healer like Nelac – they will be blind for the rest of their lives. If they live at all."

There was a sober silence. "I wonder what she meant by children being stolen for the armies," said Maerad. "Orphanages are just where people put children who have nowhere else to go, aren't they?"

"I don't know," said Cadvan grimly. "I haven't heard of child thieves, either. But children are cheap labour; perhaps they are stolen to be slaves. I can barely credit that they are kidnapped to be soldiers; but times are so evil that perhaps even that is possible. The orphanages are bad enough; squalid, stinking prisons of despair. Well, you heard Hem speak of them. Such is the legacy of the retreat of Barding. Once such children were valued and cared for. It would not be surprising, in this diseased land, if there were a trade in children." He spoke as if the words tasted bad in his mouth. "But enough of that: all the more reason for haste. *Esterine ne*, Darsor!"

Darsor threw up his head, and then plunged forward in a full gallop. Imi followed at his flank, as if the horses, too, sought to shake off the horror they had glimpsed in the desolate hamlet behind them.

For the rest of the day they rode through Edinur, through town and hamlet and past lone farmhouses. Some places were as devastated as the first they had seen, while others seemed untouched. But over everything was a pall: they frequently saw harvests lying blighted in the fields, already grey with a fungus growth that meant the corn or wheat would never be gathered and eaten; and they passed orchards in which the leaves were withered and the trees bore none of the fruit that should have been ripening there, ready to be gathered in. Everywhere were signs of coming famine, and in every town there were many beggars, turning sightless eyes towards them in a plea for alms.

As they pressed deeper into Edinur, they began to pass entire families who were heading for the towns, perhaps Aldern, with all their possessions piled on wagons drawn by horses or bullocks. Children sat at the back, their feet dangling, looking emptily towards their former homes, or shrilly bickering. The men and women stared hungrily ahead, as if they already despaired of the hope that had brought them onto the road, the hope that somewhere there might be a home for them that would be less cruel than the one they had left. Equally as often they saw single travellers, on horseback or on foot, loaded down by heavy packs. Sometimes they were barefoot, and their feet were bleeding.

These were hard sights to bear, and Maerad and Cadvan spoke less and less as the day wore on. As dusk deepened, they reached the junction where the Bard Road from Ileadh met the North Road and turned towards the Valverras, tacitly agreeing to get out of Edinur altogether before they made camp that night.

Maerad remembered this stretch of the road, which cut through copses of beech and larch trees before it ran up a high ridge. Now, as day was retreating, they saw no one else on the road; this was only a relief, as those they had met had been so desperate. On the other side of the ridge fell a wide valley of bare turf, with the Aldern River threading through its centre. The North Road plunged down the steep slope, leapt over the river on an arched stone bridge, and then turned sharply west, running alongside the river to skirt the Valverras Waste, a wide expanse of tumbled hills and bogs topped with granite tumuli.

However dour the landscape before them, Maerad felt a vast relief as they left Edinur behind. They cantered down the valley and crossed the Edinur Bridge, turning west along the

Bard Road. They trotted on while the full moon rose, swollen and yellow, until they found a grove of old willows in which they would be hidden. As she tiredly dismounted and unsaddled Imi, leaving her to graze while Cadvan prepared a meal, Maerad felt so depressed she could hardly speak. The memory of her foredream of Turbansk rose inside her, and she couldn't push away its horror, nor the trembling in her heart when she thought of Hem. She had not told Cadvan of her dream, because she couldn't bear to give it voice. This is our future, she thought blackly, this ruined world, in which everything we love is poisoned or slaughtered.

Cadvan glanced at her across the fire. "It is hard, seeing people in such straits, and being unable to help," he said, as he stirred a hot porridge of oats and dried meat.

Maerad paused. "It reminds me of Gilman's Cot," she said. "Those faces. I thought I had left that behind. But it seems to be everywhere."

They ate their dinner in silence. When they had cleaned up, Maerad stared moodily up at the sky. The moon was an ominous orange glare between dark bars of cloud. There were no stars tonight. Her body was chill, and would not warm no matter how close she sat to the fire. Her period had begun that day, but she felt more drained than even that could explain.

"We are unlucky," said Cadvan. "I think the weather is going to break."

"Just as soon as we enter the wild. Luck is in short supply around here," Maerad said, and then, to her surprise, found herself crumpling into tears. She turned away, but Cadvan had already moved close to her, and he took her hand.

"Maerad, our world is full of sorrow and evil," he said. "But there is also beauty and light and love. You must remember that." He looked earnestly into her face, but Maerad couldn't meet his eyes. She turned aside, thrusting away his hand.

"You don't know what you're talking about," she said bitterly. "There are things you don't know, Cadvan. You don't know what it's like to be me."

"No, I cannot know that," he said gently. "Nor can you know what it is like to be me."

"I don't care what it's like to be you," Maerad said, suddenly possessed by a desire to hurt Cadvan, who was always so reasonable, always so fair. "That's got nothing to do with what I'm talking about."

Cadvan sat silently, his faced shadowed. Maerad lifted her eyes, still burning with tears, to his face; but he did not meet her gaze. She looked away, through the willows into the darkness beyond. Her heart was full of an anger and pain she could not express, even to herself, but she did not want Cadvan's compassion. It made things worse: it raised a fear within her, over which she had no control. She couldn't tell if she had hurt him, or if he was just thoughtful.

"I am sorry," he said at last.

Maerad nodded, accepting his apology, but did not offer one of her own. She was taking first watch, so a little while later Cadvan rolled himself into his blanket, and fell asleep.

XI

ENCOUNTER WITH BARDS

AFTER that night, the constraint between Cadvan and Maerad became a constant thing. They travelled as had now become habit, and superficially things seemed much as they always had; they joked, and talked in the evenings, although they did not bring out their lyres. Cadvan taught Maerad how to use the blackstone, which had lain forgotten in her pack since Thorold, and Maerad developed some skill with it although it was tricky to use, as difficult to bend to the will as it was to sight or to touch. But even the brief resumption of Cadvan's teaching role could not quite drive away the shadow that now lay between them, the more powerful because it remained unspoken.

Maerad didn't really know how this had happened. She still trusted Cadvan as she always had, but she couldn't resist whatever it was within her that rebuffed him. And the less able she was to speak to Cadvan, the harder it became to find a way back to their earlier friendship. Cadvan, reserved at the best of times, was now mostly silent. She resented this as well, feeling guiltily that it was her fault, and at the same time feeling that his silence was being used as a weapon against her.

They pushed the horses as hard as they could, although after days of fast riding an unremitting fatigue was settling deep in their bones. The weather had turned, and often they beat on through driving gales, their hoods pulled down over their faces, the rain pelting straight into their eyes, and their camps were cold and cheerless. The horses had lost the glossy condition they had gained in Gent, and began to look lean. But an obscure sense of urgency pushed them all on past their limits. They began with the dawn, and if the moon, which was now almost full, let down enough light to illuminate their way, they often continued until well after dusk. It took them only two days to ride more than twenty leagues to the Caln Marish, where the road turned north again, and another three to reach the Usk River, thirty leagues further on.

Maerad remembered that it had taken them more than ten days to travel the same distance, from the Usk to the Aldern, when they had ridden over the Valverras two months before. She was glad of the Bard Road, for all its cheerlessness. It stretched before them, a white unvarying course running straight to the horizon. The road was less well tended here, and in places it had almost completely crumbled, but despite that it was, for the most part, in surprisingly good repair. On their right stretched the rocky wolds of the Valverras, and on the left the Caln Marish, with the same rattling stands of black reeds that they had seen before they entered Edinur. Many birds lived there, flying in great whirling flocks over their heads during the day or piping plaintively at night out of the still ponds and bogs. Maerad often saw eerie lights on both the Valverras and the marshes when she watched at night, but she knew better than to follow them; Cadvan had told her some of the stories of those misled by the fenlights. When the wind blew from the marshes, a foul reek of rotting vegetation tainted the air.

In all those days, they saw absolutely no one; this was not a well travelled road. Most of the time neither Cadvan nor Maerad spoke, except to the horses, and the great silence around them seemed amplified by the clatter of the horses' hooves on the road. Maerad bit down on her loneliness, as if it were a caustic seed, with an almost perverse pleasure. She felt herself hardening, feeling tempered by this punishing ride. I am stronger, she thought to herself. And I will be stronger still.

They crossed the Usk, which ran loudly over the shallow pebbles of the ford, and continued north through country less bleak, if no less lonely. They were now in the far north of Annar, in the region known as Predan. Most of the northern parts of Annar were at best sparsely inhabited, and the North Road passed through some of the loneliest parts of Edil-Amarandh.

After the unrelieved flatness of the past week, it was a balm to look on purple hills forested with black stands of pine, or to see slopes tangled with briars just now swelling their rosehips, or sloe and elder letting their faint fragrances into the air, or to ride through woods of beech and larch and hornbeam that were losing their greens to the coppers and golds of autumn. The gales stopped, giving way to days of rainless but sombre clouds, and the weather grew steadily colder. At night, despite her physical fatigue, Maerad slept restlessly, unable to escape the frost that nipped her feet and hands.

At noon on the third day after crossing the Usk, they came to a fork in the road, leading westwards to Culain and east to Lirhan. They were not planning to go to Lirigon, Cadvan's School, but to continue until they struck the Lir River. At that point there was a ford and they would cross it into Lirhan. They did not resume their guises as messengers, despite the increased risk of meetings on the road: it was simply too exhausting, and they were both worn down after the past three weeks. And they had seen no travellers for days now.

The next day, just after they had paused for their midday meal, the road entered one of the many beechwoods that dotted this part of Annar. The beeches were ancient and stately, their branches meeting over the middle of the road, which was littered with the first copper leaves of autumn, muffling their hoofbeats. The sun was out, and golden rays pierced the interlaced branches overhead, casting a vagrant warmth about their shoulders. Despite her gloom, Maerad's spirits lifted, and she sniffed the smell of the loam and the woods with pleasure, momentarily distracted, relaxing into her deep exhaustion. Cadvan too seemed similarly lulled. So it was that they did not see the Bards until it was too late.

There were two, a man and a woman, riding at a leisurely pace towards Culain. Cadvan saw them first, and turned back to Maerad.

"Bards!" he hissed.

Maerad looked up, jolted out of her reverie, and looked down the road with a sinking heart.

"We have to do the courtesies, or they will become suspicious," Cadvan said. "By the Light, I hope neither of them knows me. Cover your face, and shield yourself."

Maerad did as Cadvan bid, mentally hiding the glow by which Bards identified each other, and drew her hood over her face. They slowed to a fast walk as they approached the other riders. Maerad loosened her sword in its sheath.

Cadvan put up his right hand, palm outwards, in the traditional gesture of greeting, hoping that it would be sufficient and they could pass without comment. Maerad did likewise, looking out of the corner of her eye at the strangers; she saw with a sinking heart that the man wore a brooch that identified him as a Bard of Lirigon, while the other was of some School she did not know.

"Greetings, travellers," said the man; and then he drew up his horse in surprise. "Cadvan!" he said.

"Nay," said Cadvan, quickening his pace to pass them swiftly and making an odd gesture with his other hand. "You mistake yourself."

"It is Cadvan of Lirigon," said the woman, warding off Cadvan's charm. "Don't try to trick me with your wiles, Cadvan, lately of Lirigon; I've known you since you were a stripling." She turned to her companion. "It's the outlaws for certain, Namaridh. It was said Cadvan was travelling with a young woman."

The other Bard drew his sword, at the same time casting a freezing spell. Maerad and Cadvan both glanced it aside, but Darsor and Imi stopped fast in their tracks as if they were made of wood. Maerad struggled to undo the charm, but it held fast. There was a short, almost embarrassed silence.

"I mislike this, Cadvan," said Namaridh, looking at both of them apologetically. "It's not that I feel any enmity towards you. It breaks my heart that a man such as yourself has seen fit to betray the Light. But you will have to come with us. You are declared outlaw in this land, and you have no right to enter here. That is the law."

"My friend, you are wrong," said Cadvan. "I have not betrayed the Light."

"Some of us have longer memories, Bard," said the woman coldly. "I remember your little skirmish with the Dark. I would not trust such a man again. I never understood why you were not banned for ever from all Schools. Well, the folly of that has become very clear now."

"It is not so, Ilar of Desor," said Cadvan calmly. "I would no more betray the Light than you. You do not know the full story of what is happening in this land. And I say to you, that you cannot make us come with you, and it would be inadvisable to try. Let us pass."

"No one here has betrayed the Light, except those who cravenly obey the evil edicts of Norloch," added Maerad fiercely. "If you attack us, you are but a slave of the Nameless One."

"So speak all traitors, with tongues made slick by lies," said the woman contemptuously. "Take them, Namaridh. We can bind them and bring them back to Lirigon, to face what they deserve."

Cadvan signalled Maerad to be silent, but Namaridh had dismounted and now moved to take Darsor's reins. At the same moment, Maerad and Cadvan threw off the freezing spell from their horses, and Darsor and Imi reared back. But before she could collect herself, Maerad was hit with a stunning blast of light from Ilar that nearly knocked her off Imi.

She reacted with blind fury, without thought. She gathered up all the power she felt within her and directed it at the Bard in a bolt of white fire. Ilar simply collapsed and slithered off her horse, which skittered sideways in alarm. She fell to the ground, motionless and completely white, the only sign of injury a small, black burn in the middle of her forehead. In that instant, Maerad knew she was dead.

Namaridh stared at Maerad with horror and backed away, throwing a shield of protection around himself, before he ran to check the fallen Bard. He listened for her heart, and then picked up her body, holding it to his breast.

Cadvan swung Darsor violently around to face Maerad.

"That was not well done," he said, with cold fury. "That was not well done at all."

Maerad stared back at him, her face a mask of shock. "She was going to kill us," she said.

"She would not have killed us. And she did not deserve death." Maerad had never heard his voice so implacable, and she flinched. But now Cadvan was speaking to the other Bard, his voice steady and full of compassion.

"Namaridh," he said. "This was needless and wanton. I have no desire to harm you further. Let us pass; my errand now is of such urgency that if I do not succeed, all of Annar will fall."

Namaridh looked up at him, shaking with contempt and grief and rage, his face wet with tears.

"I know I have not the power to stop your fell deeds," he said. "I am not so powerful a Bard. But, by the Light, if ever there is justice in this world or the next, Cadvan of Lirigon, I will avenge Ilar of Desor's death. She was worth six of the likes of you. Now, get your monster to do her worst. I suppose I too must die."

He stood up, staring steadily at Cadvan with a defiant courage. Cadvan spread his hands in a gesture of peace and regret. "Nay, Namaridh. I would for all the world this had not happened. There is nothing that will compensate. I beg your forgiveness."

Namaridh spat on the ground.

Cadvan bowed his head. "This is how the Dark works, riving friend from friend," he said. "One day, I hope, the full text of this story will be known. Perhaps then you will forgive me, although nothing can forgive the wanton murder of a Bard."

The other Bard said nothing. He just stood, breathing heavily, glaring at them both.

Cadvan sighed. "I am sorry, Namaridh. I must now work a charm on you. One day, perhaps, you will know it is for all our sakes."

He stretched out his hand, saying some words in the Speech, and Namaridh's eyes closed briefly, and then opened, staring sightlessly ahead. He sat down quietly by the side of the road, as if nothing was amiss, and Cadvan turned to Maerad, urging on Darsor. "Go!" he said.

They left the scene at a full gallop, slowing to a canter a few leagues down the road, when they had left the beechwood far behind. Cadvan did not speak a word to Maerad for a long time. She cast furtive glances his way, but his face was hard and closed.

Maerad still felt shocked. The Bard's insults and then the blow – which was not, as Cadvan had said, meant to kill, only to stun – had released a deep, uncontrollable anger. She was terrified of what she had done, but Cadvan's anger was almost as frightening. She heard his words echoing in her head, icy with contempt: *nothing can forgive the wanton murder of a Bard.*

So, she was a murderer now, although she had only sought to protect them. Cadvan had himself killed Bards: yet he had forgiven himself more easily than he seemed to forgive her.

Other arguments stirred within her. The forces against them were ruthless, and they must be as ruthless if they were to achieve anything. Then she thought of what Nerili had said, ages ago it seemed, about the ethics of the Balance, and her own doubts about them. *We remember that if we did not adhere to the Balance, even in our extremity, we would become like them. And that would be the greater defeat.* Well, perhaps Bards could not afford such niceties, if they were to survive against the Dark.

She fiercely regretted killing Ilar, but she felt she did not deserve Cadvan's anger. Her shame mingled with resentment at his lack of understanding. She did not deserve Cadvan's absolute censure. She had not meant to kill; it had just come out of her, in the same way as when she had destroyed the wight. He had not been so keen to judge her then. She pushed down her knowledge that, at the instant of the blow, she had wanted to utterly destroy the Bard. She bit her lip, hardening herself, and concentrated on keeping up with Darsor, which was not easy. Cadvan was pushing the great horse almost as fast as he could go.

It was not until they struck camp that night that Cadvan spoke about what had happened that day. They had eaten in silence, and Maerad was about to wrap herself in her cloak and curl up to sleep. She now felt nothing at all: neither grief nor regret nor anger. She was just too exhausted.

"Maerad, we must talk," said Cadvan. He looked at her over the fire, its flames casting his eyes into deep shadow. "Today's task was ill done, and I hope you feel the weight of your crime. You have killed a Bard needlessly. We were not in threat of our lives, and we did not need such violence."

Maerad flinched, and looked away. His words hurt, as if they scraped her in some raw place. She tried to turn the subject.

"What did you do to that other Bard?" she asked.

"I emptied his mind. He will be perfectly calm until the morning, and then he will take Ilar's body back to Lirigon, to be attended to by those who love her."

"I'm surprised there's anybody, the way she spoke." The words came out of Maerad, vindictive and ugly, before she could stop herself, and then it was too late to draw them back. For a moment, Maerad quailed as cold anger flared again in Cadvan's face, before he mastered himself.

"It does not do to speak ill of the dead," he said softly. "It is singularly graceless when her death is on your conscience. Ilar was a Bard of great honesty and worth. If she was mistaken, it does not make her worthy of your sneers. I do not doubt that you are shocked, and I know you are very young; but that does not excuse you."

Maerad smarted at his rebuke; he was treating her like a child. She folded her lips tightly and turned away, saying nothing.

Cadvan waited for her to answer, and then sighed and continued. "Your failure is also my failure, as I am your teacher. I have not taught you as I should. And I have not had the strength to meet your need over the past days. I am deeply sorry for that; it has led to disaster. I hope it doesn't lead to further ruin."

"Meet what I need?" Maerad looked up at him. "What do you mean? How do you know what I need?"

"I know you are troubled, Maerad. And it seems that at the moment I am unable to help you, and I have failed to teach you how to use your powers as a Bard should. That is what I mean. Ilar's death lies on me as heavily as it should on you."

"I do feel sorry for it," said Maerad sharply. "Why do you think I don't? But it was me who did it, wasn't it? You don't need to get all noble and take it upon yourself as well. I did it. I killed a Bard. She was going to deliver us to the Dark, but no matter, I shouldn't have killed her. I shouldn't have killed the wight, either."

"I was not saying that." Cadvan looked to the sky, as if summoning patience. "It should not have even occurred to you to kill Ilar. Bards of the Light do not kill each other. They were not Hulls, nor even corrupt Bards. They would not have wantonly killed us, even if we had attacked them: only in the last resort, ever, would one Bard kill another human being. If you had been taught properly, you would have known that. Your power is frightening, Maerad. Misused, it is a monstrous power."

Maerad saw Namaridh's face, twisted with fear and grief, calling her *monster*. Was that what she was? Was that what Gahal had seen, when he had tried to warn her in Ossin: that she was a monster? She suddenly felt like weeping. Deep inside, she understood the enormity of what she had done; but she couldn't face it, and it could not be undone.

She almost overcame her resistance and unburdened herself to Cadvan. But something kept her back: pride, perhaps, or a shadow of the fear of Cadvan that she had felt since the voyage from Thorold. Oh, she was wrong, she knew she was wrong. But she was not wholly wrong. Cadvan was still being unjust. She drove her tears back with an iron effort of will.

"I'm not a monster. I made a mistake. You made a mistake, too, didn't you? But nobody calls you a monster."

"Some do, in fact," Cadvan responded dryly. "That is not the point. Maerad, I know what it's like to misuse power. It is a terrible thing. Out of all the terrible things that have happened to me, my own actions have been the worst. They scarred my life as nothing else has."

Maerad stirred at the urgency in his voice, but said nothing. If she broke now, she would break into pieces. She did not want to break. She felt herself hard and stern, and something in her rejoiced at her resistance.

"Maerad," said Cadvan. "Listen to me. If you do not learn how to control these powers you have, I fear for you. I fear for all of us."

Then *be* afraid, said some inner voice. She looked steadily across the fire into Cadvan's eyes. "There's nothing to be frightened of," she said. "I am sorry I killed the Bard. I won't do it again."

Cadvan held her gaze; she felt herself faltering, and her eyes dropped. She knew it was not so simple; but she pushed that thought away. She was no longer a young girl, who could be easily chastened. She was not a naughty child, to be scolded for playing with fire. She was Maerad, Elednor, the Fire Lily of Edil-Amarandh. Without speaking, she pulled her cloak around herself, and rolled over, her back turned to Cadvan, preparing herself for sleep. But she did not sleep for a long time.

After a while, she heard Cadvan begin to sing in a soft voice, a chant that she knew was a lament for the dead Bard. He sang low, so she couldn't hear the words, but the melody burned her heart like a rain of fire. She turned over, covering her ears, and her eyes grew hot with unshed tears.

Cadvan sighed, and poked the fire with a stick. Its flames flared up briefly, a frail light in the empty darkness that filled the world.

The following day they left the Bard Road and forded the Lir River into the Rilnik Plains of western Lirhan, the most northern of the Seven Kingdoms. Maerad was glad to be out of Annar; she had felt cursed as soon as they had entered that land. They bore north-east, following a track, little more than a well beaten path wide enough for a single cart, which meandered across the plains, occasionally crossed by others.

The light possessed a diamond clarity: every detail seemed to have a heightened solidity and luminosity, as if the landscape were some marvellous carving of precious stones, run through by silver rivers. They passed into wide, empty plains of grass and sedges, now yellowing and sere beneath tangles of blackthorn and gorse. The plains were punctuated by stands of ash and larch; and aspens and willows crowded the many small streams that ran down to the Lir. Before them on the horizon, faint and distant, but visible in every detail as if inscribed in ink by a master penman, loomed the Osidh Elanor, the mountains of the dawn.

It was a beautiful countryside, but its loneliness intensified the breach that had now opened between Cadvan and Maerad. The silence between them was now almost complete; they spoke only at absolute need, and then as briefly as possible. It seemed the breach even extended to the horses, who bickered uncharacteristically; Imi once nipped Darsor on the flank, and received a kick in the belly for the liberty. It was only enough to wind her, to Maerad's relief; but the Bards attended to their horses separately, rebuking and comforting them without speaking to each other. Maerad was also privately worried about Imi, whose coat was beginning to look rough and dull; she was as tough and stubborn as a mule, but this unrelenting journey was beginning to tell on her.

Western Lirhan, Maerad knew, was largely devoid of towns and villages, which tended to cluster closer to Lirigon. In the summer months it was inhabited by the southern clans of the Pilanel people, nomad horse breeders and traders who grazed their herds on the sweet grasses of the plains and moved with the seasons and their need. She saw a clan in the distance, a gathering of brightly painted caravans drawn in a circle around the rising smoke of a large fire, and she saw herds of horses grazing on far hills, but they went nowhere near the Pilanel and passed no one on the road. It felt like a cruel mercy, since it left Cadvan and Maerad to each other, and that was cold comfort for both of them; but after their last encounter she dreaded meeting any other wayfarers.

They were travelling as fast as before, both of them sure that pursuit must not be far behind, but despite this Maerad's exhaustion abated slightly. Lirhan did not erode the soul as Annar had, and perhaps that had been the greater part of her fatigue. She was very fit, after three weeks of hard riding, and her natural toughness reasserted itself.

She began now to feel the loss of Cadvan's company; always tending to the taciturn, his silence was now an impenetrable wall. Her only company was Imi, who sensed her unhappiness and would lie close at night to comfort her. She was grateful for the beast's simple understanding, but it only slightly eased the ache within her. She felt somehow exiled from humankind.

She bitterly regretted her killing of Ilar of Desor, and she also felt contrite about her words to Cadvan that night. But both were equally impossible to undo. Her contrition was somewhat tempered by a certain resentment at Cadvan's withdrawal, which felt like a punishment. She was too proud to ask for forgiveness, although she would have welcomed any softening from him. And underneath, Maerad was simply afraid: afraid of her quest, afraid of whoever pursued them; afraid, perhaps most of all, of herself.

Their ride was uneventful, except that the mountains grew slowly closer and closer and the plains lifted into highlands, growing hillier and colder. The weather held, each day dawning into clear skies in which rode huge clouds, purple beneath and gold and white above, but the sun now held little warmth and the chill of the fading year was palpable.

Cadvan had reckoned it would take about a week to ride to the Osidh Elanor. The Elanor was one of the two major ranges of Edil-Amarandh, supposed to have been formed in the devastating Wars of the Elementals many aeons before, and it was by far the highest. There were only two ways through: the Gwalhain Pass, which the southern clans of the Pilanel used in their migrations from their winter fastnesses in Zmarkan to their summer grazing grounds in west Lirhan, and the Loden Pass further east, just north of Pellinor. The Gwalhain Pass had been Gahal's main objection to their plans to travel by land: he argued that if anyone knew Maerad and Cadvan were heading north, they would simply have to wait there and ambush them.

"We shall have to count on their not knowing," Cadvan had said at the time. But the closer they drew to the mountains, the greater seemed their risk. Maerad's murder of the Bard had increased their danger sevenfold: it would be widely known by now that they had been in the north of Annar, although Cadvan considered that the Bards would think it most likely that they were heading for his home School of Lirigon. The Light may well be already hunting them through West Lirion, and it was not unlikely that others might guess they intended to go to Zmarkan; the Dark had been one step ahead of them all along.

XII

THE GWALHAIN PASS

THE mountains seemed to emerge from their swathe of distance all at once, as if the leagues of hazy air that had held them at bay, making them seem mere pictures and not real things at all, had suddenly drawn themselves up like veils and vanished. From their feet, riding eastward along the Osidh Elanor, it was as if the eye could not take in such vastness. From here Maerad could only see the lesser peaks, and even they looked grim and forbidding. They dwarfed the Lamedon, and even the mountains of the Osidh Annova where she had spent her childhood in slavery, and she couldn't see the heights that rose behind them at all.

All the tracks that trailed through the Rilnik Plains here converged into a single broader road, riven with many deep ruts and marked regularly on each side by standing stones, which threw long shadows forward as the day dipped to evening. The road travelled east along the feet of the Elanor, gradually climbing its lower slopes. It wasn't long before their way fell into the shadow cast by the steep ridges that towered above, and a deep chill settled over them despite their fast pace. Maerad shivered and drew her cloak closer about her shoulders; it was time now to take out the fleeces they had carried with them since Thorold. Cadvan rode ahead, his shoulders hunched against the cold, unspeaking and driven as he had been for the past week. It grew dark early, but they pushed on: Cadvan wanted to reach the Gate of the Gwalhain Pass by the end of their ride that day. It was a clear night, and the light from the crescent moon and the stars was enough to see by, if they went slowly. There was no wind, but the air crackled with frost.

At last they pulled up to camp. Even in the darkness, Maerad could see they had halted at the very root of the mountains: the sheer south wall of Mount Gwalhain rose straight up in front of them, glittering in the starlight, before it bent, as sharply as if the rock had been folded like paper, to its east wall. The Gate of the pass was a narrow canyon with Gwalhain on its left and the cliffs of Morchil Mountain on its right, its narrow entrance guarded by two more of the standing stones.

They camped a little way from the entrance, which looked too black and ominous to turn their backs on, next to a small thicket of dwarf birches. They lit no fire, fearing it would be seen even in such lonely country, and the horses stamped disconsolately, snorting and whickering as they grazed on the grasses either side of the road. After a poor dinner of hard biscuit and dried fruits and nuts, eaten in silence, Maerad took first watch, pulling her blanket out of her pack to protect her from the heavy dew that was already falling. She leaned against a granite rock and stared down the road away from the mountains, towards Annar. The lands fell away below them, sombre and wide under the veil of darkness, with the occasional gleam of silver where a river or a pond lay. It all looked huge and empty.

She felt as if she were taking one deep breath before she dived. Through Cadvan's silence, Maerad discerned his anxiety about their journey through the pass, and it made her feel even more nervous. And there was nothing to alleviate her fear, not even the casual banter of companionship; since the killing of Ilar, she felt as if Cadvan had abandoned her. A wave of loneliness swept over her, a fierce longing. Was there anyone in this vast empty world who cared for her, just as she was, for herself? Anyone who thought of her simply as a fellow human being, and not as some symbol burdened by a destiny she barely understood? Hem, the one person who loved her simply because she was Maerad, was probably already dead, slaughtered in the ruins of Turbansk.

She reached out with her mind, trying to touch, as she often could, that obscure sense that told her Hem was alive. She felt nothing, nothing at all, and a part of her went numb with despair.

Well, she knew about darkness now. She stared out bitterly into the night.

They broke their fast the next day in the grey light before dawn, barely able to see each other through a thick fog that had descended in the dark hours, and entered the pass soon afterwards. Here, in this deep defile, no sunlight entered: the chill was permanent. The road narrowed dramatically, becoming just wide enough for a caravan, and leapt steeply upwards. Every league or so, a bay was carved into the rock of the mountain, Maerad supposed to permit caravans to pass each other, if they met face to face, for there was no room for more than one. The rock face leapt up sheer on either side of them, with every now and then a tiny stream tumbling down in miniature waterfalls and running away in a little channel carved into the side of the road. In that dim, cold light grew only mosses and bearded lichens, trailing dull greens and yellows down the scabbed face of the rock. Sunlight was visible only long after dawn as a thin strip of light dizzyingly far above them. Not even snow could fall here in the hardest winters. They pressed on, slowed to a walk because of the steepness of the climb and because the road was slick with ice, keeping their hearing alert for any sign of ambush or other travellers.

They paused for a dismal meal, Maerad already feeling heartily sick of the gloom of the defile. It was late afternoon when they suddenly emerged from the mountainside into daylight again. The light flooded their eyes, and they stopped; but it wasn't only the light that made Maerad pause. Inside the Gate, they had climbed up into the heart of the Osidh Elanor, and now they could see across the snowfields and mountain peaks that stretched for leagues before them. Not ten paces before her the road turned sharply left, and only a low wall stood between her and a vast, cold emptiness of air.

The Gwalhain Pass was not a Bard road, although the Bards had improved it centuries before, cutting a little further into the mountain to make it broader and adding low side walls. Its origin was lost in legend; some said it had been made by the ancestors of the Pilanel, just after the Wars of the Elementals. Whoever had made it had also set the standing stones that marched alongside, now so ancient and blotched with lichens and mosses it was impossible to tell whether they had once been carved into the semblance of figures. Many had long fallen and lay broken, and others leaned drunkenly sideways.

The pass was cut into the living rock, zigzagging back and forth across the mountains and sometimes even tunnelling through the mountainside. From where she stood, blinking in the bright sunlight, Maerad could see the Osidh Elanor stretching before her far into the distance, white peak after white peak, blinding in the unreal clarity of the sunlight, with the grey scar of the road gleaming along their flanks. Across the valley in front she saw forests of spruce and fir, their greens sharp against the snow; below them was a sheer wall of rock on which no snow or soil could find purchase, and which dropped to a depth she could not measure. She could see a pair of mountain eagles circling lazily upwards from beneath their feet. She caught her breath.

Her first feeling was awe. None of the mountains she had seen had prepared her for this endless panorama. Her next was a sinking feeling akin to nausea: the cliffs above and below the road were vast, and any careless footstep could spell doom. The road wound on for leagues and leagues; they would be in this maze of mountains for days.

"It's only ten leagues to Zmarkan from here, as the eagle flies," said Cadvan, making her jump: he hadn't spoken all day. "But it is thrice that by the pass. And we cannot go swiftly here. May the weather hold!"

"Do you think it will?" Maerad said. She squinted up at the sky. It was mild and clear, without a cloud in sight.

"The weather in the Elanor is treacherous," said Cadvan. "It shifts without warning; last time I went through this pass a fog came over me, swift as a racing horse. It was so thick I couldn't see further than my nose, and had to feel my way like a blind man. A storm in these mountains is beyond description."

"Perhaps we will be lucky," said Maerad.

"Perhaps." Cadvan gathered up his reins. "If it was only the weather, I would not be so worried. If the Winterking can send a stormdog as far south as Thorold, then here will hardly be a challenge. And I do not think, Maerad, that even you could sing more than one such creature to sleep. Not in their own lands."

He smiled crookedly at Maerad, and she looked back uncertainly. This was the most Cadvan had spoken to her in a week. Did this mean he had forgiven her? She didn't feel like forgiving him so easily, as if she were a puppy to be seduced by a pat.

"With any luck, we won't have to find out," she said, more coldly than she had intended. Cadvan's face was suddenly expressionless again, and she kicked herself. If he shouted at her, it would be easier, or if they could laugh together, but there was nothing, it seemed, to laugh at. Cadvan was so often beyond her, withdrawing into some inaccessible place within himself; but now it seemed as if nothing would heal the breach. Perhaps it was partly that in some secret place within herself,

she didn't want to, that she feared their closeness. She dismissed
that thought as ridiculous; Cadvan's withdrawal made her so
miserable, how could she want it? How she wished he had not
looked at her as he had on the voyage from Thorold; everything
since then had just gone wrong.

Cadvan urged Darsor into a walk, and they started their
slow, interminable journey.

Maerad was suspended between delight at the astounding
vistas that opened up before her and a constant anxiety about
the dizzying depths and heights that seemed to wait only a few
steps from her feet. The road was lonely; they saw no living
things except the eagles and occasionally, in the distance, the
scuts of mountain hares playing on slopes and, once, a snow
lynx, which surveyed them with a mixture of curiosity and
scorn from below the road. It wasn't long before their days
assumed a pattern. The days were long and they rode from
dawn to dusk, camping each evening in one of the many bays
carved into the mountain walls for travellers, wide caves big
enough to hold two caravans, which provided shelter from the
worst weather. They protected themselves as best they could
against the punishing cold of night, waking up often with frost
in their hair and on their clothes. Maerad was more grateful
than she could say for the winter clothes they had brought from
Gent, which miraculously kept in their body heat; but even
with these, the deep cold of the mountains made sleeping difficult. Very often there was wood stacked in the bays, left there
by travelling Pilanel, and then they would light a fire; there was
precious little firewood this high up.

The first time, their third night on the pass, Maerad was surprised to see the neat stack. "Can we take it?" she asked.

"These are for the use of travellers such as us," said Cadvan.
"Look at the wall."

Carved into the rock next to the pile were two signs, which

looked very like Ladhen runes. Maerad examined them curiously: one, she thought, was the sign for light, the other she
didn't know. She looked at Cadvan, her eyebrows raised in
inquiry.

"They're slightly different from those the Bards use," said
Cadvan. "Bards adapted the Ladhen runes from the Pilanel,
who use them all the time to communicate with each other from
place to place. It means, roughly, that this wood is a gift to travellers in the name of the Light: that is the rune for Light, written
over the rune for travel, and this the sign for an offering or gift."

Cadvan began to build a fire, and when the flame leapt up
in that dark cavern, Maerad felt better than she had for days.
She took off her riding gloves, knitted of raw wool and lined
with thick silk to keep out the cold, and stretched out her naked
hands towards the warmth.

That night, Cadvan made a hot dinner, a stew of barley and
dried meat, and the tension between them subsided slightly as
they ate. Maerad could feel the cold outside the cavern growing
as the sun disappeared.

"There will be a hard frost tonight," said Cadvan, as they
tidied away the meal. "But I think we will strike good weather
for the next few days."

"It would be good to get through the pass without anything
bad happening," said Maerad sombrely.

"Yes, it would," said Cadvan. He was silent for a short time,
and then he looked directly at Maerad, his eyes dark. "Maerad,
we need to talk of what happened in Predan." Maerad shifted
uncomfortably, but said nothing. "It troubled me deeply. But
something within you is troubling me more."

Maerad looked at him guardedly. "What?"

Cadvan poked the fire as if he needed to gather his
thoughts. "It is not just that there is a wilful death, a murder,
on your conscience," he said. "It is that there is about you

something that makes me fear for you. Not just for you, but for the Light, for everything that both of us hold dear." Cadvan gazed at her soberly. "It has troubled me since leaving Thorold. Maerad, some darkness grows on you. I can see it in your light."

"In my light?" Maerad met his eyes, and then flinched away. "Well, I've been feeling a little – sad. So perhaps it makes me seem dimmer, or something. I noticed that with Silvia, whenever she was thinking about her daughter and was missing her."

"No, I don't mean that. I mean that some darkness within you might be gathering itself. Not just a sadness, but an active malice, which you must learn how to resist. I fear what it might mean, if we find ourselves again in peril. I don't know what you might do."

Maerad gasped as if he had hit her. Cadvan's words bit deeply, striking her worst fears. "How can you say that?" she asked, when she had recovered from her shock. "It's not true. Oh, Cadvan, I know I did something wrong, but you are talking as if I am something evil myself…"

"I did not say that," said Cadvan sharply. "I said that your light has changed and that within you moves some shadow. I do not understand what it is, or why it has happened, but I think your killing of Ilar of Desor was a token of something…"

"It was just a mistake!" Maerad stood up in her agitation, unaware that tears were gathering in her eyes. "I didn't mean to, Cadvan. I didn't mean to. She was just so horrible, and then she hit me with that blast—"

"I know what happened." Cadvan cut her off. "Maerad, I don't want to talk about that incident, not now. What I am trying to talk about is much more difficult. I think you need to understand what is moving within you."

"If you hadn't been punishing me these past few days, treating me like I was beneath your notice, then maybe I wouldn't feel so dark." All Maerad's resentment welled up inside her; she wanted to hit him. "You've made me feel like a piece of offal or something. Well I'm sorry for what I did. But that doesn't mean that you can treat me like—"

"Maerad, Maerad…" Cadvan stood up and took both her hands in his. She withdrew them roughly and turned away. "Maerad, I was not punishing you. I did not know what to say. I needed to think."

"About how evil I am," said Maerad bitterly.

"No." Cadvan took a deep breath. "Maerad, you have more innate power than any Bard I have ever met. Those powers are dangerous, and you have to know how to use them, so you don't hurt yourself, so you don't hurt the Light. You need to—"

"I know how to use them." Maerad glared at Cadvan. "What I don't need is you standing there telling me that I'm some kind of, I don't know, some kind of Hull."

"We all have darknesses within us," said Cadvan. "And we all have to learn how to deal with them. You more than anyone. But we have to recognize what they are first."

"I know what they are!" Maerad turned fiercely, trembling with anger. "I need to know I have friends who trust me. I need to know I have a family who loves me. And I don't have either of these things." Tears of self-pity rose in her throat, choking her, but she swallowed them down with a massive effort of will. "I'm just a tool of the Light. Those Bards don't care about me. You don't, nobody does. You just all want to use me, so the Nameless One is destroyed. Well, I can't go up to his big black tower and cast him down by myself, can I? So I don't know what I'm supposed to do. There's all this gibberish about finding the Treesong, when we don't know what it is, and being nice even when people want to kill us, and I'm just supposed to nod my head and do what I'm told and be what I'm supposed to be. Well, I'm just me, and that's that."

Cadvan had listened to her without interrupting, his face downcast, his expression unreadable. "I'm sorry I've made you feel more lonely," he said.

"I don't need your understanding," she answered harshly. "I've learned how to get along without that."

There was a long silence while Maerad, her back turned to Cadvan, tried to master herself. She wanted to fling herself on the floor and weep until she was completely emptied of tears. But she would not cry in front of Cadvan.

"Maerad, this is more important for you than anyone else," said Cadvan at last. "And I am saying it because I care for you. If you do not understand this, my heart forebodes disaster."

"I understand enough," said Maerad in a muffled voice. "I understand that I'm on my own. Well, that's no different from how it's always been."

"You're not alone," said Cadvan; but this time, she did not answer him.

After that night, Cadvan was gentler with Maerad, but once she had let out her resentment, she couldn't put it back. She rebuffed his attempts at conversation, and they rode through the mountains for the next two days in silence. The horses were also glum and unspeaking, catching their riders' moods. They didn't like the cold, and they missed their nightly cropping of grass. *Oats are all very well*, said Darsor impatiently, *but give me a sweet mouthful of grass from the Rilnik Plains any day.*

The bright weather held; Maerad's eyes began to ache from the constant glare, and she tired of looking at mountains. They stretched on ahead always, crevasses and walls and peaks, grey barren stone and blinding white snow, grim, unrelenting, mercilessly there. Despite her gloves and warm boots she had chilblains, and she was certain her nose was bright red from being pinched by frost. She was grateful for the sunshine, all the same; they had managed to keep up a steady pace, and were much more than halfway through the range now. In a couple of days, according to Cadvan, they would arrive in Zmarkan. Though what they were going to do once they got there, Maerad thought, overwhelmed by a bitter hopelessness, the Light only knew. Talk to the Pilanel? Their quest was an idiotic waste of time, a chase for wild geese, based on a couple of random guesses and some mumbled pieces of lore. And she would probably die for it.

As they prepared their camp that night, Maerad felt the air shift. At the same time, Cadvan turned his head alertly, as if he were a deer scenting danger, and sniffed the air. At that moment a sudden strong wind came up, blowing a scattering of gravel into the bay, and died away to a steady current of air; but now it was coming from the north, and it held a new chill. Neither of them remarked on the change, but it was colder that night than it had been, and when Maerad woke in the morning her blanket was stiff with rime.

They started as soon as they had broken their fast, just to get the blood moving in their chilled limbs. The sun was hidden in a swathe of grey clouds that muffled all the higher peaks and rolled in thick fogs down the sides of the mountains, where they were blown into shreds by the increasing wind. Around midday the wind picked up further, and it began to sleet. Maerad and Cadvan covered their faces with their scarves, and pressed on doggedly. The horses trudged along the pass, their hooves slipping on the icy trail, their tails miserably pressed between their legs, their ears flat against their skulls. As the afternoon wore on, the light grew worse and worse, and Maerad got colder and colder.

This was the most miserable day yet, and she almost cried with relief when they at last found a bay out of the wind and sleet, and she saw there was firewood. It took a while to light, and Maerad was almost incandescent with impatience before Cadvan coaxed a flame out of the tinder. The horses stood against the far wall, disburdened of their packs, miserably munching oats in silence, while the Bards rubbed their frozen hands in front of the fire, trying to get some blood into them, and steam rose off their soaked clothes. They each had a dose of medhyl, and then Cadvan prepared a stew for their dinner.

The bay was hardly as cosy as a cave would have been, since it was little more than a hollow scooped into the mountainside. Stray blasts of wind threw handfuls of sleet onto the floor, where they melted and ran sizzling into the fire. But it sheltered them from the worst of the weather, which from the increasing wail of the wind was getting steadily worse. Beyond the friendly flickering of the firelight it was impenetrably dark. Maerad sat as close to the fire as she could without actually catching fire herself and slipped into a stupor of miserable exhaustion.

"I hope this passes by tomorrow," said Cadvan. "A bad storm could keep us holed up here for days."

"Days?" said Maerad, starting awake. "We can't stay here for days."

"Well, it's better than being blown off the side of the mountain," he answered. "Unless that's what you'd prefer."

"I just want to get out of this place." Maerad looked despairingly up at Cadvan, her eyes ringed by deep shadows, and, for a moment, she saw an expression in his eyes she had never seen before, an unguarded tenderness. But it vanished at once, and she thought she must have imagined it.

"So do I. But not at the price of my life."

"Well, couldn't you just calm the wind, if it's still going tomorrow?" asked Maerad, without much hope. Even tonight, Cadvan hadn't used magery to light the fire; his miserliness with his powers sometimes made her furious.

"I dare not try to work the winds here," said Cadvan. "It would alert any evil creature for leagues around to our presence. Our best bet is to go on as we have, unseen."

"It's easier to hide in a storm," said Maerad stubbornly. "It's not that bad." As if to spite her, the wind rose suddenly into a high screech.

"Yes, and your body might never be found. Don't be foolish."

Maerad sulkily prepared herself for sleep. The idea of being trapped in this bay for days on end appalled her beyond measure; even walking through the sleet, as they had today, could hardly be worse.

The next day the wind had dropped, and the world was white with fog. It was possible to see only a few paces ahead, but Maerad, panicking at the thought of being stuck in the mountains, argued that they should continue regardless. Cadvan was dubious, saying that the fog could as equally thicken as lift, and that in a thick fog it was quite possible to get completely disorientated and turn back without realizing it, or fall down an unseen precipice. But Maerad was adamant, and after anxiously testing the wind Cadvan agreed to chance it, as long as they waited to see if the fog was getting worse.

After a while, it seemed to have thinned slightly, and so they mounted and cautiously pressed on. Riding through this whiteness was eerie; it seemed as if they were suspended in mid-air, in the middle of nothing. All they could see was the road, still dark and wet after yesterday's sleet, twisting for a few paces in front of them before it vanished into a white haze. The standing stones by the side of the road would loom over them suddenly, as if they appeared out of nowhere.

It wasn't long before they were soaked with dew. Maerad felt as if her ears were stuffed full of cloth; hoofbeats died instantly on the air and there were no other sounds except the snorting and puffing of the horses.

By midafternoon, the wind suddenly rose – a chill, buffeting blast. The fog began to break up, flying past them in wisps and rags. Every now and then, Maerad could see a glimpse of a mountain slope or a crevasse or a stand of trees, only to have the veil of mist instantly drawn over it again.

"Look out for a bay," called Cadvan over his shoulder. "There's going to be a storm." The wind whipped his words away as he shouted.

Maerad was too cold and tired to say anything. She just hoped there would be wood in the next bay, so they could have a fire. She started looking along the left wall; there should be one not so far ahead, she thought. There seemed to be one every league or so, and they must have gone that far by now. She scanned the rock face anxiously. It remained obdurately blank, and the wind was getting stronger every moment. Then a fierce hail started, driving almost sideways, so Imi and Darsor shied, snorting. The hailstones were big, like pebbles hurtling at them out of the sky; they hurt; and they made the stone road treacherously slippery. Cadvan signalled to Maerad to dismount, and holding their horses' reins they fought their way forward against the wind.

"If we make it to the next turn, we'll have some shelter," Cadvan shouted. Maerad could barely hear him, but nodded. On the mountain's flank, they were directly exposed to the gale, and even a little relief from the wind and hail would be better than nothing. Visibility was not much better than it had been in the fog, but at least it wasn't night; though with a sudden stab of fear, she realized that they didn't know how far the nearest bay was, and evening was coming quickly. In the fog they might have already passed one without seeing it. A night in the open in weather like this didn't bear imagining. She gritted her teeth and forced herself on, her legs feeling as heavy and cold as iron.

Then Cadvan stopped very suddenly, and Imi nearly ran into Darsor's rump. Cadvan turned around to Maerad and shouted something, but she couldn't hear him over the howling wind. With a leap of hope, she thought perhaps he had found a bay at last; but his final words were drowned in a huge crash, as if hundreds of tons of rock had smashed into the mountain. She saw that Cadvan had drawn his sword and was blazing with power, a sudden terrible light that dazzled Maerad's eyes; but she was so cold and tired, so battered by the hail, that she could barely react, and looked on in bewilderment.

Imi neighed with terror and reared, tearing the reins from Maerad's frozen hands, and then bolted back down the pass, her reins swinging wildly and the packs falling from her saddle. Maerad watched her vanish into the storm with a sense of unreality, as if she were in a dream and this had nothing to do with her, and then turned again to Cadvan. He was standing with his arms held high, shouting something in the Speech, but she could hear nothing over the storm. There was another huge crash, and a boulder the size of a horse hit the road in front of her, just missing Cadvan and Darsor, and then rebounded and plunged into the darkness beyond.

This jolted Maerad out of her stupor, and she was seized with fear. Cadvan was fighting some assailant, but she couldn't see what it was. The hail worsened, slamming into her like hammers of ice. She put up her forearm to protect her face and struggled towards Cadvan, not knowing what else to do. She couldn't go after Imi, she didn't know where she was. Perhaps the mare in her terror, already had plunged over the edge of the narrow road.

As she neared Cadvan, her head began to ring with the force of his power. He was a brilliant figure of blazing silver, globed in a shield of white fire, and she could barely look at him. She stared beyond him, into the darkness, and at last saw what he was fighting.

She knew at once it was an Elemental power, as the storm-dog had been, but she had no idea what it was. Like the stormdog, it was difficult to fix in the vision, seeming to be made of something not quite substantial; this was like a giant man hewn out of stone and ice, but it flickered with strange fires from its mouth and eyes, and parts of it would vanish when you looked at it, as if it were a cloud. It bore a huge, crude club made of rock and, as Maerad watched, it smashed the road very close to where Cadvan was standing. To Maerad, it seemed that Cadvan and Darsor must be squashed flat by that massive blow; but the weapon rebounded strangely, glancing off to the mountain wall where it struck showers of blue sparks, and Cadvan still stood, swaying a little. Darsor screamed in defiance.

Maerad was a hair's breadth from turning and bolting after Imi. Instead she gathered up what little remained of her cour-age and ran into the circle of light, touching Cadvan briefly on the shoulder to let him know she was there. He nodded without turning, his whole body tense with concentration. It was easier to think within Cadvan's shield: it kept off the bruising hail, and the noise of the storm was muted a little. Maerad focused her mind to join with Cadvan's. To her dismay, nothing happened; and before she could gather herself to try again, the creature swung at them with the club. It missed, striking the wall above, and chips of rock showered over them.

Maerad felt once more for Cadvan's mind, wondering uneasily why she couldn't join him, and asked silently: *What is it?*

A frost creature, an iridugul, Cadvan answered grimly. *We are unlucky. Or ambushed. I fancy the latter.*

So what can we do?

We can't destroy it. So we have to escape it somehow. I don't think you can sing a lullaby to this one.

Their conversation took place with the speed of thought. Everything had happened so quickly; it couldn't have been much more than a few breaths since Cadvan had halted and Imi had run away. Maerad squared her shoulders, and attempted again to join her mind with Cadvan's. This time he flinched, and the white fire dimmed.

It's not working, she said desperately.

Stop, Maerad! It's hurting me, he said. Another boulder crashed and splintered on the road beside them and he strengthened his shield. Close up, Maerad could see his face, pale and grim with exhaustion, the whip scars around his eye suddenly livid, and a terrible pain flowered in her heart. *We shall have to fight separately.*

They would be less strong that way, Maerad knew.

Try once more, said Maerad desperately, as Cadvan sent a bolt of fire straight into the frost creature's eyes, and it fell back into the void beyond the road, boiling like a storm cloud and roaring with fury.

All right. Now.

This time, Maerad was so anxious for their melding that she knocked Cadvan over. He staggered to his feet, gasping, and Maerad stared at him in bafflement: why could they not meld?

Maerad, it's like you're attacking me, said Cadvan. *If you do that again, you'll destroy me. We shall have to fight separately. We need to make semblances to confuse it. They are not clever, these creatures.*

Maerad shook her head in confusion, but had no time to think, for the iridugul had recovered itself and was now raining blows upon them in a rage. Cadvan was concentrating on keeping his shield intact, and simultaneously working a glimmerspell, a semblance of himself and Darsor, which he could leave behind him for the iridugul to attack.

Maerad cleared her mind, trying to ignore the furious hammerings of the iridugul. First she made another shield that enclosed Cadvan's, reinforcing it, and then she began to work a glimmerspell. To make even such an easy charm under such attack was difficult, but she concentrated grimly. I am Maerad of Pellinor, *Elednor Edil-Amarandh na*, she said fiercely to herself; why am I being so stupid?

Maerad's semblance took a little longer than Cadvan's, but after what seemed like an eternity they had created shining replicas of themselves. Cadvan extinguished his mage light and took Darsor's reins. They waited, choosing their time, before they slipped out of the shield of white fire and stumbled along the base of the cliff, leaving the iridugul to attack their empty images. The hail pelted into them as soon as they left the protection of the light, but Maerad put her head down and ran with Cadvan as fast as she could, hugging the wall, praying the iridugul was too enraged to notice the tiny figures scrambling along the mountainside like furtive mice. It was now nearly dark.

They had almost reached a hairpin bend in the road, when disaster struck. At the bend was a sheer precipice guarded only by a low stone wall and one of the standing stones, which rose like a black, ominous finger in the seething greyness around them. As they neared it, Maerad disbelievingly watched the standing stone rise up in the air: and suddenly there materialized in front of them not one, but two iridugul, one holding the standing stone over its head as a weapon.

Cadvan stopped dead, instantly throwing a shield around them, and mounted Darsor, who was foamed with sweat. Maerad looked back desperately; she could see the first iridugul still attacking their semblances, its fury increasing as its club seemed to pass through them without hurt. Three!

Maerad, we're going to have to blast them and run, Cadvan said into her mind. And then he noticed, for the first time, that Imi had gone. *Where's Imi?*

She ran off…

Cadvan said nothing, but reached down and pulled her into the saddle behind him. Then, without even pausing for thought, they both sent out bolts of white fire, aiming for the iriduguls' eyes, and Cadvan urged on Darsor, who leapt forward in a surge of muscle, making for the bend in the road. Maerad heard the screams of the iridugul, an unbearable noise like the tortured wrenching of stone, and just hung on as Darsor plunged forward. The great horse spun himself around the sharp bend, making Maerad's neck crack with the violence of the turn, and tore on down the road into the gale, bolting for his life.

Maerad heard the splintering of rock as the standing stone crashed into the road at their heels, and somehow Darsor sped up, his hooves skidding on the icy stones. Then suddenly an iridugul was before them, bringing down a fist like a massive rock on the cliff above them, and there was a rumbling as if the whole side of the mountain was collapsing. Maerad looked up, and with a sick horror saw a landslide of snow and boulders moving with a ghastly slowness towards them. She instinctively covered her eyes, forgetting for that moment everything except her fear of death. Darsor reared, and she fell off onto the road and rolled, coming to rest at the very edge of the precipice. She scrambled up in time to see Cadvan, his face glimmering pale, turn in shock and call her name, trying to pull up, but Darsor's reckless pace was unstoppable. She saw the great-hearted horse plunge on through the gathering shadows, still globed in Cadvan's shield of white fire, trying with his last desperate strength to beat the inexorable rockfall. She instinctively ran the other way, away from the pebbles that were just beginning to trickle down the slope, and then turned to watch, pushing her soaked hair out of her eyes, her chest heaving in great sobs of breath.

Darsor and Cadvan raced along the cliffside. It was too far to the next bend; they would never make it.

Just as they vanished in the gloom, the entire side of the mountain slid onto the road with a terrible sound like thunder that just rolled on and on and on, and the ground beneath Maerad shook and trembled so she was nearly flung off the road. Icy sludge and pebbles struck her face. The edge of the rockfall was only a body-length away, and she crawled towards the cliff face, sobbing with terror. When the noise stopped, she looked up. Where the road had been was just an impassable blankness of rock and ice: and the iridugul had vanished.

There was no chance Cadvan and Darsor had escaped. Buried beneath those mountains of rubble, she understood with an agony as clear and sharp as a fresh wound, were those she loved as much as her own life. Maerad covered her face with her hands, stunned and disbelieving. Cadvan and Darsor were dead. It couldn't be true; it must be some awful nightmare. She slid down the mountain wall, hiding her face. It could not be true: and yet it was. In a paroxysm of grief she beat her forehead until it bled, against the mountainside and fell insensible onto the frozen stone.

ZMARKAN

O raven, where are you flying
  Over the ice and snow?
O raven, surely I'm dying
  And my mother doesn't know.

Fly through the bitter weather,
  Fly through the starless night,
Where my people come together
  To sing by firelight.

Find my mother and kiss her
  For I'll not kiss her again,
How sorrowfully I miss her
  Staunching my final pain.

Find my darling lover
  Whose lips are sweeter than wine,
Tell her my life is over
  And she will never be mine.

O raven, where are you flying
  Over the ice and snow?
O raven, now I am dying
  And my mother doesn't know.

Traditional Pilanel folksong,
Library of Lirigon

XIII

THE PIPES OF THE ELIDHU

W HEN Maerad opened her eyes, it was so dark she thought she had gone blind. She tried to sit up, but her body wouldn't obey her. Perhaps I'm paralysed, she thought; or maybe I'm dead. The thought was strangely comforting, and she lay in the darkness for a long time, without memory or thought. After a while, a sharp rock pressing into her cheek became irritatingly uncomfortable and she tried to move again. This time she was able to shift her head, and, as she did, sensation flooded back into her body. She hurt all over, as if she had been beaten with sticks from the crown of her head to the tips of her toes, and she was wet through and freezing. Groaning, she managed to crawl up, and sat with her back to the cliff wall, holding her head, her body shuddering with violent, uncontrollable tremors.

As she sat there, memory crept back, first one image and then another. She did not search for it; something within her pulled back from the terrible realization of what had happened to her. But randomly, inexorably, images floated into her mind. Finally, with a numbing feeling of shock, she remembered the terrible sight of Cadvan and Darsor engulfed by the landslide. She stared blindly into the darkness, her eyes dry.

This time she really was alone. All her complaints and resentments of the past days seemed so trivial now. This was the disaster Cadvan had tried to warn her of, and she had brushed off his warnings, sure and arrogant in her power. And her power had failed her. She hadn't been able to meld with

Cadvan, as a Bard should, and she hadn't been able to work her Elemental powers either. She had cowered abjectly in the middle of herself, and she had failed. As she remembered what had happened, she was almost glad of the physical pain; compared to her mental anguish it was a relief.

Cadvan and Darsor's deaths were her fault. And Imi, she thought, had been killed in her panicked flight, or worse, lay with broken legs on some inaccessible slope, dying a slow and terrible death of thirst and starvation.

As she tasted the full bitterness of her self-accusation, Maerad considered whether to throw herself off the side of the mountain. It would be a just punishment, she thought coldly. Such a creature as she had no reason to live. Such a creature as she deserved no friends, if she failed to protect them.

Gradually the darkness became less absolute, and she could see the outlines of the road glimmering against the lighter darkness of the sky, and the huge black mass of rocks close beside her that entombed Cadvan and Darsor. She looked up and saw a blur of silver above the black blades of the mountain range where the moon, now at her full, hid behind a bank of clouds.

Maerad's face itched with blood and she clumsily tried to wipe her eyes with her gloves, which were rimed with frost. I need something to drink, she thought; and some of the generalized pain in her body identified itself as an overpowering thirst. Her lips were parched and cracked. Oh, I'm so thirsty and so hungry, she thought. But there's nothing to drink and no food...

She sat unmoving, sunk in hopelessness, and it was only when she shifted to ease the aches in her body that she remembered that she still wore her pack. In a sudden panic of haste, she fumbled it off her shoulders and started trying to open it, but her fingers were so numb they kept slipping off the fastenings. Eventually she got the pack open and found a water bottle, of

which she took a long draught, and the medhyl, which brought
a little fire into her chilled veins; and then she unwrapped some
of the dried biscuit. She ate only a little of that, because it hurt to
chew. Her lips felt as if they were on fire.

She felt restored enough to make a tiny magelight, and
with its help searched through the bag until she found some
balm, which she put on her lips and then smeared over her face,
slightly easing the stinging pain. Briefly she touched the reed
pipes the Elidhu had given her. For an instant, the light greens
of early spring woodlands filled her mind, and she remembered Ardina as she had first appeared to her, in the forests of
the Weywood, long, long ago it seemed, in another life. A bar of
a song floated into Maerad's mind.

Maerad picked up the pipes awkwardly in her gloved
hands, studying them as if she had never seen them before. She
had never played them. They were simple cut pipes such as
a child might make, fashioned of a dark purplish reed bound
with woven grasses. She wondered what they sounded like.

She ought to make a lament for Cadvan and Darsor and Imi.
That was what Bards did. And she was still a Bard, even if she
had betrayed her calling. She thought briefly of her lyre, but she
knew her hands were too numb to play it. And some other part
of her thought she was unworthy to touch her lyre, as if she had
renounced her right to that most precious of her possessions.

She sat for a long time while the night grew colder, holding the pipes loosely in her hands. At last, reaching a decision,
she drank some more of the medhyl. Then she painfully pulled
off her gloves and rubbed some of the medhyl and some balm
into her fingers. Her fingers burned unmercifully, but, at last,
she managed to make them flex and curl enough to hold the
pipes properly. She held the instrument to her lips and blew
experimentally. Her lips were so cracked that at first she could
not make any sound at all, but she persisted, and with a small

feeling of triumph managed to get a tiny sound. It made a thin, high fluting, like the wind over rocks.

She played up and down some scales, becoming, despite her extremity, absorbed by her fascination for music. Maerad had played similar instruments as a child and she had some virtuosity with them. These had an unusual richness of tone, and she found she could bend the notes expressively. When she had tested the pipes to her satisfaction, she stood up. This took some time, as on her first attempt her legs simply buckled beneath her, but she continued with a single-minded stubbornness until she was able to stand upright without having to lean against the rock wall, planting her feet doggedly on the ground.

She took a deep breath, closed her eyes, and played.

She played for Darsor and Imi, her friends, who had been with her through so much. She played for their beauty as they ran free on the Rilnik Plains, racing and kicking and nipping each other, the wind blowing out their manes in ripples of sable and burnished silver, while she and Cadvan ate the evening meal. She played for their simple, undemanding companionship, for Imi's nose leaning on her shoulder, whickering softly to comfort her, for the wordless comfort of her sympathy. She played for Darsor's dour humour, his endurance, and his plain, steadfast loyalty. And, last of all, so that it might not go utterly unremarked even if she died where she stood, Maerad played for Darsor's heroic attempt to rescue them from the landslide, for his shining, unbroken spirit and his great heart that had never quailed nor admitted defeat, even in the face of total disaster.

She finished, her eyes still shut, and bowed her head for a few moments of silence. Then she lifted her pipes again and played for Cadvan.

She had loved Cadvan, and he had loved her; and, she knew now, with an unassuageable bitterness, she had misunderstood that love. He was her first friend, the first who had seen her for who she was; he had rescued her from slavery and petty tyranny and shown her the world of Barding, a world of loveliness and humanity she had not known was possible. She remembered her first sight of his shadowed face, exhausted and sad, in the cowbyre in Gilman's Cot, and how she had trusted him, and had continued to trust him despite all the conflicts between them. She remembered the hours of his teaching, how freely he had given her the gifts within himself, how patiently he had revealed the secrets and wonders of the world to her astonished eyes. She remembered the brilliance of his rare smile, when the fountain of his joy spilled over and illuminated everything around him.

Now he was gone for ever it was as if, for the first time, she could see him clearly: imperfect, driven, haunted, stern, divided within himself; but also true, honest, generous, strong and gentle. He had been, all at once, her father and her teacher and her friend. Her grieving love welled through the pure, haunting notes, filling the desolate mountainside with inconsolable yearning for everything she had lost. Her tears spilled down her face and froze on the pipes and on her fingers. Maerad, lost in the music, did not notice she was crying.

At last, she finished. She let the notes die away into silence, and remained still for a long time, her head bowed, her eyes shut. Then she painfully took the pipes from her lips; in her long playing they had frozen there, and they pulled away the skin. She felt a little warm blood run down her chin and freeze. She straightened herself and opened her eyes.

For a moment, Maerad thought the moon itself was standing on the mountainside. She blinked in dazzlement. The bare rock of the road and the wall behind her shone like burnished silver, and behind every blazing boulder and pebble stood a black shadow. Before her stood Ardina, but she appeared neither as a wild Elidhu of the woods, shimmering naked in a bower of branches, nor as the agelessly beautiful Queen of Rachida. Maerad saw her as the songs described her, as Cadvan had sung of her once, long ago: the enchanting daughter of the moon, a being spun of sheer moonbeams, beautiful and evanescent.

Maerad was past astonishment. She thought she must be dreaming, or suffering a fantastic vision, as people were said to do sometimes in the extremity before death, and she gazed at Ardina as if it were completely natural that she should be there.

The Elidhu was suspended slightly above the ground, unmoving save for her hair, which stirred in a wind that Maerad could not feel. She seemed to be waiting for Maerad to speak. At last, as the vision did not disappear, Maerad bowed; but the movement was too much for her, and she slid down the mountain wall, until she was sitting on the ground, still staring at Ardina, her body racked again by uncontrollable tremors. At that, the Elidhu stepped towards her, putting a hand on her forehead. It felt like ice, but thrillingly alive, as if the energy of a mountain river coursed through her veins. Maerad's shuddering stopped.

"Are you dying, my daughter?" Ardina asked. "I think you have put all your life into your music. I wish I had asked you to play before; I have heard no such music since the days of Afinil. But even then, only the Elidhu could play with such wildness and such skill and such sadness."

Maerad tried to speak, but her throat was so parched she couldn't make anything beyond a croak. She just nodded, swallowing. Yes, she was dying.

"I think you did not mean to call me." Ardina laughed, her head to one side. "You forget what I said: that if you needed me, you should play the pipes I gave you. But you had another desire, I think."

Maerad did not answer, but a fresh tear rolled down her cheek, and Ardina sighed. "I warned you once, about love.

Mortals die like the reeds, and then within the world's circle is only absence. Ah, my dear daughter, there is no remedy for love or grief. They persist beyond all boundaries."

Ardina's words pierced Maerad to the quick. She bowed her head to hide her face and saw that she still clutched the pipes in her hands. With a dogged deliberateness she put them back in her pack, and then lifted her pack onto her lap and clutched it, almost as if she were drowning. She could scarcely feel it with her numbed hands, but it was solid and real, and obscurely comforting. Ardina watched her closely, but without impatience.

"Do you choose to die?" she asked, almost disinterestedly. "For I will not interfere with any choice of yours. I know what it is to desire death, and to be refused it. But if you do not choose death, I will help you. It pains me to see such suffering in thee, daughter." With that intimate address, some of the despair that had frozen Maerad's heart melted, and she met Ardina's gaze. The fey, yellow eyes of the Elidhu were soft with compassion.

For the barest moment, Maerad hesitated. It would be so easy to die, to renounce all her struggles and suffering, to escape the terrible grief that racked her spirit. But something within her refused to choose death; it would come to her eventually whether she chose or not, but an inner voice stubbornly cried out: *not now*. Slowly she said in a cracked voice, so quiet it could hardly be heard, "No, I don't want to die."

Ardina leant over her and kissed her forehead. From her cold lips blossomed a delicious glow that coursed through all Maerad's body, as if she were falling into a divinely comfortable bed and all her hurts were healed. She looked up into Ardina's wild face, and it seemed as if the entire world vanished into a golden mist: only the brilliant, unsettling eyes, eyes as yellow as topaz or citrine, burned in her mind like two lights of haven, as she drifted into the blessed shades of sleep.

XIV

MIRKA

MAERAD didn't want to open her eyes. She didn't know where she was; she knew she hurt all over, and that she had a bad headache. She was lying on something soft, and the air around her was warm. In her nostrils was a strong smell of woodsmoke laced with fish.

She lay very still, listening. She heard the sounds of someone moving around, and then a faint metallic clang, and the gentle pop of a burning fire. Gingerly she touched what was covering her: it was soft and warm, some kind of fur.

She heard someone moving towards her and tensed as a hand stroked her forehead. Involuntarily she opened her eyes. She looked into a cracked, ancient face, and a pair of very pale-blue, watery eyes.

"*Om toki nel?*" said the face. Maerad looked back without speaking, and the mouth, a cave of wrinkles, opened in a smile, revealing a few blackened teeth. "*Na, na, ek lada,*" and the face nodded. "*Na, na.*"

"What?" said Maerad. Her voice came out as a croak. "Who are you?"

But the figure had turned to shuffle back to the fire, which gave the only light in that tiny room, and was busy with a pot that hung suspended over it. She was, Maerad realized, a very old woman, smaller even than Maerad. She looked like a shapeless bundle of rags: she was wearing an unidentifiable number of clothes, oddments of furs and cloth, which all looked as if they hadn't been taken off since she had put them on. A few wisps of yellow-white hair clung to the polished dome of her scalp.

Slowly she turned around, holding a bowl in two hands, and shuffled back, carrying the bowl with infinite care so she might not spill its contents. She sat down next to Maerad on a sawn-off log, which passed for a stool, and offered her a spoonful of something. It was where the smell of fish was coming from, and it made Maerad feel slightly nauseous.

"Eat," said the old woman. "Eat. Good."

Maerad struggled to sit upright, but her muscles would not obey her. The old woman nodded to herself and pushed the spoon against Maerad's lips until she opened her mouth to protest. Before she could speak, the old woman had slipped the spoon between her teeth. Maerad choked and involuntarily swallowed. It was a thin fish soup, and despite the smell, very good indeed. The nausea she had felt identified itself as ravenous hunger. The woman waited patiently while Maerad coped with her first mouthful and then gave her another spoonful, feeding her like a very small child until she had finished the bowl.

"Good, good," she said. Her face cracked into a smile again. "Sleep now."

Maerad's eyes were already shut.

She didn't know how long she lay there in that tiny hut, drifting between sleep and brief waking. The old woman fed her soup, cleaned her and changed the furs when she was incontinent, and stroked her forehead wordlessly when, as sometimes happened, she woke from terrible nightmares of the mountainside falling, and slow, weak tears ran down her face. Sometimes daylight showed through tiny cracks in the walls like impossibly bright stars, and sometimes it was night; Maerad had no sense of continuity, and didn't know if it was one day and one night or many. The wind wailed sometimes and died down, the rain beat sometimes and went away, and through it all she heard the old woman's voice, talking to herself in her own tongue or singing or humming, a ceaseless gentle monologue like the running of a river. Time simply vanished. Maerad accepted her ministrations passively; she felt like a baby, incapable of the simplest things, of feeding herself, walking or even of speech.

But one day – a day later? a week? a month? – she could sit up and take the bowl in her hands and feed herself. And this time, when she handed the bowl back, wiping her mouth, she said, "Thank you."

"Good?" said the old woman. "*Na, na*, good." She carried the bowl back to the fire and wiped it carefully with an old cloth before she put it away on a stone shelf beside the fireplace. Maerad didn't go straight back to sleep, as she had before, but instead looked around curiously. She had never seen such a hovel, a ramshackle hut built of bits of stone and wood with rags stuffed into holes to keep out the wind, barely high enough to stand up in. For the first time, she noticed a yellow dog curled up asleep in the corner on a pile of ragged blankets, where she supposed the woman was sleeping, for Maerad had the only bed: a simple pallet piled with blankets and furs.

"Where am I?" she asked.

The old woman looked up and stared at her with rheumy blue eyes. "You Annaren?"

Maerad nodded.

The old woman pointed to the ground. "Here, Zmarkan." She pointed behind her, using the Pilanel name for the Osidh Elanor. "Idrom Uakin." Then she slapped herself on the chest with both her hands. "Me, Mirka." She grinned, showing her blackened teeth again. "You?"

"I'm Maerad."

The old woman came up to her and squinted into her face.

"You good?"

"A bit better."

Mirka nodded, satisfied, and went back to her business of tending the fire and stirring the soup. Maerad sat in silence and watched her.

"How did I get here?" she asked at last.

"You come to my door. You forget? You very sick. Aieee, very very sick." Mirka shook her head, making clicking noises with her tongue. "Bad storm, maybe you forget. I find, and bring you in. Mirka *Mikinim*, big famous once, no more, just old, just old." She cackled, a sudden younger light in her pale eyes. "You lucky girl. You dying, yes?"

"*Minikim?*" repeated Maerad. She found Mirka's broken Annaren hard to follow, and the Pilanel word defeated her.

"I forget the word. Witch? *Dhilla?* I mend people. Once."

"Healer?" said Maerad, and then tried the Speech. "*Dhillarearën?*"

Mirka paused in her scrubbing. "Yes, once," she said in the Speech. "You are a *Dhillarearën?*"

"Yes," said Maerad; it was a relief not to have to struggle through barriers of language. "No. I don't know. I haven't had the right schooling."

The woman cackled again. "Schooling? I am one of the Pilani, we don't send all with the Voice down to Annar, although some go. But that was a long time ago. I live here now, and wait for death to come and visit me. But, instead, I find you. What does that mean, eh?"

"I don't know," said Maerad. She felt confused, and even this short conversation tired her. The old woman came closer and examined her face.

"You are pretty under those scabs, I can see that. Never fear, there will be no scars; the young heal quickly, and Mirka remembers healing, even if she forgets much else. You must sleep if you are to heal." Mirka put her hand on Maerad's brow, and sleep swept through her like a wave. But then she started up, remembering something with a sudden panic.

"What about my pack? Was my pack with me?"

"Yes, my chick. I couldn't get your hands off it when you came in, you were holding it so tightly. What is so precious to you, that you cannot let it go? Nothing is that important. Sleep now…"

Time began to run consecutively, and to differentiate into day and night. Maerad managed to get out of the bed the day after first talking to Mirka, although her legs were so shaky she could scarcely walk across the hut. Mirka supported her, making clicking noises, with the dog walking at her heels, as if it too were helping. Just walking across the room made Maerad dizzy, and she had to sit down; Mirka waited until the trembling stopped, and then patiently made her do it again.

The day after that she went outside, her eyes watering in the bright daylight, and sat and watched as Mirka, who was much stronger than she looked, chopped wood and tended to her chickens, which scratched around in a little coop scarcely smaller than the hut itself. It looked as eccentric outside as it did inside, its single clay chimney crookedly defying gravity, its walls a patchwork mixture of mud daub and stones and wood, but it was strangely homely.

In the merciless light of day, Mirka looked even odder; her clothes were shapeless, clearly once having belonged to many people – men, women, children – and scavenged for their warmth. They were now all worn down to the same grey-brown colour, and seemed to adhere to her skin. She obviously never bathed. Despite this, Mirka was not unpleasant to be around; she smelt like woodsmoke and earth and some bitter herb. The dog, whom Mirka called Inka, which Maerad later discovered was the Pilanel word for dog, followed her everywhere, always at her heels. When she fished, Inka curled up beside her and went to sleep, and Mirka slept at night with the dog, by the fire. Maerad never heard Inka bark or growl, and she took no notice of Maerad whatsoever, once she had sniffed her and decided she was harmless. She was, like Mirka herself, a scrawny, tough creature – a continuous silent presence who seemed, after a time, like an aspect of Mirka herself.

The hut was hidden in a small clearing in a forest of spruce that filled a little gully on the northern side of the Osidh Elanor. On one side was an ancient wild pear tree, its gnarled branches heavy with sour green fruits, and brambles twined themselves crazily about the walls of the chicken coop. A small stream, cold as ice and flickering with minnow and other fish, ran close by the hut, and on sunny days Mirka would sit for hours with her fishing rod, catching the mountain trout that made up much of her diet. Behind her rose the staggering panorama of the Osidh Elanor, snowfield and fir forest and naked grey peaks, but Maerad couldn't see past the gully into the downlands at the mountains' feet.

Mirka told Maerad that she had lain in her pallet, barely alive, for seven days. She had simply appeared on her doorstep, and unquestioningly Mirka had taken her in, tending her and bringing her back to life. Maerad had no memory of anything after seeing Ardina, and supposed that Ardina had brought her down the pass to the old woman to be healed. She counted on her fingers; seven days made it well into autumn, about seven weeks since they had left Ossin.

"I'll have to leave soon," she said. "I've lost so much time."

"How can you lose time?" asked Mirka. "Time doesn't belong to anybody." She grinned. "You can't go anywhere while your legs are like cloth. And you need fattening." She pinched Maerad's forearm so hard that she cried out. "You are scrawny as a sick chicken."

"No, I suppose not," Maerad answered sadly. She couldn't walk across Mirka's clearing without her legs trembling; a hard journey was beyond imagining. She realized she had already decided to pursue her quest for the Treesong; it was the only way she might redeem herself in her own eyes. She met the thought without quailing. After that terrible night on the mountain, the thought of dying no longer frightened her.

"Where do you wish to go, anyway?" Mirka looked at her, her head cocked to the side like a bird.

"I have to go to Murask."

"To Murask?" A shadow fell over Mirka's face and she walked away mumbling to herself, as if Maerad were not there, and would not answer any of Maerad's questions.

Finally, Maerad said, "I thought you were Pilanel. Murask's a Pilanel town, isn't it?"

"The young, they are always impatient," said Mirka crossly, waving her hands at Maerad as if to shoo her away. She fell into her own language. "*Na, na, im Pilani.*" To Maerad's surprise, the old woman's eyes filled with tears, and then she sat down on a log and began to bawl, as unselfconsciously as if she were a three-year-old child.

Maerad was discomfited; she did not know how to respond or why Mirka was crying. In the end, she just held the woman's hand until she stopped and wiped her nose on her sleeve.

"Yes, I am Pilani," she said. "I and my family. But I have no family any more. I no longer wish to go to Murask for the winter gathering and the stories and the dances. My family is dead."

"Dead? How?" asked Mearad, and then instantly regretted asking, because Mirka started crying again. But finally she stopped, hiccupping, and looked at Maerad.

"It does good to weep for the dead," she said. "They need their tithe of tears. And I thought I was all dried up, and couldn't weep any more. Well, perhaps you have opened a new spring in me, my young chicken. I had daughters once." She chucked Maerad under the chin, and went back to splitting wood, as if nothing had happened. But she talked between the axe strokes.

"I had daughters and sons and a husband, and I thought it was good. I knew, because I was one with the Voice, that I would outlive them, but I thought to see them grow and bear their own children. But one day the Jussacks came and killed them all. And that was that."

Maerad waited in silence for her to continue. Mirka stopped to wipe her brow, and then started swinging the axe again. "I was the only one left. They said I was mad after that. Maybe I was. The sun darkened and the night was full of horror. If I could have saved my darlings by lifting the mountains with my naked hands, I would have done it. But I could not."

"Who are the Jussacks?" ventured Maerad uncertainly, afraid that she would reactivate Mirka's grief. Mirka didn't reply at first, but chopped the wood with a new viciousness, as if she were splitting the heads of her enemies. When she had finished, she sat down next to Maerad.

"The Jussacks are bad, savage men," she said. "They worship death. They keep their women in holes in the ground and they drink the blood of those they kill. They do not know what it means to have mercy."

Maerad had never heard of the Jussacks, and looked at Mirka blankly. "Do they live in Zmarkan?" she asked.

"Aie, sometimes, sometimes. They are like Pilani, they do not stay in one place, but they do not use caravans. They ride with little leather houses rolled up on the backs of their saddles, and where they want to stop they put them up. They ride very fast, and you never know that a Jussack band is coming until it is too late."

"But why do they kill people?" asked Maerad.

"I told you." Mirka began to look as if she might start bawling again. "They worship death, the Great Ungiver. It is said they eat the hearts of their enemies. They believe that anyone who is not a Jussack has no right to be on this earth. They kill us and they steal our horses."

Maerad was silent after that. Mirka sat beside her, mumbling to herself in Pilanel, lost in some other reality; she smiled and nodded, as if she were speaking to someone who was not there. She was, Maerad thought to herself, more than half mad; but there was something about her that forbade pity. She did not pity herself.

Maerad's strength returned quickly. She had not told Mirka who she was, apart from her name, or anything of her story, and Mirka did not ask; she accepted Maerad as if she were an injured bird, sent by the heavens for her to care for, who would one day recover and fly away. She no longer needed to sleep so much, and as the weather continued fine she washed her clothes in the stream, scrubbing them with some hard soap Mirka gave her, and bathed briefly in the freezing waters. She had been absolutely filthy, grimed in sweat and blood, and it was a relief to be clean again. After the first shock, which even made her teeth numb, she stood under a tiny waterfall and washed her hair, and when she stepped out of the water, her skin felt as if it were burning with life.

But as Maerad's body revived, she began to feel her grief more keenly. More than ever before she missed her brother; she wanted the closeness of kin, the wordless understanding that she and Hem had enjoyed for all too brief a time. She thought now that Hem was not dead, but she wondered if he had been captured. Or perhaps Turbansk still stood. She had no way of knowing. Not knowing was almost worse than anything.

Sometimes she thought she held his restless, bony body when she slept, as she had so often when they travelled together and his nightmares had troubled him, and she was surprised when she awoke to find her arms were empty. At such times, his absence was a physical ache; she missed him with her skin, in the marrow of her bones.

But, most of all, Maerad was tormented by regrets about her breach with Cadvan. Again and again she went over their conversations, wondering how things might have been different if she had been less angry, if Cadvan had been even a little less stern; perhaps if their minds had been able to join (and why could they not? why did Cadvan feel it as an attack?) they could have destroyed the frost creatures. She saw the final conflict as her failure, and her failure only.

She was also troubled by the death of Ilar. She could no longer hide from herself that she had intended to kill the Bard; and she wondered what Cadvan had meant by the new darkness he had perceived in her. She knew something within her was changing, but it wasn't something she could easily perceive: she simply suffered it. It was as if, at some level below speech, there were two Maerads, and she could recognize neither of them: and worse, they were at war. The only way she could resolve this inner conflict was to think of continuing her journey.

She sorted through the few scraps of knowledge she had about the Treesong: the foredream that had told her to *look to the north*; the idea that the Split Song and the Treesong were somehow linked; that the Treesong was of the knowing of the Elidhu; that a poison at the root of the Speech was to do with the secret of the Treesong. Nelac's certainty that she and Cadvan must solve its riddle comforted her; surely so wise a Bard would not have sent them on a nonsensical journey? Their quest had depended on a deeper knowing, akin to her instinctive knowledge, when she had first encountered Hem, that they belonged to each other. She had to trust that deeper knowing, as Cavdan had, and be content not to understand everything. In the cold light of rationality she had very little to go on: dreams and guesses, riddles in themselves. Perhaps Cadvan had had a clearer idea of what they might do once they had crossed the Osidh Elanor, but that knowledge was now lost to her. She was on her own.

She said nothing of these thoughts to Mirka, although they talked now in the evenings, and Maerad was well enough to help her with simple tasks. Mirka taught her how to fish, bringing out a precious second rod she kept stored in her roof, and they would sit on the banks of the stream, watching the glittering surface of the water. Maerad managed to catch a few trout, but she was by no means as skilled as Mirka: fishing was Mirka's passion.

It took a few days before Maerad felt able to broach the subject of Murask again. She chose one evening, after they had shared a stew of herbs and turnips and were sitting together looking into the fire. This time, Mirka gave her a narrow look.

"Why do you want to go to Murask?" she asked.

"I have something to do," said Maerad. "And I must go there."

"Well, then." The old woman leant forward and poked the fire. "Well, then. You are not Pilani, and you wish to go to Murask."

"My father was Pilanel," said Maerad. "His name was Dorn."

"Dorn? That's a common enough name among the Pilani. Dorn of what?"

"I don't know." Maerad felt disconsolate. "He was a Bard. A *Dhillarearën*. I never knew him, he was killed when I was a little girl."

"Dorn." Mirka's face creased up in thought. "I did know a Dorn. Dorn à Triberi, one of the southern Pilanel who winter in Murask. He was one with the Voice who went south. Perhaps it was him."

"Maybe," said Maerad. "He married a Bard, my mother."

"Dorn à Triberi was a special child." Suddenly Mirka was far away, as if she were speaking in a dream and had forgotten she was sitting next to Maerad. "A star child, one of the blessed. Not just because he had the Voice; he was born with the caul. I delivered him, and he came into the world blind and covered, and when the caul was taken away, he looked at me with his dark eyes, and he saw the whole world. Aiee, there are some babies like that, but not many in this world, not many…" She trailed off into silence.

"Do you think he was my father?" asked Maerad, reflecting again on how little she knew of her own family. Scraps and rags: a few fragmented memories, the few facts she had been told. Cadvan might have known more, but if he had, he hadn't told her.

"How can I know?" said Mirka irritably. "He might have been. He might not. There are many Dorns in the Pilani. He might be of a northern clan, they don't go to Murask, and there are many *Dhillarearën* among those people."

"Well, whether he came from Murask or not," said Maerad, biting her lip to stave off her impatience, "I have to go there. And I'd better go soon, because before long autumn will be over, and it will be winter, and travelling will be hard."

"*Na, na.* Well, you are bent on your road, my little chicken. I do not think it is a good road." Mirka gave Maerad a disconcertingly penetrating glance. "There is a shadow on you. But I do not want to know about such things, no, I have enough darkness of my own. Well, Murask it is. It is not hard to find, you follow the road, and it will take you there."

"But which road? And is it far?" asked Maerad.

"A week's walk, maybe, ten days. Not far, no. I will show you the road, when it is time. You have not the strength, my chick. Not yet. Your body is strong and you will get better, but not today, nor tomorrow."

Mirka would say nothing more of Murask, although Maerad prodded her, and in the end, feeling frustrated, she went to her pack and took out her lyre. It had lain neglected since long before the attempt on the Gwalhain Pass, and Maerad felt a thrill of recognition as she took it out of its leather case; the lyre was her oldest friend, once her only consolation. And perhaps, now, her only consolation again. She inspected it closely for hurt, but its plain wood and silver strings were unharmed; she ran her fingers over the strange carvings, the ten rune-like decorations that no one could read, and which were as familiar to her as her own skin. Finally she drew her hand across the strings, and a chord rang out through the hut. Maerad looked up, smiling, and saw with surprise that Mirka was staring at her with horror.

"What is that?" she said. "What is that thing?"

"This?" Maerad lifted it so Mirka could see it properly, but the old woman flinched back. "It's only my lyre. My favourite thing. My mother gave it to me, and she had it from her mother, and so on back through the House of Karn. Haven't you seen one before?"

"It is too big a thing for this house." Mirka's face was grey with dread. "It has seen too much grief, aiee, it has seen the rending of the world, the moon is black inside it. Put it away!" She covered her eyes with her hands and started chanting something in Pilanel, her jaw trembling.

Astonished, Maerad looked down at her humble lyre, and then slowly packed it into its case. She knew her lyre was ancient, made by the Dhyllin people in the flower of their civilization, and that however humble it looked, it was an ancient and precious instrument made by a master craftsman. But although the few Bards who knew its heritage had responded with amazement and respect when they had seen it, no one had ever reacted as Mirka had. Maerad felt disturbed and disappointed; she was full of hunger for music. She wished that Mirka was not so mad.

The old woman peeped out between her fingers and saw Maerad had put her lyre away. She let down her hands and cackled at Maerad's glum face, as if it had all been a big joke. "Did I frighten you, my chick?"

Maerad didn't say anything. She did feel afraid; although she thought that Mirka was just crazy.

"I frightened you, didn't I? I think you are not frightened enough." Mirka laughed again.

"Frightened of what?" Maerad asked. Of everything, she thought tiredly to herself. Or maybe nothing. She didn't know any more.

"There are many things to fear," said Mirka evasively. "Always is. Always was."

Maerad sighed. Her longing for music flowered inside her, an unassuageable ache. "Perhaps," she said, "we could just sing something. I know some songs."

"Maybe you only know broken songs," said Mirka, looking at Maerad with a strange slyness.

"Broken songs? What do you mean?"

Mirka didn't answer for a long time. She shut her eyes hard and rocked, as if she were trying to hear something that was too far away. When she opened them again, her slyness had vanished and she seemed merely a bewildered old woman. "I don't know what I mean," she said. "You are like a dream that has already happened to me, you and that thing you carry. Aiee, a dream, but a good one or a bad one, I don't know."

"I don't know either," said Maerad miserably. "A bad dream, I think."

"Maybe. Maybe not. Who can tell? It is said all riddles are answered by the Wise Kindred."

"The Wise Kindred?" Maerad wondered if this was some other figment of Mirka's imagination. She looked up and the old woman was far away again, her eyes blank and unfocused.

"The Wise Kindred live on the ice, far in the north, where it is always night or always day." She spoke in a monotone that sent shivers down Maerad's spine, and for a moment she thought Mirka's face blurred and she saw another face, much younger, in its place. "They are the Oldest and they remember much that was lost in the Black Days, aiee, when the evil lord held sway. They understand what is half and what is whole, what is made and half made."

Maerad's heart leapt into her mouth; she thought of Ankil's story of the Split Song. Was this what her foredream meant, when the voice had said: *Look to the north*?

"Can they tell me about the Treesong?" she asked.

"They keep the Song," the old woman said.

Maerad waited, holding her breath, but Mirka said nothing more; she was still staring into space, as if Maerad was not there. Maerad leant forward and touched her shoulder, and the old woman blinked and looked up, as if she had just awoken from a dream. Her face collapsed into a grimace of pain, and she clutched her head.

"Are you all right?" asked Maerad.

"*Na, na*, child, I am just sore headed. It happens when you are old. It will happen to you one day…" Mirka started mumbling something that Maerad couldn't understand, and Maerad thought with frustration about what she had just said.

"Can you remember anything else about the Wise Kindred?" she asked.

"The Wise Kindred?" said Mirka sharply. "What are you talking about, child? They are the stuff of children's tales, no more. Why do you ask?"

"But you just said…" Maerad began, and then gave up. Perhaps Mirka really didn't remember what she had said; but whether she did or not, it was clear she wasn't going to tell Maerad anything more.

X V

ALONE

TWO nights later, Maerad dreamed of Hem. It had nothing of a foredream's dreadful clarity; but she hoped it was some kind of true dreaming, nevertheless. She was sitting somewhere in bright sunshine, next to her brother. Hem had a big, white bird on his shoulder and he was leaning back against a dark-leaved tree. He looked older than she remembered him, taller and rangier, and his skin was darker; but he gazed at her with the same blue eyes. In his hand he held a smooth orange fruit, which he was cutting with a small, wooden-handled knife. They were laughing, although Maerad couldn't remember why.

The dream passed into other dreams that Maerad didn't remember, but she awoke with a small easing of the cold despair she had felt since she had found herself in Mirka's house. Hem was still alive, and was thinking of her; she was sure of that. She was not entirely alone in the world. And it was time for her to leave.

She didn't need to say anything to Mirka. The old woman merely looked at her and nodded.

"You are well now," she said. "You will wish to go."

"Yes," said Maerad.

They said nothing further about it until after breakfast, and after Maerad had helped Mirka with her morning tasks. Then Maerad took out her pack and sorted through it. She still had some of the hard travelling biscuit, enough to last two weeks, and some dried fruit and nuts; the cooking gear had gone with

Cadvan and Darsor, so there would be no hot meals. But it was autumn, and there would be wild berries and nuts and other things she could gather, perhaps, on her way. Her bottle of medhyl was almost full. She filled her water bottle from the stream and then packed everything away.

Experimentally, she swung the pack onto her back. It didn't feel as heavy as she had feared it would after her illness. She put it down and looked inside the pack again. She drew out the little black wooden cat she had carried since that day, long ago, when she and Cadvan had found Hem, and swinging up her pack again, went outside to find Mirka.

Mirka was not far away, sitting on her favourite fishing knoll; Inka was at her feet, snoring. Already two trout lay in the basket beside her, their iridescent scales breaking up the sunlight; she was catching as many as she could, to smoke for the frozen winter months ahead. Maerad sat down beside her and Mirka grunted in acknowledgment, her eyes fixed on the shining line trembling over the water.

"I've nothing much to give you, for what you've done for me," said Maerad. "You saved my life."

Mirka turned to face her, her blue eyes sparkling and present. "I need nothing," she said. "You were a gift from the mountains."

"I'd like to give you something, all the same." She held out the little cat, and Mirka took it. "I found this, a while ago. At the same time that I found my brother. It's Pilanel, I think."

Mirka took the little cat and inspected it. "Yes, it is a Pilani carving," she said. "Some child loved this. And it will not make Inka jealous, will it?" She prodded the dog with her foot and it opened a sleepy eye. "Not like a real cat. Thank you, my chicken."

"I think I shall start, while it's still early," said Maerad. "How do I find my way?"

Mirka fixed her rod in the ground and slowly stood up. She pointed to a winding path that led through the forest from her clearing.

"Follow that," she said. "Soon you will find the road. Then turn away from the mountains and go north. You will find Murask."

Maerad nodded, and said awkwardly, "Well, goodbye then."

"Just wait a little. I have something for you."

Mirka hobbled back to her hut. She was not gone long, and returned holding a small object in her hands.

"Take this," she said. "It is a token of trust. If you show it, you will be admitted into Murask, even though you are a stranger."

She gave Maerad a small disc carved out of yellowing bone. In the centre was a beautiful relief of a running horse, perfect in every detail, except that a small crack ran through it.

Maerad was so taken aback that for a moment she was speechless. "I can't take this," she said.

"You can take it, my chicken," said Mirka, patting her cheek. "And you will. Tell them Mirka à Hadaruk sends greetings and blessings."

Maerad nodded, and then kissed the old woman on both cheeks. "May the Light shine on you!" she said.

"It will, my chick, or it will not, whether you will or no," said Mirka. She smiled and stroked Maerad's hair. "But now I have work to do. Off you go. And go well."

She turned back to her fishing. Maerad watched her for a short time and then sighed and swung on her pack. She headed for the path and followed it through the trees. It wasn't long before all trace of Mirka's clearing had vanished from sight.

As Mirka had promised, the little path ran into a wide road of beaten earth that led straight downhill through the spruce and birches. Setting the mountains to her back Maerad walked on. Lilac bushes, currant vines, wild strawberries and low hazels grew in tangled clumps under the trees, their leaves already yellow and brown. The sky was a very pale blue with little warmth in it, good weather for walking, and she strode out, pulling the cold air into her lungs, listening to the birds squabbling unseen in the branches around her and the soft crunch of her footfalls on the ground. There was little other sound: for the first time in her life Maerad was completely alone, with no other human being in call. It was a strange feeling, but liberating; for some curious reason it made her feel less lonely.

The walking emptied Maerad's mind of everything that troubled her. She entered the rhythms of her body, letting her arms swing and her legs push her forwards, enjoying the feeling of health that coursed through her after the long, dark days in Mirka's hut. She didn't think about Cadvan or Darsor or Imi, though they lingered in the shadows at the back of her mind, regrets and griefs she would never lose.

When the sun was at its height, she stopped for a quick meal, and then pressed on. Around mid-afternoon she emerged from the forest, and saw before her the great plains of Zmarkan, which the Pilanel people called the Arkiadera or the Mother Plains. They stretched past the horizon, a flat sea of red sedges and yellowing grasses and heathers. The road ran straight on through the plains, turning neither right nor left, underneath the huge, empty sky. The only trees Maerad could see were some low, dark withies and hazels. They followed a twining course that meandered alongside the road like a drunk; Maerad guessed with relief that they marked the course of a river.

In the distance, she could see animals moving across the plains, but she couldn't tell what they were. She didn't know if they were wild, or if they signalled the presence of people.

She felt exposed as soon as she left the shelter of the trees, and although there was no one in sight, and no chance of anyone creeping up unseen on that level ground, she put on a glimmer-spell to make her unseen. It made her feel a little safer. She did not fear that she would meet Hulls or Bards so far north, but she knew that now she was within the reaches of the Winterking's domain, and she thought she felt a presence, a sense of ill will that beat on her from the north-east. It was only the vaguest of senses, but it was insistent enough to trouble her awareness. Instinctively she shielded her mind against it, squared her shoulders, and kept on.

She walked until evening, when she thought she ought to make a camp. There were no trees to shelter her, so she made a detour to the riverside and camped there among the withies. They were of a kind Maerad had never seen before, with reddish violet branches spotted with blue, their yellow leaves shivering in the evening wind. A gaggle of ducks squabbled unseen on the water, and in the distance she could hear the mournful cries of plovers. She found a place between two old trees that offered a little shelter and crouched down among the roots, the sense of well-being she had felt during the day beginning to shrink and vanish.

As soon as the sun disappeared, it began to get very cold, and Maerad was shivering as she huddled, wrapped in her blanket, trying to get comfortable among the tree roots. She felt unsafe; there was no one to keep watch, and she would have to sleep unprotected in the wild. She still wore her glimmerspell, but she knew the spells did not fool animals. And she could light no fire to cheer her, because she had nothing to light it with. She pondered briefly lighting one with magery, but abandoned the idea: a fire would attract notice, anyway.

She lay awake for a long time, listening to the night, shifting restlessly on the hard ground. The stars glittered in the darkness.

Maerad stared at the bright path of the Lukemoi, the riders of the stars, which arched right across the middle of the sky. She had never seen it shining so brilliantly. It was said that the dead walked that road on their way to the Gates. She wondered if Cadvan lingered there, watching for her even as he made his way to the Groves of Shadow. The thought brought her no comfort. No, she thought; Cadvan was long gone. She was alone.

When she woke up, Maerad had a brief moment of panic; she couldn't remember where the road was, and she couldn't see it from the river. She realized that she could easily wander in circles for days in these flat, featureless plains: the only thing that gave her any sense of direction was the road. She breakfasted quickly, and set out away from the river in what she thought was the right direction, and before she became too anxious hit the road again. The next night, when she left the road to find a camping place, she marked her direction much more carefully.

She walked quickly, taking a rest at midday, but otherwise moving all day, anxious to reach Murask before the weather changed. She had been lucky: the days were cold and clear, and there had been no rain. She had unpleasant memories of sleeping in the open in bad weather, and here it was colder than she was used to. In the morning when she woke, the world was white with frost, the dews frozen on the leaves, and the little warmth she had managed to generate overnight quickly dissipated as soon as she moved. She was glad of her sheepskins, for otherwise she might have frozen to death.

The animals she had seen on the plains turned out to be wild herds of a large, shaggy kind of deer. She never came very close to them as they avoided the road, though once she came upon a small group of about twenty before they scented her and stampeded. There were also groups of wild ponies, of the kind the Pilanel herded: tough and long-haired and wary. Otherwise she saw little creatures like weasels with glossy brown coats, and occasional foxes and hares, and birds: black-and-white terns, which hovered overhead, and enormous flocks of geese and ptarmigans migrating south for the winter, and once a pair of eagles hunting, dropping like stones to the grass and sweeping off with a small luckless animal caught in their talons.

She saw no other human beings. She didn't feel lonely; being alone was a relief. She didn't think about the incident in the Gwalhain Pass. The terrible dreams she had suffered at Mirka's, in which she endlessly relived the moment of Cadvan's death, had stopped; she was too tired, after walking all day, to dream about anything. She felt empty and dry, as if she would never feel anything again. She concerned herself with the trivial details of each day: making sure each evening that her feet were properly massaged with balm to prevent blisters, eating enough food to keep her going, and keeping alert for any sign of danger. She watched carefully for strange shifts in the wind or weather, which might signal the arrival of a frost creature or stormdog. But the sky remained clear and blue.

Doing these banal tasks inevitably reminded her of Cadvan. She realized, with a poignancy that pierced even her numbed emotions, that if he hadn't taught her these rudimentary skills she wouldn't have had a hope of surviving alone in the wild. And this induced other anxieties: even though she was travelling as fast as she could to Murask, she dreaded arriving there. What would she do when she did? Whenever she had met strangers before, Cadvan had been there, to introduce her, or to deal with any difficulties that might have arisen.

Maerad reflected bitterly that she knew very little of people; for most of her life, her world had been so small, the space of Gilman's Cot, and since then she had learned only of Bards. She couldn't speak the Pilanel language, although Mirka had said there were many Pilanel with the Gift, and being travellers, perhaps most of them spoke some Annaren. Should she just walk in and ask for help? Should she explain who she was or what she was doing, or should she dissemble? She knew nothing of the Pilanel people; even Hem would have been better prepared than she was. She was no good at the disguising charm, which, in any case, wouldn't give her the Pilanel language. She was sure that Cadvan could have passed himself off as a Pilanel if he had wanted to, as sure as she was that she couldn't; he most certainly spoke the language. And Cadvan knew the north well, probably better than any other in Annar – he had travelled its length just before he met her. Maerad had only the faintest memory of the maps she had perused at Gahal's house, and the maps of Zmarkan had been rather empty anyway. There had been no mention that she could recall of the Wise Kindred, or of where such people might live.

She went on, in truth, because she couldn't think of anything else to do. Becoming a Bard had invested her life with a meaning it had never possessed before; now that meaning had shrivelled and vanished, poisoned by her own foolish vanity. Perhaps the only way to restore that meaning was to stay true to her promises to Cadvan, to Nelac, to Nerili, to all those who had shown faith in her, and whom she felt she had so dismally failed.

When the puzzle of her Elemental nature raised itself, she simply put it aside as something she couldn't solve. She didn't understand her closeness to Ardina: why the Elemental queen called her "daughter" as if she were much closer kin than merely a distant descendent. She didn't know why she had powers that other Bards did not. She didn't understand why she was considered to be so significant, the Fire Lily, the Foretold, the One, and how that matched her feeling that she was, in truth, utterly insignificant, a tiny human being toiling along in the immense world, alone and powerless, of no more importance than any other, and of much less worth than most. Mirka, she reflected, for all her madness and grief, had made a kind of peace with herself. In her unrest and doubt, Maerad envied Mirka; all she knew of peace was the deadness in her heart.

Mirka had told her that Murask was a week to ten days' walk away from the mountains. Maerad kept careful count of the days, watching the slender moon waxing each night, and after seven days began to look around for signs of the settlement. The Arkiadera stretched away before and behind her, the huge range of the Osidh Elanor now merely a purple smudge on the horizon, the only sign that she had travelled any distance at all. She began to worry about her food supply, which would last only a couple of weeks. If Mirka was well out in her reckoning, or if she was going in completely the wrong direction, she would soon be in serious difficulties.

On the tenth day of her trek, Maerad at last began to see signs of other human beings; in the distance she would occasionally see a Pilanel caravan, or sole herders with horses. She began to think hopefully that she was indeed on the correct road, and had not been, as she had feared, simply wandering into the heart of the plains.

She kept herself unseen, out of caution, she told herself; but it was also shyness. If she had been heading to a School, she might not have felt so nervous. She wished, not for the first time, that she were not so ignorant. She often fingered the token that Mirka had given her, wondering what it meant and if it would help her, as the old woman had promised.

On the thirteenth day she saw a smudge of smoke rising before her, and guessed that she was at last close to Murask. Encouraged, she sped up and by nightfall it was in clear view; still a few leagues off, but unmistakably a settlement of many people, since the smoke from numerous fires rose into the sky. She was puzzled because she couldn't see any buildings, only what appeared to be a low hill.

She could have continued and reached Murask just after dark, but she decided against that, feeling unprepared. Instead she made camp again by the river, planning to arrive early the next day. Despite her weariness she slept badly; the moon was now at the full, and burned brilliantly in the frozen sky, throwing sharp black shadows over the sedges. Looking at it through the tangled branches of the withies, Maerad shivered; it was a powerful moon, dragging up feelings she had thought dead, but they were distorted and unrecognizable, turning strange faces towards her. I no longer know who I am, she thought to herself; I never really knew in the first place. A terrible desolation seized her heart, and she lay on her back, shivering with cold, unable to find any comfort in either her body or her mind.

She woke when it was still dark from troubled dreams that she did not remember. There had been no frost, but she was drenched with a freezing, heavy dew, and the grey world around her seemed bleak and empty. She sniffed the air; the wind was changing, bringing a colder blast from the north, and the sky was heavy with yellowish clouds. She ate her humble breakfast hastily, watching the massing clouds, and then washed briefly in the river's freezing water: as always when there was a full moon, her period had arrived, and she longed to take a bath. She cursed the timing; she felt more fragile than usual, as if she were made of glass, and now more than ever she needed to be strong. She tried to comb her hair, but it was so tangled after days of sleeping in the open that she almost broke the comb, and she gave up. At last, finding no other reason to procrastinate, but with a heavy reluctance, she began to walk to Murask.

The closer she came to the settlement, the more it puzzled

her. It did not look like a town at all. Now she frequently passed grazing herds of ponies, attended by herders in bright Zmarkan jackets, but she could see no caravans. The green hill grew bigger and bigger as she approached it; it was the only high ground in these huge, flat plains. She began to realize that Murask must be inside the hill. She grew more and more apprehensive, and part of her played with the idea of just turning around and walking away. Where to? she thought despairingly. You have no choice – if they don't let you in here, you'll freeze to death. As if in answer to her thoughts, a few stray flakes of snow started whirling idly from the sky. She put her head down, postponing all further speculation, and concentrated on walking.

She arrived at the gate to Murask by mid-morning. The countryside around her was already white with a thin layer of snow, and she stamped her feet to keep them warm as she stood before the gate, wondering what to do next. Above her loomed the hill, rising higher than two pine trees end to end, and almost as steep as a wall. Close up, it was obvious this was no natural mound, although it was covered with a short green turf that made it seem part of the plains, and hazels and small willows and thorn bushes hugged its base.

The gate itself was huge, as high as four men, and made of thick iron bars through which Maerad could see a dark tunnel lit with torches. Behind the bars stood two leaves of a stout wooden door. It was unadorned, and it somehow gave the impression of immense age. It seemed older than anything Maerad had seen at the Bard Schools; maybe it was as old as the standing stones she had seen in the Hollow Lands in Annar. Maerad swallowed, momentarily daunted. The gate was shut, and she could see no one nearby to open it. Experimentally, she set her hand to one of the bars, and pushed. As she expected, it was locked.

She looked around and this time saw a bronze bell hanging to the side, with a thin metal chain dangling from its tongue. She pulled it, and the bell clanged, making her jump; it sounded very loud in this quiet landscape. At first, nothing happened; but after a while a little door she had not seen to the left of the tunnel opened, and a man limped out, saying something in Pilanel. Maerad had never seen a grown man so short. His head was drawn down on his shoulders, and his spine was bent into a hunch; but his shoulders and arms were massive, suggesting enormous strength. She could not understand his speech, and she just stood, holding out the token Mirka had given her, waiting for whatever might come next. The man peered through the bars of the gate, looking straight at Maerad. Then he shrugged, muttering something to himself that sounded like a curse, and limped back into his room, slamming shut the door.

Maerad suddenly realized that she was still under a glimmerspell, and almost laughed. It was no use knocking at a door if no one could see her. Her heart was beating fast, and she waited a little while until she felt calmer. Then, glancing around to make sure no one was nearby to witness her suddenly appearing out of nowhere, she undid the glimmerspell and tried again.

This time the man came out more quickly. He looked annoyed, and Maerad braced herself; but when he spotted her through the bars, he simply stopped, looking surprised. Maerad held out the token, her hand trembling slightly.

"*Om ali nel*?" he said.

"My name is Mara. I am Annaren. I bring greeting from – from Mirka à Hadaruk."

The man studied her in silence for a while, and then reached his fingers through the narrow gap between the iron bars to take the token. He looked at it closely, turning it over and over, his face expressionless, and Maerad watched him anxiously.

He finally seemed to reach some decision, and took a long iron key from the bunch jangling at his waist and turned it in a lock in the middle of the gate, using both his hands. Then he took another broader key and disappeared inside his room again. Maerad was just beginning to wonder whether he was coming back when he reappeared and with another key turned a lock near the base of the gates. Then he pulled them open, beckoning her inside.

"Come," he said, speaking in thickly accented Annaren.

Maerad hesitated on the threshold, and then obeyed him. Once she was inside, blinking until her eyes adjusted to the darkness, the man repeated the laborious process of locking the gates and, without speaking further, he indicated that she should follow him.

The tunnel through the hill was very large, big enough to accommodate Pilanel caravans. There was no feeling of dampness, as Maerad had expected; the air seemed, if anything, to be warm. It was lined and flagged with roughly dressed stone, and smelt of the burning pitch of the torches that lined its length. She fixed her eyes on the humped back of the gate warden, hurrying to keep up with him. Despite his limp, he walked very quickly. He limped, she realized, because one leg was much shorter than the other, and she found herself wondering who he was, and what it was like to be him. She had never seen anyone so misshapen.

The passage had many turns, and it wasn't long before Maerad had completely lost her sense of direction. After the first three turns they came to another iron gate, again fastened with three locks, and then, not much further on, another one. Maerad noticed slits in the walls on either side of the gates, and thought they probably allowed archers to attack any invaders. Murask was obviously well defended against any attack, and Maerad uneasily wondered again how she would be received.

They seemed to walk for ages before Maerad saw daylight, an impossibly bright silver at the end of the tunnel. Perhaps Murask wasn't inside the hill, after all, she thought with relief; maybe the hill was in fact a very big wall. They emerged at last, and Maerad blinked, dazzled, and looked around in amazement. She was certainly in some kind of town, but she had never seen anything like it.

Murask, the winter gathering place of the southern Pilanel clans, was, as Maerad had guessed, a fortified settlement. It was an artificial hill, built in a time long forgotten, and it reared high over the flat plains and stretched more than a league from end to end. The "wall" was four times as wide as it was high, and was mostly hollow: most of the Pilanel dwellings were actually inside it. In the centre, where Maerad had emerged with her strange guide, was a wide flat space covered with short turf, now white with snow. Unlike the outer walls, the inner walls were all bare, weathered stone, pierced with hundreds of doors and windows. Several Pilanel caravans were drawn up against the wall, their shafts resting on the ground, and Maerad saw a dozen children playing a wild game of tag, who paused when they noticed her and stared in open-mouthed curiosity. There were a few ponies hunched up miserably against the snow, some of the heavy deer Maerad had seen on her way to Murask nuzzling aside the snow to graze on the turf, and a few thin whippet-like mongrels of the kind the Pilanel kept as guard dogs.

She didn't have much time to look around, as her guide was hurrying to a large building in the very centre of the space. It was built of grey granite and rose three storeys high, the highest storey completely covered with a thick, steep thatch of river reeds, which overhung the walls by at least a dozen paces. Its front wall was faced with some kind of plaster or stucco, and was brightly painted, like the Pilanel caravans, in geometric patterns.

Her guide walked up to a double-leafed door and rang a bell very like the one at the front gate. A tall man appeared swiftly, and the two had a long conversation. Her guide handed over Mirka's token, and he too examined it carefully, glancing at Maerad from underneath his eyebrows as he did so. Finally he nodded, and the gate warden, without a glance at Maerad, turned and went back to his post, his keys jangling at his waist.

The second man gazed at Maerad without speaking for what seemed a very long time. Maerad endured his examination, trying to appear harmless and polite, surreptitiously examining him in return. He had dark skin like Hem's, the colour of dark honey. His eyes, under thick black brows, were unreadable as deep water, and his face was stern and lean. Maerad saw also that he was a *Dhillarearëan*.

"You are Annaren?" he said at last. He had only a faint accent.

"Yes," said Maerad, relieved that he spoke her native tongue. "My name is Mara. I seek your help, and must speak with the chief of your clan."

"That you shall do, as do all strangers who enter this Howe. But in these days of distrust, we do not let many into our haven. We only do so now because of this token. I would like to know how you came by such a thing."

"It was given me by Mirka à Hadaruk," said Maerad, taking a deep breath. "She sends greeting."

The man looked directly into her face. "Mirka à Hadaruk has been dead many long years," he said. Maerad's heart skipped a beat, and she looked down, discomforted.

"Perhaps the woman who gave it to me used Mirka's name without cause, although I do not know why she would do so," she said at last. "She is very old. But she is not dead, unless she has died since I last saw her, two weeks ago."

There was a silence, and the man nodded. "Perhaps there is another story to be told," he said. "I judge that you do not seek to mislead me. You may enter."

He opened the door and beckoned Maerad inside. Before she stepped inside, she hesitated.

"It is only courtesy to ask your name, so I may thank the one who invites me," she said.

"My name is Dorn à Hadaruk," he said.

"Dorn à Hadaruk?" Maerad said, taken aback. Dorn? Her father's name? *That's a common enough name among the Pilani*, Mirka had told her... And he had the same last name as Mirka.

"Mirka is my mother's mother," he said, his dark eyes expressionless. "So you see, the question of her life and death holds a certain interest for me."

"I see." Maerad was silent for a while, thinking of the mad old woman who had been so kind to her. She had spoken of her daughter, and of her daughter's death; she had never spoken of living grandchildren. She wondered if Mirka knew she had a grandson, or if she thought he was dead, just as he thought she was. Then she realized Dorn was waiting patiently, holding the door open. She tried to smile. "I thank you, Dorn à Hadaruk," she said, and followed him into the house.

Dorn took her through a wide, dark passageway, which led, surprisingly, into a huge room that Maerad thought must have taken up the bulk of the house. Its height reached up the three storeys to the roof, and at each level ran a gallery, off which Maerad could see other rooms. At the other end was a fireplace big enough to fit a whole tree, surrounded by a mantel carved with geometric Pilanel designs; inside it was burning some kind of fuel Maerad did not recognize, a kind of peat, which threw off a huge heat and gave a pleasant, earthy smell. Otherwise, the hall was lined with polished cedar wood, covered in some places with hangings whose brightness had faded with age.

By the fire, on a carved wooden chair, sat a tall woman. Although her hair hung in two simple plaits either side of her face, and her robe, a rich purple-red, was plain and unadorned, Maerad sensed in her an aura of unchallengeable authority. And with a shiver of recognition, she understood that the woman was a very powerful Bard. She fixed her dark eyes on Maerad as she paced slowly across the room behind Dorn, her feet echoing on the wooden floorboards.

To Maerad's exaggerated perceptions, it seemed to take a very long time to traverse that room. She was conscious always of the woman's eyes upon her as she approached; it made her back prickle. At last, she stood in front of the chair, and the woman rose and turned her eyes to Dorn, who spoke in Annaren, out of courtesy to Maerad.

"Sirkana à Triberi, Headwoman of the Southern Clans," he said. "I present to you a traveller, who comes here bearing a Pilani token of urgency and trust, and the greetings of Mirka à Hadaruk, who she says is alive. The traveller is Annaren, and gives her name as Mara."

Maerad bowed, feeling very short. Standing up, Sirkana towered over her; she was taller than most men. "Thank you for greeting me, Sirkana à Triberi," Maerad said, as formally as she could manage. "I have travelled far to see you."

Instead of answering, Sirkana bent down so she could look straight into Maerad's face. Maerad's first instinct was to hide, but she blinked and bore the scrutiny. After a long pause, the headwoman straightened herself.

"It is she," she said, in the Speech. "The Chosen has arrived at last."

XVI

MURASK

DORN glanced at Maerad with a sudden amazement, and she became agonizingly aware of her filthy appearance.

"You are certain?" he said, answering in the same tongue, and Maerad gave him a swift look. The two Pilanel were staring at her solemnly, and she felt that she ought to say something.

"I am sorry to come before you in such disarray," she said at last, using the Speech. "I mean no disrespect."

"I mean none either," said the woman. "I have waited for you for a long time."

In her confusion, Maerad forgot her formality. "For me?" she asked. "How did you know I would come here?"

"It is said in the lore," said Sirkana, as if that explained everything. "It has long been known that the Riddle would begin its answer here. Our songs do not lie, and the past years have brought all the signs. It was time. Besides, your destiny is written in your face."

Maerad was speechless, and felt herself blushing.

Sirkana laughed at her discomfiture. "Your destiny is not visible to everyone," she said. "Only to those gifted with both Sight and Voice. And there are not many of those. Only myself, perhaps. Well, you have travelled far, and must be footsore and hungry. You may stay in my house; there is room aplenty. Come, we will talk more later."

She snapped her fingers, and a woman Maerad hadn't noticed stepped out of the shadows under the galleries. Sirkana spoke to her rapidly in Pilanel, and the woman nodded and then beckoned Maerad out of the hall. Maerad followed her, puzzled by both her interview and her swift dismissal. She felt as if she had stepped into the middle of a conversation she was expected to understand, and was left gaping like a fish, trying to catch up.

At least she was warm, for the first time in days. And maybe she could have a proper wash.

Maerad was taken to a small chamber that led off the highest gallery. The woman who took her there spoke no Annaren, but with gestures they managed some communication: Maerad found out that her name was Zara, and Zara, who was clearly a practical woman, established that, yes, Maerad would like to wash herself, and also would like something to eat. She disappeared, and Maerad finally put down the pack she had carried for two weeks from the Osidh Elanor. She rubbed her shoulders, and sighed.

She felt too tired to unpack; now she had arrived, it was as if a leaden weight of weariness had settled on her shoulders. She yawned hugely, and looked around the chamber. It was comfortable and snug, being just near the chimney of the fire downstairs, and like the main hall was entirely panelled in wood, here painted with murals of wolves and foxes and owls in a snow-covered forest of spruce. The painted animals were abstracted in a way that caught Maerad's attention: there was no mistaking what they were, but the artist had made no attempt to make them appear real, and their forms owed much to the geometric patterns with which the Pilanel adorned their clothes and caravans. There was a narrow bed, draped with furs, and a stool and a tall, plain cedar chest, but no other furniture.

Zara silently returned, bringing with her silver ewers of water smelling of roses, one boiling hot and one cold, a large

silver basin and some cloths; and before she left, she carefully draped on the bed some warm woollen robes like those
Sirkana had been wearing. They were dyed a purple-red; even
in Thorold, she had never seen dye of that colour. The respectful way that Zara had handled the raiment alerted Maerad that
the robes were precious, and when she stroked them she realized they were made of some very soft, fine wool she did not
recognize. They had clearly been woven with great care: even
when Maerad looked at them closely, she could see no sign of
any seam, and thought that either they had been stitched with
marvellous skill, or they were woven in one piece. She stroked
the soft material, feeling sensible of an honour of which she did
not understand the full significance, and then poured water into
the bowl and, with intense relief, washed herself properly for
the first time in weeks. There was some soft soap in the bowl,
and with it she washed her hair. She didn't know what to do
with her dirty clothes, and folded them up on the floor so they
should not soil the bed.

Then she drew the robes over her head. As well as being
softer than any fabric she had touched, they were also warmer.
She sat down on the bed and inspected her feet. They had
held up quite well through her walk from the mountains, but
her boots were looking the worse for wear; she thought they
would not last another long trek. She wondered if she could
get some new boots in Murask, and then realized that she only
had a few Annaren coins with which to buy things, for Cadvan
had carried the purse. In Schools they had never needed to buy
anything; as Bards, they had been given what they needed.
But here she was not in a School. She put that particular problem aside for another day, and began the long, slow business
of untangling her hair. Perhaps she should wear it in braids,
like Sirkana, she thought; it would be more practical. Some of
it was almost matted like felt. She finally managed, by patient

application, to rid herself of most of the knots.

Zara returned with a pair of buskins made of sheepskin for Maerad's feet, and a tray on which was a bowl of hot stew and a piece of unleavened bread covered with some kind of black seed, still warm from the oven. Maerad's mouth immediately filled with water. She was relieved that she would be eating alone, and she thanked Zara and laid the tray on the chest, which was high enough to use as a table. Zara disappeared, and Maerad devoured her late breakfast, or early midday meal, with indecent haste: she suddenly felt as if she had not eaten for days. The stew had a gamey taste, like goat, and was flavoured with sour cream and fennel, and a duck egg had been broken into it, a combination Maerad found unusual, but surprisingly pleasant. She ran the bread around the bowl to soak up every last drop.

The meal and the warm room made her feel very tired. She lay down on the bed, intending just to have a short rest while she awaited a summons. She wondered how Sirkana could have known she was the One, and what that meant in Pilanel lore; and even more uneasily, she wondered what else was known. She had thought her identity easy to conceal once she was north of the mountains, but clearly it was not so; and if she was as recognizable as she seemed to be, then she was certainly in peril ... worrying vaguely around these thoughts, she drifted into a deep sleep.

She woke with a start, and immediately sat up, instantly alert. The room was much darker; she must have been asleep for hours. She sent out her hearing, wondering what was happening. People moved in the house speaking in Pilanel; somewhere in the distance, outside perhaps, somebody was singing and she could hear the sounds of animals and children. She sighed and rubbed her eyes. Well, there was nothing to do but wait. She did not want to creep around the house like a thief. And, for the moment, she was quite content to stay where she was.

Before long, Zara poked her head around the door. Maerad smiled and nodded, and Zara came and inspected her, taking her chin and turning her head from side to side as if she were making sure she was properly clean. She adjusted Maerad's robe fussily, as a mother would a small child's, and made clicking noises with her tongue until Maerad put on her buskins. Then she took her arm and led her downstairs, back to the hall.

This time Sirkana was not alone. There were three others: two men, one of whom was Dorn, and a woman. The two Pilanel Maerad did not know stared at her as she walked towards them, not bothering to hide their curiosity.

"Welcome," said Sirkana in Annaren. "You have given us the name Mara to call you by." Maerad blushed, ashamed of her deception, and opened her mouth to say something, but Sirkana held up her hand to silence her. "I think it is not your usename, but it will do for now," she said. "There are ready reasons for discretion in these dark days. Let me present to you my friends, whom I trust with my life itself. They are Tilla à Minatar," (here the woman, who was almost as tall as Sirkana, nodded) "and Vul à Taqar. Dorn à Hadaruk you have already met."

Maerad bowed to each of the Pilanel, and then Zara, who seemed to have taken on Maerad as a personal responsibility, pushed a chair towards her, indicating that she should sit down. Maerad sat and looked enquiringly at Sirkana, wondering whether she should speak next, and what she ought to say. There was a short, slightly awkward silence.

"You are very young," said Sirkana.

"I know," said Maerad, slightly despairingly. Everyone said that; perhaps she looked even younger than she was. "But I have travelled far, nevertheless, to be here. I have a doom laid on me, a doom that concerns us all, and I seek your help."

"Our help you shall have, once we know who you are," said Vul. He was younger than Dorn, a heavy-boned man with a gentle face, and he spoke with a thick accent.

"I–I'm not quite sure how to answer that question." There was another short silence, and Maerad felt again the lack of Cadvan, his ease with strangers. She felt shy and foolish, and angry with herself for feeling these things. "I am a Bard of Edil-Amarandh, Maerad of Pellinor. Until lately I was travelling with Cadvan of Lirigon, seeking this place. He died in the Gwalhain Pass, and since then I have walked here alone."

The four Pilanel stirred at this news, exchanging shocked glances. "Cadvan was known to us," said Sirkana. "You bring grievous news. What could have killed such a powerful *Dhillarearën*?"

"We were attacked by frost creatures. Iridugul. There were three, and they brought down the side of the mountain on him. Not even the greatest of mages could have survived that."

"Iridugul?" Dorn stared at Maerad in disbelief. "What are iridugul doing in the Gwalhain Pass – and in autumn? I can scarce credit this."

"They were pursuing us." Speaking of Cadvan's death to others for the first time was like admitting finally that he was gone, and Maerad struggled with the pain rising inside her. "We were also attacked by a stormdog near Thorold. Cadvan thought it was the Winterking. We have been pursued for a long time." She stopped, biting her lip hard enough to hurt. She did not want to break down in front of these grave, dignified strangers.

"If the pass is blocked, it would explain why the clans are late in coming from the southern plains," said Vul. He looked intently at Maerad. "Is it blocked?"

"I think so," said Maerad. "There was a landslide that filled up the whole road. It would take an army to clear it."

"It seems our clans will not return from the Rilnik this year, then," said Dorn. "That is sad news."

"If you are young, you have seen much beyond your years," said Sirkana. "We do not mean to distress you." She waited until Maerad had composed herself, and then said, "I suppose, then, that Cadvan of Lirigon knew you to be the Chosen."

"I am the One. The Foretold among Bards." It was the first time Maerad had claimed this title before others, and she sat up straighter. I am the One, she thought, and I have to stop behaving as if I am not. "If that is what you mean by the Chosen, then you are correct. It is said that I will defeat the Nameless One in his next rising." She looked down at her hands, suddenly an abashed young girl again. "The only problem is, I don't know how. Or why it is me." She finished in a whisper, not daring to look up. She heard Vul clear his throat.

"And how do we know this?" asked Tilla, speaking for the first time. "I do not mean discourtesy, Maerad of Pellinor, but perhaps you or others are mistaken."

"I don't know," said Maerad humbly. "My Truename is as foretold. And I do have – I did have – an unusual Gift. I can do things that other Bards cannot."

"She is the Chosen," said Sirkana. "I knew as soon as I saw her."

"But how did you know?" Maerad looked at Sirkana, suddenly forgetting everything in her desire to understand why everyone else seemed to know more about her than she did. "I'm not even sure myself. How can you *know*?"

Sirkana looked at her steadily. "You know, Maerad of Pellinor, that like you I am a *Dhillarearën*. In Annar, any with the Voice are sent to the Schools; even here many travel south to gather that learning. But not all do. There are other ways, and I have followed those, in the fashion of my people. I also have

the Sight, which is not given to many among the *Dhillarearën*. I
see what is hidden from others."

Maerad looked up at the proud figure of Sirkana, a little
shocked. Mirka had said the same thing, but Mirka fitted much
better the usual idea of the unSchooled Bard: a tragic figure,
whose Gift, left to itself, had turned against her, or had never
developed in the way it should. But here was a woman who had
never been instated into a School, and yet who held within her
all the powers, and more, of a formally Schooled Bard. Perhaps
Maerad's lack of Schooling, which she regretted so fiercely, was
not such a handicap after all.

But now Dorn was speaking. "If Maerad speaks true, as
you say, then she is not Annaren after all." He swept his gaze
from her feet to the crown of her head, doubt clear in his face.
"She should be Pilani, although she does not look as if a drop
of Pilani blood runs in her veins. For that is also what the songs
say, that one of our blood is the Chosen."

"My father was Pilanel." Maerad shut her eyes, suddenly
overwhelmed; how was she to explain her whole life to these
people? "He married Milana of Pellinor, the First Bard of that
School, and they had two children – my brother Hem, I mean,
Cai, and me. My father was killed when Pellinor was sacked,
when we were small children."

"What was your father's name?" asked Dorn.

"I don't know his full name." Why, thought Maerad,
had she never thought to ask? Since she had been given a
full name, she had always carried her mother's. "I know his
usename was Dorn, but Mirka told me it is a common name
among the Pilanel. I don't know where he came from, or anything about him. My brother Hem looks like him, he is dark
skinned, like you. But people tell me I look like my mother."
She met Dorn's eyes. "I know very little about my family; I
was taken as a slave after Pellinor fell, and until this spring I

didn't even know I was a Bard."

There was a long silence. The four Pilanel seemed to be deep in separate contemplations, and Maerad sat still, trying to be patient. At last, Sirkana stirred, and glanced over to her companions. Maerad saw Dorn nod very slightly, as if Sirkana had asked him something. Sirkana then turned to Maerad and gazed at her for a moment, searching her face. Then her eyes became unfocused, as if she saw something very far away.

"I knew your father," she said. "And we both knew the Chosen was to be born to him. It was a curse; even then he knew it would kill him."

"And his name was Dorn?" asked Maerad, her voice very small. She had hardly known her father, and it seemed somehow unfair that Sirkana had. She wondered suddenly why Cadvan had not told her more about her father's family; surely he would have known? It would be just like him not to tell her, she thought.

"Yes. Dorn à Triberi." Sirkana breathed in hard, as if staving off pain. "He was my twin brother. He left me a long time ago, seeking the Schooling of the Annaren Bards. Missing him was a pain worse than I thought I could endure; I thought my heart would split in two. His death was a great grief to me. Well, then, you are my brother's daughter. Do you not see why I knew you were the Chosen?"

Maerad shook her head, trying to clear it. This was very unexpected; she had thought that perhaps she would have had to explain her story, in order to find help, and had braced herself to be as persuasive as possible; but she had not thought to be recognized as soon as she entered Murask, and most certainly didn't expect to find such close family. Sirkana, then, was her aunt, her father's sister.

She studied Sirkana curiously, summoning her few, fugitive memories of her father. She remembered him whirling her around while she laughed and laughed, and a faint, spicy perfume, but she couldn't make those memories match the stern woman who stood before her. But when she looked she realized that Sirkana did remind her of Hem; there was something about the shape of her eyes, her nose, the line of her jaw. Maerad suddenly wished that Hem was with her now; perhaps it would not be so strange for him.

"How did you and – my father know that the One would be born to him?"

Sirkana fixed her dark eyes on Maerad's face. The room seemed suddenly to dim around them, and she felt herself becoming dizzy, as if she were looking into a deep well.

"I dreamed," said Sirkana in the Speech. "When I was ten years old, I dreamed of a great darkness. And my brother Dorn held up a child against the darkness, and the child was made of light. And I knew it was his child." As Sirkana spoke, Maerad saw the dream vividly in her mind, as if it were her own. "When I was twelve, I dreamed again the same dream, but by then I had the Voice, and this time Dorn spoke and told me who the child was. And again when I was fourteen, and sixteen, always the same dream.

"I told my mother of the dreams. She knew I had the Voice, and she counselled me to tell the headman of the clan, which I did. But I did not tell Dorn until I was sixteen; it was the only thing I kept from him, ever. I feared what he might do if he knew. And I was right to fear. But at last I did tell Dorn, and that night he had a dream of his own, the only foredream he ever dreamt. In his dream a great darkness rose over the land, and he was swallowed inside it. He was frightened, but he said to me that he must learn what it meant. It was after that he left for the Schools of Annar, and I knew I would never see him again."

"And when you saw me, you recognized me?" said Maerad softly.

"I did," said Sirkana. "But not with my eyes. With other vision. I have watched for the signs and listened to the songs since I was a young girl. I knew the Chosen would come in my lifetime, and I have been waiting."

Maerad looked blankly at the wooden walls, which flickered with dim firelight. Since she had entered Murask, she had felt as if she had fallen into a dream herself; the ground seemed to be falling away from beneath her, tipping her into some other world. But somehow Sirkana's words comforted her, in an obscure way she did not understand; they seemed some kind of recognition. When she looked up the room was full of light again, and the other Pilanel were looking baffled.

"What were you saying?" asked Tilla. Her voice was a little shaky, and Maerad, glancing towards her, saw she had gone pale.

"Maerad is the One, and she has arrived here, as foretold in the songs," said Sirkana. "It is the final sign." She made a strange gesture, touching her closed fist to her heart and then to her forehead, and the others followed suit. "Are we agreed then?" They all nodded.

Agreed to what? thought Maerad. She still couldn't find her bearings. Everything seemed to have been settled, but she hadn't asked for anything. She took a deep breath and sat up straight, looking at each of the Pilanel in turn. "I have to find the Treesong, the root of the Speech," she said. "That is my quest. And I need your help, I have nothing..." She spread out her hands in a gesture of humility. "I don't even know where to go."

"Where do you *need* to go, little chicken?" said Vul. Maerad started at his using Mirka's term of endearment, and bridled a little. She was not, after all, a child. But Vul's face was gentle, and she did not think he had intended to insult her.

"I believe I need to find the Wise Kindred. Mirka has the

Voice, and she fell into a sort of trance and she said ... she said all riddles were answered there. I need to know about the Split Song. It's all connected." As Maerad said this, a mocking voice echoed in her head: *you don't know what you're talking about. It's words, just words...*

"There is time to debate all of this," said Sirkana. "If you need to find the Wise Kindred, then we shall help you. You cannot go there alone: it is a long journey, and a hard one, to the Labarok Isles, even without this early winter."

She turned to the other Pilanel. "I swear you all to secrecy," she said. "I do not trust all of our people enough for the news of the One's return to be widely known. There is peril enough."

Each in turn, they nodded solemnly, and Maerad felt herself sag with relief. There was, indeed, peril enough.

XVII

THE PILANEL

MAERAD was exhausted after her meeting with the Pilanel. When she returned to her little room she sat down blankly on the bed, staring into space. She felt strangely lost. Even when she was alone in the empty spaces of the Arkiadera Plains the map of her world had been certain, if perilous. But now it was as if all the familiar signs had been erased, revealing a strange new country.

Despite her close kinship to the Pilanel, she did not feel at home in Murask: it was alien and confusing, the people harsh and stern, if not unkind. She felt no echo of the strange familiarity that had puzzled her when she had first entered Innail, even though the School had been as different from her life in Gilman's Cot as could be imagined. She was sure that Hem would have felt differently about Murask. He was not immediately comfortable among Bards; she had put it down to his nightmarish childhood, kidnapped by Hulls after the slaughter of Pellinor and dumped in a grim orphanage in Edinur. But perhaps it was more profound than that, and his discomfort was the same kind of refusal that Sirkana had expressed, a belief that there were other ways of unlocking the Gift. And, unlike Maerad, with her fair Annaren skin, Hem would have been accepted as Pilanel without question.

She was glad that Sirkana intended keeping her identity secret. She thought she now understood how the Dark had known about her, why they were always, as Cadvan had said, two steps ahead of the Light. The Hulls must have known about the Pilanel prophecies; they must have known somehow about Sirkana's dream and Maerad's father's decision to move to Annar. Sirkana had said she did not trust all her people. There may well be a spy in Murask now, and it seemed there had been one here before Maerad was born. Although, she thought, Dorn might have confided in a Bard of Annar who had betrayed him. She thought of Helgar, and the other Ettinor Bards she had so distrusted in Innail; they had been spies, if not for the Nameless One himself, certainly for Enkir. Maybe Dorn had spoken to Enkir himself? It would not be unlikely; why would Dorn have mistrusted a Norloch Bard of such standing?

Restlessly, Maerad stood up and paced the room. She felt stifled; she needed some fresh air. She opened the shutters over the window, thinking to lean out and see what the world looked like – it must be late afternoon by now. There were two sets, both of thick, stout wood, bolted fast. When she opened the outer shutters they tore out of her hands, banging back against the wall, as a blast of freezing wind gusted into the room, dumping a small drift of snowflakes on the floor. Maerad had a brief glimpse of swirling whiteness before she wrestled the shutters back and bolted them closed again. She hadn't realized there was such a storm; the walls of the house were very thick. If she had been out in the open, she would have frozen to death. She had beaten the snow by one day.

The thought rattled her slightly, and she sat back down on the bed and decided to unpack. As she took out her familiar objects – her lyre, Dernhil's book, the bottle of medhyl, now quite depleted – she began to feel less displaced. She missed the wooden cat she had given Mirka, but even its absence was part of the tally of her life. When she had arranged the room to her satisfaction, she sat on her bed and opened Dernhil's book. It had been a while since she had been able to read his poems; and, perhaps perversely, she felt more Bardic than she ever had.

She wasn't at all sure of what she thought about being claimed as a Pilanel.

That night she was invited to dine with Sirkana. Zara fussed around her, even insisting on plaiting her hair, and making sure that her robes were straight. Then she solemnly led her down to the hall again, where a long table had been set, with a bench either side, full of people. The noise of conversation rose up to her as she walked along the gallery outside her room, and Maerad's heart leapt into her mouth; she had not been among people for a long time, not since leaving Ossin. Going down to meet them took all her courage. She did her best to conceal her nervousness, but it was difficult when she entered the hall and every head turned to look at her. Sirkana, who sat in the middle of the table, beckoned her to an empty place on her left, and Maerad sat down, looking curiously at the men and women who sat around her.

Sirkana was as austerely dressed as she had been earlier, except that she now wore a plain necklace made of gold links, which glinted like the gold rings in her ears. "Tonight we dine with the heads of the southern clans," she said in the Speech. "You may meet some of your kin."

Maerad looked at the dark, tough faces of the Pilanel and inwardly quailed. "What shall I say of myself?" she asked.

"As little as you may," said Sirkana. "These are good people, but a loose word may enter an evil ear. Tilla, Dorn, Vul, I trust with my life; your story is safe with them. I shall say you are on pilgrimage from Annar, and have brought word from Mirka à Hadaruk: that is enough to explain the honour we do you." She winked slyly at Maerad, an ironic smile softening her stern face, and Maerad felt herself relax.

Sirkana formally introduced Maerad as Mara, and she was toasted in welcome. Then it seemed any formalities were over, and the feast began. On Maerad's other side was a tall, stocky young man with a gentle face. He introduced himself in excellent Annaren as Dharin, and they began to chat; he had travelled widely in Annar, and wanted to know where she was from. He had never been to Thorold, and when she mentioned that she had been there he plied her with questions.

It was a high feast in the Zmarkan style, and food just kept coming and coming: first little pancakes stuffed with some kind of herbed cheese; then pickled plover's eggs; then a soup of a surprising pink colour with sour cream and dill; then a roast goose stuffed with hazelnuts and wild onions; then some kind of dumpling filled with spiced offal; then a huge side of roasted venison. And there was still more: thick spicy sausages that seemed mostly stuffed with fat, and pickled cabbage, and a number of dishes that Maerad couldn't identify at all, and, remembering her experience with mussels, left well alone. Nobody seemed to mind when she stopped eating, but she found herself amazed at how much the Pilanel could eat and drink and still stay upright.

The meal was accompanied by shots of a fiery liquor, drunk from very small clay cups, and as the evening wore on the conversation got louder and louder. Unexpectedly, Maerad found she was enjoying herself, and not only because of her conversation with Dharin. The Pilanel, for all their stern demeanour, gave themselves to pleasure as wholeheartedly as the Thoroldians. When the food at last stopped arriving there were calls for music, and three Pilanel drew out fiddles and drums and pipes and began a wild dance tune that got into the blood like a fever.

"Come," said Dharin. "We must dance."

Maerad demurred, feeling shy, but Dharin took her hand and dragged her into the middle of the hall, where there were already many dancers. Maerad was glad that she hadn't overeaten, because she would have surely been sick; Dharin whirled her around like a top. The Pilanel dances were very similar to those she had learnt in Thorold, and before long Maerad had lost her self-consciousness and entered the pure pleasure of the present. It felt like aeons since she had last been able to forget all the troubles of her life. All the fears and doubts surrounding her quest, all her griefs and regrets, were swept up into the tempest of the music, poising her exactly in the centre of the moment, a clear vessel of joy.

"You dance like a true Pilani," said Dharin, as they returned to their seats. "Life is hard, no? And full of sorrow. The Pilani dance in defiance of death and grief and hardship. They choose to burn before the darkness, rather than to gutter out like a dim flame."

Maerad looked up in surprise; she had just been thinking something similar. "Yes, it is good to dance," she said. "And it makes me feel stronger, as if I can face peril a little better."

"You are over-young to face perils," said Dharin. Maerad glanced at him ironically; she thought he was not much older than she was. He intercepted her look, and grinned. "Well, you are right, life is no respecter of youth or age. It will pour its troubles equally over all."

Some more than others, thought Maerad, for a moment lapsing into self-pity. But it made her few moments of pleasure all the more precious.

By the following day, the storm had blown out, leaving an unfamiliar white world with strange lights and glints. Pilanel children tumbled into the snow, bundled in brightly embroidered jerkins and scarves and hats, and threw snowballs at each other. Across the wide, empty turf in the middle of the Howe the snow lay knee deep, with a thin deceptive crust that broke into icy sludge. The sky was swagged with heavy, yellowish clouds, presaging more snow.

Maerad breathed in the icy air, feeling the tingle of blood rushing to her cheeks; she liked this weather. Sirkana had offered to show her around Murask, and Maerad met again some of the Pilanel she had dined with the previous evening.

When the clans came to Murask for the winter, they returned to their traditional quarters. These were – apart from Sirkana's house, which was the central meeting hall – tunnelled into the thick wall of the Howe; but to Maerad's surprise, they were far from the gloomy, airless caves she had expected. They were pleasant dwellings, with bright murals and comfortable, warm furnishings. Typically, the animals – dogs, deer, horses – were kept in large barn-like rooms downstairs, while upstairs were the living quarters. Pilanel clans varied enormously in size; they could range from five to a hundred people, and did not necessarily comprise people from the same family. They were often practical groupings arranged according to need and custom – where a clan travelled, for instance, during the summer, or how they made their living. Some worked as minstrels or sold handcrafts, some were horse breeders and traders, some were travelling tinkers and cobblers, some herded deer. When they arrived at Murask, they tended to arrange their living quarters likewise. Mostly this was established by tradition, and the same clan occupied certain dwellings for generations without count.

The more Maerad saw of Murask, the more intrigued she became. The settlement was a complex and efficient structure, like a hive, and those who had built it had been very ingenious. It had a piping system, like the Schools, and very efficient drainage; and it never ran out of water, which was supplied from a spring with outlets inside the Howe itself and in Sirkana's house. Slow, peat-burning furnaces kept the Howe from freezing even in the most savage weather, and all of it was warm. Maerad asked Sirkana how old it was, but she answered that no one knew; Murask had been there from time immemorial, and was far older than the Schools of Annar.

About half of the tunnels through the Howe were used for storage. Each year the clans would bring back supplies for the long winter – grains, oils, nuts, strings of onions, dried bunches of herbs, preserved fruits – traded over the summer. Or if they were not traders, they would lay aside hard cheeses made from milking their herds of shaggy deer, or slaughter the young animals in the autumn and smoke the carcasses in the huge smoke rooms in the Howe. Each clan brought all that they could, and the food was held in common. "We are fat together, or we starve together," said Sirkana. "And this year is a thin year. This is why it is such a blow if the Pilani who spend the summer in Annar cannot come home for winter; we were hoping that they might be able to make up the deficit. From what you say, they will have to turn back."

Maerad thought of the blocked road in the Gwalhain Pass. "I don't know," she said. "Maybe someone determined could dig their way through. If they had a lot of people with them."

"It is late in the year for such digging," said Sirkana, and sighed. "Well, they may yet come. We will not close the gates against them. But it bodes ill for us."

It was not until that afternoon that Maerad had a chance to talk about her quest. They had ended up in Sirkana's private rooms, which were not much bigger than the chamber Maerad had been given, and Sirkana made her a sweet herb tea. They sat in comfortable silence for a time, pursuing separate reflections; but then Maerad gathered herself. She was not so daunted by Sirkana as she had been, and when they had first met, Sirkana had spoken of Pilanel lore, about a riddle that might illuminate the Treesong. She leaned forward, her brows creased.

"Sirkana, do your people have a tale of the Split Song?" she asked.

Sirkana looked up in surprise. "The Split Song? Nay, I do not recall…"

"Or the Treesong?"

Sirkana shook her head. "Not that I know," she said. "And I am deeply learned in Pilani lore."

"It's something to do with the Elidhu," said Maerad.

"The Elidhu no longer speak to mortals," said Sirkana. "They departed from the human world when the great darkness fell."

"Some do," said Maerad, beginning to feel a little impatient. "I have spoken to Elidhu. But what I have to do is to find the Treesong, which is something to do with the Elidhu, and which is also – well, Cadvan and I thought – to do with this tradition of the Split Song."

"It is all riddles," said Sirkana, smiling. "We say the One is a riddle, perhaps the greatest riddle of them all. But of course I will help you."

Maerad frowned again. "Mirka said that the Wise Kindred answered all riddles, and knew what was half and what was whole, and that seemed like a clue. My heart tells me that I must find the Wise Kindred. You seem to know who they are and where they dwell. Who are they?"

"They live far, far away," said Sirkana. "In the land of ice and fire, the Labarok Islands. They live where the snow never melts, and where winter is one long night, and summer one long day."

"How far away is it?"

"No Pilani has been to the Labarok Isles in living memory," said Sirkana. "But it is said that they are thrice as far as Murask is from the Idrom Uakin." Maerad was baffled for a moment, until she remembered that was the Pilanel name for the Osidh Elanor. "It is a perilous journey, especially in winter."

"Can it be done, though?" asked Maerad urgently. It came

over her that she could be caught in Murask all through the northern winter, and then, even if her quest succeeded, it could be too late.

"Aye, it could be done, if you took one with you with weatherlore and a finding sense, and if you were lucky. We have the telling of how to get there, if the Wise Kindred still dwell there. It is not just the ice and the storms and the cruel terrain to fear. There are also the Jussacks, who prey on travellers. You will need to be well armed."

"I have some swordcraft," said Maerad. "And Barding skills as well."

"You can ride?" asked Sirkana.

Maerad nodded.

"It is yet two moons before the winter solstice; it is early for snow, and this storm should pass," said Sirkana. "It would be best to go on horseback to Tlon, where the northern clans gather. From there you will have to travel by dog. There is no other way over the snow."

"Dogs?" said Maerad, with some trepidation. She harboured a deep fear of dogs. Sirkana picked up on her tone and gave her a slightly mocking glance.

"Dharin à Lobvar, my sister's son, is an expert dog handler, and he owns a very fine team. He goes on the trading routes to the northern clans each winter. Perhaps you can speak to him; he is young and he itches for adventure."

"Is he the Dharin I spoke to last night?" asked Maerad.

"He was seated with us, yes. His mother is not here; she is south with the clans in Annar."

"But that would make him my cousin." Maerad spoke softly. This was a long way from having no family at all.

"Yes, he is. But I will not tell him of that kinship, for fear that in his gladness he might tell others. Whether you tell him after you leave Murask is up to you."

There was a short silence. Maerad studied the strange murals in Sirkana's room, pondering how she could have such close kin in Murask, and yet still feel so alien. When she looked up, Sirkana's eyes were unfocused, as if she saw something far away. Presently Sirkana blinked and seemed to return; her eyes, Maerad saw with surprise, were bright with tears.

"Aye, he is your cousin," she said. "I think he is meant to travel along your path. But it is a heavy price."

Sirkana would not say further what she meant, although Maerad pressed her. She merely said that Maerad would be equipped with everything she needed for her journey to the north, and that she would ask Dharin the following day if he wanted to go on the journey. Their quiet intimacy seemed to have been broken; Sirkana made it clear, without saying anything, that she wanted to be alone, and Maerad retreated to her chamber, filled with a sudden gloom.

Maerad was eager to leave. She was free to wander wherever she liked in Murask, but everyone seemed busy with various tasks – smoking meats for the coming winter, or putting food and grain in the storage houses, or cleaning out their winter quarters – and she most often felt that she was in the way. It had started snowing again, a seemingly unending blizzard, and if she wanted to leave Sirkana's house she used the underground tunnel that linked it to the warren of the Howe. Maerad had spent her childhood in mountain country, and was not unused to snow; but she felt the oddness of this blizzard, and did not need the Pilanel to tell her it was unseasonal, two months before the midwinter solstice, to have such heavy weather. She thought of the stormdogs, and the iriduguls in the Gwalhain Pass, and her heart grew heavy. A cold intelligence was aware of her, and brooded over her presence in the north; she was surer and surer of it. It felt like a shadow in her mind, inchoate but present, which intensified with the cold weather. Arkan, the Winterking, knew she was here.

Her single pleasure was the beginning of a friendship with Dharin. As she had promised, Sirkana spoke with him privately, and the following day he came to her at the noon meal and clasped both her hands in his. Maerad looked down: his hands were enormous, her whole hand barely covering his palm.

"Sirkana tells me you are on a quest and she asked if I would take you north, to the Wise Kindred," he said. "I will be your guide; I know the telling of the way there. No one from the southern clans has been that way since my father's father was alive. It will be a great adventure!"

He grinned, and Maerad could not help smiling back.

"She told me that we'd have to go by dog from Tlon," said Maerad. "I didn't know you could ride dogs."

At that, Dharin burst out laughing. "You don't ride them, little cousin." Maerad flinched; did he know her real identity? But he used her pseudonym Mara – Sirkana had been insistent that her real identity be kept secret within Murask. "Come, after the meal I will show you. We might be using dogs all the way from Murask, the way this snow is falling, so you should get to know them."

As he promised, that afternoon Dharin took her to see his dogs. Because of the blizzard, they went by the underground tunnels to a part of Murask that Maerad had not seen. She had assumed the Howe was perfectly round, but it was not; the dog stables, as they were called, were in another open area that was separated from the common where Sirkana's house stood. It was divided into big pens by high stone walls, and was kept apart from the rest of Murask to prevent the working dogs from hunting the livestock in the main part of the Howe. There were at least fifty dogs there, penned in groups ranging from six to more than a dozen.

It was clear the dogs were Dharin's pride, and Maerad, who could not quite overcome her fear of them, did her best to conceal her nervousness. They were bigger than any dog she had ever seen, bigger by far than Gilman's hounds – they stood as high as her chest – and were unsettlingly like wolves.

To Maerad's surprise, despite the bitter weather the dogs were all curled up outside, covered in a thin drift of snow, rather than in the shelters provided for them. Even with her untrained eye, she could see that Dharin's dogs were unusually fine: all glossy-coated and well muscled, with deep, strong chests. There were fifteen of them, grey or black with thick white ruffs around their wolvish faces, and their eyes, unsettlingly, were a light, icy blue.

"This is Claw, my leader," said Dharin, as the biggest dog shook off the snow that had curled around it and bounded up to him, its tail wagging like a puppy. Maerad had steeled herself to follow Dharin into the pen, not wanting to be thought a coward, and flinched; this close, the dog was something out of some of her worst nightmares. The dog's face was almost level with Maerad's, even as it stood on four legs before her. Its canine teeth were as long as her fingers. She could feel the dog's hot breath puff past her face, as Dharin briefly stroked Claw's ears. The dog gave a short bark and Maerad jumped.

"Do they frighten you, Mara?" said Dharin, turning quickly. "You must not show them your fear, they can smell it, and it makes them afraid. Claw, down." The dog instantly lay down on the snow, looking up at Dharin alertly, waiting for his next move or command. "Claw is the best dog in Zmarkan," he said proudly. "I have had many offers for her, but I would as soon sell my own soul. And all these," he waved at the rest of the team, "are her puppies. I have always kept the best. It makes a good team, there are no fights on my trips. Well, not serious fights anyway."

Maerad nodded, her heart in her mouth. How was she to stop the dogs knowing she was afraid? One snap from those formidable jaws would break her neck. She could use the Speech, perhaps, but she dared not; if it was impossible to lie in the Speech, it would be impossible to conceal her fear.

Dharin disappeared inside the shed, leaving Maerad looking at the dogs. They ignored her, obviously having decided she was harmless. They all stood up, their ears erect, watching the doorway. Soon Dharin emerged carrying a side of meat, which he threw to the ground. The dogs instantly pounced on it, snarling and yapping at each other, and Maerad backed away nervously. She could hear their jaws crunching on the bones. The flesh looked very red on the white snow.

"They are hungry," said Dharin, who seemed unfussed by what to Maerad looked like terrifying and threatening behaviour. "They are fed every two days; they do not need to eat more often. And they are spoiling for exercise. They are the only creatures that do not enjoy rest." To Maerad's relief, they left the pen, although Dharin remarked indifferently that his dogs could leap the high fence if they really wanted to. "Sometimes dogs will jump into another team's pen, and that is not a good thing. Not my team, but others less obedient. It makes people very angry; you can lose a good dog that way."

Maerad shuddered. Dharin's dogs were more frightening than any dogs she had ever seen. And it seemed she would have to travel with them for weeks.

"Are they wolves?" she asked, thinking that her silence had drawn out for too long.

"Not all wolf. Part wolf, and half wild still. Like all wild things, they must be treated with respect." Then Dharin noticed Maerad's white face.

"Mara, they are good beasts," he said earnestly. "Even if you are afraid of them, they know that you are under my protection, and they will not hurt you. I am the boss dog."

"I saw a man killed by dogs once, when I was a child," she said. "I used to have nightmares about it."

Dharin looked at her thoughtfully. "That is a terrible thing. But it was not my dogs who did that."

"No," she said. It was no use trying to explain her fear; it wasn't as if it was rational. "But if I can't stop being afraid, I can be a little brave, can't I? If you promise they won't bite me."

"When you are with me, they will not touch you," said Dharin.

"Well, I'm not going near them otherwise," she said.

"Well, then, we will be all right," he answered. He looked up at the sky, which was still swirling with snow. "I somehow do not think that we will be riding horses to Tlon," he said. "This snow does not look as if it is going to stop."

"It's the Winterking," said Maerad, without thinking.

"You think so?" Dharin gave her a surprised glance. "Well, perhaps you are right. There are many dark rumours these days; and no doubt you have other news."

Maerad squirmed a little. Because of his massive bulk and slow deliberate movements, she had not thought Dharin especially quick, but he seemed to have unsettlingly acute perceptions. "But you can't travel in a storm," she objected, to turn the subject.

"I have a good sled. And my dogs have run in weather worse than this," he answered. "Admittedly, on roads that I know well. I never get lost, you see; they say I am like the wild geese, who fly to the same spot each summer from the other end of the world. But true, even the best driver in the world can fall into a hole, if he can't see it in front of him."

Despite Dharin's boast about travelling through blizzards, they did not begin their journey until the snowstorm abated. It lasted for three days, dumping snow in the centre of the Howe until it reached the bottom of the lower windows. Every day paths were shovelled through the snow, but most people just used the tunnels.

Sirkana told Maerad that a winter this early had not been heard of since the days when the Winterking held sway over Zmarkan. "His power waxes," the headwoman said gravely. "I do not doubt it is him. I told Cadvan of Lirigon of this, when last he was in Murask."

Maerad's heart gave a little flip at the mention of Cadvan's name. "Yes, he believed that the Winterking had arisen. And he said he had travelled within sight of his stronghold," she said. "It seems all but certain now."

Sirkana gave her a narrow look. "I do not fully understand your quest, my brother's daughter. But if Cadvan of Lirigon was with you, then I do not doubt it is good. And I know you do not seek to deceive me; it is difficult to lie to me. Nevertheless, I am troubled. There is within you something that I do not recognize; it is not of the *Dhillarearën*, it is something else."

"It's the Elemental blood," said Maerad.

"Nay, it is more than that." Sirkana frowned. "Elemental blood, so it is said, is common among the Pilani. Still, I wonder greatly that you have spoken with such beings."

"Oh, only one," mumbled Maerad, suddenly embarrassed. "The Elidhu called Ardina has spoken with me once or twice."

"Hmmm," Sirkana's face was unreadable, and Maerad wasn't sure if she believed her or not. "There are tales that attend you, beyond your years, that is at least clear. Well, I see there are questions of high policy that are bound up with your quest, and I will not ask further. I trust you, and not only because you are my kin. I will give you what help I can."

The warmth that flooded into Maerad's breast when Sirkana said she trusted her surprised her. She blinked, feeling her eyes prickle. It seemed the first time that anyone had said such a thing to her; and since the killing of the Bard in the Rilnik Plains, and Cadvan's death in the Gwalhain Pass, she had not even trusted herself. She turned away to hide her emotion.

"I thank you, Sirkana," she said, her voice rough.

"Ah, little one." Sirkana put her hand on her shoulder, and Maerad started at the intimacy of the gesture. "It is hard to bear such a burden as you bear, even for one much older than you. You are very young. We are all mistaken sometimes; sometimes we do wrong things, things that have bad consequences. But it does not mean we are evil, or that we cannot be trusted ever afterwards."

Maerad said nothing; she felt that if she said anything she would burst into a storm of tears. Sirkana had guessed shrewdly at what tormented her.

"I loved my brother," Sirkana went on softly. "And it has been a strange shock to me to meet you, my brother's daughter. But as I have talked with you, I can see his face in yours. There is much in you that comes from him. And he was the bravest man I have ever known, and the most honest."

Now Maerad did begin to cry. Sirkana patted her shoulder until she stopped, wiping her eyes with her hands.

"I don't know," she said despairingly. "I don't feel brave. Everything's been very hard for a long time. All my life, it seems. I wish I could remember my father better. All I can remember is—" She stopped, swallowing. "The clearest memory I have is of him being murdered. It doesn't seem *fair*."

"The world is not fair," said Sirkana. "And there is nothing that can make its injustices easier to bear."

They were silent for a while, and for that time Maerad felt closer to her than she had felt to any human being for a long time: she felt that someone saw her for who she was, and simply accepted her, in all her rightness and wrongness, as bone of her bone. Once, perhaps, her mother had looked at her like that. But she could barely remember it.

Finally Sirkana kissed her forehead, and stood up. Her gentleness vanished behind her usual austere expression. "Well, I have a dispute that I must sort out between two clans, and they are awaiting me in the Hall," she said. "I am already late."

Maerad looked up, her lashes still wet with tears, and smiled. "Thank you, Sirkana," she said.

"There is nothing to thank me for," she said. "You will have what you need for your journey. If your quest succeeds, perhaps I will have to thank you."

"Not for that. For—"

Sirkana's face briefly softened again. "I know. Remember that my love will also go with you, and may it guard you well. For your sake, as well as your father's."

Dharin insisted that Maerad help him with gathering supplies and packing the sled for their journey. He said she should know what they were taking and where it was kept, and that she needed to be familiar with the sled before they left. She gladly assented; it gave her something to do.

Dharin had made the sled himself, and he knew every knot of it backwards. The long runners were made from single lengths of ash that he had cut and carefully warped upwards at one end, so the sled would ride easily over rocks and other obstacles. The runners were each about as thick as his thumb, and he had covered them beneath with a mixture of mud, moss and (he told Maerad later, when they knew each other a little better) urine, which froze hard and slick, and protected the wood. Up from the runners ran six stanchions, also of ash, each one higher than the last, which were joined by two parallel rails. At the back end, behind the hindmost stanchion, was a little platform where Dharin stood to drive the sled. He told Maerad that she would be sitting in front of him, and he carefully made her a comfortable seat well padded with furs, which she could simply slip into, like a foot into a shoe.

The base of the sled was fashioned of thick wooden slats. At the front was a curved bow to protect the sled; it was made of stout wood and covered with rawhide. When he had taken the sled out of summer storage, Dharin had dismantled it entirely and freshly lashed it together, to ensure maximum strength and because mice had nibbled the hide. The hide kept the structure flexible and strong. Over the whole he had lashed two layers of cured skins.

Dharin explained every detail of the sled patiently, running his hands lovingly over each part of it, feeling for flaws and warpings in the wood that might have occurred during the summer. Maerad couldn't imagine herself driving it, but then, she thought, there were a lot of things she had done that she wouldn't have thought possible. Very slightly, her apprehension of the coming journey abated.

Together they packed onto the sled what seemed to Maerad an enormous number of supplies. There were extra furs to keep them warm at night and a sort of tent made of oiled hide and springy willow wood. They stowed a lot of a tough honey biscuit baked especially for long journeys through the cold. There were also bags of the usual travelling food – nuts, dried fruits, cured meat – and several large leather bags of drinking water. They took a supply of peat and fire-making tools, and a small travelling stove, of a kind Maerad had never seen: it was made of iron, with a stone base to prevent it burning the wood of the sled.

Maerad's pack, which had often seemed so heavy in her travels, looked insignificant compared to everything else. And yet it contained everything she owned – her fighting gear, her treasures, her lyre. By far the most space was taken up by food for the dogs. Maerad was at first surprised by how much they were taking, but Dharin explained that while horses could usually feed themselves, everything dogs ate had to be carried.

"Unless they go hunting, but they might not catch anything, and it makes them wild," he said. "And they eat a lot. They can keep running all day. It adds up to a lot of meat. I put it at the front, it will freeze there and so it will keep."

They stood back, both admiring their handiwork. "It looks neat, well balanced," said Dharin, his head tilted to one side. "Well, Mara, we're ready to go any time now. Just say the word."

Maerad looked out through the open doors into the wide yard. She couldn't see to the further end; the view was white with snow.

"Do you think we ought to leave in this weather?" she asked dubiously. "Are you really as good a driver as you say?"

Dharin glanced at her. "We can wait," he said. "Even the best driver avoids blizzards if he can."

Maerad considered. "Let's wait a day," she said. "I don't think I have a lot of time, so maybe if this snow doesn't stop, we should think about going anyway. If you think it's all right."

"I await your word," said Dharin, giving her an elaborate bow. Maerad pretended to be unamused by his foolery and waved him away, like an arrogant queen. He shuffled out of the shed backwards, dangling his hat in his hands, and fell over backwards in the snow.

Maerad laughed out loud, and Dharin came back inside, brushing snow off himself.

"Sorry, Queen Mara," he said. "I'm not much good as a slave."

Maerad laughed again, and brushed more snow out of his hair. "Neither was I," she said.

XVIII

WHITE

THAT night, alone in her room, Maerad was afflicted by a terrible melancholy. In the few days she had been in Murask, she had found a part of her family she hadn't known anything about. And although she felt a closeness to Sirkana she could not deny and even to Dharin, she also knew she was different from them in a way she was sure that Hem was not. Hem would have fitted in seamlessly, right down to the endless meals. She smiled, thinking of Hem's bottomless appetite. It was impossible to be in Murask and not to think of Hem; his vivid face came into her mind's eye again and again. That afternoon she had seen a young boy whose lean, dark features were disconcertingly like her brother's, and she had almost cried out his name, until he turned and she realized he was quite different. Hem would belong here, perhaps as she felt she belonged among the Bards. Or *had* felt, in the past, before … she flinched from the painful thought that her actions might have exiled her from the Schools for ever.

She lay on her bed for some time, staring sightlessly at the ceiling. Soon – tomorrow, perhaps – she would be starting another stage of her quest. She knew nothing of where she was going, and it was possible that she might not come back. And if she did not, Hem would never know of his family in Murask…

She remembered her terrible foredream of the sack of Turbansk, and felt a suffocating despair rising in her breast. What hope did she or Hem have of surviving their different perils? How could she know that Hem was not already dead? And yet, with some unshakeable knowledge deeper than her doubt, Maerad was certain Hem was still alive. It was as if the two of them were connected by an invisible filament, immeasurably fine and delicate, which vibrated with his presence in the world. She was sure that she would know if Hem were dead. Hem was alive, then; she had to believe that. And while heart beats hope lingers, she said firmly to herself. She could not let her fear or hopelessness rule her actions; that way lay certain defeat.

Maerad reached a sudden decision. She got up from her bed and rummaged through her pack, looking for the writing materials she kept in there, wrapped carefully in oilskin. She spread the precious paper on the trunk, took out the pen and dipped it in black ink, and then paused for a moment, wondering how to begin. Then she started writing with a desperate industry.

My dear brother, she wrote. *I am writing this letter in Murask, a Pilanel settlement in Zmarkan. I hope this finds you well, and that Saliman (greetings, Saliman!) has taught you enough script for you to be able to read this on your own. I am full of sad news: Cadvan, our dear friend, perished in the Gwalhain Pass on our journey here, with Darsor and Imi. There are no words to express my sorrow.*

I reached Murask on my own and am now about to travel further north with a Pilanel guide to find a people called the Wise Kindred, who may be able to tell me something about the Treesong. I hope I am right, and that this is not a mistake. I may not return, and there are some things that I want you to know, in case I am not able to tell you of them myself.

I have found our father's family here. My guide is called Dharin à Lobvar, and he is our cousin: our father's sister's son. I have not been able to meet his mother, who is not in Murask at present, but the headwoman of the clans, Sirkana à Triberi, is another of Dorn's sisters. She is a Bard like us and she is Dorn's twin sister. I feel quite sure that if you came to Murask, you would feel completely at home; you already know that you are Pilanel, in a way that I am not, for all that we are kin. And the Bards among the Pilanel have other ways of using their Gifts than being instated to a School. If the School of Turbansk does not suit you, perhaps you might find a place among them. Whether you find yourself a Turbansk Bard or no, I believe that you must one day journey to Murask and speak to your kin here.

I write this with terrible sadness. I miss you more than I can say and every day I wish that we were together, and not separated by so many leagues. I have heard of war marching on Turbansk, and I fear for you. We are born into such dark times. But I also write this with hope and love, until one day I embrace you again, my dear brother.

Your sister,
Maerad

When she had finished, she read it through. It didn't really say what she meant; she hadn't the words for so many things, and she still found writing a difficult labour. But it would at least give Hem this knowledge, if she could not – if the letter ever reached him through the war-torn land. She sealed it with wax, pressing her Pellinor brooch into the seal, and then addressed it: Hem (Cai of Pellinor), by way of the hand of Saliman of Turbansk, at the School of Turbansk, in the Suderain. Then, possessed by urgency, she went to Sirkana's room and knocked on the door.

Sirkana answered, looking weary. Maerad thrust the letter towards her, hastily explaining who it was for and what it was, and asking if it could be sent as soon as possible. Sirkana's eyebrows lifted, and she took the letter, looking at Maerad's anxious face.

"Perhaps there is a way of sending it before next summer," she said soberly. "There are other passes through the mountains than the Gwalhain, and sometimes we have traffic through Annar even in wintertime. If your brother is in Turbansk, he is very far from here, and the roads are very dangerous now, but our people have secret ways. I will do my best."

Speechlessly, Maerad flung her arms around Sirkana's neck. Then, feeling a little better, she returned to her room.

The next day, the storm had blown itself out. It was now Maerad's fourth day in Murask, and she was itching to leave; the clear weather seemed like a sign. For the first time since arriving in the Howe she was able to throw back her shutters and let in some fresh air. Although it was not early, outside it was still the darkness before dawn; the days were already shortening. A strange blue light entered into the room, reflected back from the whiteness of the snow, and she breathed in the icy air. With a feeling of lightness she had not had for weeks, she began to dress for the journey.

Dharin had taken charge of Maerad's travel clothing, a task he had approached with the utmost seriousness the previous day. Sirkana had given him the keys to the clothing stores, and he had taken Maerad into a series of rooms that had impressed her deeply – here was kept the community's entire stock of spare clothes, which were given to anyone in need. There were shelves of hats, boots, jerkins, trews, dresses and coats.

Dharin had chosen heavy fur-lined boots that reached up to Maerad's knees, and shown her how to bandage her feet with strips of cloth before putting them on; this would protect her better against frostbite. He closely inspected her silk-lined woollen gloves, frowning slightly, and then chose some fur-lined mittens, suggesting she wear the woollen gloves underneath them.

"Can't I just wear the gloves?" asked Maerad. With her hands covered in so many layers, she felt very clumsy. "I can't pick anything up."

"You'll have more trouble picking things up without any fingers," said Dharin, with a sharpness in his tone she had not heard before. "Believe me, Mara, your worst enemy out there is the cold. It is nothing like the cold in Annar. I have seen frostbite. It is not something that you want to risk."

Maerad subsided, feeling rebuked, and meekly looked at the growing pile of clothes. They all looked very heavy, she thought. Nearly everything was lined with fur. Then they went back to her room and Dharin inspected her travel clothes and suggested she wear all of them, in several layers. Her leather trousers passed inspection, but he told her to pack her cloak away; it would be useless. Then he gave her a thick jerkin and trews, both woven out of the same soft wool as her robes. She was to cover everything with an ankle-length, fur-lined leather coat with a hood that almost covered her whole face.

He made her put it all on, waiting outside her room while she did so, and then inspected her critically. He drew the hood more closely over her face, so it shaded her eyes. "You must keep it like this," he said. "Otherwise you will go blind from looking at the snow." Maerad, who could already feel the sweat running down her face in the warm room, merely nodded. She hadn't realized northern travel was so complicated, but the seriousness with which Dharin was speaking impressed her deeply.

"You see, Mara, proper clothes can make the difference between living and dying," he said, when she begged to take them off. "There is almost nothing more important."

"The only real problem now is that I'm going to die of the heat," she protested. "I'm not in the ice yet!"

Dharin obviously thought she was taking the subject too lightly, but he reluctantly let her take the furs off. "You'll see, and you'll be grateful that you have these things," he said seriously.

"I know, Dharin," Maerad said, her face pink, as she thankfully threw the coat onto her bed. "But now I'm just *hot*."

This morning she put on everything except the coat, checked that all her possessions were in her pack, and went looking for Dharin. He was, as she had expected, in the dog stables. The sled was already out, and he was inspecting the dogs' paws, lifting them up one by one and carefully checking them. He looked up when Maerad arrived, and smiled.

"Are we off, then?" he said.

"Now?"

"Why not?" Dharin grinned. "I just have to harness the dogs, and then we can go."

Maerad was used to formal farewells, and felt somewhat taken aback.

"I don't have my coat with me," she said. "And my pack is back in my room. And I must say farewell to Sirkana, and thank her."

Dharin patted the dog he had been inspecting, and sent it off to join the others. "I've finished here," he said. "I'll come with you."

They returned to Sirkana's house. Maerad collected her things, and then with Dharin went to Sirkana's rooms. She wasn't there, nor in the Hall; after asking around they found her in the Howe itself, making an inspection of the food stores.

"We've come to say goodbye," said Dharin, without preamble. "It's a perfect day for travelling."

"I thought you would be leaving." Sirkana studied both of them in silence, as if she were judging how prepared they were for the journey. "Well, Dharin, sister son, have you the telling of how to find the Labarok Isles?"

Dharin grinned and tapped his forehead. "All in here," he said. "I won't get lost."

"Good." She gave him a long, slow look, which seemed to Maerad full of sadness, and then embraced him. "Travel well, and take no risks. You will have danger enough." She kissed him on both cheeks and then turned to Maerad.

"You won't find a better guide," she said. "He is young, but there is much knowledge in his bones."

"I know," Maerad answered. "And I am grateful. And I thank you for your generosity to me, and your welcome."

Sirkana stroked her cheek and then kissed her.

"Go then. And may you find what you need." She returned to her interrupted task, her back straight and unyielding. With misgivings, Maerad felt Sirkana's sternness concealed a deep sorrow.

From the storehouse, Maerad and Dharin went straight back to the dog stables. Maerad watched from a safe distance while Dharin skilfully harnessed six of the dogs. "The others can run behind until we get out of Murask," he said, looking up. "They won't fit through the tunnels if I harness them all. We can both walk alongside until then."

They left the Howe through another tunnel by the dog pens. It was much shorter than the winding tunnel through which Maerad had entered, since the wall here was scarcely thicker than the length of a man, and was obviously designed for the dog sleds. It was guarded by a warden who, in comical contrast to the man who had let her in, was taller even than Dharin and thin as a stick. He was, however, equally silent as he went through the laborious system of locking and unlocking the three gates; Maerad wondered why Murask specialized in such surly door wardens.

They emerged onto a flat area high over a snowy slope: before them the side of the Howe swept down like the side of a mountain, smoothly covered in snow. It would be impossible to climb, Maerad thought, as she looked down the slope. But going down was another matter. The sled sat on top of a drift of snow, like a boat on water; it reminded Maerad of nothing so much as the *White Owl* perched on the crest of a huge wave in the storm, in the breathless moment before it plunged into an abyss.

Dharin told Maerad to get into the sled, and then began to harness the rest of the dogs. They were whining now, eager to go, their tails wagging. In a surprisingly short time he had harnessed them all, and the fifteen dogs fanned out in a row, testing their shoulders against the weight of the sled, but not as yet moving. Maerad was surprised; somehow she had expected them to be harnessed like oxen to a cart, one behind the other.

"This way, every dog sees what is in front," said Dharin, when she asked why. "They perfer it. Though they all still follow Claw."

He climbed on to his perch behind Maerad, made one last check that everything was in place, and cried out "*Ot!*"

The dogs immediately started running, and with a jerk the sled moved over the lip of the slope. Then they were moving downhill, gathering speed at a reckless rate, the dogs fanned out in front of them. Maerad clutched the side rails until her knuckles were white and shut her eyes. Her stomach seemed to have been left on top of the Howe wall.

Just as Maerad had decided they must crash, or at least run the dogs over, the sled righted itself with a slight bump, and slowed down. She opened her eyes and looked around cautiously.

At first they ran alongside the high wall of Murask, its shadow falling chill across them, but in a very short time they had passed it and were running over the Arkiadera Plains. But they were not the plains as Maerad had walked them so short a time before: they were now a brilliant expanse of white stretching in every direction, broken only by the dark line of trees that grew alongside the river. Maerad leaned over the side of the sled to look behind them for a last glimpse of Murask. Covered with snow, the Howe seemed even stranger than it had before, a huge solitary mound risen from the shadowless flatness of the plains. It was now falling swiftly behind them.

The glare thrown up from the bright sunlight was dazzling, and remembering Dharin's strictures about blindness, Maerad drew her hood over her face so her eyes were shaded. The icy wind blew into her face, stinging her skin, and her heart rose in sudden exhilaration. She turned to Dharin.

"This is wonderful!" she said.

He grinned down at her. "I told you," he said. "There is no better way to travel. Who needs roads?"

They continued all day, heading in a north-easterly direction. Every now and then the dogs would get their traces tangled, and Dharin would stop and sort them out. It was a chance for Maerad to get out and stretch her legs, before she climbed back into her seat.

After a while, the motion of the sled lulled her asleep. She dreamed she was in a ship of bone, sailing across a sea of ice; it seemed she was looking for another dream, but she couldn't remember what it was. High above her in the sky hung bright curtains of light, and she reached up her hands to touch them. They were very cold, sending an icy thrill through her whole body, and afterwards her fingers fell off her hands. She looked at her fingerless hands with neither surprise nor horror, thinking to herself that she didn't need fingers to play music, but then someone who was both present and absent, someone with Cadvan's voice, said, "Nonsense!" and she woke up with a start.

The sun had moved across the sky in its low trajectory along the horizon, but the landscape looked no different.

"It's easy for some," said Dharin.

Maerad sat up, rubbing her eyes. "It's very warm and comfortable, with all those furs you put here," she said. She looked at the dogs, who were running as swiftly now as they had when they had first started. "How do the dogs still run so fast?"

"They are very strong. And they are eager."

When the sun was close to the horizon, they stopped for the

night. Dharin unharnessed the dogs and fed them, while Maerad prepared a meal from their stores. Then Dharin put up the tent, an ingenious device made of springy canes of willow wood and well oiled skins. When it was unfolded, it miraculously snapped open to make a small two-man tent with a firm, waterproof floor. At the front of the tent were long flaps of skin which could be lashed to the sled itself, at its uncovered end, anchoring the tent to the ground. It made two different quarters: a very small space where Maerad and Dharin could sit and eat, warming themselves by the stove; and the sled, where they slept. Maerad was enchanted by it, and made Dharin open and close it a few times, just to see it spring up; and Dharin, who had made the tent, was quite happy to oblige her. To Maerad, who had been used to sleeping in the open in all sorts of weather, a tent was a luxury; but Dharin laughed when she said this, and commented that in the north shelter was no luxury, but a necessity, if she did not want to become a human ice block.

They both ate their evening meal sitting outside on the toe of the sled, watching the sun sink over the plains, a burning globe of fire in an orange sky that cast a deep golden light over the snow.

"It's beautiful," said Maerad dreamily.

"It is," said Dharin. "Perilously beautiful. When we get past Tlon, we begin to reach the real winter land. That is lovely beyond description, and deadly."

"Have you been there before?" asked Maerad.

"Once. I travel far; it irks me to be shut up all winter, which is the best time to travel, although I like to be in Murask for the midwinter festival. I first went to Tlon when I was ten, with my father. He traded furs and other things with the northern clans. He was a great driver."

"Is he dead now, then?" Maerad squinted across at Dharin, examining his face.

"Yes. He did not return, five years ago now. I was eighteen and already a man. It was a great grief to my mother. She joined another clan, and now goes south each year. She has not been able to return this year. I hoped to see her before I left, but I could not."

"And do you have brothers and sisters?" asked Maerad.

"No. There were none after me. My mother was very ill after I was born; I was a very big baby, and she nearly died in labour."

They both sat in silence, eating their meal. Maerad thought about Dharin's life, which seemed in a different way as harsh as hers, and wondered whether to tell him who she was, and that they were cousins. Something held her back; perhaps principally the thought that doing so would entail her telling him that she had deceived him in the first place.

Despite being only a passenger, Maerad felt strangely exhausted, and as soon as it was dark they prepared for sleep. Dharin tethered the dogs to the sled, and they curled up, nose to tail, and went to sleep on the snow.

"Should we set a watch?" asked Maerad, ready to volunteer to be first. But Dharin laughed.

"We could not get a better watch than these dogs," he said. "They will rouse us if anything stirs within a league. They have better ears than either of us."

Possibly not, Maerad thought, thinking of her Bard hearing; but she did not demur. It was a relief to think that she would have unbroken sleep for a change.

They slept side by side in the sled. Ordinarily Maerad might have felt self conscious about this arrangement, but Dharin was so casual about it that she didn't feel bothered at all and he was, after all, kin. He simply settled himself among the furs, said, "Dreams of Light, then," and was almost instantly asleep. It took Maerad a little longer to sleep, but not much.

In less than two days, Maerad felt that she had always lived this way, travelling in a sled through the snow. The landscape seemed endless and unchanging; they had left the river line behind and now swept over the heart of the Arkiadera Plains. She saw many birds – strange birds with feathered feet, which could run across the snow, and big crows, startlingly black against the whiteness. More occasionally, she spotted hunting eagles, circling on updrafts of wind. She also saw little white animals that Dharin told her were a kind of weasel called zaninks which the northern Pilanel trapped for their warm fur. "The fur in your jacket is of this kind," he said. "It is the best protection against the cold that you can find."

Occasionally they saw herds of the shaggy deer, which Dharin told her were of a northern species the Pilanel called oribanik, and which were herded for their meat and milk. They were very big, sometimes standing higher than a horse, with dappled coats, and the males had huge branching antlers.

On the third day, the clear weather turned. The temperature dropped perceptibly as a bitter wind began to blow from the north-west. Dharin wrapped a cloth around his face to stop his nose from freezing, so that all that was visible was the glint of his eyes. Maerad did the same. Dharin had been right, this was a different kind of cold. As the day continued, the wind picked up and a thin snow began to fall. "It will be a cold night," said Dharin that evening. "And I think a blizzard tomorrow. It is a strange wind. A gift from the Winterking."

Maerad looked up sharply. "Do you think so?" she said anxiously.

"Oh, that is a saying among my people, for weather from the north-west. It blows bitterly."

"Still, you could be right," said Maerad broodingly. "He has pursued me since Annar."

Dharin was silent for a time, and then said, "Perhaps, Mara, you can tell me what it is that you are doing. Sirkana told me that you were on quest to see the Wise Kindred, that if I took you there, it could be perhaps the most important thing I had ever done. But she told me no more. I had guessed that it was something to do with the Winterking, but nothing else."

Maerad studied Dharin's face. He looked back earnestly, his gentle eyes enquiring and a little shy.

"You're right," said Maerad. "It is not fair to ask you to risk your life for me, without knowing why. Well, it is a long story."

Dharin settled back. "I like stories," he said.

"First, Mara is not my real name," said Maerad. "My proper name is Maerad of Pellinor, and I am a *Dhillarearën*, a Bard."

Dharin's eyebrows went up. "I did not guess that," he said. "Although I knew there was more to you than there seemed. But then, I'm surprised that you are frightened of the dogs. If you are a *Dhillarearën*, you can speak to them in a way I cannot."

Maerad nodded, and then pondered the truth of what he said. She had not used this aspect of the Speech much, except with Imi, whom she still missed with a fierce ache. And she was not otherwise afraid of wild creatures.

"Fears don't always make sense," she said. "I have been too frightened to speak to them. Well, I have never seen dogs like yours before. Maybe I will try later."

"So, your real name is Maerad." Dharin did not look surprised, and Maerad supposed he had already guessed that Mara was not her real name. "And what is your story?"

"Well, actually, I am your cousin. My father was Dorn à Triberi, Sirkana's brother. My mother was First Bard at the School of Pellinor. But I scarcely knew my father, he died when I was very little."

Now Dharin did look surprised, but he smiled. "I should have known we were kin," he said. "I felt as if I already knew you. Good, good. Well, Mara – I mean, Maerad – you must tell me everything."

Even in their small tent, crouched over the stove, the air was cold. Outside the wind was beginning to howl, and the thin skins flapped. Maerad shivered and drew her furs closer around her; she was glad even of this small shelter. She took a breath and began the story of her life, which she had told, how many times now?

Dharin was a good listener; he sat in attentive silence for the whole tale. When she had finished, Maerad looked up at him. His eyes were downcast.

"Thank you, Maerad," he said. "I think it is a very sad story, yours. Well, I understand a little now. And I understand why Sirkana said to me what she did."

Maerad was grateful for his simple acceptance. She had felt guilty about deceiving him, and fearful that her deceit would harm the trust between them.

"I'm glad you're my cousin," she said. "I wanted to tell you before, but I felt I couldn't."

"There is no need to excuse caution, in days like these," said Dharin. Despite herself, Maerad yawned, and he smiled gently. "We will have a tough day tomorrow," he said. "We must sleep." He put out the stove, storing it carefully by where their feet would be when they lay down. Then he kissed Maerad on both cheeks. "Sleep well, cousin."

"Sleep well," replied Maerad. That night she slept almost as soon as her eyes closed.

The next few days' travelling was not as pleasant as it had been. It was not quite a blizzard, just endless snow and cold air. Dharin slowed their pace, watching anxiously for signs of trees or other obstacles. Maerad covered her face, and then tried to snuggle under the skins and sleep. She was mostly bored; there was nothing to look at, and it was very cold.

Living so closely with the dogs did much to allay Maerad's fear of them; they were savage and half wild, but they did her no harm, treating her, she thought, with a kind of friendly contempt. She began to tell one from the other, and to see their different personalities. She could recognize Claw, with her black coat and dramatic white ruff. She was sober and responsible, and kept the team in line. There was also a young grey dog called Ponto, the youngest on the team, who often annoyed the older dogs by trying to chew their tails and wanting to play when they were all resting, and who somehow reminded her of Hem; and a big grey-and-black dog called Neck, for the strange white dapples around his throat. She still got the others more or less mixed up, but she was learning.

Since the beginning of their journey, Dharin had insisted that Maerad should learn to drive the sled, and one afternoon she gave in. She stood on the ledge at the back, while Dharin sat in her usual place, and she took the harness in her hands. "Now, say: *Ot!*" said Dharin, giving her the Pilanel word for "go". She said it, but nothing happened. "Say it again, but more firmly," said Dharin. She tried again, but still the dogs took no notice. This time, Maerad felt a bit annoyed, and before Dharin could give her further instruction, she used the word from the Speech: "*Imil!*"

The dogs all leapt forward. With a certain smugness, Maerad could feel their surprise, and she opened her hearing; as they ran they were complaining to one another. *Who is she?* And *You never told me she was a wolf tongue!* and *Shut your jaws, wooden teeth, and keep running.* Maerad laughed out loud, and Dharin looked up at her, impressed.

"That made them take notice," he said. "Well, maybe I do not have to teach you anything. All the commands are by voice: you say, 'right', 'left', 'stop', as you wish."

"I know nothing of this land," said Maerad. "Or where I am

going. It's no use being able to tell them to go, if you do not know where you are going."

Despite the team's sudden obedience, Maerad found driving unnerving; she felt out of control. When it came time to disentangle their leads again, she handed the reins back to Dharin. "If you want a rest, and can tell me which way to go, then I am happy to drive," she said. "But I don't want to cause an accident."

"I'll take that offer," said Dharin. "It's easy through the Arkiadera; it's just flat and there are no rivers in this part of the plains. All you have to do is keep driving straight."

After that, Maerad took the reins at least once a day. The more she drove the sled, feeling the team's responsiveness to her voice and hands, the more her fear of the dogs subsided, although she was always careful to remain respectful. In a few days, she was helping to feed them and could watch the dogs with equanimity as they snarled and snapped at each other and tore apart the frozen joints of meat.

The journey to Tlon was less than one hundred and twenty leagues north-west, as the crow flies. Their route was slightly longer, as Dharin was skirting the river that curved north of Murask. They reached Tlon in five days, and it was only then that Maerad appreciated how fast they were travelling.

From the outside, Tlon looked very like Murask, a huge snow-covered hill in the otherwise flat plains, but Maerad never had a chance to look inside. Dharin had packed enough supplies in the sled for four weeks' travel, and here he merely stopped to chat with the door warden to find news of conditions further north. Maerad stood behind him, stamping her boots on the snow, her breath making ice on the fur of her hood, as he rang the bell. She thought that with such clothes, she had no need for disguise; no one could have told whether she was a man or a woman.

The door warden answered quickly, greeting Dharin

enthusiastically by name. Unlike those at Murask, the door warden of Tlon was a fount of information. He whiled away his boring job by talking to anyone he could, trading titbits of gossip, weather lore, rumours and news. Dharin clearly knew him well, and they chatted for a long time. Maerad couldn't understand what they were saying, as they spoke in Pilanel, and she was getting colder and colder standing about in the wind, so she walked around in circles, kicking at the snow.

Unlike the snow surrounding Murask, which had been soft and powdery, this was deeply packed and harder than earth; it had been snowing here for much longer than it had down south. Dharin confirmed this when he stopped talking to the door warden and came back to the sled, where the dogs were lying down in their traces, snapping idly at the snow as it circled around their heads.

"Nok was saying that they've never had a winter this early. Nearly ten clans are not home yet, and they have short supplies. And those that have come from the north talk of treacherous conditions, and Jussack raids, many more than in other years."

"Jussacks?" said Maerad. "Mirka spoke of them."

"The Pilani Howes were built long ago, long before Jussacks appeared in the north. But they have served us well," said Dharin. "There were other enemies then, who have now passed beyond knowledge. The Pilani have always returned to the Howes – to tell our stories, to share, to court, and for the midwinter festivals. But for many years now, they also return for safety."

"But Mirka said the Jussacks attack on horses," said Maerad. "Surely they are not a threat in the winter?"

"In summer they use horses, which they steal from us. No Pilani clan goes out unarmed these days. But the winter settlements have rich stores, and if the Jussacks could conquer them, they could rid Zmarkan of all the Pilani peoples. They have tried more than once, but the Howes are strong. They will not rest until the Pilani are driven from the face of the earth.

"The Howes used only to have one gate, and that one was always open. Not any more. Jussacks use sleds, and they are a danger in winter as well as summer. But we are stronger than they realize, and we are stubborn." Dharin grinned, his teeth gleaming through the shade of his hood. "They will not defeat us."

XIX

THE NORTH GLACIER

AFTER they left Tlon their course changed, bearing more directly north. That night, as they crouched inside their tent, which shuddered under the pressure of the wind, Dharin explained that the Arkiadera Plains, which stretched over all Zmarkan, here met their northern border. "From now on, we will be journeying through Hramask, and we soon reach places where the snow never melts," he said. "But no one lives in the centre, it is too harsh; the Hramask peoples all live on the coast."

"Are we nearing the Winterking's realm, then?" said Maerad.

"No. We are moving away from it," Dharin said. "He rules the north-east, it is said. Well, there are those who say that the Winterking's stronghold does not exist, even if it once did. But whether it does or no, no Pilani willingly travels far north-east."

Maerad pondered this. "So who rules the north-west, then?" she asked.

"No one. Or no one that I ever heard," Dharin said. "The snow and ice is its own master."

Maerad tried to recall what she had been told of the Winterking. His name, she remembered, was Arkan, and like Ardina he was a powerful Elidhu. He had been Ardina's adversary during the Elemental Wars, long ages before, and he had allied himself with the Nameless One to crush the Light, which had led to the Great Silence. The ice creatures, the iridugul, had been his creations, and also the stormdogs. Even his emissaries were more fearsome than almost anything she had seen.

"What do you know of the Winterking, Dharin?" she asked, at last.

"Oh, he is but a legend to the Pilani peoples," he said. "Though some say he is worshipped by the Jussacks, and their persecution of us is his revenge. For it is said we helped to cast him down after the Great Cold, when the Iron King, him you call the Nameless One, covered all this world in terror and darkness. Then he was bound to remain beyond the Ice Sea, in the far north, and was not permitted to dwell in his stronghold, the Arkan-da, near the Idrom Unt, those mountains that you Annarens call the Osidh Nak."

Maerad nodded. "And the Arkan-da is to the east, then?" she said, trying to get her bearings. "Well, I am glad if that means we are travelling away from the Winterking. The further I am from him, the better I feel."

This was not strictly true: Maerad still felt a cold will pressing on her mind. She automatically shielded herself against it as soon as she woke up, and kept a private vigilance for any sign of the Winterking's creatures. But Dharin's words comforted her all the same.

Over the next few days the wind fell away, leaving behind it cold, blue skies, and Maerad was able to see that the landscape was at last beginning to change. To their right, in the distance, she could see the ghostly outlines of mountains, and they began to strike little woods of spruce and firs, startlingly green against the snow. The land here was hilly rather than mountainous, with more pitfalls for the unwary driver: stumps of dead trees, or lichened rocks that jutted out of the snow. Dharin drove with greater caution and Maerad only took the reins when he could clearly see the way ahead.

Six days from Tlon, they came over a huge ridge, sparsely dotted with firs, and saw before them a wide expanse of ice more than a league wide that filled the valleys between the white hills.

Dharin stopped his team and looked over it, shading his eyes.

"This is the Ippanuk Glacier," he said. "Probably the most dangerous thing we have to cross."

"Glacier?" asked Maerad.

"A river of ice. It comes from the Votul, the mountains you see there." He waved his hand to their right, where a ghostly range vanished into the hazy distance. "Well, there's no time like now," he said, squaring his shoulders. "We can see well, and from here I think we can pick a safe path. *Ot!*"

It was the first time Dharin had betrayed anything like anxiety, and Maerad looked at the glacier with doubt; if he said it was dangerous, it must be dangerous indeed. He drove the dogs slowly down the ridge and on to the glacier, bumping over the boulders and lumps of dirty ice that littered its edges. The sound of the sled changed as soon as they hit the glacier, becoming a scraping noise rather than a smooth swish through the snow. As they moved towards its centre, Maerad realized that the glacier was not silent; it made strange grinding sounds, like rock on rock, and ominous creakings, and sometimes it sounded like the cry of some strange creature. With a shudder, she realized that it was a faint echo of the cries of the iridugul, when they had attacked her and Cadvan in the Gwalhain Pass.

The ice itself varied. Sometimes it was clear as an emerald, and she could see through green depths to what she was sure was the rocky bed of the glacier, far below them; but most often it was opaque, full of flaws and cracks. It was hypnotically beautiful. Sometimes she saw strange things, like visions, emerging through the clarities: a green tree, its branches bent as if it were caught in a storm, but utterly still, or a cloud of boulders suspended as if in midair. Once she had a glimpse of a huge beast with heavy furred shoulders and long white tusks. Dharin was frowning in concentration, so she didn't ask him if he knew what it was. It wasn't long before she saw why he moved with

such painful caution over the glacier; the dogs' claws, sharp as
they were, often slipped on the ice, and the whole was riven by
deep crevasses, which could appear without warning just below
their feet. They went too close for comfort to one, Dharin's cry
to halt causing a scrabbling of claws as they backed away from
a crevice that Dharin had not sighted earlier, its treacherous
blue-green edges opening to a bottomless darkness like a terrible mouth. The dogs liked the glacier as little as Dharin; they
kept their tails low down, and every now and then one of them
would whine with anxiety. The short day was nearing to a close
before the dogs came to the end of the glacier, their ears pricked
forward with relief, and heaved the sled up the opposite ridge.

After the glacier, they faced nothing worse than the deep
cold. Now their course was north-west again: Dharin was aiming for a point on the coast about forty leagues from the glacier,
along one of the many fingers of land that thrust out into the
frozen sea. The Labarok Isles were west from there.

"Do we sail to the isles, then?" asked Maerad, thinking about
her previous experiences of sea travel, and wondering where
they could find a boat in such uninhabited country.

"No, we drive the sled over the sea," he answered.

Maerad thought he was joking until he explained that the sea
was frozen, and they would be driving across thick ice. "Maybe
very thick, given this early winter," he said. "The Labaroks are
islands, to be sure, but in winter they might as well not be. The
sea freezes and joins them all together, except around the Isles of
Fire."

As they moved away from the mountains they started
travelling more swiftly. In less than two weeks, through the ever-
shortening days, they had traversed almost the entire expanse
of the frozen north lands, and the dogs still ran as eagerly as
they had on their first day out of Murask. Maerad's respect
for their toughness and loyalty had increased as her fears had

vanished; sometimes she even chatted idly with Claw, whose harsh, unwavering determination stirred a sense of recognition within her own breast. These dogs obeyed stern laws of necessity, which were not as strange to Maerad as she might have supposed; she had suffered a harsh childhood, and understood more intimately than most Bards the crude politics of survival. Claw referred to Dharin as "Master", and she bowed to no one else, human or animal. Since finding that Maerad possessed what the dogs called the "wolf tongue", Claw treated her with tolerance and respect, but she also made it clear that Maerad's authority over her was limited. *I will obey you*, she said. *But you are not my master.*

Three days after they had crossed the glacier, they stood at last on the shores of the Ipiilinik Igor, the Sea of Fire. They camped before heading out across the ice, and when the day was still dark and the stars sparkled frostily above them in a clear, frozen sky, they began the final leg of their journey. Travelling over the sea ice was a little like riding over the Arkiadera Plains: it was flat and they could make good speed.

The sun rose, a ball of cold flame, and Maerad looked around with wonder. The flatness of the sea was punctuated by high towers of ice, blinding white with blue shadows, which were sculpted by the wind into a multitude of bizarre shapes. Dharin told her they were icebergs, mountains of ice that had not melted over the summer and had now been trapped by the frozen sea. It was, Maerad thought, utterly strange and utterly beautiful, like something from a dream. After a couple of hours, she saw in the distance what seemed to be a great fountain of steam spouting high into the air.

"That is the first island," said Dharin. "We do not go there."

"What is it?" asked Maerad.

"These islands have many mountains of fire," he answered. "They heave up melted rock from the heart of the earth, and they make these hot fountains. Nothing lives on that island, it is scalded every two hours by boiling water. We call it Terun-Ol, the Island of Heat. If you wait, you will see the fountain disappear. There is another island, further away, that is made of mountains that make fire, the Irik-Ol. But we shall not be passing there, since it is so hot that the sea does not freeze around it, even in midwinter."

As they neared the island and then passed it, Maerad watched the plume of steam lessen and then finally disappear. Then, after a long interval, it suddenly spouted up again with a noise like thunder.

Maerad thought to herself that if anyone had told her about such a thing, she would have dismissed it as a fanciful traveller's tale – it seemed so bizarre that such extremes of heat and cold could exist in the one place.

She at first mistook the next island for another iceberg: a sheer needle of rock, it thrust straight into the sky like a high tower. Dharin said it was called the Nakti-Ol, Bird Island, because in summer huge flocks of birds would nest there. "They say that they rise in the sky like a great swarm, so many that they darken the sun," he said. "I am sad that they are gone, and that we will not see it."

The sun was already beginning to dip beneath the horizon when Dharin pointed to a low, dark rise of land ahead of them. "That is the Tolnek-Ol, the land of the Wise Kindred," he said.

Maerad squinted through the gathering darkness. The long journey here, with all its difficulties and wonders, had pushed the Treesong to the back of her mind. It had been a relief to briefly forget about who she was, to merely live with Dharin and the dogs. The quest rushed back into her mind, and apprehension tightened her breast. Now, perhaps, she might find some answers. The only problem was, she wasn't at all sure that she knew the right questions.

X X

INKA-REB

THEY reached the shore of the island well after dusk. Dharin would not set foot on the Wise Kindred's land after dark, and so they camped on the sea ice for the night. The weather was clear and still, and the countless stars opened above them, seeming like brilliant cold fruits that Maerad could simply pick out of the sky. Dharin and Maerad fed the dogs and then sat outside on the sled talking, the tent seeming too close on such a night, despite the bitter cold. It would still be some hours before they felt ready to sleep.

In the distance Maerad could hear a strange barking, which echoed through the deep silence that surrounded them. The dogs pricked up their ears, but subsided when Dharin told them to be quiet.

"What is it?" asked Maerad.

"Seals, I expect," said Dharin. "There must be a seal ground not far from here. Well, that is good news; I will ask the Wise Kindred if I may hunt here. I need more meat for the dogs."

The traditional Pilanel "telling" of the northern journey included the courtesies expected of strangers who visited the Wise Kindred. Dharin now instructed Maerad in the Pilanel tellings of the northern peoples, and she listened gravely.

"You must understand," he said seriously, "that those we call the Wise Kindred are only one of many peoples who live in the cold north. The Pilanel tell of at least twenty different peoples on the coast of Hramask, from Orun to Lebinusk, and there are probably more. And you must not think that one group is the same as the next: they have different customs and they speak different languages. The Wise Kindred are understood to be the oldest of all. Their name for themselves, Inaruskosani, means 'those who first walked on the earth'."

Maerad nodded humbly, reflecting, not for the first time, how little she knew of Edil-Amarandh and its peoples. They were more various than she had ever supposed; every time she thought she was beginning to understand the world, some other aspect would open and reveal a new ignorance.

Dharin talked on softly, enumerating the different names of the peoples of the north, and what he knew of their customs. The different peoples very seldom fought among each other; Dharin said it was because their lives were so harsh that they had no time for war.

There was, he said, a common language called Lirunik, which was used by the northern Pilanel clans and the various peoples of the far north when they needed to speak to each other. Dharin had spoken this language since he was a child, as his father had been a great trader, and he would act as interpreter.

After a while, silence fell upon them, and they just sat, listening to the sleeping grunts of the dogs and the distant coughs of the seal colony. A waxing moon let fall its chilly light over the endless white sea. To the south, Maerad could see a red glow on the horizon, where the fiery mountains of the Irik-Ol poured out the molten heart of the earth. Here, she thought, all is water, ice, fire, stone and air; the anguish of human beings seemed trivial beside such huge, elemental forces. She felt a great peace descend on her heart.

They had sat thus for some time when Maerad felt a tingling in her skin, and at the same time became conscious of a strange noise that she couldn't locate. It sounded at first like a very distant whistling, then like the ringing of countless tiny silver bells. The noise reminded her of the voice that had spoken her Truename, Elednor, when she had been instated as a Bard. It grew in intensity, sounding now like ringing, now like a hissing of water or wind, now like a faint crackling, and she turned to Dharin, a question on her lips. But Dharin had turned around, facing north, and was staring at the sky. Maerad followed his gaze and gasped.

The entire northern horizon, from east to west, was alight with curtains of quivering green light. As Maerad watched, her mouth open, the curtains shimmered and parted, revealing yet more luminous veils, which themselves vanished and reappeared in a stately dance. The colours shimmered through the entire spectrum of green, from the palest spring yellow to a deep emerald shot through with glorious purples. An awe fell over them, and they watched for an unguessable time, enraptured, until at last the dance began to flicker, and then slowly dimmed and went out.

Maerad sighed with pure happiness. "What are they?" she asked, turning to Dharin.

"We call them the heavenly dancers," he said. "Some say the lights come from the realm of the dead."

"From beyond the Gates?" Maerad looked up at the now still sky, where the Lukemoi, the pathway of the dead, blazed its white trail from horizon to horizon, barely dimmed by the moon.

"Yes. They are supposed to shine when the Gates open slightly, and the border between life and death becomes less certain. For that reason, some people fear to see the lights."

"I didn't feel afraid," said Maerad. "It was like the voices of the stars." She was silent for a time, absorbed in thought. Perhaps here she had been vouchsafed a glimpse into the pure heart of the Light: beyond the depths of the White Flame, into something stranger, colder, infinitely more mysterious.

"What do think the sound was?" she asked at last. "Was it the light singing, do you think?"

"What sound?" asked Dharin. "I heard nothing."

"There was a music. A strange music…"

"There are things you might hear, cousin, that I cannot."

"Well, whether they are to be feared or not, I am glad I saw them," said Maerad. "I will never forget them."

"Because they are beautiful, does not mean that they are not perilous," said Dharin. "But I, too, am glad."

They waited until the sun rose the following day, and in its dim light drove the sled onto the Tolnek-Ol. The island was rocky and flat, with no trees anywhere, and looked very dreary under the grey flat light. The first sign of human dwellings was what looked like columns of white smoke, which Maerad took for signs of cooking fires. But Dharin told her it was steam from hot springs. They turned towards the steam columns, and soon arrived at the island's main village, Imprutul.

They were greeted first by the barking of dogs. Several children, who were so heavily swaddled in furs they seemed almost circular, spotted them and ran towards the village, shouting. Dharin drove the sled into a clear space surrounded by a scattered collection of low, round houses made of stone and ramped with earth, which backed onto a low rocky cliff. There were a number of deer corralled by the houses, and three or four large dogs came forward, barking and growling aggressively. For a moment Maerad feared there would be a fight, but the local dogs remained at a distance.

Dharin glanced at Maerad and she sensed, with faint surprise, that he was nervous. "I hope the Telling of the Pilani is still correct," he said. "It is long years since any of our people have come this way, and things change. If they are hostile towards us, we will have to leave quickly."

Maerad nodded, her mouth suddenly dry.

"If things go well, someone will come soon," Dharin said, climbing out of the sled and sharply telling his team, who were trading insults with the village dogs, to be silent. "We just have to wait. Do not look afraid."

Soon someone came. Two people emerged from one of the houses and walked slowly towards them. Maerad couldn't tell what sex they were; she found later they were two elders, a man and a woman.

Dharin put out his hand in greeting, speaking in Lirunik. The elders nodded, and each one in turn grasped his hand, holding it gently for a time and then letting go. Dharin introduced Maerad, and they greeted her in the same way, nodding solemnly. Maerad smiled back, wishing she were not so ignorant of their language. She stood by, waiting, while Dharin and the elders conversed, trying not to look too bored or cold.

Dharin turned to Maerad at last. "I've told them who we are, and that we have come because you seek their wisdom on an important question. I have also said that I wish to do some trading. The man is called Ibikluskarini and the woman is Gunisinapli. They have told me that what wisdom they have is ours, and that they have furs to trade, and they've invited us inside."

So far, so good, thought Maerad, wondering how she was to explain to these people why she had come so far north. Because of a dream, because of a few clues scoured here and there, from a half-mad old Pilanel woman and a wise goatherd in Thorold – what sense could they possibly make of what she told them?

Dharin returned to the sled and took out a package wrapped in oilskin. He told the team to remain silent, and they sat down in the snow, their ears pricked and their tails beating on the ground, whining. The local dogs seemed to have accepted that the visitors were not a threat, but still hung around, now curious. One of the elders gave a sharp command, and the dogs sprang back and sat by the doors of their houses.

"We do not want a dogfight," muttered Dharin, as they walked towards the nearest of the round houses. "And these dogs will fight to the death, if they get in a scrap."

Then he bent to enter the low doorway of the house. Even Maerad had to stoop: the doors were made as small as possible to conserve heat, and the interiors of the houses were windowless, lit by smoky lamps burning some kind of fish oil. The smell was at first overpowering: a mixture of human fug and sour fat and fish and smoke. Maerad's eyes smarted, and it took a little while before her sight adjusted to the dim light. It was very hot: she started sweating instantly. Both she and Dharin took off their overcoats of fur for the first time in days.

She had entered a room that was much bigger than she had expected. She realized that the houses continued back into the cliff itself; there was another entrance at the far end covered with a hanging woven of some kind of rough wool. Inside were about a dozen people: an old man was working on an ivory carving, and several children, the smallest of whom was completely naked, were playing a game with some large knuckle bones. Two women and a man were working a skin, kneading it with their fingers from different ends to make it pliable and soft, and another woman was feeding an infant. They all looked up and nodded when the strangers entered, and then went back to whatever they had been doing.

In the centre of the room was a round white rug, made of many furs stitched together, and Dharin and Maerad were invited to sit down. They were given a clear spirit to drink in small round cups. The elders nodded solemnly, and Dharin nodded back (Maerad, closely following Dharin's lead, did the same) and then they downed the spirit in one big gulp. Maerad did her best, but the drink was so harsh that she nearly choked;

it was as strong as voka, a spirit distilled from turnips and other root vegetables that the men brewed in Gilman's Cot, and had as little subtlety of flavour. She recovered herself as quickly as possible, shut her eyes and finished the cup. It burned all the way down to her stomach, leaving a numb feeling behind it. She hoped fervently that custom did not dictate a second cup, and to her relief no one refilled it. Now she was so hot she desperately wanted to take off more of her many layers of clothes, but she didn't know if it would be considered rude.

Dharin was unwrapping the package he had taken from the sled. To Maerad's surprise, inside were two beautiful examples of Pilanel wood carving, delicately fashioned and enamelled in a shiny black. One was of a wolf and the other was of a ptarmigan. He gave them to the elders, bowing his head as he did so. They took them solemnly, admired them both from every angle, and then bowed their heads in thanks.

It then seemed the formalities were over, and Dharin and the elders, whose many-syllabled names Maerad could not, for the life of her, remember, plunged into a lively conversation. Maerad wiped the sweat off her forehead and tried to concentrate. Dharin told her afterwards that they were simply swapping news: news of the weather, of hunting grounds, speculations on the early winter, and general conditions in the north and in the southern plains.

It seemed that the Wise Kindred were themselves suffering a thin year after several poor summers, and although they were not yet facing famine, they feared another year would bring them to hunger. Maerad caught the word "Jussacks" once or twice; Dharin had asked if there was news of Jussack raids in the far north and told of what he had heard in Tlon. The elders told him that there had been rumours from other peoples further down the coast, but no Jussacks had ever been seen this far north.

Once the news had been exchanged, Dharin began to include

Maerad in the conversation. It was laborious, translating her questions and then translating the answers, but fortunately the elders seemed endlessly patient. Yes, they did have a story about the Song. Maerad's neck prickled. Yes, even this far north, they had memories of the terrible darkness and winter that had almost destroyed their people, many generations ago, and they had seen signs in the sky and in the snow, and in the entrails of animals, that made them fear that such times might be returning. They remembered both the Winterking and the Nameless One, although they had different names in the songs of their people. But no, although they kept the stories, they could not tell Maerad what the Split Song was. And as for trees, there were no trees this far north.

At this answer, Maerad was instantly downcast. Had she come this far, only to find that the answer lay elsewhere? But the woman was still speaking.

Dharin nodded, and then turned to Maerad. "Gunisinapli says that you should speak, if you wish to know about such things, with their Singer. He is called Inka-Reb. He lives by himself with the wolves, a little distance from here. She warns that he does not speak to everybody, and may refuse to see you. But they say of him that he walks between the living and the dead, and that he knows what the dead know."

"Could he be a *Dhillarearën*, then?" asked Maerad. Dharin asked Gunisinapli, and she simply lifted her hands in a gesture that seemed to mean, maybe, maybe not.

"Well, if he is, I can speak with him," said Maerad. "Well, I suppose that is what I should do. How then should I visit him?"

There followed a list of instructions to which Dharin listened intently. He turned to Maerad. "You will have to purify yourself first. That means that you must live alone in a special hut in the village for a day and a night, fasting and preparing your mind and soul and body with song. You must not sleep. First, before you sing, you must bathe yourself in the spring. After you have sung, you must again wash, and dress yourself, and without speaking to anybody else walk humbly to his place with a clear heart, or a clear desire, the word's not quite translatable. You must take an offering; they say that he usually likes to be given meat. They will leave the offering for you by the door of the hut. Then he may choose to speak to you."

"How will I find the way?"

"They will tell you beforehand. They say it is easy to find."

Maerad nodded, thinking that if the springs were hot, then she could actually have a bath, a luxury she had not enjoyed for so long that she had almost forgotten what it was like. "And when they say "prepare yourself with song" do they mean special songs? Or can I sing my own?"

Dharin asked, and this led to a long debate between the elders. Finally he said, "They have their own songs for their own people, but they think it best that you use your own."

"When can I begin, then? I should prepare as soon as possible."

"You can go to the hut when the sun rises tomorrow. Then at sunrise the next day you can see Inka-Reb."

"That sounds good," said Maerad. "But what will you do, while I'm there?"

"I have work to do," said Dharin. "We need meat. The elders have given me permission to visit their hunting grounds."

Maerad took the instruction to prepare herself with song as a chance to play her lyre. Apart from her clothes, it was the only thing she took with her into the hut. It was a smaller version of the village houses, windowless, with a small door fastened with two layers of hide, and a chimney, which let out smoke and steam. Inside was an oil lamp and a stone seat, and a rough stone bath into which bubbled warm water. Maerad tested it, wondering how hot the water actually was; it was deliciously warm. With a feeling of luxury she threw off all her clothes and climbed in, at last dissolving off her body the accumulated grime of weeks of travel. When she had had enough, she stepped out, dripping onto the stone floor, and then wondered how to dry herself; there was nothing like a towel to hand. In the end, since the hut was so warm, she just sat naked on the seat until she had dried off. Then she put on some clean silk underclothes she had preserved since Murask, and thought about song.

It had been a long time since Maerad had played much music. A long time, really, since she had felt like a Bard at all. She lifted her lyre and softly stroked the strings, noticing that the calluses on her fingers had softened from not playing. The lyre had been hers for almost as long as she could remember; it had once belonged to her mother, and that was principally why she treasured it, although she knew now there were other reasons why it was precious.

Well, she thought; how shall I begin? She sat in silence for a time, gathering in her body's memory, where they were stored in her hands and her heart, all the songs she had been taught and had heard over many years, wondering which one was the best to begin with. At last, she realized the answer was obvious: *The Song of Making*, the first song of Barding, which told of the creation of Edil-Amarandh. She drew her fingers over the strings in the familiar chords, and began, singing in the Speech rather than in Annaren:

First was dark, and the darkness
Was all mass and all dimension, although without touch
And the darkness was all colours and all forms, although
    without sight

And the darkness was all music and all sound, although
    without hearing
And it was all perfumes, and all tastes, sour and bitter and
    sweet
But it knew not itself.

And the darkness thought, and it thought without mind
And the thought became mind and the thought quickened
And the thought was Light.

First was dark... Maerad mused over the words. She had never really thought about this before. Was it the same Dark that hunted her, or another Dark, perhaps, in the same way that the heavenly lights she had seen the night before had been the Light, but not the same Light that the Bards spoke of, the White Flame of Norloch. She let the thoughts run through her mind like ripples through a stream, letting them flow each into the next, and felt the music moving through her, calming her mind and waking some deep part of her that she hadn't known was asleep.

Over the rest of the day and through the long night, Maerad played until her fingers were sore, and her voice hoarse. She did not sing all the time. She would pause between songs, and think, and all the memories they recalled would swell inside her: the dour face of Mirlad, her first teacher, bent over his harp, or Cadvan singing in the Hall at Innail. She had not played for so long that she felt like a starving person who is suddenly offered a feast; and the words of the songs seemed fresh in her mind as if she had never heard them before, or had failed to understand them until now.

The day and night passed more quickly than she had expected. When she saw the first light gleaming through the edges of the doorway, she bathed again and dressed herself carefully. Then, packing her lyre into its case and slinging it on her back, she took a deep breath and walked outside. By the doorway, as promised, was a package of seal meat for her to take to Inka-Reb. She picked it up; it was big and heavy.

The world seemed very bright to her raw eyes, and she shaded her face. She walked as she had been instructed along a path lined with white stones that led away from the houses towards another part of the springs. Shortly she arrived at the mouth of a big cave. She saw, with deep alarm, that a magnificent white wolf stood by the cave mouth. It looked at her with ice-blue eyes and vanished inside. Maerad stood for a moment to gather her courage, and then followed it.

The light from the cave's entrance went back quite a distance, and she saw that its walls narrowed and then seemed to come to a dead end. There was no sign of the wolf, and she realized that the cave must turn further in. Treading carefully, she walked forward and found it made a right-angled turn into a low, dark passage. About a hundred paces away she saw a dim light.

Slowly Maerad walked along the passage, wondering what she would find at the end. A pack of wolves? She was terrified, but some deep calm persisted from her day and night alone, and she pushed down her fear and walked on. It seemed to take a long time, but at last she emerged at the other end of the passage into a huge round chamber. Here, on the threshold, she stopped.

There was, indeed, a pack of wolves in the cave, and the first thing she noticed was the feral stink of predators. Bones were scattered on the floor; they were probably bones from deer, but to Maerad they looked unsettlingly human. There were between twenty or thirty wolves, all seated on the floor in a semicircle with their eyes fixed upon her. None of them moved.

In the centre of the circle was the biggest man Maerad had

ever seen. He seemed almost twice her height, and was enormously fat. His long black hair was plaited in a dozen greased braids that hung down to his waist, and he was naked, his skin smeared with what seemed to be a mixture of fat and ash. He wore a bracelet made of carved bone around his upper arm, and a pendant of black stone hung around his neck from a thong of leather. He was squatting next to a pot suspended over a small fire, in which he was cooking some sort of stew. He turned his head and stared at Maerad, and, very slowly, stood up.

There was a long silence. Maerad wondered whether she ought to offer greetings, or whether to wait until he acknowledged her. At last, when the silence and the stillness had stretched her nerves to breaking point, she spoke. Without thinking about it, she used the Speech.

"Will you speak with me, Inka-Reb?"

At the sound of her voice, the wolves' ears pricked forward. Maerad realized she hadn't asked what happened to those with whom Inka-Reb would not speak. Were they eaten by the wolves? Perhaps the bones on the floor were all those luckless enough not to pass the test, whatever the test was.

But Inka-Reb spoke. His voice was deep and liquid, and boomed across the cave.

"Why should I speak with you, daughter of the Voice? What have you to say to me, that I should listen?"

"I know not, Inka-Reb," said Maerad. "I do not know what you like to listen to. But I hope that you will share your wisdom with me."

At that Inka-Reb laughed. "I think, daughter of the Voice, that you have nothing to say to me. Leave, and I will tell my wolves not to eat you."

"No," said Maerad, with more temerity than she felt. "I won't leave. You don't know what I might ask you."

"You won't leave?" Inka-Reb made the smallest gesture,

and the wolf pack slowly rose from their haunches, snarling and baring their teeth. Maerad gave them a terrified glance and swallowed.

"No. I ask something that may help your own people as well as mine. I have travelled very far to see you. I won't leave until you answer me."

The low growl of the wolves rumbled through the cavern and Maerad felt her legs beginning to tremble. She hoped it wasn't obvious. "And so you threaten me?" said Inka-Reb, drawing his eyebrows together in a massive frown.

"No, I do not threaten you." Maerad licked her dry lips. "I beg you. Not only for my sake. My life is a small one and doesn't count for much. But I am Elednor, the Fire Lily of Edil-Amarandh, the One who was foretold. And I need to know what the Treesong is, if the Dark is not to hold sway again in this land and in many others."

Inka-Reb put out his hand, and to Maerad's unutterable relief the wolves subsided, lying down on the ground and putting their heads on their front paws.

"Is that so?" said Inka-Reb. "So, it was you of whom the dead warned me, in my dreams. Well, maybe I will talk with you. But what have you brought me?"

"I–I brought this," said Maerad, holding out the seal meat. Inka-Reb looked at it briefly, and nodded, but did not move forwards to take it, leaving her unsure whether or not he had accepted it. "I wanted to ask – to ask you if you knew what the Treesong is. And where I could find it."

There was a long silence while Inka-Reb looked steadily at her, his face expressionless. Then he stepped forward and took the meat, and returned to his pot.

"I think you are a liar," he said. "And I do not see why I should speak to a liar."

Maerad was so taken aback she just gaped at him. Then,

with crushing contempt, Inka-Reb squatted down as if she were not there, and poked his fire. She was already dismissed.

All the blood rushed to Maerad's head, and she lost her temper. Entirely forgetting the wolves who sat around her, poised to tear her limb from limb, she marched up to Inka-Reb. Although he was squatting, she was no taller than he was.

"I have come countless days, through great dangers, to speak to you. And you say, without knowing who I am at all, that I am a liar." Maerad's voice was shaking with rage, and there seemed to be a red mist before her eyes. "I have lost my dearest friend who – who *died* so I could reach you, I have suffered and wept and toiled, and given my all. And all you can say is, go away, I will not talk to a liar. How *dare* you, you selfish, fat—"

Inka-Reb turned around to face her, and this time Maerad felt his power. At the same time that she realized that here was a *Dhillarearën* who possessed powers at least the equal of hers, he took her hand in one of his massive paws.

"I will speak with you then," he said. "Since you desire it more than your life. That is worthy of praise. But I still say you are a liar."

Maerad stood before him, her chest heaving, and met his eyes. He seemed to be laughing at her.

"Why do you say I am a liar?" she asked pugnaciously. "I don't lie."

"Daughter of the Voice, every human being in the world lies. Some know they are lying and some do not. I think you do not know you are a liar. But still you are a liar."

"If I don't know I'm a liar, then how can I tell the truth?" asked Maerad.

"Exactly," said Inka-Reb.

Nonplussed, Maerad stopped and swallowed. Her anger passed as swiftly as it had risen, and she was suddenly uncomfortably aware again of the wolves. They lay just as they had before, their heads on their front paws.

"All I want to know is what the Treesong is. And where I might find it. That's all."

"The Treesong." Inka-Reb gave her a long stare, and then, leaving her in the middle of the semicircle of wolves, stepped out towards the walls of the cavern. In little niches on the walls flickered oil lamps, and there were also dozens of objects: carvings on bone and stone, and other things that Maerad did not recognize. Before long he came back, holding a tusk. He handed it to Maerad.

"This is half of the Split Song," he said. "I think you know of the Split Song?"

Maerad nodded, her heart hammering in her chest.

"Take it and look at it," said Inka-Reb.

Maerad took the tusk. It was clearly very old, the ivory yellow and cracked. On its surface were carved some strange characters. They seemed unaccountably familiar, and Maerad rubbed her fingers over them. Where had she seen them before?

"Do you know what this is?" asked Inka-Reb.

"No," said Maerad.

Then Maerad almost dropped the tusk. With a shock of recognition that went down her spine like a wash of cold water, she realized that she knew the shapes of the carvings as well as she knew her own hand; she had stroked them over and over again all through her childhood, trying to puzzle out what they were.

They were the same ten runes that were carved on her lyre.

She looked up at Inka-Reb in wonder, her fear and irritation forgotten. "I do know these runes," she said.

"Each one of those marks is a tree," said Inka-Reb. "And each one of those trees is a verse, and each verse is a mark of time. But it is only half the Song."

"But how can I read it?" asked Maerad in despair. "I don't know how to read it. And where do I find the other half?"

"I read the stars and the wind and the bones of animals," said Inka-Reb. "I can read stone and shadow and snow. But I cannot tell you how to read this Song. It is a blasphemy." He spat on the ground.

"You think that the Light will find the Song and make it whole, and then the world will be well. But I say that if either the Dark or the Light unite the halves of the Song, then that day will be catastrophe."

"What do you mean?" Maerad looked up at him. "How will it be catastrophe? And do you know who could tell me what it means?"

"You ask too many questions." Inka-Reb stared over her head. Now he looked bored. "I have told you what you asked for," he said. "I can tell you nothing more. Now you can take your lies and go."

Maerad looked up, another question on her lips, but Inka-Reb's face told her the interview was over. He held out his hand for the tusk and she gave it back to him, bowing her head.

"I thank you," she said.

"Go," he said. The wolves were beginning to stand up, and were looking at Maerad with less-than-friendly eyes, their hackles rising, their lips drawing back from their teeth.

She went.

XXI

THE JUSSACKS

MAERAD dreamed. In her dream she stood in the ruins of Pellinor, not as she had last seen them, fleeing as a terrified child with her mother through the burning streets, but as they must be now. She stood among broken stone walls, their blackened outlines softened and sometimes completely concealed by ivies and other creeping plants, in what must have been the central circle of the School. The remains of paving still existed, broken by weeds and even a sapling here and there, but it was still mainly a clear space. In the middle of the circle, at a distance, she saw a figure bent over a fire, cloaked and hooded in black. At first she thought it was a Hull; then she realized it was a Bard. It reminded her of Cadvan, and she almost cried out his name; then she remembered that Cadvan was dead, and the figure disappeared.

She woke, and the dream vanished completely from her mind, leaving behind it a ghost-print of grief. It was still some hours before the sun would rise. Beside her Dharin snored gently, and outside the tent she could hear a dog growling in its sleep. Inside her furs she was warm, but her nose was very cold. Soon it would be time to rise and to prepare for their long journey back south. And what then?

She lay on her back, her heart heavy as a stone in her breast, trying to rally her spirits. She had completed part of her quest; but, all the same, her feeling of failure was overwhelming. All she had discovered on her long journey north was that she had carried the Treesong with her all her life.

It was like some bad joke, she thought. Even though she knew the Treesong as well as her own hands, unlocking its riddle was as far beyond her as it had ever been. Even a Bard as learned as Nelac hadn't recognized the runes, let alone known how to read them. Her dream of the destruction of Turbansk came back to her with agonizing clarity: all those who had put their trust in her had been mistaken. Cadvan and Dernhil, Darsor and Imi, had died for nothing.

It was no use having the Treesong if she did not know what it meant.

She battled her despair all that day, as she and Dharin packed to set off once again over the ice sea. They took their leave of the Wise Kindred, who pressed on them gifts of food: unprepossessing packages of meat that looked to be mainly fat, and two yellow ivory tusks, on which were carved the images of a seal and a fish. Maerad had bowed, touched, and accepted the gifts feeling that she was a fraud.

Since Maerad had returned from Inka-Reb's cave and reported that Inka-Reb had spoken to her, she and Dharin had been treated with respect bordering on awe; it seemed that he barely deigned to speak to anybody. But this only compounded her feeling of failure. It might have been better if Inka-Reb had said nothing; what he had told her had made her more responsible than she had been before, without giving her any clue what to do about it.

Dharin had merely asked her if she had found out what she needed. She told him briefly what Inka-Reb had said, and he had shrugged. "Well, then, we must find someone who can read the runes," he said.

Maerad looked at him. "Where?"

"I don't know," he said, smiling. "But if they are written, they must be able to be read."

Not if the only people who can read them are dead, thought

Maerad; but she didn't say it out loud.

Dharin asked nothing further, and didn't mention her quest again. Maerad was very glad of his easy, undemanding company over the following days. They retraced their route over the sea and back down through the Ippan Peninsula towards the Ippanuk Glacier, easily falling back into the routine they had established on their way there. The weather continued fine, and they travelled through days of icy, clear skies and nights of still cold. In five days they reached the glacier and re-crossed it without incident. Dharin estimated that they would be back in Murask within a week, if the good weather continued. Maerad dreaded returning; she had the Treesong, or at least half of it, but what could she do with it? What was she to do next?

On the day after their crossing of the glacier they had stopped in a dip for the hourly untangling of the dog traces. They worked from different ends of the team, meeting in the middle, so it took very little time. Maerad's fear of the dogs had now completely vanished, and she worked in a methodical, businesslike way.

They had just finished their task, and were deciding whether to have their midday meal before moving on, when the team began to bark and howl, straining at their traces. Maerad had never seen them do this; they were, as a rule, silent when they were working. She looked towards Dharin, and saw with alarm that he was running to the sled, standing on the driver's ledge, and was waving her to get in. She looked around wildly, but could see no sign of any disturbance. She sent out her hearing, and realized why the dogs were barking: there were sleds nearing them, from either side. She saw with sudden dread that the hollow in which they had stopped was the perfect place for an ambush. And the air was so still that even the dogs had sensed no one near until it was too late to avoid them.

Maerad instinctively felt her side for her sword, and realized, cursing, that it was in the sled. She had fallen out of the habit of carrying it, finding it too clumsy with all her winter clothing. She ran to the sled and climbed into her usual seat, dragging her sword from where she kept it. Dharin set the team running so quickly she nearly fell out.

"Jussacks!" shouted Dharin. "We'll have to outrun them. There are at least two sleds, probably more, and we can't outfight them."

"I think there are six, or more," Maerad said. She looked back, and saw four sleds appear over the ridge. Their sleds were much lighter than Dharin's, and each carried a single man. She saw with anxiety that even though their dogs were not nearly as powerful as Dharin's team, they were faster.

The Jussacks themselves were, like Maerad and Dharin, dressed in heavy winter clothing. Each man carried a weapon like a mace in one hand, steering his sled with the other. They had fair beards, plaited in two ropes from their chins, and there was something odd about their faces, something misshapen, that Maerad could not make out at that distance.

The dogs were running at a reckless pace. There was no clear path and the risks of hitting an obstacle grew the faster they ran. Then she saw two sleds ahead of them. There was no escape to either side; they were now running headlong down a narrow valley. Dharin urged the dogs on, his voice sharp, and they somehow managed an extra spurt of speed. It was hopeless; they could not turn back, and passing the Jussack sleds ahead of them was their only chance.

Maerad stood up, holding to the rails to keep herself steady, and threw up a shield to protect them. Then she prepared to blast the Jussacks aside, to allow their sled to pass. She gathered the power inside herself, feeling a sudden gladness as she felt an infinite energy surge through her veins, and cast a bolt of light towards the nearest sled.

Nothing happened. Maerad staggered and almost fell. It wasn't like the Hull with the blackstone, which had eaten up her power and then cast it back twofold; nor was it like the impotence that had afflicted her in the Gwalhain Pass. This was something else altogether; she felt herself to be powerful, and knew the magery was glowing within her. But for some reason she could not use it.

Dharin was looking at her in awe, and she realized he had not seen her in her power before. She straightened herself and tried again, steeling her will. Again nothing happened. She shook her head, bewildered, but by now they were almost level with the sleds, which had turned to block them. Dharin's team swerved violently to avoid a collision. He was making for a tiny space between the right sled and the rise beyond, calling his dogs to bunch together. If they made it through, they might have a chance.

Wildly they raced for the gap, and at the last moment the Jussack urged his sled out of the way. Maerad glimpsed his face as they passed, his eyes cold, his blond beard forking down from his chin. For a moment she thought he was not human at all, and then realized that his face was tattooed, with strange blue marks curling around his cheekbones and eyes, making him look savage and alien.

Then they were past the sled; they were flying along the valley. They might just make it. Maerad's heart leapt in hope.

But suddenly Dharin slumped forward with a grunt. The traces went slack and the dogs, bewildered, became tangled and lost their direction.

Maerad turned, her mouth open, and saw that an evil-looking bolt was protruding from just below Dharin's collarbone. It had passed right through his back. She hadn't even heard it. So her shield wasn't working either. What was wrong with her? But she had no time for thought: their sled struck a spruce with a splintering crash, shivering Maerad to the bone and pulling the dogs up so sharply that some tumbled over in their traces. Dharin was flung over the rails and landed on Maerad.

Forgetting everything else, she lifted him off her with a strength she had not known she possessed, and straightened him lengthwise on the sled on his side. The black feathered shaft of the arrow stuck out from his back. She bent over him, trying to pull the arrow out through his chest, her fingers slippery with blood, but he lifted up his hand and clasped her fingers. He opened his eyes and looked up into Maerad's face. His eyes were very blue and clear, and his face was very pale.

"It is no good, Maerad," he said, gasping for breath. "The life already goes out of me."

Maerad stared at him, all the love she felt for this gentle young man welling into her heart. "No!" she said. "You can't die. I can heal you."

"They will kill you, too. I hope your death is as merciful as mine. I am told—" Dharin winced, and a trickle of blood came out of his mouth. "I'm told that it is often better to kill yourself, rather than to be captured by these people. I'm sorry, little cousin."

Maerad could find no words to answer him, and bent over Dharin, clasping his hand and stroking his face. He pressed her hand gently, trying to say something. She pressed her ear to his mouth.

"If you are not killed – if you ever speak to my mother – say my farewells for me. I will see her beyond the Gates."

"I will. I'll do anything. I love you." Dharin's blood seemed to be all over Maerad, in her hair, on her clothes, all over her hands; and still more poured out of him. "You have nothing to be sorry for; it's my fault. It's all my fault. You can't die."

"Nay." Dharin drew a shuddering breath and tried to smile. "Nay. It is not your fault. I love you too, cousin. I am glad that I

knew you." His breath now bubbled with blood, and he tried to
say something else, but Maerad couldn't hear it.

"What?" she whispered, her face close to his.

"It doesn't hurt. Don't be afraid." Then he shuddered and
went still, his eyes turning up into his head, and Maerad knew
he was dead. She closed his eyelids with her fingers and kissed
his forehead, remembering how she had done the same for her
mother, so many years ago. Was she cursed, that she caused the
death of anyone who loved her?

She had been so intent on Dharin that she had not realized
that his team was howling. The mournful cries echoed unbearably through her body, like the sound of her own grief. She stood
up and saw the Jussacks had already reached the sled and were
walking over the snow towards her. There were two, with four
more behind them. She drew her sword, snarling. She was not
afraid any more. She had nothing left. Her powers had deserted
her. She had failed. All that lay before her was darkness.

Out of the corner of her eye she saw Claw biting at her harness, trying to get free. She looked as though she would tear
out the throats of any Jussacks who came near. Maerad felt like
Claw: she would fight to the death, since death was all that was
left her. With her sword she slashed the great dog free of her
restraints, and then launched herself off the sled with a wild
cry, suddenly glad that she would die.

The Jussacks were almost twice as big as Maerad, but
they were not prepared for the ferocity of her attack. As one
approached her, she sliced off his arm with a double-handed
stroke, jumping back and spinning to counter the other. But he
hung back, keeping out of reach of her sword until the other
sleds drew close and he was joined by the other Jussacks. The
man she had maimed lay twisting on the ground, screaming,
blood blossoming from his body and steaming on the snow.
Suddenly a huge shape launched from behind Maerad, and

leapt snarling onto the injured man. It was Claw, the cut traces still dangling from her harness. He screamed high, and then stopped, and the second Jussack ran to Claw and hit her on the head with his mace, as Maerad ran up to him yelling. Claw turned, snarling, ready to bite, but then, with a dream-like slowness, tripped and fell into the snow, and did not get up. Maerad launched herself at the Jussack who had killed Claw, freshly enraged, but again he retreated beyond her sword, unwilling to engage her in combat, and at this point the other Jussacks reached them.

One of them, Maerad realized instantly, was a sorcerer, but he was exerting some magery that Maerad had not encountered before. He raised his hands, speaking words she did not recognize, and suddenly Maerad's mind became vague, tipping over into a darkness like sleep. She stood like one in a daze, and her sword fell to the ground out of her nerveless hand. So, that's why my magery failed me, she thought, with a kind of wonder. A huge dark smoke seemed to be filling her mind; she struggled against it, trying to bend down to pick up her sword, but her body would not obey her. Is this death? she thought. Dharin was right, there is no pain... And then the darkness overwhelmed her, and she knew nothing more.

ARKAN-DA

Up then stood the Wolf King Nardo,
Bravest of his kin and kindest,
Savage hunter shod with silence,
Fearless singer in the moonlight,
Standing high so all could hear him
On the peaks of Idrom Uakin,
To the snow hare and the eagle,
To the elk and fleet-foot zanink,
To the horse herds sadly waning,
To the moose herds weakly starving,
Spoke then with a voice of thunder:
"I will journey for our hardships
To the fortress of the Ice King,
To the mountains of the Trukuch
Where he rules in his dark palace.
I will seek the season's changing,
Winter dark to silver springtime,
Hammer hail to gentle summer.
Of all creatures I am swiftest,
Of all fighters the most deadly,
I fear not death nor what comes after.
I will take this task upon me."

From *The Kilibrikim* (Pilanel Lore,
Library of Lirigon)

XXII

DELIRIUM

MAERAD was lost in a desert of dream. Strange orange dunes rose ahead of her, wave upon wave, like an endless ocean of sand. A golden snake was swimming through the sand before her; it turned and fixed her with a ruby eye. She fell forward into the eye, which grew huge, like a pit of fire, and its flames licked painlessly about her. Her skin curled and blackened and flaked away. She was bones on sand, an endless desert of thirst; she cried out, and her mouth filled with water, or blood. She couldn't move her arms or her legs, and she burned all over, with cold or heat, she couldn't tell. She struggled weakly, as if she were drowning, and the blackness rose up out of the ground and reclaimed her.

Maerad was on a sled, bound hand and foot. The white sky passed endlessly above her. She could hear the panting of running dogs, their almost silent padding through the snow, the swish of a sled, hoarse male shouts in a language she did not recognize. She looked to her right: alongside were running white wolves, strong and fast. One looked at her and grinned, its red tongue lolling from its mouth; and then, as she watched, its shoulders swelled and sprouted wings, and it flew up into the sky. She turned away, frightened, and a blond, bearded face looked into hers. Filled with a sudden hatred, the reasons for which she did not know, she tried to spit; but her mouth was parched. Hands raised her and gave her water. She swallowed; it burned her mouth like fire, but she had moisture in her mouth. She spat into the light-blue eyes. They blinked, and disappeared, and the darkness swept over her.

Maerad's mother, Milana of Pellinor, stood before her in a tower of glass. Her face was marked with inconsolable grief. In her arms she clasped Hem, not as Maerad had last seen him, but as a baby. Both of them turned to face Maerad, who was outside the tower. There was no door. Maerad was overcome by a longing to join them, to be held again in her mother's arms. She beat her hands against the glass until they were bloody, but she could not break it; she beat and beat, until she could see the bones of her hands, like broken white twigs in a mess of blood and flesh.

After that dream, Maerad awoke. The world around her seemed to be real. Hem is dead, she thought; the dream told me. He is dead, murdered, like everyone else I have ever loved. The thought brought no tears. She was beyond tears, beyond grief; she was empty of all feeling, a shell as light as a feather. All her body burned with pain, apart from her left hand. Her left hand was almost completely numb.

She was bound; that was no dream. She seemed to be tied to a sled. Slowly she remembered what had happened to her; she remembered Dharin's death, and the final fight with the Jussacks. She blinked, trying to work out where she was. She was on a sled, being driven over the endless plains of Zmarkan. She had been captured by the Jussacks. Dharin had said they would kill her, but they had not killed her. She wished they had.

All Maerad wanted was to die. Even that had been denied her. She had thought about killing herself once before, after the death of Cadvan; but then the life in her had cried out, had pleaded for its existence. But now even that visceral pleading of the body was gone. The darkness was friendly and warm; it waited for her, a dark pool into which she could slide her body and rest for ever, free from grief, free from torment: free, most of all, from her failure.

When the blond face appeared again, she turned away and shut her eyes and mouth, so she could not be given food or drink. Her head was lifted, and water was forced between her lips from a leather bottle. She was too weak to keep her jaw clamped shut, and when the water dribbled into her mouth she automatically swallowed. She tried to spit out the next mouthful, but could not. She tossed her head from side to side, but someone held her head firmly, so even that protest was thwarted. Some warm soup was forced into her mouth and she nearly choked before she swallowed. I could kill myself by choking, she thought, and the next mouthful of soup she took eagerly, trying to fill her mouth so much that she could not breathe, so that the soup would go into her lungs and drown her; but despite herself she swallowed it. The same thing happened again, until she had finished the bowl.

Then she was left alone. Maerad lay on the jolting sled, tears at last spilling from her eyes. Even her body betrayed her.

Time no longer existed. Life was an unending torment, rushing forward through an endless night, slipping between evil dreams and worse wakings. The Jussacks did not want her to die; they were going to a lot of trouble to make sure that she didn't. She was fed and even kept clean, no easy task in the harsh conditions. She barely needed to be tied; she was so weak that she could not even lift her arms. Sometimes the wind howled and snowflakes settled on her face; and until someone noticed and she was covered, being unable to brush them away was a worse torment than almost anything else.

When she could feel any emotion, she felt hatred. It was like a cold poison in her soul. Her body's ills she learned to ignore, except for the times that the pain was so overwhelming it filled her whole mind, so that she felt she would go mad, if she were not mad already. She was racked by fever and chills, almost convulsive enough to break her bindings. But despite this, her body began to heal. After a time, the convulsions stopped, and she was merely tormented by the cold. The Jussacks gave her enough furs to keep her from dying, but not enough to keep her warm. She dreamed that her left hand had frozen and fallen off, a chunk of ice, and woke surprised to find it was still there.

She stank of blood. Dharin's blood had soaked into her fur coat, and although the worst of it had been cleaned off, the fur along her collar was rough with it and she could feel the dry clots in her hair. It was Dharin, the last thing she had of him, and she did not complain. And then her period began and she felt as if her whole body was weeping blood, that she slept and woke in its sour smell.

There was one man who, it seemed, had been given the duty of keeping her alive. At first, he looked to Maerad like all the other Jussacks: they were all as pale-skinned as Maerad, with long blond hair, long plaited beards and pale blue eyes rimmed by blue tattoos. She didn't seek to differentiate one from the other: to Maerad they were all nameless savages.

This Jussack was not quite as tall as the others and, despite the tattoos, in other circumstances Maerad might have thought he had a pleasant face. When he needed to clean her, which he did using a cloth soaked in a kind of clarified fat or oil, he was always respectful, almost apologetic. And his feeding of her was, if practical and brusque, not without gentleness. Maerad noted these things unwillingly. She did not spit in his face now, but she would not respond to his attempts to communicate, even though sometimes it was clear that he was trying to tell her his name and was asking hers. She pretended she didn't understand.

Shortly after dreams and reality untangled themselves, she was inspected by the sorcerer, who was the leader of the small troupe. He looked her over as if she were goods that must be brought intact to their destination. The sleds had stopped, and as she had been every night, Maerad was carried into one of the Jussack tents and laid on the floor. The sorcerer entered, stooping in the tiny space, and inspected her. Maerad became aware of his gaze and opened her eyes. He was clearly a *Dhillarearën*, and the bile rose in her throat. There was a wrongness in his Gift that she had not sensed in the other Unschooled Bards she had met – Sirkana, or Inka-Reb. But he was not a Hull. Somehow, thought Maerad, he was something worse: darkness twisted within him like a poisonous smoke.

"Who are you, to look at me?" she said in the Speech. Her voice was harsh with disuse.

The sorcerer looked back at her expressionlessly, although she saw the muscles around his eyes flinch in distaste. "I am who I am," he said. "You are no one, to ask such a thing."

"You murdered my friend," said Maerad. "Why have you not killed me?"

"You killed a man," said the sorcerer. "The punishment for that is death. But we have other plans for you. They are not your concern."

"You are all base murderers," answered Maerad. Her mind was slow and thick, and she felt too tired to argue. "That man would not have died if you had not attacked us. It's your fault he died, not mine."

"Be that as it may," he answered. "You are ours now."

"I belong to no one." A dull rage rose inside her. "You have no right…"

He stared at her with contempt. "You are a woman. Be silent."

If Maerad had been in possession of her powers, she would

have blasted him into nothing with no compunction. She stared back at him with loathing, refusing to lower her eyes. Something faltered in his gaze, and instead of challenging her, he turned away.

"Why have you captured me?" asked Maerad. "Where are you taking me?" But the man would not answer her.

He examined her as if she were a piece of livestock, looking at her teeth and inside her mouth and checking her limbs. Furious at the indignity, Maerad bit his hand, and he hit her across the jaw with a casual violence. What he saw clearly did not please him, and he spoke sharply to the Jussack, who trembled at his side, his head bowed in fear and humility. He picked up her left hand and pressed it. A little feeling came back into it, mostly pain. Then he gave the other Jussack what was clearly a long list of instructions, and left the tent.

After that, her situation improved slightly. Maerad was given more furs and did not suffer so much from the cold. She was also untied, so she had some freedom of movement on the sled. She thought of casting herself off into the snow, but there was plainly no way she could do so unseen, and she would immediately be picked up and probably bound again.

At this time, she also realized that Dharin's sled travelled with them. It was being driven by one of the other men. She wondered what had become of the bodies of Claw and Dharin; no doubt they had been left, unhonoured and unburied, in the snow. The thought was agonizing. And where was her pack? Her lyre? They must be in the sled… But she was still too tired to think properly, and her thoughts slid into a confused maze.

She was bewitched by some spell she did not recognize, in a way that paralysed and sickened her. The enchantment came from the sorcerer, and she began to push against it. She felt his will resisting her, and she was sure that she was a stronger *Dhillarearën* than he was; but no matter how she tried, she could not unlock the spell. It held her fast.

Sometimes Maerad thought she could see pale shadows running at a distance, parallel to the sleds. They looked like wolves, but if she tried to stare straight at the movement she could see nothing but bare snow. No one else seemed to notice them, and she dismissed them as hallucinations.

At night, she dreamed of wolves.

The days passed, each one identical to the next. Maerad tried, with little success, to work out how long she had lain insensible; time then had ceased to exist. She made little scratches on the wooden rail of the sled. If she had been delirious for seven days, she had been their captive for two weeks now.

She began to be able to tell her five captors apart. The Jussack in charge of her was clearly the youngest and the lowliest in rank; he seemed to be about Dharin's age. The others were all grown men, who looked to be between thirty and forty. Maerad thought them brutal thugs: they reminded her of the men in Gilman's Cot, among whom she had been raised. The recognition called within her a deep contempt, which fed her hatred. The sorcerer, who was called Amusk, was the chief among them, and all the others deferred to him with varying degrees of fear.

Despite herself, she began to feel some sympathy for the young man in charge of her. Although he tried to give no sign of it, Maerad thought that he disliked the sorcerer Amusk as much as she did. His sled was usually the leading one, and after a while Maerad realized that he had a gift similar to Dharin's, that he had an infallible sense for knowing where he was. It explained, Maerad thought, why so young a man had been taken on a mission with the older men.

And she began to understand that these men considered it to be demeaning to look after a woman, and that the youngest

Jussack's task was a humiliation for which he was often teased
by the other men. Their comments made him angry, and once
she saw him draw a knife on one of his tormentors, who backed
away, shaking his head, his arms spread wide, clearly not wanting to fight. Despite this, the Jussack looked after her diligently.
She noticed that he only attempted to speak to her when no
one else could overhear, and when the other men were nearby
would sometimes speak harshly to her, as if to conceal any
empathy he felt.

After the sorcerer's visit, Maerad did not ignore the young
man the next time he tried to tell her his name. He put his hand
on his chest and said: "Nim." Then, plainly asking, he pointed
to Maerad.

"Maerad," she said. "I'm Maerad."

For the first time, she saw him smile. It transformed his face,
and she realized for the first time just how young he was. He
might even be as young as I am, she thought. "Nim. Maerad,"
he said, pointing from one to the other. Maerad nodded.

He disappeared out of the tent and returned with a warm
meat stew. Maerad was now able to feed herself, although when
she was not on the sled her feet were tied to prevent her attacking anyone or escaping. Nim handed her a steaming bowl.
"*Hulcha*," he said. "*Ij lakmi.*" He mimed the actions of eating.

"*Lakmi?*" said Maerad. "Eat? I eat?" She pointed to the bowl.
"*Hulcha*," she said. Again Nim nodded and smiled.

Well, I might as well learn Jussack, thought Maerad, as she
began to eat the soup. It's not as if I have anything else to do. But
then, with a cold shock, she realized she was beginning to think
kindly of one of Dharin's murderers. She suddenly felt sick and
pushed the bowl away, and would not speak to Nim any more.
When she did not answer him he looked disappointed and
hurt, almost like a small child who had been snubbed, but he
covered it swiftly and said something to her that sounded like

a curse, and laughed in the way the older men laughed, with a crude, knowing brutality. Then he took her bowl and ate the soup himself, hungrily.

After that a diffident relationship developed between Maerad and Nim. Maerad learned the Jussack language quickly, and over the next few weeks they began to have simple conversations. Although their talks were always underlain by a mutual wariness, something grew between them which, in different circumstances, might have developed into a friendship. As things were, it was a kind of tacit alliance.

It was Maerad's only comfort, if their often difficult and uneasy conversations could be called comforting. Her loneliness was almost unbearable, and her secret talks with Nim were the only human contact she had. Some stubborn will reasserted itself as her body slowly strengthened, although she was always tired from her unceasing battle with the sorcerer's will. She felt little power within her. It was a strange emptiness, as if a limb were missing, but still she resisted. Although she had no hope for herself now, she did not feel entirely hopeless. There were still things she could do, perhaps, even if she faced certain failure. It might not be entirely vain to attempt to escape.

The first thing she wanted back was her pack. When she saw that the Jussacks had brought Dharin's sled and dogs with them, she realized that her pack must be there as well. It contained everything that mattered to her in the world, including her lyre. When she and Nim talked, she told him of her longing for her music, for her lyre. He stared at her with his pale-blue eyes.

"You might want to trick me," he said. "I know you are a witch, and you may have something for your spells in there."

"No," said Maerad. "There is a lyre. A harp. For music." She hummed, hoping that Nim could understand her broken

Jussack. "It belonged to my mother. She is dead."

"My mother is dead, as well," said Nim. He pondered in silence for a short time, and then drew out a circular pendant from underneath his jerkin. It was made of black, polished stone. "This was hers."

Maerad was unexpectedly moved, and reached out and gently touched the pendant with the tip of a finger. "Beautiful," she said.

Nim looked at his pendant and then put it back inside his clothes.

"I will get your things for you," he said. "But if you decide to do magic or to escape because of what I have done, I will be killed."

Maerad looked at him as straightly as she could. "I can't escape," she said. "And I can't do magic with my lyre. I would like to hold it again." As she spoke, it was as if a hunger flowered in her fingers.

"I am stupid to do this," Nim said. "But I will do my best. I do not know why, but I do not think you lie to me. Perhaps you are a good liar."

Maerad smiled, thinking of Inka-Reb. "A wise man once said I was a liar," she replied. "Perhaps he was right. But I am not lying to you."

"How would I know?" said Nim. "I am only a simple man. I don't know why we had to travel so far to find you. Amusk cast runes all the way there to track you. I think they take you back to Arkan-da."

Maerad looked up in confusion: this was the first she had heard of where she was going.

"Even I can see that though Amusk has bewitched you, you are powerful; I have never seen him afraid of anyone except you and the Ice King. If the Ice King wants you, then you must be powerful."

"If I was powerful, I am no longer," said Maerad. Amusk was afraid of her? "But I can still play music. Maybe, if you can get my pack, I can play you a song of my people."

Nim sighed. "If you do, they will hear, and I will be punished," he said. "But I would like that." He looked down at his hands again, and suddenly seemed very shy. And Maerad was at once aware of him, simply as a man, not as a Jussack or an enemy. For the first time in her life, it did not make her feel afraid. She wondered at this: she had more reason to be afraid than at any time since she left Gilman's Cot; perhaps she had been through so much that things that once frightened her now seemed trivial. Or perhaps, somehow, she trusted this young man.

Nim had nursed and washed her throughout her illness, even though such tasks were demeaning to him. The thought of those intimacies made her blush. He need not have been gentle, but he had been. And he had never been anything but respectful of her. Perhaps it had been out of fear at the Winterking's displeasure should she sicken and die. But Maerad now thought that it might also be a simple kindness.

"Are you really taking me to Arkan-da?" she asked. "Do you mean the Winterking?"

"I think that is what the Pilani call the Ice King, curse them."

Maerad was silent for a while. "Why do you curse them? They are good people," she said at last. "My father was Pilani."

Nim looked up quickly. "I am sorry to offend you. The Pilani have taken over our land. We want it back."

"And who told you that?" asked Maerad, wondering. "The Pilanel have been in Zmarkan since the beginning of time. They can't have taken your land. And isn't there enough space in Zmarkan for everybody?"

"Everyone knows that it is true," said Nim, with absolute certainty. "They are an evil people."

Maerad wanted her pack back, and she didn't want to make him angry, so she didn't argue. But the night's conversation gave her something to think about the following day, when she was put into the sled for the next stage of their interminable journey.

That night, although Maerad half expected that he wouldn't, Nim brought her lyre, in its leather case. He had not brought her pack. Reverently, her hands shaking with feeling, she took out the instrument and showed it to him, brushing her fingers lightly over the strings to make a faint chord. His eyes widened in wonder.

"I wish I could play," she whispered.

"I wish that too," he said. "I have never heard anything so beautiful."

"Thank you, Nim," she said. "I won't forget, ever." She looked up and saw in Nim's eyes a wakened longing that made her pity him.

"Perhaps you could go to Annar one day," she said softly. "People there are good. They are not cruel, like Amusk. And then you could hear the music."

Nim suddenly looked ashamed, as if she had seen him naked, and turned away, speaking no more that night; and the next day he was harsh with her when he put her in the sled. But Maerad felt no animus towards him for that; she knew the pain of awakenings. Once she too had protected herself against her own feelings as Nim did. And no one was going to rescue Nim and show him a new world, as Cadvan had rescued her from Gilman's Cot. Not, she reflected sadly, that anyone was going to save her now, either. But having her lyre back made her feel slightly less helpless. Even though she could not play it, she caressed it at night, running her swollen fingers over the runes, wondering if she would ever know what secrets they contained.

Nim had told her that Amusk was the most powerful of all the Jussacks. Maerad had thought about this; it meant that her capture had been carefully planned, perhaps after the failure of the stormdog and the iridugul. Her journey with Dharin had been doomed from the beginning. She remembered Sirkana's sadness when she had farewelled them, and was sure that Sirkana had foreseen his death. Why, then, had she let him go with Maerad?

But she flinched from thinking too much about Dharin; it raised too many painful memories. Dernhil, Cadvan, Dharin; Imi, Darsor and Claw; how many had died to protect her? The Pilanel had told her that the Jussacks worshipped the Winterking and if such an important man as Amusk had been sent to capture her, it meant that the Winterking wanted her badly. She was a trophy, she thought bitterly; not only for the Dark and the Light, but now the Elementals. No doubt the Winterking would deliver her to the Nameless One himself.

When she was next inspected by the sorcerer Amusk, he was not so displeased with her condition, but he looked closely at her left hand and pursed his lips. Three fingers were a strange colour, a dark purple, and she could not feel them at all. He did some healing magery, but it made very little difference.

This time Maerad could follow the conversation a little, though she kept her knowledge of the language secret, in part out of natural caution, and in part to protect Nim. She gathered they were not far, perhaps a week, from their destination. She was briefly amazed; they had traversed the vast expanse of the Arkiadera, from one side to the other. She had twenty-five scratches on the wooden rail. Even given that she didn't know how many days she had been unconscious after her capture, they were travelling swiftly.

Maerad inspected Amusk closely. He did not look at all like Nim; she wondered now how she could ever have confused them. His face was thin and cruel, and it seemed to Maerad that he looked much more drawn than when he had last come into the tent. Good, she thought; he battles hard to keep me under his control. Alerted by Nim's comment, she looked for signs of fear when he inspected her, but his eyes were cold and did not reveal anything. An arrogance within her stirred under his cold regard, and she would not avert her gaze, although she could tell he was used to people lowering their eyes in his presence. Especially women, thought Maerad. But if he wanted her in good condition, he could not punish her too much. And, indeed, he did not punish her.

This time she did not try to speak to him, and he did not speak to her at all. When he left, Nim confirmed they would soon be at Arkan-da.

"I suppose then I shall not see you again," he said.

"I will escape," said Maerad. "And I will go to Annar. You should too."

"I have to look after my grandmother and my sister," said Nim. "My father is dead, too, and there is no one else to care for them. I cannot leave my people."

"Then maybe we will not meet. Unless one day there is peace in our lands, and perhaps then we could visit each other's homes." It was a childish fantasy, but Maerad said it anyway. Speaking of any future was only dreaming.

Nim laughed. "My people are not peaceful," he said.

"Peace is better than killing," said Maerad with feeling.

"I think so too." Nim was silent; he seemed to be remembering something. "I used to like gathering the wildflowers with my sister. We were sent out to get berries and we would gather flowers instead. My mother would be very angry."

Maerad looked at him curiously. "An old woman told me that the Jussacks keep their women in holes in the ground," she said.

"That's not true. Pilani lies," Nim spat.

"Well, maybe the Jussacks tell lies about the Pilani, too.

The man you killed – my cousin, Dharin à Lobvar – he too might have gathered flowers instead of berries."

Nim was silent for almost an hour after that. Maerad settled down to sleep, her eyes heavy. She still found moving difficult, although she did not feel as sick as she had. She was quite certain that Amusk had almost killed her when he had captured her. All her hatred now focused on him, and on the Winterking. She brooded, wondering what she would find at Arkan-da.

"I do not know much of the world," said Nim, breaking into her thoughts. "Perhaps you are right. You know different peoples and different languages. All I know is my people and my language."

"I don't know that much," said Maerad sleepily. "Some people have taught me some things."

"Well, you are lucky," said Nim. "Maybe they are lies they tell about the Pilani. But would we stop warring against them if there were no lies?"

"You might." Maerad leaned on her elbow and looked at him.

"And we might not," said Nim. "I don't know."

"Maybe you will become the big chieftain and stop them," said Maerad.

"And maybe then I will visit you in Annar."

They smiled at each other, each knowing the impossibility of what they were saying. For a moment, they were like children playing a game in which, for a short time, they could hide from a cruel adult world.

The next day Maerad saw a range of mountains in the distance ahead of them, a low purple shape on the horizon that might have been clouds. Nim told her that they were mountains, the range his people called the Trukuch. The ground began to rise, and the flatness was relieved by hills and low ridges. Maerad began to see dwarf hazels pushing through the crust of snow, and then groves of spruce or fir.

They drew ever closer and closer, until they were running in the mountains' shadow eastwards to Arkan-da, along a road marked by standing stones. The Trukuch mountains rose on their right, sharp blades against the gloomy skies, their sheer sides naked of snow, their crowns shrouded in dark clouds, and Maerad's spirits dropped again to their lowest ebb. The mountain walls seemed like the outlying ramparts of a vast fortress. She began to realize how foolish it was to believe that she could escape the Winterking's stronghold, once she was enclosed within it. The little hope she had distilled from her friendship with Nim evaporated and vanished.

Her continual silent battle with the sorcerer briefly intensified. She was maliciously satisfied to see his drawn face grow greyer, his eyes bloodshot, his thin mouth yet thinner. But he still had the upper hand; she could struggle against his enchantment, but she could not break it. Perhaps, though, she was breaking him.

She hated Amusk with a passion that contained all her grief and love for everyone she had lost. She would have liked to make him so strained that his heart burst and he fell to the ground, his eyes turned up, the blood from his mouth staining the snow as Dharin's had stained it, steaming in the cold. The image give her a grim pleasure. But Amusk did not break.

Nim and Maerad's conversations almost ceased when they came close to the mountains. Nim also looked strained, for reasons Maerad could not guess, and he was as sharp with her as he had been when she was first captured. But Maerad did not mind; she was past caring about herself now. She felt a rising gladness that she was being taken to face her enemy. The Winterking had sent the stormdog against them in the Straits of Thorold, and the Winterking had killed Cadvan in the

Gwalhain Pass, and finally he had murdered Dharin. Perhaps, as Inka-Reb seemed to, he knew about the marks on the lyre, and wanted them for himself. Whatever he wanted, Maerad was not going to gratify him. He had taken such care to ensure that she survived that she was sure the way to disappoint him was to bring about her own death.

She had already decided that she could not do so while she was in Nim's care; she could not bear the weight of his inevitable death on her conscience. She waited, while the sled swept past the mountains, which grew higher and grimmer the further they journeyed.

I feel you, my enemy, she said to the night. I feel you closer and closer. At last I will look on your face. Something within her laughed, but it was not joyful laughter; it was the defiance of someone who faced certain death, and no longer cared. I will not die a slave, she said to herself. I have earned that much.

The day before they reached Arkan-da, a heavy mist rolled down from the mountains, enclosing the sleds in an eerie white silence. Their pace slowed considerably, and Nim was sent ahead to track the way. Maerad sat on the sled before him indifferently. The mist seemed full of frightening apparitions that dissolved as they neared them, and they could hear dreadful noises that seemed to be the very stones groaning and crying out in pain or rage. Maerad could feel the fear of the men in the sleds behind them. But the apparitions and the noises had no effect on her; nothing frightened her any more. She pushed against the sorcerer's spell and felt Amusk weaken. Even he is afraid, she thought. He still wants to live, he still wants to have power in this world. I do not, and so I am not afraid.

That night, Nim and Maerad spoke for the last time. Maerad searched through her clothes; she badly wanted to give him something. She unpinned her silver lily brooch, the sign that marked her as a Bard of Pellinor. He would be able to hide it from the others, and she would not be needing it any more. She stroked it, remembering the gentle, stern woman who had given it to her: Oron, First Bard of Innail.

Perhaps Oron would not think it amiss that she should give away this token for the sake of the rough kindness Nim had shown her. It was in Innail that Maerad had first understood the value of human kindness. She remembered Silvia telling her: *The law is that the hungry must be fed, and the homeless must be housed, and the sick must be healed. That is the way of the Light.* Maerad smiled at the memory, so distant from her bitter present, and ran her fingers over the lily sign of Pellinor one last time.

"Nim," she said. "This is for you." She handed him the brooch.

He took it with wonder, his eyes widening. "It is a lovely thing," he said. "A precious thing. I have nothing that I can give you in return."

"You have given me much," said Maerad. "This is to thank you. You have been kind to me. You didn't have to be."

She saw a flush run up his neck and over his face, and he took the brooch awkwardly, and put it inside his clothes.

"I will not forget," he said, and turned away.

The sun no longer seemed to exist. The day was distinguishable from night only because the shadows were slightly less dark. The mist enveloped the sleds so they were barely visible. There were no stars: the ground threw up a white glimmer, as if it were itself a source of light, and was the only thing that kept them from moving through complete darkness.

When they had begun that morning, the teams had turned south and started running swiftly along a narrow mountain pass. The standing stones loomed out of the mist and vanished, and Maerad thought of those she had seen along the Gwalhain Pass: the same people must have made this road, in ages long past. The air was still and freezing.

Maerad sat on Nim's sled, ahead of the others, hugging her lyre between her knees. She felt dizzy, unable to think; she could feel the closeness of the Winterking in her mind, the shadow that had been pressing upon her ever since she had set foot in Zmarkan. Waves of blackness broke over her; she sank into them, as she had when she had first been captured, to re-emerge not knowing how long she had been unconscious. She could feel Amusk's spell pressing harder against her, and his sense of triumph as he felt her resistance waver, and a reflexive contempt stirred in her stomach. It was not Amusk who made her falter.

It was certainly night when they reached a lofty arch of black stone. Its keystone stood high over the road, and, as they neared it, Maerad felt dread tightening her stomach. The road ran through it into a natural courtyard walled by high buttresses of stone. At the far end reared the dark flank of a mountain. The arch seemed to be made of some kind of polished basalt covered with strange reliefs; the carvings looked as sharp as if they had been finished the day before, and yet the arch seemed ancient. It stood all by itself, with no buildings of any kind around it. Its power made Maerad feel faint.

The dogs would not pass beneath the arch, despite being severely whipped, and finally, cursing, the Jussacks stepped out of their sleds. Maerad was ordered to walk in front of them. The men's fear was palpable. Maerad hurriedly grabbed her lyre, slinging it in front of her under her coat, and stepped onto the ground. Immediately her knees buckled beneath her. Somebody kicked her, and she curled herself into a ball around her lyre, feeling the ground cold against her face, suddenly indifferent. They could kick her as much as they liked. Let them kill her.

There was more cursing; an argument was breaking out between Amusk and two of the other men. Nim was silent. Finally she was pulled upright, and her arms were slung about the shoulders of Nim and Amusk, so that her toes scraped the ground. The other three Jussacks stayed behind with the sleds.

As they passed under the arch, a great coldness fell on her heart, as if everything inside her turned to ice.

XXIII

THE ICE PALACE

MAERAD thought she was dreaming. She was deliciously warm; warm as she had not been since she had left Murask eight weeks before, and she was curled up in a bed of surpassing comfort. She was dressed in a long nightgown that stretched down to her toes. Her skin felt silky and clean, and her hair was spread out over the furs, freshly washed and smelling of sweet herbs.

She sat up and looked around in amazement. She was in a room that seemed to be made of something like moonstone: the walls were translucent and shimmered with a dim light. She reached out and touched the wall; it was cold, but not unpleasantly so. Before her was a doorway covered with an unfigured azure hanging, and on the floor, which was made of the same substance as the walls, was a rich rug of the same colour.

She brushed her hair out of her eyes, blinking, and then stopped and looked down at her left hand. It was the wrong shape. She dropped it on the fur coverlet, as if it didn't belong to her, and looked again. Something was wrong. She had a thumb, a forefinger, half of her middle finger, to its first knuckle, and then a clean, white scar. There was no pain.

She studied her hand with a kind of dazed wonder, and then spread out her right hand next to it on the fur. She wore the golden ring Ardina had given her on her right hand, on the third finger. For a while, as if to steady herself, Maerad stared at its delicate pattern of entwined lilies. When she didn't look at her left hand it felt exactly the same as it had before, as if her mind made ghostly fingers to replace those that weren't there. She curled her left hand, feeling its new shape, and then hid it under the coverlet. It's just an ugly claw, she thought. How am I going to play? And then she looked around. Where am I? Am I dead, after all? But if I were dead, would my fingers be missing?

She shook her head in bewilderment. Her last memory was of passing under the black arch on the road in the mountains. She had known already it was the entrance to Arkan-da, the stronghold of Arkan, the Winterking, and she had been consumed with dread. But here she felt only peace and light.

She looked around the room again: it must be enchanted, but she couldn't sense any magery around her. The room was very beautiful, as beautiful as some of the rooms she had seen in Annar, but stranger: there were no lamps, although the room was softly illuminated, and no furniture apart from the bed, which was little more than a mattress on the floor, and a strangely carved black stool. Against the stool leaned her pack, and her lyre in its leather case. She stared at them, feeling more amazed by their presence than almost anything else; what were they doing there? They must have been placed there by someone, as if she were a guest in a Bardhouse.

She searched within herself, looking for her own magery, but nothing was there. Once I was the most powerful Bard in Edil-Amarandh, she thought to herself; and now I am nothing. What has happened to me? Where did my Gift go? But no self-pity or despair stirred with these thoughts; all she felt was a kind of blank amazement.

I must be dead, she thought again. But I don't feel dead. Unless the dead can feel exhausted … and why wouldn't they? She took her left hand out from under the cover and looked at it again. It looked like an injury that had happened years ago. Where her fingers had been was just smooth white skin. She felt a sudden pity for her maimed hand, and stroked the scar; it was a little sensitive, but that was all. Then she hid it again and lay down and shut her eyes.

If I am not dead, she thought, I must be alive. But if I am alive, where am I? The questions circled around in her head like aimless flies, bumping into each other and reaching no destination until exhaustion crept up on her again, and she drifted back into sleep.

When Maerad next opened her eyes, she was still in the same warm bed, and her fingers were still missing. What woke her was thirst; her mouth was parched. She sat up, wondering where she was going to find some water, and saw that next to the bed there was now a table, made in the same style as the stool, and on it was a crystal decanter and a cup. She awkwardly poured herself some water and drank it greedily, struggling to use her maimed hand.

She swung her legs out of the bed and put her feet on the carpet. It was thick and warm, and involuntarily she wiggled her toes. To be comfortable, to be warm, to be clean, to feel her body sighing out in relief; these were seductions that were hard to resist after the hardships and harshness of her recent life. But her mind felt alert and suspicious. This was surely enchantment, of a most powerful kind, and she felt she ought to resist it. But not now. Not now.

She walked over to her pack, her legs wobbly and weak, as she had not walked for many weeks, and picked it up. The familiar smell of its worn leather was reassuring. She emptied it onto the bed. Everything was there, apparently untouched: her spare clothes, her blue cloak, the oilskin-wrapped book of Dernhil's poems, her almost-empty bottle of medhyl, the pipes Ardina had given her, the ivory carving of the fish from the Wise Kindred, even, to her surprise, the blackstone. Her fighting gear, her sword Irigan and her helm, were missing, but her mail coat was folded up where she had left it in the pack. The small dagger she had carried since leaving Gilman's Cot was also missing. She slowly re-packed everything, caressing each object as she did so, and put her bag back against the stool. She picked up her lyre, holding it in the crook of her arm, although she did not take it from its leather casing.

It had been ages since she had looked properly at her possessions. It was like a retelling of herself. Since Dharin's murder she had been in and out of a twilight of the soul, scarcely remembering who she was, wanting to die. *I am Elednor,* she said fiercely to herself. *That means something. But what?* answered that other mocking voice in her head. *What does it mean?*

"It means I have failed," she said out loud, and felt her despair surge back in a dark, heavy wave. She thought of the Bard Ilar, whom she had killed in Annar, and of the deaths of Cadvan and of the horses. She flinched away from the memory of the landslide, only to see a vivid image of Dharin, his face still in death. She had murdered the Bard from Lirigon: was that why Cadvan and Dharin had died? Was it a kind of payment? She wasn't able to think about what that might mean. At least she had not seen Dernhil die. *Some mercies,* she thought bitterly, *are very small.*

She got back into her bed, holding the lyre in her arms. She didn't want to play it; she was too frightened to try. It was quite likely that she would never play anything again.

Maerad hadn't seen anyone since she had first woken, but at some point, while she had been unconscious, someone had washed her and dressed her and put her into bed. And someone had placed the water and the table by her bed while she had been asleep. The thought was disturbing.

She walked to the doorway and pulled back the azure hanging. Outside the room was a windowless corridor illuminated with the same soft, sourceless light as her chamber. The ceiling was high and vaulted, and she could see doorways leading to other chambers. She looked up and down, but she couldn't see any sign of life. For a moment she toyed with the idea of exploring, but her knees were shaking from the small effort she had expended in walking to the door, and she was afraid of getting lost. She went back to her bed and picked up her lyre again.

Maerad was hungry now. Perhaps someone would bring her food, as someone had brought her water. She might be able to ask where she was.

She sat on the bed and waited. For the moment, there was nothing else to do.

She didn't know how long it was before someone finally appeared. The light in her room was unchanging, giving no idea of the passing of time. She struggled against the overwhelming temptation to go back to sleep: she was determined to be conscious next time someone came into her room.

But after a time somebody did come, and they seemed reassuringly human. A small, fat old woman wearing a scarf knotted around her head entered the room without announcing herself, carrying a tray on which was laid a bowl full of something steaming.

"Hello," Maerad said in Jussack, thinking this the most likely language to try first.

The woman smiled, her face creasing into a cobweb of wrinkles. "You are awake, then. I will tell the master."

"The master?" Maerad eyed the bowl, which smelt tantalizingly delicious, but she did not stretch out her hands to take it: more than food, she wanted information. "Who is the master?"

"He is our kind lord and master," said the old woman. "He will see you soon."

"But what is his name?"

"He does not have a name," said the woman. "He is too big for a name. He is our master. Here, take the soup." When Maerad would not take it, the woman laid the tray on the table beside the bed, and turned to leave.

"Then what's your name?" asked Maerad hurriedly, wanting her to stay. "And where am I? And what happened to my hand?"

"You are here, in the palace of the master. And my name is Gima, young fish. Oh, you were a sick girl when you came in." She clicked her tongue, as Mirka had done. "The frost bit your fingers off, silly girl. But now you are getting better, no? Soon you will be well enough to meet him."

"Do you mean the Winterking?" asked Maerad.

"I don't know who that is," said the woman cheerfully. "Maybe someone calls him that. Here, he is just the master."

Maerad gave up; her stomach was growling, and it seemed that Gima had no intention of telling her anything useful. "Will you come back?" she asked, as the woman left.

"Soon, soon…" She lifted the hanging, and was gone.

Maerad devoured the meal ravenously. She had been starving. She pushed the bowl aside, feeling more substantial than before. Perhaps she could think about walking a bit. She massaged her legs, which looked thin and wasted, and then thought that she ought to get dressed. She had just decided to unpack her spare clothes, filthy as they were, when Gima came in again, bearing a long robe lined with white fur, a rich crimson dress and fine woollen leggings, and some finely embroidered felt shoes.

"I will wash these for you," she said, gathering Maerad's clothes up and slinging them over her arm. "These are for you, as ordered by the master."

"But who is he?" asked Maerad, irritated. "And where am I?"

Gima simply chuckled and patted her head. "Don't you worry about that, little fish. Just get dressed, and then maybe we will take you to him, eh?" She took the tray and disappeared.

Maerad shrugged. It would be better to put on clean clothes. And if she were to see the master, whoever he was, it would be better to be finely dressed. She put on the dress and robe, stood up, and tried walking from one end of the room to the other. Her legs were not so bad; maybe she had just been hungry.

As if Gima had been waiting, she entered the room almost immediately. "Good," she said cheerfully. "You are dressed. Well, come along."

Maerad, whose only thought had been to get out of the chamber and to see where she was, immediately felt rebellious. "Where?" she snapped. "Why won't you answer? Are you stupid?" She used a Jussack word for "stupid" that she knew was particularly insulting, but Gima didn't even blink.

"Oh, you are so full of questions. Silly, silly girl. Come, come." She chivvied and coaxed Maerad as if she were a particularly slow child, and Maerad found she was following Gima along the white corridors. She was suspicious of everything in this strange place, and inclined to be hostile rather than not: but she was also consumed by curiosity.

The corridor turned into a wider passage. This was also vaulted, and was higher than the other, and every now and then they passed underneath an arch of black iron, with architraves wrought skilfully into strange geometric shapes, not one the same as the next. They were curiously beautiful. Before long, Maerad and Gima had reached a big double-leafed door.

Here Gima paused, her composure slipping; Maerad noted with interest that her face was suddenly pale. Then she took a deep breath and pushed the door. It opened silently under her hand, and they passed inside.

The room reminded Maerad of nothing so much as Ardina's hall in Rachida, only instead of silvered wood, the walls and ceiling were made of iron and white, translucent stone. The high ceiling was supported by black beams of iron that were wrought into the same abstract shapes Maerad had seen in the corridors. The walls were covered by tapestries, rich in shape and colours, but which had no figures that Maerad could make out; they seemed like the sun dazzling on snow and breaking into all its colours, or the strange hallucinatory shapes she had seen in the glacier. In the centre was a rectangular pool carved out of the translucent stone, and there the light was brightest: a cold, beautiful light that evenly illuminated the room, so there were no dark corners. At the far end was a low dais, and on the dais was a high black throne, which was utterly plain, and two low stools. On the throne sat a man. He watched Maerad and Gima in their slow progress across the hall.

Strangely, Gima's fear made Maerad feel less afraid. She straightened her back as they walked, so she should not seem deferential, and as they neared the throne she met the man's eyes.

He was an Elidhu: he had the same unsettling inhuman eyes that Ardina had, with their cat-like pupil, but while Ardina's eyes were yellow his were a very pale blue. His hair was black and long, and braided into two plaits that fell onto his breast. He was bare-headed, dressed in a light-blue tunic, richly embroidered with silver, with a long cloak of midnight blue springing back from his shoulders. On his naked arms were bracelets of silver and iron, intricately worked and set with white gems. His skin was absolutely white, but his pallor gave no sense of weakness: he looked strong and muscular, and as Maerad neared him she sensed, with a shiver, his keen vitality. Like Ardina, he seemed ageless, neither young nor old: his face was unlined, like that of a young king in the first flowering of his manhood, but his gaze was ancient.

When they reached the foot of the dais, Gima prostrated herself, tugging on Maerad's arm to indicate that she should do the same. Maerad had no intention of doing any such thing, and shook off Gima's hand. She stood and looked at the man, her face expressionless. So, I meet you at last, my enemy, she said to herself. And I have nothing left except my pride: but you cannot take that away from me. For surely this was Arkan, the Winterking, the author of her sorrows: murderer of Cadvan and Dharin, of Darsor and Imi, ally of the Nameless One, evil tyrant of the north. He stared back at her, unblinking. Then he waved his hand.

"Out, Gima," he said in Jussack. His voice was deep and gentle, and Maerad, who had been expecting a harsh command, was surprised. "Leave us."

Gima scuttled backwards on her hands and knees before she stood up and backed out of the room, almost falling into the pool. Maerad turned and watched her with astonishment: why didn't she turn around, so she could see where she was going? Finally, the old woman reached the door and slipped out.

Maerad turned back to face the Winterking, and found he was regarding her with something like amusement. Despite herself, she almost smiled. This piqued her pride, and she decided to show nothing. She met his eyes as coolly as she could manage, and schooled herself to wait.

"Welcome to you, Elednor of Edil-Amarandh," said the Winterking, now speaking in the Elidhu tongue. Maerad started; how did he know her Truename? "At last you have arrived, and I see what shape it is that so disrupts the stars."

He paused, perhaps waiting for Maerad to speak. She said nothing.

"It would be better if you sat down, instead of standing there," he said. "Come, sit beside me."

Maerad shook her head, and he sighed, as if he were a patient king dealing with one of the more querulous of his ministers. "As you wish, then," he said.

"I wish to leave here," said Maerad, looking up again and defiantly meeting his eyes. Like Ardina's, his gaze was unsettling, disturbing hidden depths within her. "Would you say 'as you wish' to that?"

"Why do you want to leave? Do you not think my palace beautiful? Does your chamber displease you? Is the food inadequate? I agree, Gima is a little tiresome; but she is also kind. I can find you another servant. My desire is to please you."

"You murdered my friends. My cousin." A hot feeling spread in the pit of Maerad's stomach; a deep anger. "Why should I wish to remain in the same house as my enemy?"

Arkan let his gaze rest on Maerad's face, and something in her flinched, and she looked away. "I am sorry for the sins of my servants. I can punish them, if you like," he said. "I was not pleased with the state in which you were delivered to me: I could see you had been ill-treated. But how else could I bring you here?"

"You could have asked me," said Maerad hotly. "Instead of attacking me in the middle of nowhere with a bunch of–of thugs."

"I shall punish them for you," said Arkan indifferently. "If it makes you feel any better."

"Not Nim," said Maerad. "He was kind to me. If I'm alive at all, it's thanks to him." Her legs had started trembling with weakness, and she swayed slightly. "Punish Amusk. He's an evil man."

"I do not understand what you mean by evil," said Arkan. "It seems to me that when humans make war, they say: this is good, this is evil. But the good and the evil often seem the same to me."

"They're not," began Maerad passionately, and then thought

of Enkir of Norloch, and of her own murder of the Bard of
Lirigon, and bit her lip. "I mean, people do good things and evil
things, but…" She stuttered to a halt, confused and dismayed;
this was not at all how she had imagined her meeting with the
Winterking.

"Are you so sure you can tell the difference?" said Arkan.

Maerad looked at him, at his strange blue eyes, which
seemed lit with a cold laughter, and straightened her back. Her
legs were trembling badly now.

"Yes," she said. "I can tell the difference. People are both
good and bad. But there are those who choose only to have
power. And they are evil."

"Your friend, Cadvan of Lirigon. He is a powerful Bard, and
has worked all his life to be a man of power. Is he then evil?"

The unexpected mention of Cadvan pierced Maerad like a
dart, and she gasped. "How do you dare speak of Cadvan to
me!" she said. "When you—" She swayed again; the pain in
her legs was almost unbearable now. "He never chose to have
power. I mean, over other people. Everything he did was for
the Light." She clenched her hands, trying to impose her will
on her body, and feeling once again with a shock the absence of
her fingers.

"Ah, the Light." Arkan's voice was expressionless. "But
what is the Light without the Dark? It cannot be. And the Dark
was first."

"That darkness was a different dark," said Maerad. "It was
the night, it was innocent…" She drew in a shuddering breath,
and there was a short silence.

"You are just out of your bed," said Arkan. "I think you
ought to sit down." He again indicated the stool next to
his throne. Maerad stubbornly shook her head, and almost
immediately her legs bent involuntarily beneath her and she
stumbled forward, and found herself kneeling in front of

Arkan, clutching the dais. Humiliated, she pulled herself up.

"It would be more prideful to sit than to kneel," said Arkan dryly.

Maerad sat on the floor where she was. "I'll sit here then," she said.

"As you will." Arkan suddenly looked bored. "Well, Elednor of Edil-Amarandh, I did not bring you here to debate the virtues or otherwise of this and that."

"Why did you, then?" Maerad looked up, anger stirring again inside her. "I didn't choose to come here. And I want to go."

"Go where, Elednor of Edil-Amarandh? Back into the snow, to give it your other fingers? The snow is always hungry."

"I–I have things I must do," Maerad answered. An overwhelming desolation swept over her. I want to go home, she thought; but I have no home to go to. An image of Hem leapt into her mind, turning towards her with his vivid, mischievous smile, and a piercing sense of how much she missed him filled her whole body. She didn't want to sit any longer on the floor of this throne room, being toyed with by the Winterking.

"What things? I suppose you have business with my old acquaintance, Sharma. You would be the merest morsel to him, I fear." Arkan laughed, and Maerad felt a shiver run down her back. Sharma, the Nameless One. "There is much you do not understand. No, I brought you here because I wish to talk to you. We have much to talk about, you and I."

"Do we?" Maerad stood up; her legs were shaky, but she could stand. "I think not, Winterking. What could you have to say to me that could possibly interest me? Why don't you just kill me? It would probably solve a lot of problems for your old acquaintance, Sharma." She spat the words out, and turned to go.

"My old acquaintance, my old enemy," said Arkan softly.

"Sharma threw me to the dogs of the Light; he betrayed me. He was once not without charm, for a human. He deceived many, who now only remember that he deceived me and choose not to remember that they too were fooled. He betrayed all Elidhu."

Maerad stopped, her spine tingling, but did not turn around.

"He stole something precious from us," said Arkan. "But he could only use its half; and the other half is in your keeping."

Maerad involuntarily spun around and stared at the Winterking in wonder.

"I want my Song back," said Arkan.

There was a long silence.

"How do I know it's your Song?" said Maerad coldly. "It might equally be Ardina's Song. Ardina, who is your enemy."

"Ardina is not my enemy. The Song is of us both."

"I don't believe anything you say." Maerad turned and walked from the throne room, not looking behind her, and she felt the room momentarily darken, as if she had finally succeeded in disturbing Arkan's calm. But he did not call her back.

She met Gima by the door. For once, the old woman didn't say anything; she seemed awed and shaken. She led Maerad back in silence to her chamber. Once there, Maerad sank gratefully onto the bed. She had managed to stay upright on the walk back, but it had taken all the will she possessed.

One to me, she said to her lyre. Twenty to him, but one to me.

XXIV

THE GAME

MAERAD dreamed of Cadvan. He was not dressed in his usual worn travelling clothes, but as for a festival, with a long cloak edged with silver embroidery and the brooch of Lirigon shining on his breast, and in the dream Maerad had forgotten he was dead. He stood before a long table laden with food of the kind Maerad had not seen for months – Annaren food. There were fresh breads of rye and wheat and linseed, salads of lettuce and radish and mushrooms and herbs, delicately roasted and potted meats, bowls of strawberries and damsons and currants, and tarts filled with apple and pear – crystalline with honey and spices – and plates of sweetmeats, candied apples and sugared chestnuts. Tall glass decanters filled with rich wines stood among the feast like glittering jewels. Maerad's mouth filled with water, and she stepped forward eagerly to the table, but Cadvan took her arm, holding her back.

"I'm so hungry," she said.

"Elednor," said Cadvan, using her Truename for the first time since her instatement. "All this is yours. You just have to take it."

Maerad turned to him in surprise.

"But you're stopping me," she said.

"No," he said. "It is you, stopping yourself." And when she looked again at her arm, she realized that he wasn't holding her back at all.

Oh, she thought; I was just imagining it … but then the dream dissolved into other dreams that she would not remember.

When she awoke, for a moment it was as if the past few months had not happened: Cadvan and Dernhil and Dharin were still alive, and she was neither hunted nor imprisoned. She was back in Innail, a young girl released from slavery and tasting freedom for the first time. She rolled over, completely relaxed, and opened her eyes; but instead of the bright casement of her chamber in Innail, she saw the translucent moonstone of the walls of Arkan-da. She blinked, and woke up properly, rubbing her eyes.

When she opened them again, she did not see the strange but beautiful chamber she had already become used to. The air she breathed was piercingly cold, and before her was a wall of black, undressed stone in which flickered a crude oil lamp, a wick floating in oil in a stone bowl. She sat on a thin pallet, covered in furs, on the freezing floor. She blinked, and the walls shimmered as if they were not quite substantial, but they did not vanish. Her left hand hurt her and she looked down; her fingers were missing, but instead of a long-healed scar she saw a healing wound. She stroked it and flinched, and as she did she saw with amazement the wound heal before her eyes, and the strange sourceless illumination returned. When she looked up, the chamber was again made of moonstone.

She tried to trace what she had been feeling when the room changed, and then remembered her dream. Cadvan, she thought; maybe he speaks to me from beyond the Gates. But instead of a feast, he seeks to show me famine ... typical. The edges of her mouth quirked up with sardonic humour, but inside she felt a sudden warmth, as if she were not quite so alone. Immediately the moonstone walls became transparent, as if she were seeing through them into another reality.

I am in a dungeon, she thought with wonder. But it is an enchanted dungeon...

This time she tried to will the other vision. She wanted to see if her lyre, which she had laid by the chest, was present when the room changed, or whether it vanished. But now the dream sense had vanished, and she could not see the reality of her cell. She sighed, and finally stepped out of bed, curling her toes in the warm rug, stepped over to the lyre and picked it up.

Elednor, she thought, returning to her bed. How did the Winterking know my name? Is that how he ensorcels me? Is this how my power has suddenly vanished? The more she thought about it, the more certain she was. Maybe it had been the case even in the Gwalhain Pass, when she and Cadvan had been attacked by the iridugul and she had not been able to join with him to fight them off. The Winterking had been working against her for a long time now, ever since she had left Thorold. Or perhaps earlier. No doubt he had seen her in the pool in his throne room: Ardina had used a pool to see events in distant places, and Cadvan said the Landrost, the Elidhu he had been fleeing when they met, had a pool that he used to see what he willed. But how did the Winterking find it out? The only people who knew her Truename were Cadvan and Saliman and Nelac, and she knew that none of them would betray her.

My name was foretold, she remembered suddenly. Any fool who read the prophecies aright would know it. A cold fear stirred in her heart: how was she to escape Arkan if he knew her Truename, if he wielded such power over her that he could fool her hands, her eyes, her very skin? And even if she did escape his stronghold, how was she to remain free, how was she to regain her full power, if he could take it from her again?

No, she said to herself. No, it can't mean that. But in her heart she knew that it was true. Any Bard whose Truename was known by an enemy was crippled.

She sat despondently for a while, holding her lyre. But

something within her was stronger today; perhaps some of the warmth of the dream still clung to her mind. Finally she sat up straight and shook herself. Well, she thought, I'll try the lyre, and see what happens. A song for the Winterking, maybe. Perhaps his ensorcelment can make my injured playing into a real song. She fiddled around for a while, trying to adjust her grasp of the instrument to her missing fingers, and, shutting her eyes, drew her right hand across the strings.

She instantly realized what she had been unable to admit to herself: she would not be able to play the lyre again. She could no longer use her left hand to pluck or block the strings to make chords. The pain of her loss of music seemed to go from her missing fingers right into her heart, and she rested her forehead on the instrument as the notes died away into silence, breathing in the smell of the fragrant almond oil with which she polished it. But then she took a deep breath. Well, I have only one and a half fingers and a thumb, she thought, but I have other bits of hand. Perhaps I can still play a little.

She sat up straight again and this time tried a simple chord, one that only needed her forefinger and thumb. It rang out musically into the room, and as it did the moonstone vanished and she was suddenly in a dungeon. She stared at the oil lamp on the wall before her, noting how it dimmed and vanished as the chord died on the air. Then she set her lips and tried another, more difficult, chord. This was fumbled; she could not get it true. But the enchanted room still vanished.

She put the lyre down and thought for a while. This must be her lyre; no illusory lyre would hold enough magery to contest the Winterking. But then why had he given it to her? Surely he would have expected her to find out that it dissolved his sorcery? She tried the chord again, getting it true this time. The same thing happened. But as the sorcery vanished, her hand hurt, and after three chords she had cracked the scabs and they were already bleeding. She put the instrument down and stared at it as if she never seen it before.

Even with the knowledge that the Treesong was inscribed on her lyre, she began to think it was more enchanted than she had realized; more enchanted than the Winterking knew, or why did he let her have it?

The Winterking did not want her dead; without the enchantment, the dungeon was merely cold and uncomfortable. She had been colder in her pallet at Gilman's Cot without taking harm. She thought of her weakness the day before, when she had stood before the Winterking. Her body was not strong enough, yet, to rely on. She must heal and strengthen herself before she could think of escaping. The Winterking wanted the Treesong, and somehow she was important to him as well. She must find out why. She must find out everything she could: and then she must escape him and go back to Annar.

She had just reached this conclusion when Gima entered with a meal, some fatty meat smoked and then fried and a sort of mash of vegetables flavoured with dill and sour goat's milk. For the first time, Maerad smiled at Gima, and the old woman smiled back. Maerad ate the food hungrily. She didn't dare to think what it was really like – maybe it was something else, something less appealing – but it was hot and the feeling of solidity it gave her was reassuring.

"You're eating well today," said Gima. "You'll be a fat little fish if you keep on."

"It's really nice," said Maerad. "Did you make it?"

"Oh, bless you, no," said Gima, cackling. "The master has cooks enough in his kitchens to keep me away from the pot. I just bring it."

"How many cooks is that?" asked Maerad.

"Oh, he has forty or fifty at least. And more to make the beds and to keep the palace clean, and to keep us all safe from wolves and suchlike."

"He must be a good master, then."

"A good master. Oh yes, he's a good master. We all love him."

Maerad kept chatting while she ate, and Gima sat herself comfortably on the chest, happy to talk. Gima told her that the Ice Palace was very big, bigger than Gima knew how to say, with countless rooms, and that many people lived there. Maerad chatted mindlessly, drawing out the old woman, who seemed relieved that she was at last being friendly, and responded enthusiastically, speaking now of her chilblains and next of how she had entered the Winterking's service. Maerad remembered back to the map in Gahal's room in Ossin: the Osidh Nak branched out north-east from the Osidh Annova, where the Osidh Elanor met them. And if she had it right, the Loden Pass to Annar would be due south about eighty leagues from Arkan-da. It was a day's walk either way out of the mountains.

"Oh, but a hard walk," said Gima, shuddering with the memory. "Such chasms on one side would make your heart stop still, and those cliffs! But it was all worth it when I got here."

"Why was it worth it?" asked Maerad curiously.

"Oh, you've seen the master," said Gima comfortably. "We all work hard for him. We all are happy here, in this beautiful palace."

Horrible dungeon more like, thought Maerad, but kept her thought to herself. The more she talked to Gima, the more sorry she felt for her. But maybe she was right to be happy, even if her present life was nothing more than a powerful illusion; in her former life she had been a slave, and was married off when she was younger than Maerad to a man who beat her. She had borne him three dead children. After the third child he had thrown her out of the house, saying that she had cursed him, and she would have died homeless and alone if she had not been taken into Arkan's service.

It seemed that Maerad was again to see the Winterking, and she let Gima fuss around her, putting on the elegant furred robe and brushing her hair. She felt more prepared than she had the day before. Her legs were much stronger today, and she merely felt tired as they wound through the long passages to the throne room.

As before, Arkan was seated at the far end of the room, but this time Gima, who was visibly quaking, stayed by the door instead of entering with Maerad. Maerad wondered what she meant by saying that she loved the Winterking; if she showed any emotion in his presence, it was naked terror. Perhaps the sorcery also works on feelings, she thought, so terror seems like love. She wondered briefly why she was not afraid; perhaps Arkan did not want her to be frightened. Or maybe (she thought with a flicker of hope) it was because she truly wasn't afraid. After all, she thought, I am partly Elidhu.

When she reached the dais, she looked up into the Winterking's icy eyes.

"Greetings, Elednor," he said. This time she thought she detected a flash of mockery as he said her name. "Did you sleep well?"

"I slept as well as could be expected," she answered coldly. "And you?"

"Me?" Arkan looked at her expressionlessly. "I do not sleep."

Maerad suddenly wondered what time was to an entity that would not die. It could not be the same as it was for her, a straight line that led into darkness. Or was it like that? she mused, distracted; perhaps it was a river that meandered and branched into ever-widening deltas before it merged into an immense, boundless sea. She suddenly realized that the

Winterking was speaking, and she had not heard what he had said.

"I'm sorry?" she said. "I was – I was thinking about something else."

Arkan regarded her sceptically. "I said that perhaps today you should sit down. Or will you manage to remain upright during our conversation?"

Maerad considered briefly. "I will sit down, I thank you." She lifted the hem of her robe and stepped onto the dais, passing close before the Winterking to reach the black stool that stood by the throne. Her skin bunched up in goosepimples as if she passed before an icy blast, but she did not look at him. She settled herself.

"That is wiser," said Arkan. "You humans are so – frail." It was not quite a threat; but having decided that she did not want to die, that she wanted to escape, Maerad almost felt her mask of composure slip.

"We are," said Maerad. "But that does not mean that we are weak." She paused. "When did you learn my Truename?"

"I know the names of everything," said Arkan.

"That's not true," said Maerad, without rancour, and then added on an obscure impulse: "I'll warrant you don't know the name of my brother."

"Your brother? I know his name, as I know the names of your mother and father and all else about you, more than you know yourself, Maerad of Pellinor, Elednor of Edil-Amarandh." A shiver went down Maerad's spine, but not an entirely unpleasant one.

"What is his usename, then?" she asked politely.

"It is Cai of Pellinor, of course," he said.

"No, it's not," said Maerad. She looked back at him scornfully, and for an instant his gaze faltered.

"You lie," he said.

"I do not lie," she answered. "Although one has called me a

liar, I did not know what he meant."

Arkan laughed, a long low laugh. "Was that the wise man you travelled so far to consult?" he said, at last. "And he called you a liar? Ah, that is amusing."

"Then do you know what he meant?" From here, Maerad could look Arkan in the eye. She could tell he was not used to such a straight gaze, and felt it as an affront, as certainly as she knew he would say nothing about it.

"Lying is not the same thing as not speaking the truth," said Arkan. "Elidhu do not lie. Why should we lie? Only humans lie, because they think that language can give them another reality. And then out of their lies they make that reality. Have you not understood that yet? Why do you think Sharma is as he is? He is the Great Liar, and his lie almost became the whole world."

"But it was still a lie." Maerad found these conversations disconcerting; they never seemed to go in the directions she imagined. "He wanted to destroy truth."

"The truth that he wanted to destroy was the truth that he must die. I have seldom met a human being who really wanted to die. Sharma found death a great insult, and he envied the Elidhu, because we do not die. Why do you think he stole our Song? But even he, one of the greatest mages of a golden age of Bards, could not make the truth as he wanted it."

"So he wished to destroy all truths," said Maerad.

"No," said Arkan. "He did know one truth: power. And power is the only thing that humans understand."

"No, it's not," said Maerad stubbornly. "There are other truer truths." She stared at Arkan, thinking that his veins, if he indeed possessed any, probably ran with ice water; how would he understand the truths of love, of kin, of blood? Of unassuagable grief and longing?

"I know what you think," said Arkan. He glanced at her, and it went deeply into Maerad, like a lance of ice. "What of love? What of sorrow?"

"I don't think you know what those things are," said Maerad sharply.

"You have no idea what I know." His scorn was naked, and she flinched. "No human knows anything of truth. Could you pick the smallest pebble out of a stream and tell me the truth of it? Could you tell me its story of long aeons of water and wind and ice and fire? No, to you it would be just a pebble, resting in your hand, of note only because you had picked it up. But that is not its truth."

"Does that make me a liar?"

"Perhaps."

"I do not claim anything," said Maerad, and suddenly felt forlorn. It was true: she did not, and could not, claim anything. "That doesn't explain why Inka-Reb said I was a liar. He meant something else. If you know everything, perhaps you can explain that."

"I do not know why the Singer said you were a liar," said Arkan indifferently. "I think you are a liar because you think you know what is true. You think you feel what is true. But you do not yet know what you do feel and what you do know. You desire and do not take, you love and are too afraid to feel your love, you conceal your vanity and pettiness from yourself, you are afraid to look into your soul and see what you are. That is why you are a liar."

Maerad was unexpectedly stung, and glared at Arkan. "You have no right to say such things," she said.

He shrugged. "You asked. You know enough to know that I speak truly."

Maerad stared down the throne room towards the pool. *Arkan is right*, she thought. *It's what people mean when they mention how young I am.* "What if I do learn truth?" she asked at last.

"Then you will be miserable," said Arkan. "So, you see, it is easy to understand why humans are such liars." He seemed to be laughing, and Maerad stared at him defiantly.

"Why would a human not choose what is true?" she asked.

Arkan held her gaze, and then glanced away; and as he did so the throne room seem to shiver, as if it were made of water instead of stone, and his face seemed like a double face, as if a mask had slipped. It revealed something dark and cold and dangerous that made Maerad feel really afraid for the first time. Then the mask was back, but the impression remained, like an after-image of a brilliant light. Her heart started beating fast. He did not seem so duplicitous now; his face was comely as before, but now it had dimension, depth, weight, darkness. Maerad was suddenly deeply unsettled.

"I have only once known a human choose what is true," said Arkan. "Why should they? They do not live long enough to find out anything: they are like snowflakes, that die in the air and disappear."

"To you it seems that way," said Maerad. "But time feels different to us than it does to you."

A silence fell between them. Maerad was thinking of her dungeon, which his illusions made into a luxurious chamber. Perhaps the Winterking thought that was really what she preferred and was, by his standards, being kind.

"Why did you capture me?" she asked at last. "I know nothing of the Treesong. I have been told I must seek it, so that the Nameless One will not prevail in his new rising. And I have been told that you ally yourself with him, and that he released you from your banishment. Is this true?" She paused. "And you still haven't told me how you know my Truename."

"So many questions! You are impatient," said the Winterking. "It was not difficult to know your Truename. If you truly were the Foretold, then you would have no other name. A flaw in the plans, yes? For anyone who is attentive to the signs and knows the lore will be aware of your name. Your prophets were far sighted, but not wise." He smiled at her and Maerad shivered: the Nameless One, too, would know her Truename.

"And is the Nameless One your ally?"

Arkan's mouth thinned. "I would not call him an ally. Yes, it is true: he broke my banishment. You cannot understand what a terrible punishment it is to be exiled from my mountains, my rocks, my place … it is something no human can understand. It is to have no body, no mind, no home, no life." He looked directly at Maerad, and, as if a door had suddenly opened, she felt a desolation that staggered her. She knew what it was to feel homeless, to be alone and abandoned without kin, but Arkan was speaking of something else: millennia of exile, of unbeing. She blinked.

"So you owe the Nameless One your gratitude," she said.

"I owe him nothing." The throne room flickered with icy rage. "Do not be so stupid. It does not become you."

"Then what do you want from me?"

"I told you what I want."

"But I don't have it." Maerad studied his face, looking for any sign that he knew she was not telling the truth.

"Of course you have it. Or you have the half that Sharma desires. Do you think me a fool?" Maerad felt his displeasure; the room darkened, as if a shadow fell over the pool, and for the briefest second the throne room was as cold as ice. "You do not understand that it means nothing."

To Maerad's alarm, the Winterking stood up. He was very tall, much taller than a man. He stepped off the dais and walked towards the pool, moving with the fluid, predatory grace of a snow lynx. When he reached the pool he stood there with his back to her, dark against the glow, a halo of frosted light about his form.

"It means nothing to me," said Maerad angrily. "It is of no use to me at all. I don't know what it is and I don't know how to read it."

"Do you know where it is?" said Arkan.

Maerad bit her lip. Arkan was tricking her, confusing her with his talk of exile and right and wrong; she was being slow witted. She had just admitted that she had the Treesong. "What do you mean, 'where it is'?" she asked, trying to buy time.

Arkan turned violently, his face dark with anger, and strode back to Maerad, standing above her. "Do not play these childish games with me," he said. "I am not interested in your lies; you are here because I wish to speak with you, and to speak anything but truth is a waste of time. I know perfectly well that half of my Song is written down on your lyre."

Maerad's heart sank into her boots. "Then why don't you just take it, and give it to the Nameless One?" said Maerad bitterly. "And that will be the end of love and truth and all those things that you say don't exist, and then you can just cover the whole earth with snow and ice. Isn't that what you want?"

"Did you hear nothing that I said?"

"I don't trust anything you say to me."

"You should." Arkan grasped Maerad's shoulder, and she started and tried to move away, but could not: the cold pierced to her bone with a strange thrill. "We have interests in common, you and I."

Arkan's eyes were alight, but not with laughter; it was some other intensity she did not understand, and it frightened her. She pulled away from him. "Let me go," she said. "It hurts." He released his clasp. "I don't understand," Maerad said passionately, her fear flaming into anger. "You have murdered my dearest friends." An ache gathered in her throat. "You sent stormdogs and iridugul to kill us. You ordered those Jussack thugs to capture me, and they dragged me hundreds of leagues, half dead, across the winter lands. I am your prisoner, held here against my will. And then you say to me, we have things in common. We have nothing in common."

Arkan sat down again on his throne, his face turned from Maerad, and there was silence for some time. Maerad rubbed her shoulder where he had touched it, trying to get some warmth back. At last, he stirred and spoke.

"I am not used to speaking to such as you. I do not wish you to be afraid, and I do not desire your anger. I regret your sorrow."

"Yet everything you have done has made me full of sorrow and fear and anger," Maerad said. "Should I now forgive you those things?"

"Your sorrow evades me," Arkan answered. "It is prideful and full of anger against death. All those you say are dead, they are merely in another place. There is another sorrow, the sorrow of deathlessness, which humans do not understand."

"Except the Nameless One," said Maerad.

"Except Sharma. But he does not understand it in the way of the Elidhu. For him endless life is endless torment. It is not so with us."

There was another pause while Maerad tried to sort out her thoughts. She remembered her vow to escape, her need to find out what Arkan knew.

"You want a Song that I don't understand and can't read. You know it is written on my lyre, but you say it's no use to you. You say you know more about me than I do, but you won't tell me what you know. If there's no point to my being here, and you don't want to kill me, why don't you just let me go?"

"There is something that I do not know," said Arkan.

"That I do know?" Maerad looked at him questioningly. "What do I know? I don't know anything."

"Knowing and being are not so different." Arkan fixed

Maerad with a penetrating stare. "Do you not understand that you are part of the riddle?"

"Part of what riddle?" asked Maerad with exasperation. "I thought the riddle was the Treesong."

"Aye," said the Winterking. "And you are part of the Treesong. It will not be free unless by your hands."

Maerad looked at Arkan in disbelief. "What do you mean? I have to play the Song?"

"It must be released, to be given back. You are the player, and the singer as well as the seeker. Did you not know that?"

Maerad held up her maimed hand and thrust it into Arkan's face. "I cannot play anything now," she said passionately. "Let alone a Song that I do not understand. I am crippled, you understand? And I can't read like Bards can. My whole life, I was a slave. But even if I wasn't, even if I was wise as wise, I still couldn't read it. Even the most learned Bards can't read that script."

Maerad paused, breathing hard, and stared bitterly at Arkan. "I have failed. I have failed everyone I love, everyone who loved me. I have failed my name and I have failed the prophecies. And now I have even failed you. Why don't you just let me go?"

"Why do you wish to leave here? It is comfortable, yes? But perhaps that is not enough for you. Say what you desire, and I will do what I can to provide it."

Maerad paused and thought. She desired her freedom, but clearly that was the one thing Arkan would not give her. "I don't like being shut in my room," she said, in a softer voice. "I would like to look around the palace. I would like to go outside."

"You cannot leave here, Elednor of Edil-Amarandh. I think you would do well to remember that, instead of wasting your time in futile efforts to escape." As Arkan said her name,

Maerad felt as if she jerked a tight leash on her mind, reminding her of his power over her: but this time she sensed something, a weakness. Perhaps his control was not as complete as he had thought.

"And how long do you plan to keep me here?"

"You will stay so long as I need you to. While you are here, Sharma cannot take you: he has not the power to challenge me in my own domain. You do not know how much he desires to find you, nor how fortunate you are that I found you first. You cannot outrun Sharma's spies and servants; they are everywhere, and they all seek one thing: you. Do not believe that they will not find you. They will."

Maerad shuddered, remembering her nightmares where Hulls reached for her, the foredream where the darkness sought her.

"The Nameless One is cruel, as I am not," said Arkan. "You would not be permitted the escape of death: your most secret mind would be open, skinless and raw, to his hatred and malice. You could hide nowhere. Your existence would be an endless torment. There would be no resistance; he would break you, and you would do anything he desired."

Maerad considered this. She thought that Arkan was probably speaking the truth. And it seemed clear that the Winterking was pursuing his own interests; she found it difficult to believe that anyone so arrogant would consent to serve another. She studied him mistrustfully.

"I thought you and Ardina were enemies," she said at last. "And yet you say you are not."

Arkan made a dismissive gesture with his hands. "In the deeps of time we waged different wars," he said. "Things change."

A terrible thought occurred to Maerad: had Ardina delivered her to the Winterking? Had she betrayed Maerad? She thought of Ardina, the beautiful, amoral Elidhu she had first met in the Weywood, the wise and just Queen of Rachida, the blazing Moonchild. Ardina was a creature of many faces: Maerad had no reason to believe that she would not have betrayed her. The thought made her feel miserable, and she realized that she was exhausted. She looked down at her hands: they were trembling.

"I want to go back to my room," she said.

"As you like," said Arkan. "We will speak when you next wake. You have the freedom of the palace; you may wander where you will."

Maerad stepped off the dais and walked towards the door of the throne room without saying anything further. At the door, she turned and looked back. The king's throne was empty.

Once back in her room, Maerad flung herself on the bed and covered her face to shut out the sight of the chamber. Her conversations with the Winterking seemed to turn everything on its head. What was real and what was illusion? She felt as if she didn't know anything any more. She sat up and put her hands in front of her eyes. Was it illusion that her hand was mutilated? But no, when she had played the lyre her fingers were still missing: only then they were not so well healed. Or maybe her wound was an illusion as well? How was she to tell? On a sudden impulse, she scratched her right hand viciously with her left forefinger, hard enough to draw blood. It opened a wound: but, as she watched, the skin joined and healed, and it seemed as if she were not scratched at all.

That, at least, could not be real.

She picked up her lyre and slowly stroked a chord. As the notes rang out, she saw the scratch open on her hand, the blood running down into her palm. It tickled, and she licked the blood off her hand thoughtfully until the music faded and her hand was whole and she was back again in her beautiful prison of ice.

The more she thought about it, the more she thought that Arkan was being honest with her. She did not trust him, but she believed what he said about the Nameless One, and his story of betrayal. Perhaps it was Arkan himself who had revealed the Treesong to the Nameless One – she wished fiercely she knew more of the history of the Dhyllin, of the legendary citadel of Afinil, when Bards and Elidhu had sung together, before the Great Silence. She would be better able to judge his tale then: she would know whether he sought to mislead her, whether he warped the truth to his own ends.

Ardina had told her she was neither of the Dark nor the Light. Arkan had more or less said the same thing. They were very different from what she had been told of other Elidhu like the Lamedon. She struggled to remember what Cadvan taught her. No one knew how many there were, and when the Great Silence had fallen on Annar they had withdrawn from human affairs, and would no longer take human shape. Except, she thought, Arkan and Ardina, who had domains over which they ruled as king and queen. Ardina had done so for love: or that was the legend. But Arkan – why had he? Was it also for love of a human being? Perhaps – she dismissed the thought as ridiculous almost as soon as it occurred to her, but it returned and she puzzled over it, wondering if it was perhaps not so far-fetched – perhaps Arkan had loved Sharma, and perhaps he had been betrayed by him. Love would explain why Arkan spoke of the Nameless One with such bitterness, and also, maybe, why he might have given him the Treesong. If he had. After all, there were many stories of love between Elementals and humans. But the Treesong, she thought suddenly, did not belong only to Arkan. Did he want it only for himself?

Maerad felt dizzy. She lay on her back and shut her eyes.

Beneath all these thoughts was the necessity of escape.

Whatever Arkan wanted of her, he had no right to keep her against her will. She had no doubt that he was not exaggerating the dangers of the Dark in Annar: even the Light had been conscripted against her. Yet some deep instinct, beyond her desire for freedom, told her that she must get back to Annar.

Hem needed her; maybe he was the only person who really needed her – not as an embodiment of prophecy, not as the final hope of the Light against the Nameless One, but as his sister. And Saliman could help her quest; he was almost as powerful a Bard as Cadvan. But how could she possibly find them? The chaos of war must be everywhere by now: perhaps Turbansk was already fallen, and Annar itself riven by civil war.

Arkan was confident she could not escape him; so confident that she felt a little hope. She did not think that he knew that she had pierced the illusion of his ice palace. But it was possible that he was toying with her: he knew, after all, that the Treesong was written on the lyre, and perhaps he knew of its power to break his sorcery. But Maerad thought that he did not know, and it was much better that he didn't.

Perhaps he underestimates me, Maerad thought hopefully. In which case, I am a little freer: he will not watch me so carefully. And if I am careful enough, if I am clever enough, perhaps I will find a way out of here.

She pondered for a while whether she was capable of being careful and clever enough to outwit the Winterking. She felt somewhat dubious. But, she thought, she had little to lose by trying. Living in Gilman's Cot, she had played private games to escape the misery of her life. Here life was not so miserable: she was more like an honoured hostage than a slave. It would be a game, a game with high stakes, a game for her freedom, for her truth.

A thought struck Maerad like a hammer, and she sat up. Perhaps Arkan could read the runes on her lyre.

Could she risk showing the lyre to Arkan and asking him? Could she risk not doing so? If it was Arkan who gave the Song to the Nameless One, he may have had a part in making the runes. Perhaps he understood what they meant. It might be her single chance to decipher the runes.

Maerad lay down again. She was so tired... She tried to weigh the risks of taking her lyre to Arkan against the possible gains, but sleep blanked out her mind before she reached any decision.

She woke knowing she had dreamed, but without any memory of dreaming. Again she felt a little easier in her soul, as if sleep had offered her some respite. She opened her eyes and saw that the walls were the rock walls of a dungeon. She rubbed her eyes and the dungeon shimmered and faded, and in a few moments her comfortable chamber had returned.

Perhaps – perhaps there was a way out.

It struck her that she had had no idea what the time was since she had been in Arkan-da. There was no window in her room, and the light, anywhere she walked, was always the same soft illumination. It always seemed to be night, and she had lost her bodily sense of time: she ate when she was fed, rose when she woke, slept when she was tired, with no idea whether it was morning, noon or night. It was disturbing. It also occurred to her that although Gima had said that hundreds of people lived in Arkan-da, Maerad had seen no one except Gima and the Winterking. There were not even guards at the door of his throne room.

Her question had answered itself while she slept. She would take the lyre to the Winterking. She would have to be wary, and careful not to reveal that she saw through the enchantments of his stronghold. But it did seem the best chance she had of reading the runes. It was possible that even if he could read them, he would not tell her what they meant; although if he wished her to play the Song, then surely he could not keep the meaning from her?

That day, Gima took her to a bathroom, and she was able to wash. Steaming hot water fell in a constant waterfall from a pipe carved as the mouth of a fish, and it was caught in a deep and narrow stone bath. To sit in it she had to draw her knees up to her chest; the water reached her shoulders. There was no soap or lavender oil, she noted regretfully, but there was no shortage of hot water. As the water foamed around her neck, she wondered whether it was real or not. Perhaps she really sat in a freezing cold pool, or maybe there was no water at all. Maerad decided she didn't want to know. She would enjoy the bath anyway.

She stepped out at last, her skin pink and steaming, and changed into the clean clothes Gima had put out for her. They were very warm; there was finely spun woollen underwear and several layers of woollen garments before she put on the fur-lined robes. If they were what they seemed, she thought, they were not utterly impractical; she might not die of cold if she escaped. When she went back to her chamber she played a few chords on her lyre, and was surprised to see that her clothes remained unchanged, although they were less rich in colour.

Probably he doesn't want me to freeze to death in my dungeon, she thought. She felt cheered by her discovery, and inspected her pack again. Her cloak was folded up, and her spare clothes had been washed. She didn't know where the warm overcoat Dharin had given her was; she would need that. If she had the freedom of the palace, she might be able to find it, or at least a coat that would be warm enough to protect her from the weather.

She took out Dernhil's book of poems, unwrapping it carefully from its oilskin. It was a small book, not much bigger than her hand, with a tooled calfskin cover, and each page was exquisitely illuminated in bright inks and gold leaf. The book fell open on a poem without a title. On the facing page was a detailed picture of a landscape, with a silver river winding away through green fields towards mountains ghostly with distance. In the foreground sat a young man playing a flute, his head bent in concentration. It looked very like, and probably was, somewhere in the valley of Innail, and Maerad felt a sudden pang of longing for its gentle green landscapes, so different from the harsh beauty of the north. In her mind's eye she saw Silvia, grave and merry and beautiful all at once, turning towards her with her face full of light, her lips open with what she was about to offer – a song, a joke, a kiss.

Maerad began to read the poem silently, moving her lips as she did; and as she read she heard in her mind the cadence of Dernhil's voice reading it to her, in another age of her life, in his rooms in Innail:

The breath of heaven teases my lips
With a single petal dislodged from the sky:
My love you are that single petal.

The gazelle looks up from the pool
Blinded by one spark of Light's radiance:
My love you are that single spark.

The peacock cries in the empty garden
For the memory of a tear outshining him:
My love you are that single tear.

O petal that is my garden of delight!
O spark that is my heart's conflagration!
O tear that is my swelling ocean of sorrow!

An icy splinter seemed to melt in Maerad's heart as she read, and she looked up blindly from the page, her eyes full of tears. Dernhil would never read that poem to anyone again, would never sit gravely in his study with his cloak thrown carelessly on a chair nearby, surrounded by crooked towers of books, oblivious to everything but the scratching of his pen on parchment. Yes, we are frail, thought Maerad; but within that frailty is such strength and such beauty, such love … surely it is not all for nothing? Surely it means something, even should the dark overwhelm us utterly?

Sorrow flooded though her, and she hid her face in her hands. She couldn't remember the last time she had cried. She had not been able to weep for Dharin's death. Her despair had shrivelled her soul: she had been too hurt for such a generosity as tears. At last she mourned him, his gentleness, his courage, his friendship, the wound his absence left within her. She wept for Dernhil and Cadvan, for Darsor, for Imi, for Hem and his broken childhood, for her mother and father, so cruelly killed; and lastly she wept for herself. And as she wept, she felt as if all those she loved and missed, the dead and the living, were somehow present, and in her sorrow was a painful comfort.

At last, her tears ceased. She blinked, rubbing her eyes, and saw that she was in the dungeon, not the enchanted room. It was cold, and she wrapped her robes tightly around herself, and looked back down at the book. Its colours seemed brighter still in the dim, flickering light of the oil lamp.

I am free, Maerad thought. I am here, imprisoned; but at last I am free.

XXV

THE SONG

MAERAD decided to take Arkan at his word and, since Gima did not come to her chamber again that day, she began to explore the Ice Palace. Her moonstone chamber was back, but it had now a sense of unreality, as if it were slightly less stable than it had been. She took care to remember her route; she didn't want to get lost. She decided to use a system of counting, as if she were remembering a complex piece of music, so she could find her way back. No one stopped her; no one was there to stop her. She didn't see anyone else at all.

Arkan-da was eerie and deserted. It seemed to be a busy place, where people lived and made things and ate, but wherever Maerad walked it was as if they had abandoned their tasks and left just before she got there. There were endless corridors with scores of doorways, and when she lifted the hangings that covered the doors she saw a bewildering variety of rooms. Some seemed to be bed chambers, furnished simply, but beautifully, with personal belongings scattered on the bed or the floor, as if someone had just walked out. She saw a place that seemed to be a kitchen, with black iron implements hanging from the ceiling and an iron cauldron suspended on a tripod over a fire, bubbling, but no one was there.

There were many grand halls with pillars of iron and stone, so big that the columns marched off into long distances; and store rooms with shelves full of dried or smoked foods, sides of meats or long sausages or onions; and she saw armouries, with rows of pikes and maces and strange leather helms.

She looked always for an exit or a window, but she didn't find any until she entered a high, wide passageway supported by iron pillars. She was just about to turn to find her way back to her own room when a difference in the light at the other end made her look again. Although her legs were already beginning to ache, she made herself walk to the other end, and as she did she saw that she had indeed found a door. And the door was open.

The passageway was as deserted as the rest of the palace had been, so no one stopped her from stepping outside. The air was freezing, but very still. And the relief of knowing what the time was, the delight of seeing the stars, of walking on snow, made her eyes prickle with tears.

The sky was clear, the stars scattered in hard brilliance over a deep-blue field. She squinted through the darkness. Before her glimmered a long, snow-covered slope, running between two sheer rock walls, which met further down to form the high black arch. She was as sure as she could be that the arch was the one she remembered passing beneath when she had arrived at Arkan-da. But she did not remember seeing any palace beyond it, or anything at all, apart from more mountains. She looked behind her, and saw that no palace stood at her back: she stood at the open mouth of a large cave, and above her stretched the sheer cliff of a mountainside. Beyond the arch a path continued a little way before it ran into a road that curled itself around the side of the mountain. One way went north and one south; but which was which?

Suddenly the silence was rent by the howling of a wolf. Maerad started, remembering the wolves in Inka-Reb's cave, and the wolves she thought she had seen as she was carried across Zmarkan by the Jussacks. In her mind's eye she saw again Claw's savage beauty. She realized she wasn't afraid of dogs any more; maybe not even of wolves. And then, with a pang, she thought: They are free, and they sing their own song. She listened until the eerie ululations died away into the stillness of the night.

Maerad stood there as long as she could bear the cold, breathing in the fresh air with a sense of exhilaration. Her escape from the Ice Palace now seemed possible: she had found a way. She sighed in pure happiness.

"The mountains are very beautiful, are they not, Elednor of Edil-Amarandh?" said the Winterking, at her shoulder.

Maerad jumped with shock, and turned around. Arkan was standing just behind her.

"You were thinking, no doubt, how easy it would be to walk out of Arkan-da," he said.

Maerad saw no point in dissembling. "What would stop me?" she said. "The road is just over there."

"You could try," said Arkan easily. "I think you would find it interesting. If you watched that arch long enough, you would see that not even birds fly over it."

"I remember coming under that arch," said Maerad. "But nothing more. And I would probably freeze to death out here before anyone found me, if I swooned again."

"Do not fear," said Arkan. "I always know where you are."

Maerad felt uneasily that this was true, and that Arkan had followed her meanderings around his palace that day.

"I would like to come out here again," she said. "I am happy to see the stars and to breathe the wind. I find it hard to live without windows. I miss the sky."

"There is no harm in that," said Arkan. "And how did you find my palace?"

"It is very beautiful," said Maerad truthfully. "But odd. I didn't see a single person all day. Gima said hundreds of people live here, but I didn't see anybody."

"Does that disconcert you? They have been told to avoid
you, for fear that you may be frightened. But you are shivering; perhaps we can go back inside." Arkan turned, courteously
offering Maerad his arm as if they stood in a hall in Annar, about
to enter a feast, rather than on the bleak side of a mountain. She
hesitated, and then took his arm, feeling a numbing chill in her
hand as she did so, and they walked back inside. Immediately
it was warmer, and Maerad looked along the ice-white walls
with their rows of iron pillars. Beautiful, she thought, but very
stark; everything here is ice and iron. Perhaps the Winterking
can imagine nothing else.

"I was remembering Innail today," she said conversationally.
"It was the first School I ever saw, I mean, apart from Pellinor,
which I don't remember very well. It is a lovely place."

"I have never been there, though I have seen it in my mind's
eye," said Arkan. "Yes, it has a certain beauty."

"I miss green. Green fields, green trees, flowers…"

"Such green withers and dies," said Arkan. He disengaged
Maerad's hand, and pointed towards an alcove carved out of
polished black stone. "Look at this."

Maerad saw with a gasp of astonishment that the alcove
housed a great, perfect diamond, almost her height; it was
much bigger than the crystal of the White Flame in Norloch,
and was incomparably beautiful. Light broke on its facets into
every colour, and as she gazed she felt almost hypnotized, as
if she could fall into its glittering maze and never find her way
out again.

"This is better than your green," said Arkan. "It will not
die."

"Only because it is not alive," said Maerad, freeing herself
with difficulty from the fascination of the diamond. She looked
up into Arkan's face, feeling an amazement growing within her
at the strangeness of their conversation. Arkan seemed different

to her since she had seen the shadow of his wild being; when she had first met him she had thought him handsome, but cold and somehow loathsome. Now she was aware of his vitality, an energy like a storm that made her skin tingle.

"I live," said Arkan, with a peculiar arrogance as they walked. "And I do not die. The wind lives, the snow lives, the ice lives, the mountains live. Rock and ice have their own voices, their own lives, their own breath, their own pulse. Do you deny them that?"

"No," said Maerad, unable to conceal the sadness in her voice. "But I like flowers."

"I will make you flowers, if you desire them."

"They would be flowers of ice. Beautiful, but cold. It wouldn't be the same. But thank you."

They walked in silence for a time through the endless, beautiful corridors, and despite herself Maerad found she was admiring the beauties of Arkan-da with different eyes. The design of the pillars had changed subtly, she thought; she saw flowers within them, all with six petals, but infinitely various and intricate. She was always conscious of the man pacing beside her, although she did not look at him.

"Why do you wish to please me?" she asked, breaking the silence. "You could just as easily cast me into some dark dungeon. What difference would it make to you?"

"It is better if you do not hate or fear me," said Arkan. "Song cannot be made out of hatred and fear. That is what Sharma failed to understand."

"What is needed to make song, then?"

Arkan turned and looked her full in her face, and Maerad's heart skipped a beat. "Do you not know?" he asked.

Maerad looked down at the floor and watched her feet. She did not want to answer.

"Love," said Arkan at last. "Love is what is needed to make

the Song. Love is why the darkness blossomed into light. Love is why the Earth spoke and became Elidhu."

Maerad blushed furiously, and did not dare to meet the Winterking's gaze. It was the first time he had addressed her so familiarly, and the intimacy struck a resonance through the depths of her being. She felt herself shaken with sudden desire, like a tree that fills with a wild light when it is touched by storm.

What do I know of love? she asked herself fiercely. And now this man, this Elidhu, this creature of ice and storm and stone, wants to show me? And then, fearfully, she asked herself if he mazed even her feelings, manipulating her as he manipulated the perceptions of Gima.

She waited until the wild beating of her heart calmed down, and then turned to the Winterking, careful to betray nothing of what she felt. "Was love why the Song was lost?" she asked boldly.

Arkan turned from her gaze, with a trace of bitterness. "Perhaps," he said.

"And is that why the Song split in two?"

"It can only be sung with love. And love can neither be stolen nor feigned." He gave her a swift, piercing glance, and Maerad felt herself tremble. "It can only be given."

And yet he keeps me prisoner, Maerad thought, averting her eyes. Hypocrite. But underneath her confusion, she knew that the answering leap within her was not commanded by the Winterking.

Maerad was silent for a long time after that, as they wound back through the Ice Palace into the heart of the mountain. She felt at once troubled and confused and strangely exhilarated. She was quite certain that when Arkan spoke of love, he meant something different from what she understood to be human love; and yet she did not know what to do with the desire that suddenly blazed within her, a desire she had never permitted herself to feel before. Some part of her, the Elemental part, she thought, stirred in response. Why now? she cried to herself in exasperation. And yet she lingered, nodding when Arkan pointed out some new beauty of his palace, agonizingly aware of when he took her arm, when he moved closer to her, when his robe brushed hers.

She thought of Cadvan, of Dernhil, of Dharin, of Hem. I cannot stay here, she thought. I must not... At last she took a deep breath.

"I can't play a Song I cannot read," she said. "Even if I still had all my fingers. Could you read the runes on my lyre?"

Arkan turned and regarded her thoughtfully. "Will you show them to me?"

Maerad reflected that Arkan could no doubt look at the runes, without her permission, any time he liked. "I'll bring my lyre tomorrow," she said. Whenever tomorrow is, she thought, in this dayless time. "Perhaps you can help me understand them."

"Perhaps," said Arkan. "Well, here we are at your chamber. Good morrow, Elednor of Edil-Amarandh." He bowed, and then his form began to glow with an intense light, which became so bright that Maerad blinked. When she looked again, he was gone.

Back in her chamber, Maerad walked restlessly from one end of the room to the other. The moonstone walls had seemed transparent before, less substantial; now they looked more solid and real. Maerad stared at the glowing walls with despair.

Am I to be betrayed by my own heart? she thought. That is what Arkan wants. At last, she sat down on the bed and picked up her lyre. She began to strum a simple song using the two or three chords that she could play without difficulty. The light changed and she looked up; to her intense relief she saw that the walls had vanished again, revealing her rocky dungeon.

She continued to play, seeking comfort in the music, although the scabs on her left hand broke and began to bleed. She put down the lyre and rummaged about in her pack until she found the healing balm. There was a little left, and she smeared her hand until the stinging was slightly numbed, and then she returned to the lyre. She played a ballad she had sung with Cadvan; the chords were easy if she did not pluck the melody. It was the ballad of Andomien and Beruldh, a short song that introduced a longer lay. Maerad sang the old story of Andomien's imprisonment and death in the stronghold of the sorcerer Karak, of the love she had for her brothers, of Beruldh's love for her, with new feeling; it was as if she had never properly sung it before, as if she had never really known what it meant. Perhaps Cadvan had guessed that it somehow foreshadowed her own fate, on that evening so long ago when he had played it in a birch dingle called Irihel, just after they had left Gilman's Cot. She saw his grave, dark face in her mind's eye, and realized again with undiminished anguish how much she missed him.

I must leave here soon, or the Winterking will bewilder me utterly, she thought, putting the lyre carefully back into its case. I am Elidhu, and Bard, and Pilanel too – and each part of me pulls in different directions. How am I to work out which is me? Can I ever be whole and true to myself? And how can I leave, anyway? Arkan is so certain that I can't. Maybe he is right.

Some part of her leapt up in gladness at the thought, but she sternly confronted her feelings, examining them as neutrally as she could, neither judging nor rejecting them. So, she said steadily to herself; I find I desire the Winterking. That doesn't mean that I will permit him to imprison me. If I am Elemental, I am a wild thing, not to be caged or bound: I am like the wolves in the mountains, and must sing my own song. He must know that. He cannot keep me here unless I want to stay.

She saw Hem's thin face before her, his dark-blue eyes haunted by deep shadows. I must find Hem, she thought passionately. He's all I've got left. And he needs me, more than anyone else in the world. A grieving love filled her body, a sweet, unassuagable ache that seeped through her from the marrow of her very bones. Hem, my brother...

With a thrill, she felt magery begin to run through her veins, a fiery illumination that spread from her heart to the soles of her feet and the tips of her fingers and the crown of her skull. She had forgotten what it was like to feel that power: it felt so long since it had lived within her, free and undimmed. For weeks now, she had resigned herself to its lack. She looked down at her hands with amazement and relief: they glimmered with silver magelight. She saw that her left hand had now five fingers of light: in her power, she was whole, unmaimed.

Slowly, reluctantly, she let the light dim. I must shield myself, she thought. The Winterking must not know. But how could he not feel the surge of her native power? She wondered if, with her returned magery, she could now make herself unseen. It could be no glimmerspell: it would need to be something deeper. She reached inside herself and concentrated.

The moonstone walls wavered and vanished.

Immediately Maerad released the charm, and the enchanted room reappeared. Then she shielded herself, fearing that Arkan would already know that her magery had returned. She needed to know more; she needed to know the limits of the Winterking's knowledge and power. For he did not know everything; and deep inside her, she was certain his power was not absolute.

Tomorrow, she thought, I will walk to the door and see the sky again.

*   *   *

Maerad woke from disturbed dreams and lay in bed, sending out her listening. The palace was silent, as it always was. She heard no distant footfalls on stone, no murmur of conversation, no bustle of activity. Next to her bed was a bowl filled with a hot gruel, which was still steaming. She had not heard anyone come in, but she heard one set of footsteps retreating, with a slight limp: Gima's footsteps.

There is no one here, she thought. There was never anyone here, except me and Arkan and Gima. It is all illusion. The Winterking is the mountain, and the mountain is the Winterking. I am trapped inside his mind.

She got out of bed and dressed, and ate the gruel hungrily. Then she wended her way through the endless corridors, remembering the way from the day before, counting it out like a piece of music. She made no mistakes, and came straight to the front door. It was daytime. A pale, bright sun struck up from the snow, momentarily blinding her. She shaded her brow with her hands, waiting for her eyes to adjust, and breathed in the cold air.

Now she could see the mountainscape, snowy slopes rising to sheer grey rock pinnacles, interrupted only by stands of pine and fir. She studied the sun, working out her bearings; after a while she was sure that the south road ran alongside the Winterking's mountain. The Trukuch range did not seem as high or as harsh as the Osidh Elanor. Perhaps she could walk the width of the range in a day, if Gima was correct and Arkanda was in the centre of the mountains.

She walked across the snow to the black arch and cautiously examined it, careful not to pass beneath it. It emanated a power that made her hair stand on end. Carefully keeping her magery shielded, she tried to measure it with her mind, trying to decide if she could break through it using her own powers.

She wondered if perhaps the lyre could help, since it seemed to dissolve Arkan's illusions, but she could reach no conclusion. And if I try and don't succeed, I won't get a second chance, she thought. So it looks like I'll have to try blind. And then what? If I do escape, he'll send the frost creatures after me. He might come himself. And I'll just be freezing to death on a mountainside.

If I were a gambler, she thought, I would not hazard anything on me.

Perversely, the thought cheered her, and she turned to walk back to the cave mouth, the door of the Ice Palace, half dreading, half hoping that she would find the Winterking waiting behind her. No one was there, but a prickle of presentiment made her look back again.

High on a slope beyond the arch there stood a huge white wolf, staring at her with yellow eyes.

Maerad stared back. The wolf did not seem to be threatening; but it looked as if it were waiting for something. For me? she thought, and almost laughed.

Yes, said the wolf into her mind. *I am waiting for you.*

Maerad was struck speechless with surprise, and merely stared.

Do not speak, said the wolf. *You will be heard. Listen. Remember. Triple tongued is triple named.*

The wolf loped off without waiting for a reaction, vanishing swiftly over the slope, and Maerad shook her head. It had left no footprints: the snow where it had been was utterly unmarked. Was it another illusion? Or some kind of wer? Or was it simply that she was losing her mind?

It is, thought Maerad, quite possible that I am going mad.

Triple tongued is triple named.

She stopped dead, realising what the wolf meant.

Three tongues: Human, Bard, Elidhu. Three names. She must have three names. Maerad, Elednor ... and another, which even she did not know. A deeper Truename.

The Winterking did not know her third name.

She wandered back to her chamber without meeting anyone. She found Gima waiting for her in agitation. "The master waits you, he waits you," she hissed. "Where have you been?"

"He knew where I was," said Maerad calmly. But she did not feel composed; standing outside, her attempt to escape had been a certain thing, something she had decided. But the thought of seeing Arkan made a void open in the pit of her stomach.

"Come, come, come," said Gima, on the verge of panic. "Come, there is no time, he is impatient."

"There's no hurry," said Maerad. While Gima fumed impotently, Maerad picked up her lyre and looked slowly around the room to check if there was anything else she needed, although she knew there was not. "I'm ready now."

Deliberately slowing her pace, she followed Gima, who hurried down the corridors, turning at each corner and hissing for Maerad to catch up, to hurry. But Maerad refused to walk any faster. I shall come in my own time, she thought. He cannot make me run.

The corridors darkened as they neared the throne room, and Gima hesitated, trembling. Maerad took pity on her. "It's all right," she said. "I know the way."

"You must go there," said Gima. "He is waiting. He must not wait."

He can wait, thought Maerad. "I will go straight there," she said. "Do not fear."

She walked on, leaving Gima standing where she was, clasping and unclasping her hands, neither daring to walk with her, nor to go back. The light in the walls was like stormlight, bright and angry, not the soft illumination she had become used to.

She reached the double doors of the throne room and paused, swallowing hard. She could feel the Winterking's wrath: the iron door seemed to pulse with it. Slowly she pushed it open, and walked in.

The hall seemed bigger, stretching back with a strangely distorted perspective, and from the pool poured a livid illumination that threw strange lights on the ceiling. The dais was in shadow: all she could see was a dark, ominous form. Maerad's nerve almost failed her, but she took a deep breath and straightened her back. Slowly she walked into the centre of the room.

"Elednor of Edil-Amarandh," said the Winterking. Maerad flinched; when he said her name it hurt her like a whip. "You arrive at last."

Maerad stared at the shadow, and gradually the darkness lifted from the dais. The Winterking stood before his throne, dressed in robes of a blue so dark they might have been black. About his brow was a crown of flickering blue lightnings, and his eyes blazed green fire.

Maerad licked her dry lips. "You are angry?" she said meekly. "I thought time was of no account to you."

"You have sought to deceive me," said the Winterking. "You are insolent, in so abusing my hospitality."

"I don't understand." He knows, she thought with sudden panic: he knows my magery has returned. "But how can I deceive you, in your own palace? You told me I could not."

"I told you not to play me for a fool." Arkan took a step towards her, and the lightnings about his brow grew more dangerous. "I know you have tried to hide from me. I do not permit it." So he had sensed her shield.

Maerad outfaced him with all the haughtiness she could muster. "I did not realize your hospitality meant that you can witness all my privacies," she said.

"Here you may have no privacy," said Arkan. "You have not earned such trust."

"And why should I trust you?" said Maerad hotly. "What do you think it feels like, being watched all the time, like a–a captured animal? What right have you to accuse me? I have done nothing wrong."

"I will not countenance you opposing my power," said Arkan.

"How can I oppose your power?" asked Maerad bitterly. "Here, you say, I have none."

"If I chose to take all your power, you would be unable to move a single finger without my permission." The Winterking stared at her with withering contempt. "I leave you a little, as a courtesy. You are unwise to use it against me. Even in your full power, you could not challenge me."

"It's strange, for you to speak to me of courtesy," she answered angrily.

"Silence!" This time the Winterking exerted the full force of his power over her. Maerad felt as if a rope jerked her hard; she gasped in pain and fell forward onto her knees. "Elednor of Edil-Amarandh, I have been patient with you. I have spread before you the riches of my palace. I have refused you nothing. But perhaps you prefer this treatment? I can easily oblige you."

Maerad, her head bent, said: "I don't understand. What have I done?"

The Winterking stepped down from the dais and walked towards her, and then bent down and took her chin in his hand. His hand was cold as ice, and its strength inexorable, but his touch was gentle. Maerad looked up into his eyes and instantly forgot everything in a rush of desire. She blinked with humiliation, seeing a flash of triumph in Arkan's eyes, and tried to hide her face.

"You are the Fire Lily," said the Winterking softly. "And I am the Ice King. Does fire melt ice? Or ice put out fire? Or may they come together, fire and ice, neither melted nor quenched?"

Maerad blushed, and turned her eyes away. Arkan let go of her chin, and she bowed her head, looking at the floor. She was trembling all over, with fear or longing, she could not tell.

"I do not know," she whispered at last.

"I thought to honour you as my queen," said the Winterking. Now his voice was sad and full of longing, a young prince wounded by his unfaithful lover. "And I think in return you betray me."

Maerad reeled in shock. She shut her eyes for a moment, gathering her breath and her will, carefully shielding her mind. She could feel her pulse throbbing hard in her neck. He doesn't know I have any power, she thought; not for sure. Very slowly, she stood up and looked Arkan in the eye, refusing to lower her gaze.

"You said that love could not be feigned, and could not be stolen," she said passionately. "And now you say that I will be your queen. And yet you imprison me, and give me no freedom. You know what it is like to be caged. It is a death. You tell me I cannot hide from you, and yet you punish me for hiding. You say you do not want me to fear you, and you treat me as if I were a slave. Forgive me, My Lord," and here she bowed her head sadly, contrite and meek, "I do not understand your anger. I do not understand why you are punishing me for something that you say I cannot do. I do not understand your love, if this is the love you offer me."

The Winterking turned on his heel, and she looked up as he walked away from her. She could feel his doubt, as slowly the light in the throne room softened, and the shadows faded. He does not know, she thought. He still thinks his power is enough.

"I do not desire a slave," he said, at last.

"I am not a slave," said Maerad.

Arkan glanced at her swiftly. "Forgive me, if I made you afraid," he said. "I am not used to dealing with mortals, and perhaps I am impatient."

Maerad nodded her head very slightly.

"Come, sit with me. We will forget this ever happened." He turned back and offered his arm, and Maerad smiled wanly, taking it hesitantly. She shivered at his touch: now it burned her like ice.

"I see," he said, "that you brought your lyre."

"As I said I would," said Maerad. "I don't know how to read the runes."

They didn't speak again until they were seated. Maerad already felt exhausted: she knew she must deceive Arkan if she was to escape, but the only way she could deceive him was by revealing the truth. The problem with the truth, she thought despairingly, is that it is true. She stared at his mouth, noticing its cruel sensuality. To kiss him, she thought, would be like kissing a river; I would faint and drown. She dug her nails into her palms, trying to stop the dizziness that his closeness induced in her, trying to keep her mind clear and alert.

It was no use thinking like this.

She handed him her lyre with a strange reluctance; it was as if she were giving him her heart. But it is mine, cried a voice inside her; it belongs to no one else. His fingers closed on it covetously, and she felt his grasp on her most loved possession as a deep pain, and momentarily shut her eyes.

He must not know I feel like this, she thought.

She opened her eyes and smiled.

"Can you read the runes?" she asked.

Arkan stroked his fingers lightly over the carvings, and Maerad shivered. "Yes," he said. "I can read them. Shall I tell them to you?"

She didn't trust herself to speak, and just nodded.

"I remember when these runes were made, many many wanings of ice ago." Arkan's voice was suddenly tender, and Maerad looked at him in surprise. He was far away, in some memory of his own. "They should never have been made," he said. "But they were. That was the first ill."

"Did the Nameless One make them?" ventured Maerad, looking at the strange carven forms. They seemed too beautiful to have been made by him.

Arkan's eyes were suddenly opaque and private. "Nelsor himself made these runes. He was told the Song, and its potency and beauty amazed him. And secretly he made the runes, so he could have it for his own. He was always the greatest of the Bards; none other had the power to do such a thing. Nor the audacity. He captured the Song of the Elidhu, and now it sleeps within these runes."

"Who told him the Song?" asked Maerad; but Arkan gave no sign that he heard her. He brushed the ancient wood with both his hands, and then shut his eyes and touched the first of the ten runes with his forefinger.

"These runes embody many things," said Arkan. "That was Nelsor's genius: he saw how the Song's powers might be captured, like a flower in ice. This is his greatest work. He did not know that it would lead to such disaster."

Maerad looked at her lyre, and then back to Arkan. In her little time at the Schools, she had learnt how letters held meaning, and how they could be magical, but Arkan seemed to be talking of something more.

"There are three dimensions to each rune," Arkan went on. Triple tongued, thought Maerad, with a sudden clutch of excitement.

The Winterking opened his eyes and looked at Maerad intently. "This first rune is Arda, the first of the moons. It is the new moon, and it is the fir tree. And it is also this stave: I am the dew on every hill."

Maerad blinked in confusion, and then nodded. If she did not understand, she could at least remember. "So," said Arkan. "First the moons." He shut his eyes again, and read each rune with his fingers. "This is the rune Arda. This the rune Onn. This the rune Ura. This the rune Iadh. This the rune Eadha. The new moon, the waxing moon. the full moon, the waning moon, the dark moon."

Maerad stared at the runes, and then looked up at Arkan.

"They're not a song," she said.

"Listen. This is how the Song is made. Fir, furze, apple, poplar and yew." Arkan turned his eyes upon Maerad, and she swallowed nervously. She pointed to each rune, and said, as if she were learning a lesson: "Arda, fir, the new moon. Onn, furze, the waxing moon. Ura, apple, the full moon. Iadh, poplar, the waning moon. Eadha, yew, the dark moon." She looked up, suddenly realizing something. "They're letters!"

"They are time written down," said Arkan absently. He was frowning in concentration. "These are the staves of the moons, beginning with the new moon:

I am the dew on every hill
I am the leap in every womb
I am the fruit of every bough
I am the edge of every knife
I am the hinge of every question

The words went deep into Maerad's soul, as if they stirred memories from before she was born. She sat silently, fixing the runes in her mind; she recalled Ardina as she had last seen her, dazzling with silver light, beautiful and ambiguous, the daughter of the moon.

"What are the others?"

Arkan looked up, his face unreadable. "These are the runes of spring and summer," he said heavily. "They are Forn, for middle spring; Sal, for late spring; Hrar, for early summer; Dir, for Midsummer's Day; and Tren, for middle summer. The rest of the year was lost when Sharma stole the runes. That was the second ill."

"He took the winter?" said Maerad softly.

"Aye."

"How were those runes lost? Did no one write them anywhere?"

Arkan didn't deign to answer her. He was tracing the runes again, his eyelids closed. Maerad watched him. With his eyes shut, he appeared more human; in repose his face was very beautiful. She shook herself, and concentrated.

"Forn, the alder," said the Winterking. "Sal, the willow; Hrar, the whitethorn; Dir, the oak; and Tren, the holly."

He was silent then for a long time, and Maerad waited patiently for him to speak again. When he did not, she asked: "And are there staves for those runes?"

Arkan opened his eyes and looked directly at her. His expression held a desolation that took her aback.

"The runes are empty," he said. "They are dead. To speak them on the air is a horror."

Maerad didn't know what to say, and looked down in confusion. Arkan sighed heavily.

"I will say them one time. You must remember."

Maerad felt the light in the throne room dim. She waited, feeling her heartbeat loud and heavy in her throat. At last, after what seemed an endless silence, Arkan spoke, his deep voice echoing around the room:

I am the falling tears of the sun
I am the eagle rising to a cliff

I am all directions over the face of the waters
I am the flowering oak that transforms the earth
I am the bright arrow of vengeance

When he had finished speaking Arkan covered his face with one hand, and the throne room filled with a bleak stillness.

"There is no music," said Maerad.

"The music does not live in the runes," said Arkan. "The runes are dead."

"I can't play the Song, without music," she said. "How am I to find the music? I can't play this Song."

"Do you think anything can be alive, when it is cloven in half?" Arkan glared at her, his eyes hard and icy, and for an instant Maerad thought he would snap her in two with his bare hands. He thrust the lyre back into her arms, as if it burnt him.

"Go," he said to Maerad. "Leave me."

The corridors were cold now and the light seemed sinisterly beautiful; she felt as if the walls were full of eyes, which watched her as she stumbled. She was amazed that she was still able to walk; her legs shook underneath her as if they might give way at any moment. Gima was nowhere to be seen.

She found her room and collapsed onto her bed. She lay on her back, staring at the ceiling, too exhausted to move.

She remembered with a shudder the Winterking's face as he had told her the runes, how his black eyelashes rested against the marble skin of his cheeks, the fire that leapt in her veins at his touch. And yet she knew he was ruthless and merciless; Cadvan and Dharin had died by his orders. She had no doubt that he would kill her without compunction, if she were no use to him.

The thought seemed to make no difference.

I must find Hem, she said to herself. I have to find Hem. But there was no answering resolve within her. She found she could not picture Hem's face; her memory of him seemed abstract and distant, and she had to build the picture laboriously, instead of summoning a vivid, precise memory. She turned her thoughts to Cadvan, and realized she couldn't remember his eyes. They're blue, she thought fiercely: *blue*. But she could only see the icy blue of the Winterking's eyes, their strange slitted pupils, how he had said, *I thought to honour you as my queen*.

I'm so tired, she thought. So very tired. I can't undo his ensorcelments. I can't turn my face from him and pretend that I don't feel as I do. She was certain the Winterking had spelled her; and yet she was, at the same time, quite sure that what she felt was not false. She didn't want to leave the Winterking, even for her own sake, although she knew she must.

Gradually her limbs stopped shaking, leaving her bleak and empty. She picked up her lyre, which lay on the bed beside her, and very slowly drew her right hand over the strings, so each note sounded out singly. The icy light glimmered and faded, revealing the rough rock walls of her dungeon, and she began to feel a little less weak. Ten strings, ten notes, ten runes, she mused distractedly. Three tongues, three names, three meanings. That makes nine, and leaves one over. The keystone of the music, the answer to the riddle. What would that be?

She plucked each string again, wondering if each note also belonged to a rune. She couldn't see how they would, and she thought that it would probably make no sense unless she had the runes the Nameless One had stolen. There must be twenty runes, if the Song was split in half. Did the Nameless One have a lyre as well, with ten strings?

She sat upright, irritated with herself, and, as she did, it dawned on her that she did know how to deceive the Winterking. He knew when she was absent, when she vanished from his view. So she must make a semblance, which was like her in every respect, to replace her when she used her own power and vanished. She was never disturbed when she was asleep, so she must appear to be sleeping. If it worked, she would have a few hours' start before her absence was noticed. The best time would be right now; the Winterking was sure of his power over her and he would be unwary. And perhaps, after reading the Song, he too was exhausted, although she did not know if Elidhu felt weariness. Perhaps his vigilance had lapsed.

She considered the idea, turning it over thoughtfully, prodding it for flaws. There were many. She had only made a semblance twice before, when she studied with Nerili in Thorold and in the mountains to trick the iridugul, and although she knew she could do it, and could remember the charm, it wasn't as if she was practised. She had never worked two charms at once, and she did not know if it was possible. If she tried and failed, she would be discovered, and she didn't want to think what might happen to her. She put that thought out of her mind. Instead, she placed her lyre carefully in its case and packed it away with her other belongings and, without taking off any of her clothes, got into bed and drew the covers over herself.

She would first have to make a shield that would hide her magery from Arkan, but would not hide her. Beneath that shield, she could weave the semblance, preparing it to the point where she need only set the charm that would manifest it. Then she would have to vanish, ensuring that the two spells were so finely co-ordinated that her vanishing and the manifestation of her semblance were seamless.

It all seemed impossible, and she sank into black thoughts for a few moments. But then she remembered the wolf that had spoken to her. Unless she had imagined it, which she did not think she had, it had been waiting for her. Perhaps someone, hearing of her capture, had sent it to help her. It could not have been an ordinary wolf. Perhaps she would not be entirely without help. It was a slim chance, perhaps suicidally slim, but it was the only hope she had.

Maerad brushed her doubts aside, and focused on the first question: getting out of the palace itself. She would have to do all the spells lying down in her bed, looking as if she were sleeping, which was not the ideal pose for magery. She lay on her back, as straightly as she could manage, and then, tightening her lips, began on the shield.

This took a little time, since it had to be detailed. She concentrated on concealing any magery beyond the little the Winterking believed she had regained, but not concealing so much that she might appear to vanish. It was risky, since her magery would not be concealed until she completed it, and she had to make it slowly, bit by bit, cautiously releasing her power in increments so it could not be perceived. She kept her senses keen for any changes in the palace, any shift of the light that might alert her that she had been detected. She closed her eyes, mentally said the words that activated the spell, and cautiously tested it. It seemed, as far as she could tell, to be good, and, as far as she could tell, it had not been noticed.

Then she began work on the semblance. Making the semblance took some considerable time; it could not be merely a rough form, meant to fool from a distance. It would not only have to look like Maerad, but feel like Maerad too. She worked in layers. She visualized her mind first, the colours of her emotions, the charge of her power, and carefully wove its outlines, testing them as she went to ensure they felt true. When she had finished, her mind held a replica of itself, a shell which, when she plucked it, seemed to resonate with her self. Then she started on her body, weaving it through the spectre of her mind: bone, blood, veins, muscle, and lastly skin and hair.

The semblance now existed in her mind, precise in every detail, and only awaited the word of power to make it appear, to set it breathing. Maerad took a deep breath, and prepared herself for the final, most difficult part of her task: the creation of the semblance and her simultaneous vanishing. She had emptied her mind, patiently gathering together her power, when she heard steps approaching her chamber. It was Gima.

Maerad cursed silently and paused, teetering on the brink of releasing her power. It was as if she had gathered herself for a leap, and then had been forced to stop, holding all the energy in check, without falling over, without losing the momentum of her jump. She heard the curtain over the doorway pulled aside, and the steps approached the bed. They stopped, and she could hear Gima's heavy breathing. Then she turned and left the room.

Maerad waited until she was sure the footsteps had retreated far enough, and then took another deep breath. Her mind was hurting from holding both charms in abeyance, and her body was trembling. Then, very carefully, she released the semblance and, drawing on deep powers within her, made herself vanish.

She didn't get it quite right; there was the smallest moment when there were two Maerads, side by side on the bed, and she disconcertingly found herself looking into her own face. She got out of the bed and listened, all her senses agonizingly alert for any disturbance in the palace. It was blanketed in silence, apart from the retreating footsteps of Gima.

Maerad bent to pick up her pack and realized that she had made no semblance for it; Gima might notice it was missing. That charm was easy after the spell she had just made, and this time she managed the timing perfectly, vanishing one as the other appeared. She fumbled around for her pack. Then she swung it onto her back and looked around the room that had been her prison for the past few days, pushing down a sudden sharp regret. The Winterking would believe her to be a traitor. He had no right to think that, given that he had captured and imprisoned her, but he would think it all the same.

On an impulse, Maerad drew one of her precious pieces of paper and her pen and ink out of her pack. She sat down and smoothed it out on the chest, and then paused. She didn't know if the Winterking could read Bard script, but somehow she felt she owed him some acknowledgement, even though, she thought, by all accounts of fairness she owed him nothing at all.

She bit her lip, and then carefully wrote the rune Eadha, the yew rune, the rune of the dark of the moon: *I am the hinge of every question.* She pushed her sleeping semblance, who stirred and gave a sudden loud snore, and she hid it underneath its body. Then, feeling oddly relieved, she shouldered her pack again and walked into the corridor.

In her power, the enchantment of the Ice Palace dissolved. It hit her then that she did not know the way through the unenchanted palace. She knew her way through the illusory corridors, but now it all looked completely different: she walked into a corridor that was black as pitch. She rocked on her heels, completely taken aback: she had not thought about this at all. There could be other corridors leading off the halls that could confuse her. She could still be winding through the heart of the mountain, lost and bewildered, as the Winterking discovered how she had tricked him. The thought made her go cold.

I could go back, she thought, I could undo all the spells, and then no one would know. The idea tugged at her painfully; she was already so tired, and it was a long way through the palace; and even if she made it out, she did not know how she would pass through the archway, and what would happen afterwards. She had no plans at all, beyond escaping the palace. She could try again tomorrow, and in the meantime find out more. She almost turned back to her chamber.

Some deep stubbornness flickered in contempt at her weakness. And something else ran beneath all her doubts, a deep current of urgency, which she realized had been driving her since she left the throne room. Time was running out; she did not have the luxury of tomorrow. She took a deep breath to steady herself, and began to wend through the darkness, running her fingers lightly against the walls. She would have to remember the way by touch; she dared not set a magelight.

She went carefully, fearful of making a mistake, stopping often to run through the way in her mind, sending her hearing before her. She could hear a light breath, which might be Gima sleeping, the drip of water in distant caves, the stirring of nameless creatures in the deeps of the mountains; but she could hear nothing else. The way seemed much longer in the darkness, and after a while she began to wonder if, despite her carefulness, she had made a wrong turning. Strange lights began to appear before her eyes, and her legs became heavier and heavier, and the pack felt like lead on her shoulders. Her left hand was aching badly.

She had almost convinced herself that she was completely lost, when she felt the smallest whisper of cold air touch her face. It was fresh and clean, unlike the slightly heavy air of the palace: she was going in the right direction. Encouraged, she pressed on, and before long she saw the mouth of the cave emerge from the darkness, limned silver by starlight.

Almost dizzy with relief, Maerad stepped out onto the snow and looked up into the sky. Automatically she searched for Ilion, the star of dawn and evening, which she thought of as her own, but she could not see it; it was probably deep night. The air felt like blades of ice as she drew it into her lungs, but she breathed deeply, savouring the taste of freedom.

Within moments, she was shivering with the cold. She took her cloak out of her pack, remembering how Dharin had cast it aside as inadequate, and wishing fruitlessly that she had not lost her warm fur coat. Dharin had been right, the cloak could not offer the kind of protection against the cold that she needed.

Maerad looked down the snowy slope towards the stone arch that stood over the road. This, she was sure, was the Winterking's most powerful defence; no one could enter or leave the palace without passing under it, and the Winterking had told her that even birds would not fly over it. If she could not find a way to pass it unseen, all her magery had been in vain. And she did not know how. Yet. And even if she did manage to pass it, what then?

She squared her shoulders, trying to will away her tiredness, and walked slowly towards the black arch.

XXVI

WOLFSKIN

MAERAD was not entirely surprised to see the wolf standing on the slope beyond the arch, its form frosted by the waning moon. It was standing very still, staring straight at her despite her charm. A terrible doubt rose inside her, constricting her throat: had her charms been unsuccessful? Was the Winterking, even now, laughing as she walked into an elaborate trap?

She bit down her doubts and stopped an arm's length away from the arch, looking through it to the road beyond. It ran on about twenty paces before it met the snow-covered mountain road, which glimmered slightly as it wound around the mountain wall and disappeared. She deliberately didn't look at the wolf. Unwillingly she dragged her eyes back to the arch and pondered her next step. She could feel the power invested in the stone from where she stood: it seemed to bear down on her with a malevolent vigilance. Its message could not have been clearer if it had been written in letters of fire: *You shall not pass.*

I have to pass, thought Maerad. But it will take everything I have left, and it will probably be for nothing.

As she took a deep breath, gathering herself for one last exertion, she heard a voice in her mind.

Do not speak until you pass the Arch, it said.

Maerad nodded.

You cannot pass the Arch, it went on. *It will reveal you. You must become wolf.*

Maerad looked at the wolf in bewilderment, and silenced

the questions that rushed into her mind. Wolf?

The wolf sat down on its haunches, still looking at her. The starlight sparked cold off its eyes.

Become wolf, it said again. It settled down casually and put its head on its paws, looking for all the world like a domestic dog lying down in front of a fire. Maerad stared at it in exasperation, thinking it could at least have given her a clue. After a few moments, the wolf pricked up its ears and looked at her.

You do not have long, it said. *The stars will soon begin to fade.*

Maerad gave the sky a swift glance and saw the wolf was right. It would not be long before daylight, and she would need to be well away from Arkan-da by then if she was to have any hope of escape.

She tiredly put down her pack, sat down on a rock and put her face in her hands. The cold pierced her clothes, and she was shivering. Inside her a voice said, You can't do this. You're mad to try. You can still go back to your chamber and undo the semblance and make everything as it was, and the Winterking will never know. And underneath this voice there was another, which whispered: and you will then see the Winterking tomorrow.

Maerad miserably let the implications of this rise in her mind. Leaving here would mean that she would never see Arkan again. Despite everything – despite the wrongs he had done her, despite his tyranny, despite his cruelty during their last meeting – something in her cried out in protest. She could remember only his face in repose, his cruel, sensual mouth. My enemy, she thought bitterly; my own heart. It calls me back into prison, even as the gate opens. But how can I leave my heart behind me? It would be a maiming deeper than the loss of my fingers. Then even my heart would be songless.

Maerad didn't know how long she sat, shrouded in her unhappiness, forgetting the wolf, forgetting that she sat at Arkan's very door, insensible even to her present peril. She felt

as if she were being very slowly torn in two. At last, the wolf
called her back to herself.

Become wolf, it said again. *Or you will be a tame dog for ever.*
Maerad looked up, startled, and realized that the sky was
beginning to lighten. She was almost frozen, her hair iced and
her feet numb. The wolf was standing up again, and it seemed
to be looking at her with something like scorn.

Maerad closed her eyes.

I choose to leave, she said steadily to herself. She felt as if
she had stepped out into an abyss. Now she could not turn
back.

As the decision formed irrevocably within her, she realized
that she did understand what the wolf meant. Of course she
could transform into a beast. It was not the magery of Bards,
which could only work such a transformation in seeming; it
was part of the knowing of the Elidhu: and with it, she could
worst the Winterking's powers.

She stood up slowly, her limbs cold and stiff, and deliberately shouldered her pack, which had to transform with her.
She looked the wolf in the eye; it stared back at her unblink-
ingly. Without hurry, as if she had done it a thousand times,
she focused deep within herself, sinking through layers – slave,
Bard, Pilanel, Maerad, Elednor, woman – deeper and deeper,
until she came to a place where all the skins fell away and she
had no name at all, and her mind was as empty and clear as
water. Now she sought the still point of transformation, the ful-
crum on which all turned; she found it and balanced, swaying
easily like an eagle on the wind.

Be wolf, she thought; be my heart, my hunger. Be my freedom.

For a heartbeat her whole body was racked by terrible pain,
as if she had been thrown into a furnace; but that passed almost
as soon as it arrived, giving her no time to do more than gasp.

The next thing she knew, she was overwhelmed by a new sense, the sense of smell; her tongue and her nose were suddenly flooded with odours, so rich and detailed that they were like brightly coloured images.

She could smell the arch; it smelt like burned metal, hot and dangerous, the smell of sorcery. Her hackles rose, and she leaned forward and sniffed the stone tentatively.

It will not burn you, said the wolf. *Hurry. You have wasted much time.*

Maerad did not stop to wonder that she was standing on all fours. She gathered herself and leapt through the black arch, and felt its power part before her and close seamlessly behind her, as if she were a sleek diver who left not a ripple of water in his wake. When she landed on the other side she left no mark in the snow, although she could see her human footprints all the way back to the door of Arkan-da, already beginning to blur under a thin layer of snow.

Without speaking, the wolf turned and began to lope very fast down the south road. Maerad leapt forward in its wake, her heart suddenly soaring. All tiredness seemed to have fallen from her. She was a wolf, lean and swift and strong, and if she wanted she could run all day and night. She felt the pleasure of her muscles sliding over each other, the heat of her running, her inextinguishable energy.

She was free.

The darkness faded slowly out of the sky as the sun rose above the mountains, staining the barred clouds red. The snow fell lightly, whirling idly about the wolves, and rising in small puffs of white where their paws struck the ground. They were running at an even pace that ate up the ground, and they were already far from Arkan-da, following the pass that led through the mountains. Maerad could sense now that the road was winding down, and that they would soon be out of the mountains and onto the plains.

She was beginning to tire, panting as she ran, and her left forepaw was aching fiercely; but the other wolf led her on without pausing, without even turning to see if she still followed. Maerad made no protest; fear drove her past her weariness. She now wanted to get as far away as possible before the Winterking discovered she was gone.

Maerad's semblance would last about half a day, but she thought it likely that her absence would be discovered before that. Perhaps Gima would leave her alone out of pity, but it was likely she would become alarmed if she tried to rouse her and could not, and her stratagem would then be revealed. She had no idea what would happen when the Winterking found that his captive had fooled him, but she knew that the anger he had shown in the throne room would not be a tithe of his rage when he discovered her escape. And his arm was long; he had sent his stormdogs to Thorold and attacked her in the Osidh Elanor; he had captured and imprisoned her when she was on the far side of Zmarkan. What real chance of escape did she have in the shadow of his own mountains?

For all these reasons she kept running; but another part of her ran for the sheer joy of it. Even her tiredness could not abate her pleasure in her freedom. Her senses rang with the sharp smell of pine sap, the scent and scuffle of a hare bounding for its lair, the sudden strange stink of a fox, the clean, empty taste of snow dissolving on her hot tongue. She could feel the ground stretching far beneath her paws, turning in its ancient unchanging rhythms as the wolves skated over its surface, leaving not even a mark on the snow; transient and silent as snowflakes. Only the sharpest eyes could have seen them as they ran, white ghosts slipping through shifting curtains of snow.

At about midday, they left the road and climbed to the top of a snow-covered ridge. Maerad found herself looking down on a forest of spruce, which stretched from the knees of the mountains southward. Here, at last, they stopped. Maerad drew up beside the wolf and stood, her sides heaving, too spent for the moment to speak.

We have travelled well, said the wolf into Maerad's mind, after she had caught her breath. *But further would be better.*

Yes, said Maerad, speaking for the first time since she had fled Arkan-da. She turned and looked into the wolf's eyes, resisting the urge to sniff, overcome by curiosity. *Who are you?* she asked. *You are no ordinary wolf, surely. Why did you help me?*

You know me better than you think, answered the wolf. *I have my own reasons for helping you.*

You're Ardina, said Maerad, with a sudden conviction.

The wolf looked at her, and Maerad realized it was laughing. *I might be Ardina, if I were not a wolf*, she said. *You have a sharp wit. Not even Arkan himself would know me in this guise.*

The two stood companionably, staring down over the ridge. Maerad did not feel surprised: somehow it seemed completely natural.

Then Ardina's ears pricked up and she sniffed the air. A moment later, Maerad heard a low rumble behind her and turned her head to look. At first she saw nothing; but then a black cloud rose over the shoulders of the northern mountains. She watched as it boiled upwards into the sky, blacker than any cloud she had ever seen, shimmering with forked lightning. Black twisting vortexes snaked down from its belly, striking the mountainside like giant whips. It was spreading out across the sky with a terrifying speed. She strained her ears: could she hear the baying of stormdogs? Maerad flinched and moved closer to Ardina.

The Winterking comes in wrath, said Ardina. She showed no fear. *We must move.*

The great wolf leapt over the ridge and ran down the long slope towards the forest. Maerad ran at her shoulder, her tiredness forgotten in a fresh surge of fear. She could see the edge of the forest in the middle distance, and the wolves could move very swiftly; but Maerad could feel the storm racing up behind them, swallowing up the thin winter light. He will find me, she thought, and all will be lost...

They reached the forest just as the outriders of the storm hit the trees, a gale so strong it sent their branches thrashing like reeds. At first, plunging through the darkness of the forest, Maerad was grateful for its shelter; but a branch broke and crashed behind her, just missing her tail, and she realized that it had its own dangers. She thought of the iridugul with their clubs, or the paws of the stormdogs; they could easily flatten the whole forest.

Do not fear, said Ardina, as if she heard her thoughts. *The Winterking cannot identify us, and neither can his minions, so long as we are creatures.*

We do not have to be seen to be crushed, thought Maerad, as they threaded their way through the pale trunks, which glimmered through the forest shadow. Huge hailstones began to clatter through the leaves. One hit Maerad's flank, and she jumped sideways with a yelp; it was like being struck by a hammer. Now she was sure she could hear the baying of stormdogs, tearing screams that rose above the howl of the gale and turned her blood to ice. There was more than one, she was sure. Out of the corner of her eye she saw a lone deer bolting blindly in panic, crashing into trees and falling and scrambling up to run on again, beyond anything but its own fear.

Ardina suddenly turned and disappeared, so quickly that Maerad almost fell over her paws trying to follow her. She scrambled down into a narrow gully. At the bottom was a trickle of frozen water running through a thin layer of old grey snow, banked on either side by a tangle of thorns and dead grasses. On the floor of the gully there was just enough space for a single wolf to push through. Instantly they were sheltered from the worst of the storm, although hailstones as big as pebbles still showered into the gully. One hit Maerad above the eye, and she began to bleed.

For a moment, both wolves stood erect, listening; there was a huge crack not far away, as if a tree had split in half, and Maerad saw uneasily that the forest above them was beginning to glow with a weird greenish light. She remembered that light from her encounter with the stormdog in the Straits of Thorold. She didn't know how many raged above the trees here, but she could hear baying from at least three directions. She cowered on the ground, pressing her belly close to the snow as if to meld herself with the earth.

Ardina began to wind her way through the gully, her nose to the ground, and Maerad followed her as near as she could. Even though the wolf was just in front of her, she could barely see her pale form in the gloom. Every moment it was getting darker, as if the very light was being devoured. Soon the only light anywhere was the strange greenish glow, which illuminated nothing, and Maerad was navigating by smell alone. It is as black as the Winterking's palace, she thought; I have not escaped him yet. She shuddered and pressed closer to Ardina's tail.

At that moment, the storm hit its height. The baying of the stormdogs reached a crescendo that made Maerad stop to try and cover her ears with her paws. It felt like an explosion inside her head, making her skull ring with unbearable pain. Something huge was stamping through the trees nearby; she could hear the earth shuddering beneath its heavy tread, and the smash and crack of branches breaking. Shaking with fear, Maerad sprang forward, bumping into Ardina. More than anything in the world, she wanted to hide from this black fury of destruction, this terrible chaos. If she could have dug herself into the earth, she would have.

And then, above all the fury, as clearly as if they spoke together in a quiet room, she heard the voice of the Winterking.

His voice was gentle and sad. *Elednor*, he said. *Elednor, why have you betrayed me? Come back to me. Come back to where you belong. I alone need you...*

Maerad cringed into the ground, writhing in terror and desire and shame. Her mouth was full of dead bracken and frozen soil. In her mind she saw, with an awful clarity, the Winterking's face, his pale beauty, his dark rage; she remembered how his touch scorched her with longing. Besides those memories, everything else – even her own life – seemed suddenly trivial and empty.

I didn't want to, she cried out into the earless ground. *I didn't want to leave.*

Don't answer him. Ardina nipped her shoulder and Maerad looked up into her eyes, dazed. Ardina's eyes were burning with red fire. *Don't answer him,* she said again, her teeth bared in a snarl. *He will know where you are.*

Maerad scrambled to her feet and stood miserably before Ardina, her head bowed in shame. *I think I did,* she said.

Ardina nipped her again, chivvying her along the gully. *Pray then that your voice did not reach him. Did you say his name?*

No, said Maerad.

Well, perhaps then he did not hear you. We have not far to go. Hurry, hurry...

Maerad stumbled behind her through the chaos of the storm, blind with misery. Whatever I do is wrong, she thought. The Winterking is right; I am a traitor. Not to him; to myself. But how can I be true to myself, when all my selves have different truths?

She could not understand now how they could possibly

escape. It sounded as if the forest was being torn to pieces around them; had they not found this gully, they would have been flayed by the wind, crushed by the Winterking's monsters, blown off the face of the earth. It was only a matter of time before their frail hiding place was exposed and she would be dragged, trembling, before the Winterking's wrath. Her joy in her wolfishness was utterly extinguished; she stumbled with exhaustion, and her front paw burned as if it were on fire.

Hurry.

Ardina bit her, and Maerad forced herself on, feeling her legs shuddering beneath her. She could not go much further, even though her life depended on it. She heard a crash close behind them, as a giant tree, violently uprooted, fell across the narrow gully. Somehow she found another reservoir of energy. She limped after Ardina, freezing and shaking, conscious of nothing but the iron will she needed to put one paw in front of the other.

Suddenly Ardina disappeared. Maerad blinked stupidly and looked around, but she could see or smell no sign of her. She sat back on her haunches, too tired to think what to do next, too tired to move, too tired even to feel despair. Ardina had abandoned her. Now she could do nothing except wait.

But then Ardina reappeared, snarling, her eyes blazing. *What are you doing?* she snapped. *Get in here.*

Maerad looked up and saw that Ardina had climbed into a hole above them in the side of the gully. Feeling as if it were the last thing she would ever do, Maerad somehow scrambled up into the entrance of the hole and followed Ardina inside. It smelt of earth and rotting leaves, and from it breathed a sharp animal stink. Ardina was already a long way in front of her.

Maerad crawled on and on, deeper and deeper into the earth, her ears flat against her head, thinking the tunnel would never end. It felt like a tomb: cold as death, utterly black. Eventually she would not be able to crawl any further, and she would just die there, her bones crumbling to dust for aeons as the seasons flickered and changed far above in the world of daylight. But, unexpectedly, the walls disappeared and, unable to stop herself, Maerad fell forward into nothingness. Automatically she put her legs out to break her fall, and landed with a heavy bump on stone.

She lay where she fell, her eyes closed, her flanks heaving.

Ardina's voice came through the darkness as if from a great distance. *We outran the storm*, she said. *The Winterking will not find us now.*

Slowly Maerad's breathing returned to normal and she opened her eyes. She could see nothing in the absolute darkness, but she didn't need to. She could hear the sound of beasts all around her; she could smell wolves. She stood up stiffly, sniffing the air. She was in a large space, a cavern she supposed, and wisps of air travelling through it told her it had three exits. She picked out six individual wolf scents besides that of Ardina, and the smell of meat, both fresh and old. There was a carcass nearby; she could smell its bloody hide, the marrow of cracked bones, the urinous odour of the creature's fear as it had been killed. Her mouth filled with water, and she realized she was starving. But with that realization came a more urgent one: she was thirsty. She lifted her head, swallowing: there was water not far away, she could taste it on the air. An underground river, she thought. She could hear its gentle murmur through the rocks.

Drink, if you wish, said Ardina.

Maerad walked jerkily in the direction of the water, aware of the other wolves, whose attention was focused on her. There was a small brook close by, cold as ice; it numbed her mouth to drink, but she lapped thirstily until she had taken her fill. Then she returned to her place and sat by Ardina's side, wondering what would happen next.

There was a thick silence; it seemed the wolves waited too. Not one moved a whisker, and only the low whisper of their breathing sounded through the cavern.

Very slowly, slowly enough to let their eyes adjust as it rose, a light began to glimmer in the cave. Soon it was almost as bright as soft daylight, and Maerad looked around. Six wolves sat on their haunches in a semicircle, staring at Maerad and Ardina.

Look well, friends, she said to the wolves. *This is the prize the Ice Witch desired so and whom you travelled so far to find.*

The wolves looked intently at Maerad, although they looked away when she met their eyes. She tried not to shift uncomfortably under their gaze.

Will you guide her? said Ardina.

The biggest wolf, a huge male with a white ruff, walked delicately up to Maerad, sniffed her all over, and then returned to his spot.

She can share our kill and drink our water, he said. *We will give her the protection of the pack.*

Maerad stared at the male, her mind whirling. If he was not the wolf who had greeted her at the entrance to Inka-Reb's cave, then he was his twin brother. But what would Inka-Reb's wolves be doing, so far from home? She hadn't any time to think further, as all the other wolves came up to her and started licking her face and mouth, and nudging their heads under her chin. A couple of the younger wolves crouched down and looked up at her winsomely, their eyes warm and adoring. Their sudden affection nearly knocked her over a couple of times, but she felt strangely elated and stood as straightly as she could, her eyes shining. The male wolf stood apart impassively, watching the greetings.

When the pack had finished, they returned to their places and looked expectantly at the male. It seemed the formalities were not yet finished. The wolf yawned extravagantly, showing his long fangs. Then he fixed Maerad with his eyes.

I am Ka, he said. *I call no one master, but I serve the great Dhillarearën.*

Inka-Reb? said Maerad. A look of affront crossed the wolf's face, and she almost bit her tongue in annoyance with herself; clearly Ka was not a wolf who suffered interruption. But he continued to speak graciously.

I know not what men call him, he said. *He is the wolf spirit who lives between the stars and the ice, the living and the dead. As the moon swelled to its last full, he walked among the stars and saw what no other sees. He often walks thus. When he returned he asked us to make a big kill. We brought back a bull deer and he read its entrails. He said to me that he wanted a great favour. He said that the Dhillarearën who had come to his cave to ask him a great question would need guidance. He asked us to seek you and follow you, and he gave us his blessing on our brows.*

Ka paused, this time elaborately scratching himself, and Maerad nodded her head, hoping it was the polite thing to do. She did not want to interrupt him again.

We set off at the next light to follow your trail. On the day of the full moon, we found your mate dead, and a great dog, one almost as great as a free wolf. Maerad flinched and looked at the ground to hide her anguish at the thought of Dharin's corpse, abandoned like so much rubbish, with Claw at his side. It seemed so wrong. *We treated his body with honour*, Ka said, and his eyes softened. *We understand that sorrow that burns for ever, when the mate of your life is dead. Such is the world. There was another there, but we did not honour him.*

Good, thought Maerad, the desire for revenge hot inside her. But then she was horrified at herself; perhaps even that Jussack did not deserve to be dishonoured in death. She suspected that he had been eaten. Later she wondered if the wolves meant that they had honoured Dharin by eating him, and dishonoured the Jussack by perhaps urinating on the body; but she never dared to ask.

We followed their tame dogs, Ka went on. *The moon shrank and vanished and came back, and we went far out of our lands, further than our kin had ever been. But the blessing of the Dhillarearën is on our brows, and no other wolf dared to challenge our passing, even though we crossed their high roads and hunting fields. We came at last to the highlands and followed the man road, although it stank, to the arch that burned the air. We knew you had been taken through it, and we could not follow you. Instead we followed the men who had taken you, and we took our Dhillarearën's revenge upon them.*

Maerad could not remain silent. *All of them?*

This time Ka did not look so insulted. *There was a man of power among them, he said, but he could do nothing against the blessing of our Dhillarearën, and we tore out his throat. There were three other men who tried to run, and we hunted them down.*

There was a young man, said Maerad. *Not much more than a boy—*

There was one more. Ka clearly was not going to be hurried in his story. *He smelt of you most strongly, but your smell on him was not the fear smell. Our Dhillarearën warned us not to kill without need, to be just in our revenge, lest the blessing fade. We let him go free.*

Maerad breathed out with sudden relief. At least she did not have Nim's death on her conscience. She thought of Amusk with his throat torn out and felt no pity at all.

It was after that we saw the Daughter of the Moon, as we had been told we would. Here Ka courteously bent his head to Ardina, who had sat silently throughout his narration, and she gravely bent her head in acknowledgement. *She brought us here and told us to wait for you. And so we have, and now we have come to the present time.*

I saw you, said Maerad. *I saw you from the sled. But no one else saw you.*

That was the blessing of our Dhillarearën, said Ka.

I thank you from my heart, said Maerad, wondering if that was the correct thing to say to wolves. Ka seemed satisfied with her reply, and the atmosphere in the cave relaxed perceptibly; a couple of the wolves started scratching, and one pair began to lick each other fondly. The formalities, it seemed, were over.

You have hunger? asked Ka. *You may eat. You may drink. We cannot leave until the storm has spent itself. That will take a light and a dark. We have all we need here. Then we will guide you to the mountains as swiftly as we may. Six lights and we will complete our journey.*

Maerad salivated again at the thought of food. She paced over to the deer haunch, which was already half eaten. Another two lay behind it. She began to tear at it with her teeth, pulling off chunks of flesh and barely chewing them before she swallowed. When her hunger was sated, she came back to a place by the cave wall where there was a slight dip in the rock and curled up around her bulging belly, nose to tail, utterly content. It was not until then that she remembered that under normal circumstances such a meal would have made her retch with disgust.

Ardina nudged her with her nose, and Maerad sat up, blinking.

I will leave you now, she said. *I must go back to my own.*

I thank you, Ardina, Maerad said, and instinctively she leant forward and nuzzled Ardina underneath her chin. Ardina stretched out her neck with pleasure and Maerad reflected with wonder that she would never normally dare make such a gesture with the Elidhu. There was no impertinence in it now, and there seemed no need for other words.

Then Ardina leant down and licked Maerad's left paw. She flinched; it hurt very badly now. Instead of her mutilated hand she had now a maimed paw, with two toes missing, and the scarcely healed skin had torn on their long run through the mountains. As Ardina licked the wound the pain ceased. For a wild moment Maerad thought her paw was whole again, but she looked down and saw that her toes were still missing. But where they should have been the skin was black and smooth.

Remember your wolf heart, said Ardina. *The Winterking has no power over that. And where he has no power, he cannot see.*

But he can see me as a Bard? asked Maerad, in a small voice. Must she remain a wolf for ever?

He knows your Bard Name, said Ardina. *That is the choice of your heart. And remember, daughter, it is for no one else to say the wrongness or rightness of what you do. I would not have helped you to escape from his stronghold if you had not wished it. Even though your presence there was not something I would want. Not even I can see all ends; but I have been in this world long enough to know that a choice forced is no choice, and breeds slow ills, even were it done for the highest reasons.*

Maerad listened in silence, a heaviness on her heart lifting at Ardina's words.

Farewell, she said, and the two wolves touched noses. Then Ardina turned and loped out swiftly, and as she left the light in the cavern dimmed and went out.

Maerad slept the sleep of utter exhaustion, barely stirring for a long time. She was woken by Ka.

You must eat, he said. *Now we run.*

With the rest of the pack, Maerad ate what was left of the carcasses in the cave, even crunching up and swallowing the bones. Then Ka led the pack out of the cavern along a narrow cave that ran south. Maerad knew the direction by some new sense, as if her brain now contained a compass. They filed through the cave, walking at their leisure, some of the wolves playing together as they went, nipping each other or rolling over in mock fights. There were other animals in these caves, no doubt having fled there from the storm, but the wolves took no notice of them, even of the hares, which cowered by the cave walls as they passed; their bellies were full and they had no need to hunt. Every now and then, they would pass under sleeping colonies of bats, which hung overhead in bunches like strange leathery grapes. The smell of their dung made Maerad's lips curl over her teeth in distaste.

They emerged at the bottom of a rock face that stood out of the trees. Judging by the angle of the sun, it was about noon.

They were still in the forest, Maerad saw, but it bore the marks of terrible devastation. It seemed almost every tree trunk was snapped, and everywhere was a jumble of torn branches and leaves and, sometimes, the corpse of some luckless animal. There had also been fire: Maerad saw trees that must have burned like huge torches, now sad blackened skeletons, although the fires had not spread far because of the cold. It looked like the aftermath of a war, and was tense with an eerie silence. She stood behind the rest of the pack, her ears pricked, trying to sense the presence of the Winterking; she could feel him faintly, very far off, brooding, preoccupied.

The wolves picked their way through the ruined forest, always heading south. They went in no particular order; it seemed that Ka was the wolf with the most authority, but he was not an absolute leader. They were mostly led by a she-wolf called Neka, who was, it seemed, most skilled at finding a way through this tumbled and chaotic terrain. Despite the debris, they moved swiftly.

Towards evening, they reached the outer edges of the forest

and entered a landscape like the Arkiadera Plains – flat, tree-
less tundra. Now the wolves stretched out their lean, muscled
bodies and began to run over the snow. The pack settled into
a graceful, loping rhythm, which it could maintain for hours.
They ran far into the night, as the half moon rose into a clear
sky and spilled its silver light on the snow.

As Ka had predicted, it was six days' journey to the Osidh
Elanor. Maerad was staggered by the wolves' endurance, their
relentless pace. Bad weather made no difference; if it snowed,
the pack ran closer together, so they would not lose each other,
but were no less swift. The wolves were in a hurry, and only
hunted twice, on the third day, and the sixth, although at various times during their run they chased down a hare or a mouse
that had been unlucky or unwary enough to cross their path.

Despite their pace, being with the wolf pack was, Maerad
found, unexpectedly fun. The wolves seemed addicted to play.
There was one young she-wolf called Skira who especially liked
bouncing upon the others when the pack halted; she would
stalk up behind an unwary wolf and suddenly spring onto his
rump, giving it a sharp nip before she tore off. Sometimes this
would result in a wild chase, with the offended wolf finally
catching her, the two rolling over and over in a rambunc-
tious bundle of teeth and claws and fur while the rest of the
pack barked at their antics, a noise Maerad soon recognized as
wolf laughter. One evening the whole pack, even Ka, became
involved in a crazy game of tag, skidding over the snow like
nothing so much as a bunch of romping children. Maerad didn't
know where they got the energy; at the end of the day she was
usually too tired to do more than give a yelp of protest if someone jumped on her.

Maerad was treated as an honoured guest, but despite their
friendliness she felt a little outside the close-knit relationships

of the pack. She understood after a couple of days that they had left the younger and older wolves with Inka-Reb; Ka had only taken the strongest from his pack. One night, the wolves sang for those they missed, standing in a circle and singing long ululations of a strange beauty that made Maerad shiver.

Unlike Dharin's dogs, there were very few scraps; occasionally Skira might go far enough to offend Ka's dignity, and would warrant a snarl and a nip. Maerad began to understand that for all their wildness, the wolves were gentle beasts. At night, they slept close together for warmth, and often she would wake with a wolf's forepaw slung over her back in casual affection.

Ka and Neka were mates, and the pack leaders, either one taking charge according to need. Neka was usually the leader as they travelled, being the more skilled at finding routes, and with the most sensitive nose; she could smell a deer from more than a league off. Ka was the better hunter, although both were very skilled, as Maerad discovered when they made their first big kill.

The pack was subdued on the third day, with no teasing or games, as hunger began to gnaw at them. Maerad was starving; the huge meal she had devoured before they left had been digested, and all she could think about was her need for food. The pack strung out as they ran, questing for a recent scent. Towards midday, Neka found a fresh trail, a small herd of deer, and the pack turned east to follow it, travelling against the wind. When they drew near to the herd, they stopped.

Only three wolves hunted: Ka, Neka, and another younger male, Oraka, who was almost the image of Ka. The rest of the pack simply lay down and waited, happy to rest, flicking their ears and licking themselves. Maerad was curious to see the hunt, but clearly the other wolves had to stay out of the way: this kill was too important to be disrupted by inexperienced hunters. She pricked up her ears; she could smell the wolves, but she could not hear a sound as they stalked the oblivious deer. A little later there was an explosion of activity: she heard the sudden rush as the three wolves leapt at the deer, the herd's stampede of surprise and fear, its cries of alarm, the terrified grunting of a dying animal. She was so hungry that she felt no pity; instead she began to drool, and waited impatiently for the signal to come and eat.

Before long, Ka trotted back and the pack leapt up eagerly and followed him. The hunters had killed two deer, thin scrawny beasts barely scraping through a hard winter, but still good to eat. They began to tear at the warm carcasses, eating ravenously. As they ate, two big ravens flapped down at a respectful distance and waited for their chance at the carcasses.

The wolves rested after their meal, dozing or playing idle games, until Ka shook himself and stood up. Then they were off again.

Maerad smelt the mountains before she saw them: it was the scent of pine, pungent on the cold air, drifting from the forests at their feet. They entered the forests on the fifth day, following a trail made by humans, although they did not use the track and instead ran beside it. They reached the mountains the next day, just after they had killed again.

The pass began, as the Gwalhain Pass had, with two standing stones. From there Maerad could see the road winding around the base of the first mountain. Warily the wolves crept up to the pass, alert for any human scent; but they could smell nothing. No human had passed this way for weeks.

Peering past Ka towards the standing stones, Maerad wrenched her mind back to her human memory, which in her wolf life had sunk to the back of her mind. This was, she knew, the Loden Pass, which led into the north-east corner of Annar. She tried to remember what Gahal had said of it in Ossin, but nothing came to her mind. Where was she to go now? Her only thought was that she had to find Hem.

We have come at last to the parting, said Ka. *May you travel well, and blessing travel with you.*

Maerad stared at him, momentarily bewildered. She realized she no longer needed the pack to guide her, and that it would be dangerous for the wolves to travel into Annar; but she felt a sharp pang at the thought of leaving them, a wolfish dislike of being alone. She gathered herself and replied, with the dignity she had learned was befitting of a wolf.

I sorrow to leave you, she said. *Henceforth my heart will be dark. I thank you for your guidance and protection.*

We have done what was asked, Ka replied. *Now we return home.*

May you travel safely, said Maerad. Then she was surrounded by noses and tails, as the pack crowded around her to say good-bye. She touched each wolf on the nose, farewelling Ka and Neka last of all. Then, without looking back, the pack turned and trotted away.

Forlornly, Maerad watched them until they vanished among the trees. She sat on her haunches for a few moments after they had gone, lifting her snout to catch their dwindling scents, and then she turned and loped towards the pass.

XXVII
PELLINOR

THE Loden Pass was neither as high nor as long as the Gwalhain. It took Maerad two days to reach the other side. She went as swiftly as she could, a lone wolf moving faster than a pack. She feared that she would be hungry before she reached Annar; she knew already that she had few skills as a hunter, and she did not fancy hunting in the mountains. She avoided the road, using it only when she had no other choice, preferring to run alongside it on the snowy slopes of the mountains.

It was a melancholy journey. She missed the company of the pack, especially at night, when the cold pierced her for the first time since she had been a wolf, and she felt vulnerable without them. She saw no humans and very few animals apart from the birds, although she could smell the presence of other beasts. No doubt they were keeping out of her way.

The sun was already high as she passed through the standing stones on the Annar side of the pass. The highlands of North Annar, covered in a thin snow, stretched below her in gentle undulations, with bare winter trees black against the white, and she felt a momentary leap of delight. This was not the place of wide skies and endless flat plains that she had left, but a landscape familiar and dear to her. But she did not pause to savour the moment; she felt little triumph in coming so far, against such odds. Instead she pressed on southwards, wondering what she should do next.

She kept her wolf shape, mindful of Ardina's warning that

the Winterking might sense her if she were a Bard. She was not yet sure enough of her feelings about the Winterking to risk changing back. It could be that her desire to see him would outweigh her longing for freedom, and would betray her. And it was easier to travel as a wolf, despite her lack of skill in hunting, which was much more difficult than the other wolves made it appear. After a few unsuccessful attempts to track rabbits and a farcical moment when she leapt on a surprised squirrel, only to see it leap with a panicked shriek from underneath her forepaws, scratching her nose and then vanishing with a flick up into a tree, she was beginning to feel very hungry.

The following day she came across an isolated hamlet. She waited on its outskirts until nightfall, hiding in a ditch, her nose alive to the smell of sheep and cattle and chickens, pangs of hunger ripping her stomach.

It was thick with the more disturbing smell of human beings, and she prickled with wariness as she crept towards the houses. There were only three, clustered together with their shutters tightly fastened. She discovered that the animals were shut inside large barns attached to the side of the houses, no doubt to keep them safe from marauders such as herself.

Maerad chose the barn closest to her ditch and stood for a time outside the door, sniffing until she was sure there were no humans inside. Then, very carefully, she unlatched it with her teeth and crept inside. Just near the door were several sleeping fowl. She managed to kill one, breaking its neck with a quick snap, before the others awoke and started squawking in panic, waking the other animals. Outside a dog started barking. Maerad grabbed the corpse, slipped out of the barn and fled. A man emerged shouting and waving a pitchfork, but by then Maerad was well away.

She felt better after eating the chicken, which was fat and juicy, although when she had finished it she wished that she had had time to kill another; it had taken the edge off her hunger, but not its substance. Then she curled up in the hollow made by the roots of an ancient willow and slept soundly.

She woke early the next day and continued her journey south under an overcast sky. She had no clear idea of what she was to do; her only thought was to travel as quickly as she could, to find her way to Turbansk, to track down Hem. She saw no more hamlets; this part of Annar was sparsely inhabited, although sometimes she saw abandoned houses, their doors hanging drunkenly from broken hinges, their shutters flapping in the wind.

All morning a fine, freezing rain had turned the snow into a muddy sludge and added to the air of melancholy that filled the countryside. Maerad welcomed the rain; she wondered how long it had been since she had heard its gentle murmur, how long since she had been travelling through frozen lands. It seemed for ever.

She began to have a strange feeling that she knew where she was, as if she had already visited this land in a dream. It was then she realized that she must be close to Pellinor, the School in which she had been born. This must be the Fesse of Pellinor. It had once been a thickly inhabited region, but it was now abandoned and empty, the only sign of what it had been the sad remains of houses she passed more and more frequently.

Maerad had not been to Pellinor since she was a small child, since the terrible day that it had been sacked and burned to the ground and she and her mother had been taken into slavery. She was suddenly consumed with an overwhelming desire to see her birthplace, ruined and dismal though it must be. Perhaps, in the place where her mother had been First Bard, in the home where her mother and father had loved each other and borne their children, some inspiration might come to her, and she might know what to do next.

She knew the School was nestled against the mountains, and keeping the Osidh Annova to her left she ran on through the desolate winter countryside. It was a relief to have some concrete aim, and she pressed on swiftly now, keeping alert for any sign of the School. The rain stopped, leaving swags of dark clouds that promised more.

Just before noon she found the ruins. She came over a rise thickly wooded with leafless beech and larch, and saw a broken stone wall less than half a league before her. Behind the wall rose the remains of what had been a high tower and several other buildings.

Maerad paused, suddenly hesitant. It looked even more wretched than she had expected. But her desire to see Pellinor overrode her doubts, and at last she loped down the hill towards the broken archway, which had been the gate of the School.

Almost as soon as she passed beyond the wall, Maerad was sorry she had come; but she also could not leave, as if to do so hurriedly, without looking properly, would indicate disrespect or a lack of courage. The walls rose around her, most of them tumbled and broken, covered with brown, leafless creepers that the wind rattled against the stone. The stone in many places was still blackened by fire, and amid the tumble of wreckage, now covered with a winter detritus of dead weeds, she could see charred beams and broken doors and pieces of brightly coloured glass. The stone roads were broken and clogged with dead grasses, but unless a wall had collapsed into them they were still passable. A cold wind made a thin whistle as it blew through the gaps in the walls.

Sometimes she would pass a house that was almost intact apart from its roof, which had long fallen in. Occasionally, miraculously, one window pane remained unbroken, or she could make out the remains of what had once been a mosaic of coloured pavings, with in one corner an undamaged design

– the shape of lilies intertwining, or a bird in flight. On the ground she saw the remains of statues, their faces shattered, and the remnants of what had been a lintel carved with flowers, and an iron pan, now dimpled and red with rust. Once, winding through the ruined ways of Pellinor, she emerged into a tiny court in which there was a marble fountain that was almost completely undamaged. It was a carving of a beautiful woman holding a ewer, out of which the water had once poured into a small pool. The marble was streaked with green slime and the empty pool around it was clogged with dead leaves.

Nothing stirred in Maerad's memory as she walked through the ruins of Pellinor. This sad deserted place did not match her few memories, which were full of colour and light and song; it revealed nothing but its own desolation. All that remained was a bleak, wintry absence. It filled her with an overpowering sorrow, and her thoughts turned to her foredream of Turbansk, long, long ago, in Ossin. Was this, then, the fate of Turbansk? Was that, too, doomed to become a haunting, pitiful ruin? Perhaps the city had fallen already, its light and beauty extinguished for ever.

She turned her thoughts away from Hem. She was sad enough already.

Maerad wandered miserably through the ruins, her tail dragging behind her, until she came into an open space that had obviously been the central circle of the School. As soon as she entered the circle, Maerad stopped dead in her tracks.

It seemed that the School of Pellinor was not entirely deserted: a man still dwelt amid the ruins. She scented him first, and then a pungent smell of wood smoke and meat, which made her mouth water. She saw that a horse was grazing on the far side of the circle. She had not smelt the smoke or the man earlier, preoccupied as she had been with her gloomy thoughts, and the wind had blown the scent away from her. Now she cursed her inattention.

For reasons she did not wholly understand, Maerad did not slink back silently to hide among the tumbled stone walls. Perhaps the man would give her some of his food; or if he did not give it, perhaps she could take it. She stood tensely by the edge of the circle, and watched the man closely.

He seemed to be a traveller. He was bent over the fire, poking it with a stick. After a short time, he seemed to become aware of Maerad, and turned his head and looked directly at her. She sensed rather than saw his eyes upon her.

The man stood up, but still she did not flee. Hesitantly, ready to turn and run in an instant, she stepped a few paces out into the open and there halted, her heart hammering. The meat smelt delicious, and she put her snout up into the air, tasting it. The man did not seem dangerous. If she walked towards him very slowly, showing that she meant no harm, perhaps he would give her something to eat.

The man watched her closely as she paced towards him, but he did not move. She could not see his face, as it was hooded in a black cloak. Maerad could not sense that he was afraid, and this frightened her a little, but he was not angry either. He was nothing at all: he simply stood and waited.

She was so hungry. Averting her eyes from his to indicate that she meant no harm, she moved closer and closer, halting every few paces. At last they stood only a dozen paces apart.

Samandalamë, ursi, said the man in the Speech. His voice was kind and warm. *Welcome, wolf. You look hungry.*

Maerad looked up into his face, and recognized him at last.

She couldn't react at all. She simply stared at him, her mind completely blank.

It was Cadvan; and there, coming up behind him warily, staring at her, was Darsor. It was Cadvan's face, his cloak, his sword. He looked tired and worn, and his clothes were more ragged than when she had last seen him, but he was as alive as she was.

Maerad's heart burst with a wild joy, and she bounded towards him, wanting to embrace him, to say she was sorry, to cry, to shake him for making her suffer for so long, all those tears, all that grief and regret, when he hadn't died at all. He leapt backwards with a sharp cry, drawing his sword, and Maerad, on the point of running into the blade, had to swerve violently sideways, and tumbled onto the paving stones.

I do not wish to harm you, said Cadvan. *His voice was still gentle. You need not kill me for food.*

Maerad picked herself up, shocked at his reaction, and belatedly remembered that she was a wolf. To Cadvan it would have seemed that she was attacking him.

She sat down on her haunches and took a deep breath. It was easier this time. She focused deep within herself, sinking through layer after layer until she found the point of transformation. *Be Maerad*, she thought. *Be Me.*

Next came the moment of awful pain, the feeling of being thrown into a fire: and then Maerad was sitting on the ground in front of Cadvan, looking up into his astonished face, her eyes shining with tears.

"I suppose," said Cadvan, after a long silence, "that you would still like some stew?"

Maerad laughed. She threw her pack on the ground, scrambled to her feet and flung her arms around him. He rocked back on his heels as they embraced for a long moment, and in that embrace much was healed: long weeks of loneliness and grief, endurance and suffering. Maerad had never been so purely happy.

At last they stood apart and studied each other's faces.

"I thought you were dead," said Maerad. "Why aren't you dead?"

"I'll tell you after you've eaten," Cadvan answered.

"You're almost as thin as when we first met."

"And what are you doing here?"

"I was waiting for you, of course. I had no idea that you would turn up as a wolf. I should have guessed that Maerad the Unpredictable would not choose something conventional. I hope you will forgive my discourtesy. It was merely a misunderstanding."

Maerad's mouth twitched, and she bowed. "I might forgive you, if the stew tastes as well as it smells. And if your explanations are sufficiently entertaining."

"I doubt they'll measure up to yours." Then Cadvan saw her left hand, and looked stricken. "Maerad! Your hand…"

Maerad felt obscurely ashamed, and hid it awkwardly in her cloak. "I'll probably not play again," she mumbled. "It doesn't matter…" But Cadvan took her maimed hand in his, and gently traced the terrible scars where her fingers had been shorn away, saying nothing. His face looked immeasurably sad.

"Maerad," he said at last. "I have had much time to think over the past weeks. I am sorry for my unkindness, before we lost each other. I have rued it often and deeply; and often I have wished I could tell you so, and feared that I would never be able to."

"I've regretted many things as well," said Maerad quietly. "But look! We're alive."

Cadvan smiled, and his stern face lightened with sudden joy. "We are," he said. "That you are here seems a miracle beyond hope."

"And Cadvan, I've found the Treesong. Or half of it. It was on my lyre all the time."

Cadvan gave her a long look, his eyes dark. "That is great news," he said soberly. "But I should have been as glad to see you if you had not found it."

At first, Maerad wondered why Cadvan was not more joyous

at her news, but then she remembered how she had accused him of using her as a tool of the Light. The memory hurt, and she could think of no words to assuage it.

"You have paid a great price for that knowledge," said Cadvan gently. He stroked her maimed hand once more and let it go. "We have much to tell each other. But even the best stories go better after eating."

"Yes," said Maerad. "But I must speak to Darsor first." She walked up to the great black horse and put her arms around his neck. He nuzzled her shoulder.

Welcome, Maerad, he said. It was the first time that Darsor had ever said her name. *I always said you were a great mage.*

Maerad kissed his nose. *Finding friends I thought were dead is better than any amount of greatness*, she said.

Many mages would disagree with you, he answered.

Maybe that's why they're not great, said Maerad, kissing his nose again.

Darsor whinnied with equine laughter and returned to his own meal.

Cadvan and Maerad ate the rabbit stew together, falling easily back into their old companionship. And then they talked for hours, huddled by the fire as the skies cleared above them and the shadows lengthened into evening. The white stars came out one by one in the black wintry sky above them, and still they talked.

The first thing Maerad wanted to know was how Cadvan had survived the landslide. "We were lucky," he said. "The road ran into a tunnel through the mountain side. Darsor ran in as the mountain collapsed, but it was a near thing."

Maerad was silent for a time, reliving the terrible moment when she thought she had seen Cadvan and Darsor die. "Why couldn't I see it?" she asked at last. "If I had known – if I had even had a little hope…" She thought of how things might have been different, and then considered whether, if they had been, she would know what she now did.

"It was dark," said Cadvan. "Darsor saw it after you fell off, that's what he was racing for. I didn't even know it was there until we were inside."

They had waited until the landslide had subsided and the iridugul had vanished, and then had ridden to the other end of the tunnel. Leaving Darsor to wait on the other side, Cadvan had climbed over the mountain to get back to the road where they had fought the iridugul, which took him until dawn the following day. He had found the road entirely blocked by the landslide, and no sign at all of Maerad.

"I thought you had been crushed beneath the rocks, or taken by the iridugul," he said. "I have never felt such blackness. All seemed vain. I went back along the pass a league or so and ran into several caravans of Pilanel, who were heading north to Murask. They had Imi with them; she had run back along the road in a panic and literally crashed into them."

Maerad cried out gladly. "Where is she?"

"She had bruised herself, but nothing worse. I don't know how she didn't bolt off the side of the mountain that night, but it seems luck was with her, too. And she is, after all, of mountain stock. She is still with the Pilanel; they are kindly people and will care for her. She was heartbroken that you were lost, and did not wish to come with me.

"The Pilanel had not seen you, and I did not think you would have gone back that way, although you might have passed them easily with a glimmerspell. I didn't know whether to search, or whether it was useless; and if I was to search, where should I look first? I told the Pilanel about the blocked road, and they decided to clear it. They had strong men and tools, but unless they had more hands they thought it would take two weeks to dig out that rock."

"So what did you do?" asked Maerad.

"I could not afford to wait so long, and, in the end, Darsor decided me. I could not leave him, and he was on the other side of the tunnel. I climbed back over the mountain and we talked for a long time. Darsor is a wise animal: he said that he did not believe you were dead, though he could not tell me why he thought so, and that if you were alive you were either taken by the Winterking or would continue the quest. So we continued over the pass into Zmarkan, looking always for signs of you. But we found nothing."

"So why did I not see you at Murask?" asked Maerad. "I arrived there, oh, three weeks afterwards. Surely they would have told me."

"Because you seemed to have vanished into thin air, I thought it more likely that if you were alive you had been captured," said Cadvan. "I decided to go to Arkan-da first."

Cadvan had ridden hard over the Arkiadera Plains, reaching Lake Zmark in less than a week. There he had disguised himself as a Jussack and journeyed through the Jussack settlements dotted around the lake until he reached Ursk, the major Jussack town, which nestled at the foot of the Trukuch Ranges forty leagues west of Arkan-da.

"The Jussacks have been under the sway of a black sorcerer, a minion of the Winterking, for twenty years now," he said. Maerad thought of Amusk, and shuddered.

"I think he is now dead," she said. Cadvan shot her a surprised glance. "He was killed by wolves," she said. "I'll tell you in a moment." Cadvan nodded, and continued his story.

"Ursk was an evil place to be; in the hall of their chieftain some Jussacks tried to rob me. They suffered for their pains; after that, they were afraid of me, but even so they would not or could not tell me anything of a young girl called Maerad of Pellinor.

"I went then to Arkan-da, and wasted many fruitless days trying to find a way into his stronghold. But in my searching, I had no rumour of you. I was sure that I must know if you were there, even through the Winterking's warding of his stronghold, and at last I thought I must have made the wrong guess, and that perhaps I would find news of you in Murask. The snow had begun early, and it took a little longer to retrace my steps across the Arkiadera, otherwise I might have caught up with you. I reached Murask three days after you had left with Dharin. I planned to follow, but Sirkana told me there was no team of dogs faster than Dharin's, and so I decided to await your return."

Maerad and Dharin had been expected back after four weeks, and after five Cadvan began to be anxious. After six weeks, frantic with worry, he went to Sirkana begging the use of a sled to trace Maerad's path north, but she would not permit it.

"She said, *I have already paid the price for your quest, twice over,*" said Cadvan. "*I will sacrifice nothing more.* My heart failed me, because I knew then that something must have gone badly wrong. She told me that she had foreknown that Dharin would die on his journey north. She knew nothing of what would happen to you.

"I wanted to shake her until her teeth rattled for permitting you to leave Murask when she knew already that your journey was doomed. But she said to me: *It was the right decision, although it broke my heart. I loved Dharin as my own son, as dearly as my own brother, who also died for the Light. There was no other way that the One could know what she needs to know.* And, after that, I could not rebuke her."

Maerad thought of Sirkana's stern, beautiful face. She was amazed by her strength; she could not imagine making the same decision. And she thought sadly again of Dharin, her cousin, his lifeblood spilt onto the snow.

"I still did not know what had happened to you, or where you were, and Sirkana said she knew nothing beyond what she had told me," said Cadvan. "I had no idea where, in that wide empty land, I could begin to search for you. I was in great despair. But that night I dreamt of Ardina."

Maerad sat up attentively. "Ardina?" she said. "I have seen much of her."

"That does not surprise me. I think there is much at stake for Ardina in this whole question of the Treesong," said Cadvan, giving Maerad a penetrating glance. "She appeared to me as the Moonchild, and she said: *If all goes well, seek the Lily in her birthplace on Midwinter Day.*" He stretched out his legs and sighed. "I didn't much like that phrase, if all goes well," he said wryly. "But I had no better plan. She could only have meant Pellinor. So I made the journey with Darsor back along the Murask Road and through the Gwalhain Pass, which was cold and long, and difficult with the snow, but this time not especially perilous, apart from the danger of freezing to death. And then I rode hard across Lirhan to Pellinor, dreading to miss Midwinter Day. I arrived here yesterday, and this morning I caught a rabbit and thought I would make a stew. And so you find me."

They sat ruminatively for a time, staring across the ruined Circle of Pellinor. Then Cadvan stirred and said, "Well, you have heard my story. But I'm sure yours is more interesting."

Maerad told him the whole tale of what had happened since their separation in the Gwalhain. Cadvan listened attentively, his face downcast, and did not interrupt once. By the time Maerad had finished talking, the crescent moon was high in the sky, and a heavy dew was beginning to fall. It was very cold: there would be a frost that night. He put more wood on the fire, and it flared up, a column of sparks and flame, into the still night.

"Perhaps the most astounding thing is your third name," Cadvan said at last. He studied Maerad as if he were looking at her for the first time. "Triple tongued, triple named ... it is a great strength, Maerad. There is still some power in knowing your Bard Name, clearly, since the Jussack sorcerer and the Winterking could use it so blackly against you: but I suspect that if you knew your Elemental Name, your Bard Name would cease to hold that power."

"It's a bit confusing," Maerad said. "There seem to be so many of me."

Cadvan smiled. "We are all many," he said. "But most of us don't have the privilege of understanding that as clearly as you do. It is hard, to know oneself, but until we do, we cannot know why we act as we do. It's a lifetime's quest, and it never ends."

Maerad stared at Cadvan, who was broodily poking the fire again. He seemed not to be speaking of her, but of himself.

"And the Treesong was on your lyre," Cadvan said. "I wonder that we never thought of that possibility."

"How could we know?" said Maerad. "Even Nelac could not read the runes."

"True." Cadvan stared into the fire. "I thought the runes were most likely the name and the story of the Dhyllic craftsman who made it. But now it is likely your lyre was made by Nelsor himself. The greatest of all Bards. And from what you say, it seems that Nelsor and the Winterking were lovers."

Maerad turned away from Cadvan, hiding her face. It was difficult for her to think of Arkan; and the thought that he had loved a Bard struck a hollow place inside her breast.

"I didn't know what to think of the Winterking," she said at last. "He's neither good nor evil. He has no great love for the Light, but I do not think that he gives his loyalty to the Dark; he spoke of the Nameless One with disgust, and said that he had been betrayed by him."

"He is a powerful Elidhu," said Cadvan thoughtfully. "I think you are right; he would not consent to be enslaved, like the Landrost. I wonder what part Ardina plays in all this?"

"I don't know," said Maerad. She stared out into the night; there were many forces at play, and she could not follow them. A silence fell, and to break it Maerad went to her pack and took out her lyre.

"I'll read the Treesong to you," she said. "Arkan said it was dead, that the runes had no music. I don't really understand what he meant by that, but he told me these meanings." She went through them one by one, stroking each rune as she named it. As she did so, she remembered the Winterking's face as he had taught her the runes, and a sharp pain went through her. She did not regret leaving the Ice Palace, but she wondered if she would ever be free of the memory of Arkan.

"It is beautiful," said Cadvan, when she had finished. "Well, Maerad, we've come a long way. Though I do not doubt there is much more to the Song than these runes. And we know also that the Nameless One seeks you, not just because he fears that somehow you will cause his overthrow, but because he needs you. As much as he needs the other half of the Song."

"Arkan said that I was the player," said Maerad softly. "But I do not know how to play music that I have never heard."

"No. Well, some things begin to make sense, but they only raise more questions," Cadvan said. "If the Nameless One has the other runes, I doubt it will be easy to get them back. And Annar grows ever more dangerous: war comes near, and not only from the south."

"Civil war?" asked Maerad.

"I have no doubt of it. But not only that. If Turbansk falls, things will go ill with Annar." Cadvan stretched, grimacing. "Though it could be that the chaos of war might make it easier for us to slip through the nets of both the Light and the Dark."

"I suppose now we storm the Iron Tower or something," said Maerad. "But we can think on that tomorrow."

"Well, if you escaped the Ice Palace, why not the Iron Tower?" said Cadvan, smiling.

"I almost didn't escape," said Maerad. "I–I almost didn't want to."

She hesitated, feeling intensely shy, and then said in rush: "I think I fell in love with the Winterking." She was glad it was dark, because she knew she had blushed deep red.

Cadvan looked at her for a long moment. "Love is one of the true mysteries," he said at last. "The truest and the deepest of all. One thing, Maerad: to love is never wrong. It may be disastrous, it may never be possible, it may be the deepest agony. But it is never wrong."

"He is cruel and ruthless, and he desires power," whispered Maerad. "But by his own lights he was kind to me. Sometimes I even felt that I understood him. But all the same, I feel – ashamed."

"I doubt whether the Winterking would have given you the meaning of the runes had he not known that you loved him," said Cadvan slowly.

"Yes," said Maerad, looking down. Tears prickled her eyes. "But I think he was right. The Treesong belongs to the Elidhu, not to the Light or to the Dark, and we have to give it back to them. It is not something that the Light should have. But, then, you see, I betrayed him. Although if I had stayed, I would have betrayed everyone else…" She trailed off into silence.

Cadvan leant forward and brushed Maerad's hair out of her eyes.

"Look at me, Maerad," he said. Unwillingly she lifted her eyes to meet his. "I had already begun to think that this is a matter of undoing what Light or Dark should never have done," he said. "If that is so, then that is what we must do. And you could not complete that quest while you were bound in the Ice Palace. Perhaps you have not betrayed the Winterking, after all.

Perhaps you have helped him not to betray himself."

Maerad nodded. Cadvan gazed at her with a tenderness he had never shown her before.

"Never be ashamed of your love," he said gently. "The only thing to be ashamed of is denying your love. That is what makes the shadow grow within your heart, that is the darkening of the Light. And we all have many loves."

"I remembered the other people I love," said Maerad, her voice rough. "I remembered Hem most of all. And I dreamed of you, even though I thought you were dead. It gave me hope. But it was still almost the worst pain I had ever felt in my life, leaving the Winterking."

She began to sob, and leaned on Cadvan's shoulder. He wordlessly stroked her hair, saying nothing, until she had cried herself out and sat up, wiping her eyes with her sleeve.

"I want to find Hem," she said.

"We'll start tomorrow," answered Cadvan, smiling gently. "In my heart, I, too, think we must find him. But right now I feel as tired as ever I have in my life."

Maerad gave him a wobbly smile. "Tomorrow, then," she said.

That night, Maerad dreamed she was walking through a green meadow full of wild flowers, with grass almost as high as her knees. She reached a high hedge, and unlatched a gate and passed into an orchard of apple trees. It was early spring, and all of them held a heavy burden of pink-and-white blossoms. Blossom littered the ground like snow, and among the white-starred grasses nodded daffodils and bluebells and crocuses of many colours.

She wandered through the orchard into a garden just now greening from its winter slumber, and continued over a path of raked white gravel towards a beautiful house. Maerad knew it was her home, although she had never seen such a place before. It was a long, double-storeyed building of yellow stone, with wide windows that shone in the sunshine.

When she reached the front door it opened of its own accord, and she passed inside. She entered every room, seeking something, but they were all empty. She ran upstairs, breathless, beginning to feel distressed, flinging open every door in an increasingly desperate search, but no one was there. A panic seized her, and she ran down the stairs and out of the house into the garden, tears falling down her cheeks.

And then she saw Hem among the apple trees, a half-eaten apple in his hand. He waved and started running towards her, his face radiant with joy.

He was coming home.

HERE ENDS
THE SECOND BOOK
OF PELLINOR

APPENDICES

THESE notes are intended to be supplementary to and in some cases to update the Appendices to *The Gift*, the first volume of Pellinor, in which I sketched an introduction to the history and society of the Bards of Annar, and discussed briefly the central importance of the Speech to Bardic power. *The Gift* comprises the first two books of the *Naraudh Lar-Chanë*, the Riddle of the Treesong, the great Annaren epic that chronicles the Second Rising of the Dark in Edil-Amarandh. The Riddle is translated from Books III and V of the *Naraudh Lar-Chanë*.

The complex and fascinating world of Edil-Amarandh is one of the fastest growing areas of contemporary scholarship, with branches in the disciplines of sociology, literature, history, anthropology, archaeology, linguistics, women's studies and even in the sciences; and it is consequently almost impossible to keep up with all the ongoing research. These notes cannot be anything but the briefest introduction to this field, but I have done my best to ensure that they accord with the most recent scholarship available.

THE PEOPLES OF
EDIL-AMARANDH

Annar and the Seven Kingdoms[1]

Edil-Amarandh is a general term for the continent that stretched from
the deep North down to beyond the Suderain, from the Western Ocean
to the wilderness beyond the eastern side of the Osidh Annova. It is
a term from the Speech, which can be translated variously as Earth-
Throne or Navel of the Earth, and referred to the whole of the known
world. Maerad's Bardic Truename, *Elednor Edil-Amarandh na*, was similar to saying, in modern English, "Maerad of the World".[2]

The Bards used two calendars, referred to as the Afinil and the
Norloch yearcounts (A and N). The history of Edil-Amarandh was
divided[3] into three main Ages. The Age of the Elementals ended
approximately 5,000 years before the time of the present story and concerns mainly the Wars of the Elementals, especially the War by Arkan,
the Winterking, against the Elidhu of Annar, led by Ardina. Legends
and songs, such as the many lays concerning Ardina, were preserved
in tradition from this time, and were written down later.

Second was the Dawn Age, when the culture of the Dhyllin flowered across Annar, centring on the legendary citadel of Afinil. The
Afinil yearcount started on its founding. It is reckoned that Bards, or
Dhillarearën, appeared in Edil-Amarandh shortly before the Dawn Age,
in a period known as the pre-Dawn, or Inela. The Afinil yearcount
starts in the Dawn Age, and it continued until A2041, when Sharma,
the Nameless One, overthrew the forces of Imbral and Lirion in the
Battle of the Firman Plains and began the tyranny of the Dark, which
became known later as the Great Silence.

Lanorgil named the third Age the Restoration, and it dates from the founding of Norloch, and institutes the Norloch yearcount. At this time, Maninaë founded the Schools and the Monarchy of Annar.

The Great Silence, which lasted more than a millennium from A2041 to A3234, was not counted as an Age.

The largest realm in the continent was Annar, but within Annar the different regions were widely diverse; there were huge differences between, say, Innail and Il-Arunedh, despite their speaking a common language. The diversity of Edil-Amarandh was even clearer in the Seven Kingdoms, which were distinct both from Annar and from each other in their cultures and languages. The sharing of power between Bards and what might be called for convenience "civil authorities" varied in each of the Seven Kingdoms. But perhaps because they were relatively small, and also because they were (despite being called kingdoms) not strictly speaking monarchies, conflict between the dual authorities was extremely rare and never reached, as it did in Annar, the point of civil war. In two of the kingdoms – Amdridh and the Suderain – civil authority was determined by heredity, although a ruler could be legally deposed by the other authorities if they were considered by the population to be exceeding or abusing their powers. This, in fact, happened only once, in Turbansk in A1333, when Aleksil the Tyrant, who was mightily resented for the crippling taxes he instituted to finance his opulent court, was overthrown in a bloodless coup after a popular uprising supported by the School of Turbansk. More common than hereditary succession were varying degrees of democracy, ranging from full enfranchisement (Lanorial, Culain, Lirhan), where every adult citizen was expected to vote, to partial, as in Thorold and Ileadh, where village Mayors or Thanes would represent popular interests and vote for the Chamber in Thorold, or the Parliament, in Ileadh.

The relationships between these different authorities were extremely complex, and varied from kingdom to kingdom, but they worked effectively to balance the possible extremes of each. Bardic authority was complementary to the civil authority of non-Bards, and

each took supreme authority in different areas. Bards in the Seven
Kingdoms were greatly respected: they provided education, expertise
and training in various arts and crafts, the rituals of the year such
as the Midsummer rite described in Thorold in *The Riddle*, spiritual
authority and (not unimportantly) a great deal of entertainment:
music, in particular. Civil authorities took care of most areas of justice,
administration and defence, although there was a lot of crossover
– for example, a plaintiff could appeal to a Bardic tribunal if he felt
aggrieved by civic justice, and Bards, both as soldiers and mages, were
important contributors to a region's military power.

By their nature, the civic authorities tended to be parochial in
their concerns, whereas the Bards' view was wider. In practice, this
led to cultures of negotiation and diplomacy, and mitigated against
any tendencies to absolute rule. It also led to frustrations: the Bard
Liric was not alone when he complained peevishly during a dispute
over the placement of a bridge in N356 that the Councillors of Lirhan
were "stiff-neck'd and ignorant" and that Lirhan's citizenship was
"barell-headed" for electing them, and many Bards complained over
the centuries about the conservatism and resistance to change of
many of the civic authorities. There were frequent arguments about
trade and other interests between the different kingdoms: most of
these kinds of disputes were resolved through the mediation of the
Bards. However, despite these hiccups, nothing disturbed the model
of dual authority in the Seven Kingdoms, and in the presence of
external threat it was proverbial that all smaller disputes were forgotten to protect their common interests. The Seven Kingdoms were
proud that they had been the centres of resistance to the Nameless
One during the Great Silence, and both the civic authorities and the
Bards nourished that tradition, represented by a common code of
fealty to the Light and the Balance, which, at its best, balanced both
local and general interests.

Although it was by far the largest in area and population of all
the realms of Edil-Amarandh, Annar's rule over the surrounding

territories was non-existent: it was a relationship of co-operation, promulgated in large part by the practical unity of Bards. Any attempt by Annar to assert central rule was always resisted fiercely by the Seven Kingdoms.

The most serious crisis before the events of this book occurred during the Long Wars (N710–N751) when Dhuran the Red (so named for his red hair and bad temper) proclaimed the Annaren Empire and himself Emperor after a coup in which he assassinated his brother, Ilbaran III, in N710. His claim to rule the Seven Kingdoms by Right of the Triple Sceptre led to open warfare between the Seven Kingdoms and Annar. He launched invasions against Lanorial and Ileadh after they sharply rejected his authority as both illegitimate and a corruption of the Balance and the Light. The actual invasions were easily beaten back, since Dhuran was simultaneously embroiled in ruinous civil war against the sons of Ilbaran, Baran and Ebaran, and did not have the resources to mount an effective offensive. For most of the four decades of conflict that followed, the Seven Kingdoms, after severing their alliances with Norloch and Annar and strengthening their defences, remained warily aloof from these internecine wars, waiting to see who would win. None of the claimants for the throne was an attractive prospect: the two sons of Ilbaran were as ruthless in their pursuit of power as Dhuran, and the fourth possible candidate, Dhuran's daughter Ilseticine the Fair, was murdered by Baran early in the Long Wars. When Dhuran was cast off the throne by Baran in N749, the new King's first act was to take the title of the White Flame (the prefix *Nor*), an act of staggering hubris that signified his appropriation of the traditional authority of the Bards. The newly styled Nor-Baran instituted a tyranny crueller than that of his predecessor: exacting an implacable revenge on anyone he knew or suspected of opposing him, and imprisoning and executing his brother, Ebaran, for treason. He also announced that the Schools would now exist only by Royal favour, and that any Schools that did not acknowledge this would be destroyed by force of arms. Even Dhuran the Red had not dared to alienate the Bards.

At this point, the Seven Kingdoms became deeply alarmed, as they rightly guessed that armed invasion of their territories was not far away, and made open alliance with the Bards of Annar. Nor-Baran's defeat and death in battle occurred two years later.

The Long Wars led to the final overthrow of the monarchy, the end of the line of Maninaë, and the subsequent rule of Annar by the Norloch Bards. This outcome was often considered, especially in the Seven Kingdoms, a calamitous result, since it upset the balance between civil and Bardic authority, although two centuries ensued of wise and fair rule by Noldor (First Bard from N745–N866) and Nardil (N866–N939). However, Enkir's reign as First Bard from N939 amply bore out their forebodings.

The history of the relationship between the Seven Kingdoms and Annar was, therefore, by no means untroubled. This background contributed to the disquiet with which the First Bards of the Seven Kingdoms had been watching developments in Norloch after the sacking of the School of Pellinor in N935, ten years before the events recounted in the *Naraudh Lar-Chanë*. Although Enkir was a practised politician, and was careful to stress his fealty to the Light, his uncompromising insistence on the necessity of central authority and his increased campaigning against female Bards, ensured that his rapid rise to power and his appointment to Norloch's First Circle in the early decades of the N900s was viewed with alarm in the Seven Kingdoms. The First Bards and civil rulers were disturbed enough to strengthen what had always been an unofficial alliance designed to protect the Seven Kingdoms against the machinations of Annar.

All their fears were confirmed by Enkir's extraordinary Edict of Loyalty after the Burning of Norloch, which demanded their allegiance in terms that entirely rewrote the old alliances, and the Kingdoms began to arm themselves against Norloch. Annar itself, with Schools and Fesses across the realm differing sharply in their responses to Enkir's Edict, seemed to be dangerously close to the brink of civil war; even as massive forces from Dén Raven marched against the fortress cities of the Suderain with the aim of taking Baladh, Turbansk and Car Amdridh, and acquiring bases from which to attack Annar itself. Sharma, the Nameless One, was marshalling his armies to war against Annar and the Seven Kingdoms at a time when the forces of the Light had never been more bitterly divided.

The Pilanel

The Pilanel[4] (or the Pilani, as they referred to themselves) were a nomad people who inhabited the northern land of Zmarkan, a wide tundra that stretched north of the Osidh Elanor. No records exist of when they first settled the Arkiadera, or the Mother Plains, but it was probably before the time of the founding of Afinil, after the end of the Elemental Wars.

The Pilanel did not keep written records as the Bards did, having an almost completely oral culture, and so it is much less well documented than Annaren culture. They did invent a system of runes, which the Bards adapted and extended into the Ladhen runes. Unfortunately, all we know of the Pilanel writing is what remains in the Ladhen runes, since no examples have so far been found; it seems likely that the Pilanel runes were simply scratched at need into trees and stones, to be read by other travellers. Such knowledge as we do have of the Pilanel peoples comes mainly from those Pilanel *Dhillarearën* who became Annaren Bards, and wrote about their own people in Annaren script. However, even those records are full of elisions, as it was forbidden for Pilanel to reveal many of their customs and beliefs to non-Pilanel.[5]

The extant records portray an extremely resourceful and adaptive people who possessed a rich and ancient visual and oral culture of their own with roots that went back, unbroken, to before the Great Silence. They had their share of *Dhillarearën*, some of whom, like Maerad's father, Dorn à Triberi, went south to the Schools to be trained in Annaren lore. Those who went to the Schools seem to be the exceptions, rather than the rule, and Pilanel with the Voice (as they referred to those born with the Gift) held honoured places in Pilanel culture. These roles were similar in some ways to those Bards held in Annar and the Seven Kingdoms. However, the Pilanel did not have the system of dual authority that held sway in the south and it was not unusual for the chieftains of the tribes to be *Dhillarearën*. Lineages of the Howe leaders recorded by Anarkin of Lirigon, himself a Pilanel Bard, mark about half the Pilanel rulers as *Dhillarearën*.[6]

The Pilanel divided themselves roughly into two major populations, the Northern and the Southern Clans, who were identified by the Howe – Murask in the South or Tlon in the North – to which they travelled to spend each winter. There was no clear division between the Northern and Southern Clans, as intermarriage was common, and some clans would regularly swap between the Howes. A clan was a loose grouping generally, but not necessarily, related by blood, who travelled together during the summer months; they varied in size from perhaps half a dozen people to several dozen. Moving between clans, through marriage or need or inclination, was also not uncommon.

The Southern Pilanel were famous horsebreeders and trainers (most of the Bard horses were bred and trained by Pilanel) but they also pursued a bewildering range of crafts and employments during the summer months. Some were traders, selling goods made during the long winter months in the Howe, and would also travel as far as the Suderain to buy goods in the markets, which they would then sell in Annar; some were hawkers and tinkers, repairing household goods; some became itinerant labourers and worked on Annaren farms during the summer. The Northern Pilanel traded furs, textiles and carved goods, and also herded and bred the oribanik deer, which they used for milk, skins and meat.

The Howes, giant earth and stone fortresses capable of housing several thousands, were some of the most ancient structures in Edil-Amarandh, dating (like Turbansk, the great city of Suderain in the South) from the Inela, the time after the Age of the Elementals and before the Dawn Age. There is an extremely detailed description of the Murask Howe's sophisticated heating and water system by Belgar of Gent at the Restoration,[7] and there is every reason to believe that the Schools borrowed and adapted the Howe systems for use in their own Schools. Murask Howe is described in detail in the *Naraudh Lar-Chanë*, as is the Pilanel's communal style of living.

The Jussacks

The Jussacks first appeared in Zmarkan in the mid-N800s, and it is thought their arrival coincided with Arkan's return to the Trukuch ranges – his original home, from which he had been banished after the Great Silence – and that they originated from the shores of the Ipiilinik Darsk (Ice Sea), in the area known as Norsk. Arkan was forbidden by the Elidhu to venture further south than Norsk, and he made himself a stronghold somewhere on the eastern side of the Ipiilinik Darsk. The relationship between Arkan and the Jussacks is the subject of some debate, but it seems generally agreed among the Bardic authorities that the Winterking exerted authority over the Jussacks and used them for his own purposes, including that of revenge: many believed that the Jussack's hatred of the Pilanel was fostered and encouraged by Arkan, as retribution for the Pilanel resistance to his power during the Great Silence.

The Jussacks, a fair-haired and fair-skinned people regarded as barbarians by both the Pilanel and Bards, made an aggressive move south to Unt, colonizing the eastern reaches of the Arkiadera and slaughtering without mercy any Pilanel clans they encountered. By N900, the Jussacks had established a number of settlements around Lake Zmark and the Trukuch ranges, of which the chief centre was Ursk, from which they mounted regular attacks against Pilanel clans in the Arkiadera, and also mounted offensives against the Howes.

Nothing is known of the Norsk people from whom the Jussacks are believed to be descended, and so it is impossible to know whether their warlike mores predated Arkan's influence. Jussack society in N945 was almost totally militarized: boys were trained as warriors from the moment they could walk, and they were feared as ruthless and merciless fighters, slaughtering or enslaving anyone they defeated. Women held little authority in Jussack society, being regarded as little better than slaves. In the summer months they ranged across the Arkiadera on horseback in small bands, sleeping in tents, and pillaged and slaughtered any Pilanel clans they came across. There is no evidence that they developed anything but the most rudimentary of agricultures, depending for most of their supplies on what could be won by hunting or force of arms.

At this time, the defences of both Howes were strengthened, although Murask, being much closer to Lake Zmark, was attacked more regularly than Tlon. Pilanel resistance to the Jussacks was fierce, but over the decades their traditional summer grazing grounds were steadily pushed further west and south. By N900, the southern Pilanel clans no longer travelled north-east to the shores of Lake Zmark in the summer, and after negotiations with Lirigon began to graze most of their herds on the Rilnik Plains, making the arduous journey through the Gwalhain Pass, rather than risking their traditional grazing grounds in the Arkiadera.

The Peoples of the North

Of the peoples who lived in the deep north even less is known than of the Pilanel, who after all had frequent dealing with the peoples of Annar and the Seven Kingdoms. In the *Naraudh Lar-Chanë*, Dharin á Triberi speaks of at least twenty distinct peoples speaking different tongues who lived along the coastlines of the northern continent. "The Pilanel tell of at least twenty different peoples who live on the coast of Hramask, from Orun to Lebinusk," he tells Maerad, "and there are probably more. And you must not think that one people is the same as the next: they have different customs and they speak different languages. The Wise Kindred are understood to be the oldest of all peoples. Their name for themselves, Inaruskosani, means 'those who first walked on the earth'."[8]

Unfortunately, this mention in the *Naraudh Lar-Chanë*, and the description of the Wise Kindred, is the most comprehensive reference to the peoples of the Far North yet to be discovered. That more was known at the time is evidenced in the detailed maps of the North the Bards left among the Annaren Scrolls. Perhaps such teasing hints will be fleshed out as more documents come to light, since a great percentage of the Annaren Scrolls still remain undeciphered and this is still a very new area of study.

THE ELIDHU

THE Elidhu, also called the Elementals, are the most puzzling and elusive entities of Edil-Amarandh. Among the extant scrolls are literally thousands of references to Elidhu, but apart from a couple of notable exceptions it is hard to reach any concrete conclusion as to who they were, or even what they represented to the peoples of Edil-Amarandh. The Bards who wrote of them after the Restoration of Maninaë spoke of them mainly with distrust – as dangerous, unpredictable forces who needed to be either controlled or avoided – and often argued that the downfall of Afinil was brought about by its close association with the Elidhu where, for the only time in Edil-Amarandh's history, it was said that the Elidhu mingled with the Bards of the Light in human form.

One of the more intriguing aspects of the *Naraudh Lar-Chanë* is its unusually detailed portrayal of Elidhu. If we accept, as most scholars do, that the *Naraudh Lar-Chanë* was in fact written by Cadvan of Lirigon and Maerad of Pellinor rather than later chroniclers, then it records first-hand Bardic encounters with the Elidhu for the first time since the Dhyllic civilization of the Dawn Age. Most references to the Elidhu in the extant post-Restoration scrolls are hearsay or legend, and many Bards in the later years frankly doubted their existence. We must remember that it was very unusual for the Elidhu to be the architects of decisive interventions in human affairs, as both Ardina, Queen of Rachida, and Arkan, the Winterking, are in the *Naraudh Lar-Chanë*, and that these Elidhu were consequently far from typical. In this tale, the fate of the Elidhu and their relationship to human affairs take centre stage.

All the documents portray the Elidhu as representations or personifications of the forces of the natural world (as is reflected in their Annaren name, *Iltaranaeren*, which I have translated as Elementals). Every Elidhu is linked either to some natural phenomenon – Ardina, for example, is a manifestation of the moon – or to some feature of landscape or place (the Landrost, the Elidhu who captures Cadvan at the very beginning of the story, is, for instance, synonymous with the mountain he inhabits; another aspect of Ardina is as a forest Elidhu). It is also generally agreed that they have supernatural powers and are immortal, that their eyes have irises like those of a cat, and that they are capable of manifesting in different forms, both animate and inanimate. After the beginning of the Great Silence, most of the Elidhu withdrew from the human world, a withdrawal that persisted after the Restoration, although whether this was their own choice, or because after Arkan's alliance with the Nameless One they became distrusted among Bards, remains unclear. It seems most likely that the breach was a result of both.

Thus far all the documents agree. But beyond this it is very difficult to draw conclusive interpretations of who or what the Elidhu were. It is difficult to characterize precisely how the Elidhu were regarded by the peoples of Edil-Amarandh – it is tempting to see them as personifications, for instance, of an animistic religious sense, similar to the pantheon of Greek gods, but this seems to me to be not quite accurate. Elidhu were linked with local superstitions and customs all over Edil-Amarandh, and were often called on like votive gods in specific circumstances – to find lost property, for example, or to bless a venture. However, the peoples of Annar and the Seven Kingdoms were used to asking Bards for similar blessings or charms, and Bards, for all their spiritual status, were not by any means regarded as gods. Despite their immortality and supernatural powers, there are no records in Annar or the Seven Kingdoms that speak of the Elidhu being worshipped as gods, or of shrines or rites accorded to them that could in any sense be recognized as organized religion[9], and the rise to prominence of particular Elidhu is not anywhere traceable to the rise of particular families or regions to power (as the importance of Athena, for example, rose with the importance of Athens).

The Winterking's assault on Edil-Amarandh in the Age of the Elementals can be read as a parable of an Ice Age and as an explanation of certain natural phenomena, such as the Osidh Annova, but again this seems not quite satisfactory in the context of later writings about the same Elidhu. The casual references in the Afinil documents to conversations with Elidhu, the portrayal of Ardina and Arkan as real entities in the *Naraudh Lar-Chanë*, and scores of other references can only lead us to conclude that to the people of Edil-Amarandh the Elidhu were real and present in ways that we may find difficult to accept.[10]

There is a lot of speculation in the *Naraudh Lar-Chanë* about Elemental magic: unlike the magery of Bards, which depended crucially on the Speech, it seemed to be unrelated to language. Elemental magic depended rather on influencing the material nature of things, a type of magic considered among Bards to be the chief of the mysteries, and the most difficult and dangerous to practise. It is also, clearly, an emotional, rather than an intellectual, magic, although Bards would consider this a puzzling and false division. These differences, which remain mysterious, go some way to explaining the amazement among Bards at Maerad's powers, which operated outside the arenas of most Bardic skills and gifts, as well as their distrust of them.

Ardina

Ardina was by far the most celebrated of the Elementals among the Restoration Bards. Her love for Ardhor, the first King of Lirion, with whom she forged the decisive alliance that helped to defeat Arkan the Ice Witch, the Winterking, at the end of the Elemental Wars, was a favourite subject of Bardic song[11]. In those tales, she is also associated with spring, and is a symbol of fertility. She is often represented, like the goddess Isis, crowned with the horned or full moon, and Annaren women would call on her help in childbirth or for difficulties with menstruation. She was regarded as one of the most powerful of all the Elidhu; it seems that her status as an earthly incarnation of the moon meant she was not restricted to place in the way that even Arkan, the Winterking, appeared to be, and she seemed to be able to appear in various physical or dream guises in any place in Edil-Amarandh.

During the Great Silence, Ardina disappears from Bardic history until the *Naraudh Lar-Chanë*, and the discovery of the people of Rachida, the only descendents of the Dhyllin people remaining in Annar[12]. She is, in many ways, a baffling figure, presented at once as a figure of ancient legend from the Age of the Elementals and the Dawn Age, as the wise and great Queen of Rachida, the secret realm in the midst of the Great Forest described in Book 2 of the *Naraudh Lar-Chanë*, and as a "wild and fey," Elidhu, separate from and somewhat mocking of trivial human affairs.

Ardina is described by the Bard Menellin in Afinil: "The Daughter of the Moon, Ardin Ilya Na, often comes to our halls, to sing and to speak with us, and her radiance outshines our humble lights as the Moon outshines the Stars. But it seemeth to me that her beauty is made infinitely more piquant by her sadness; for although it may be an impertinence to observe so, when she looks upon the beauty of the halls, and the flower of Manhood which gathereth here, she is reminded of her lost love, the King Ardhor, and her joy is tempered thereby. She steps among us sometimes as a great Queen, arrayed in raiment of pearls and silver; and at other times as a slender young girl dressed in the simplest robes of white, which falleth from her figure in flowing motions, and seem themselves to be woven of Light. But at all times her beauty is of the kind which pierceth the heart. It is said among Bards that she will join her love in the deathless glades beyond the Gates, and although that would be a glad day for her, whose love is as immortal as her flesh, it would be a day of great loss for us, who are so ennobled and delighted by her presence."[13]

Arkan

Arkan, known also as the Ice Witch, the Ice King or the Winterking, gets a bad press from the Restoration Bards. "When he took on human form, he was evil incarnate," wrote Piron of Il-Arunedh in N562, in a not untypical description. "He was treacherous and slippery as a cold snake. His skin was white and bloodless as snow, his nails long as claws, and the malice and cruelty of his countenance could not but strike terror into the human heart. His brow was aspected by fearsome lightnings which made his chilling visage all the more terrible."[14]

Arkan was considered second only to the Nameless One as a threat to the Light: he had covered all Edil-Amarandh with ice in the Elemental Wars, causing unprecedented destruction and forcing the Elidhu to raise the Osidh Annova and Osidh Elanor as defences against him. Before the Great Silence, he had allied himself with the Nameless One, and after their joint victory had spread his influence over all of the North and Northern Annar, withdrawing only when Maninaë finally defeated the forces of the Dark in the Battle of Malinau in A3234. After that, Arkan was forced to leave Arkan-da in the Trukuch Ranges and was banished to the deep North, a banishing effected by some council or gathering of Elidhu and Bards of the Light apparently convened by Ardina. There is no description of this mysterious meeting anywhere in the records, and after its brief mention in Lanorgil of Pellinor's *History*, Elidhu disappear from human affairs for nine centuries.

There is little doubt that the Annaren Bards had good reason for their loathing of Arkan – his treachery was the most grievous blow against the Light in Lirion and Imbral, and it was probably his decisive influence that led to their downfall. But in his own way Arkan is as puzzling and ambiguous a figure as Ardina. Documents dating from the Dawn Age often paint a very different figure from that described by Piron above: a being of somewhat perilous charisma and personal beauty. "The Elidhu Arkan is like to a spirit of winter, in human form, and his beauty is both stormy and still," writes a clearly infatuated

Elagil of Afinil. "He hath skin that glitters as white as unblemished snow, and his eyes are of the glancing blues of a clear wintry sky. Yet cold though he be, he is not unmoved by feeling: he hath both the passions and gentleness of a wolf, and speaks often with a loving delicacy of many marvellous and strange things that exist in the world. He is a being of unmatchable beauty and charm; of all the Elidhu, only Ardina can rival his presence in our halls. If he is a being of frost and ice, then surely such passions as he evinces should melt him: but his fiery glances only serve to intensify his dazzling allure."

Others refer to his generosity in sharing his knowledge with the Dhyllin: and in particular, there are tantalizing hints of a love that sprang between the greatest of the Afinil Bards, Nelsor, the inventor of the Treesong runes, and Arkan. Although no documents to date speak directly of this, various attributions and dedications by Nelsor himself to Arkan confirm at least the existence of a profound friendship. The sources suggest that the Treesong was indeed revealed to the Bards by Arkan, who may have actively participated in the creation of the runes. Intriguingly, the only contemporary references that speak of the relationship between Ardina and Arkan show no sign of any enmity between them, despite their bitter opposition during the Elemental Wars and his later banishment, but rather suggest at least mutual respect, or even friendship.

THE TREESONG

R ELATIVELY speaking, we have a lot of information about the Treesong, mainly from the *Naraudh Lar-Chanë* and most notably from Cadvan of Lirigon's extensive study of it in his crucial scroll *The Treesong Alphabet*, a document that has been preserved almost complete. Nevertheless, what the Treesong was, how it was created and what it meant remains as essentially mysterious as the Speech itself.

It is generally agreed among the Bardic sources that the runes were made by Nelsor of Afinil, who also invented the Nelsor script most often used by Bards, and that they were stolen by Sharma who attempted to use them to create the binding spell of immortality and to give himself the powers of the Elidhu. As we know, he only half succeeded in his aim, and after this the Treesong was hidden or lost. Some sources have speculated that Maerad's lyre was made by Nelsor himself, although there is no proof; what the presence of the runes on the lyre does suggest is that the runes were not complete without music, that they were crucially performative in their making.

Maerad's lyre had half of the twenty runes of the Treesong: those with the phonetic values A, E, I, O, U, F, S, H, D and T. In an unpublished monograph[15] Professor Patrick Insole of the Department of Ancient Languages at the University of Leeds has made a thorough study of the extant sources on the Treesong, and on the symbolism of the runes. I have drawn extensively on his monograph for this book, and Professor Insole, generally regarded as the foremost authority on the scripts of Edil-Amarandh, has kindly permitted me to quote extensively from his monograph for these notes.

The Treesong Runes

The letterforms, though having nominal letter and phonetic values, were almost certainly never used for everyday writing. This is evident from the relative complexity of the individual symbols and the diversity of the alphabet as a whole, compared to other ancient writing systems. It can be seen that the forms themselves are of a composite nature, which is to say that they have been "assembled" from two or more simpler forms, and were intended to embody and express particular themes, many of which will undoubtedly have been lost. The only purpose we know the alphabet served was the expression of the Treesong itself, each letter signifying a particular stanza. However, it is reasonable to assume that the alphabet could have been used for other ritualistic/magic purposes and possibly, given its seasonal/lunar structure, it may have served in the recording or measurement of time.

The difficulty in interpreting the signs comes from the very fact that their use is so rare, even in contemporary sources. However, an interpretation of their component signs, if not their underlying significance, can be attempted.

The alphabet is divided into five groupings, which can be identified as Vowels (or Moon signs), Winter, Spring, Summer and Autumn. Each group, vowels excepted, is indicated by a strong central symbol, coupled with one or more other symbols that refer to individual trees and/or its stanza. It should be noted that these interpretations are conjectural at best, and in many instances the sign has become so encoded and simplified that its origin remains unclear.

The runes on Maerad of Pellinor's **lyre, and the stanzas and values pertaining to them:**

A   I am the dew on every hill
O   I am the leap in every womb
U   I am the fruit of every bough
I   I am the edge of every cliff
E   I am the hinge of every question

F   I am the falling tears of the sun

S   I am the eagle rising to a cliff

H   I am all directions over the face of the waters

D   I am the flowering oak that transforms the earth

T   I am the bright arrow of vengeance

Vowels/Moon signs

U	Ura	Full Moon	Apple
I	Iadh	Waning Moon	Poplar
E	Eadha	Dark Moon	Yew
A	Arda	New Moon	Silver Fir
O	Onn	Waxing Moon	Furze

Consonants/Seasonal signs

F	Forn	Spring	Alder
S	Sal	Spring	Willow
H	Hrar	Summer	Whitethorn
D	Dir	Midsummer Day	Oak
T	Tren	Summer	Holly

Some conjectural interpretations of the rune designs

SPRING is indicated by a rising-sun motif, perhaps representing growth or the coming of light.

 S appears as an eagle rising.

 F shows a rising arrow shape, which may, in a stylized fashion, represent rays of light.

SUMMER is indicated by a circle, representing the sun.

 T represents both the pointed holly leaf, and the "arrow of vengeance".

H shows, essentially, a compass rose, indicating "all directions".

 D represents midsummer, indicated by the circle within a circle. The curving line is less clear, but could refer to an oak leaf or, more abstractly, it could imply growth and transformation.

VOWELS are represented by signs that refer to the phases of the moon.

 A represents the New Moon by virtue of a dot on a vertical line. An arch shape could indicate a hill.

 E represents the Dark Moon; a circle within a circle possibly indicates a lunar eclipse. The rest of the sign is unclear, but may represent uncertainty.

 I shows a familiar crescent shape referring to the waning moon. The horizontal line supported by two uprights probably represents a cliff.

 O again utilizes a crescent, this time suggesting a waxing moon. The upward arching T form could indicate leaping (cf S), or may represent the womb.

 U represents the full moon – note that the circle is fully enclosed within a leaf shape, which differentiates it from the summer symbols where the circle binds the other elements. The surrounding shape could be a generalized fruit symbol.

1   Jacqueline Allison's monumental and pioneering study of the
     histories of Edil-Amarandh, *The Annaren Scripts: History Rewritten*
     (Mexico: Querétaro University Press, 1998) remains the standard
     reference, and I have drawn from it considerably in these notes.

2   In the context of Annaren naming, Maerad's Truename would
     have been considered nonsensically grandiose. Annaren naming
     systems generally based themselves on place names (eg, Dringold
     of Fort) or occupations (Dirrik Dhurinam translates literally
     from the Annaren as Handfast Horsebreeder). Surnames as we
     understand them were unknown. In the Seven Kingdoms, the
     most common were systems of patronymics or matronymics
     ("son of" or "daughter of"), although there were no hard or fast
     rules. Bardic usenames were much more formalized: Bards were
     always named after the School in which they were instated or (in
     the case of the First Bards) the School over which they presided.
     Bards' Truenames were kept secret and so very few are extant in
     the records: what little we know suggests that they were generally
     one-word names, with no qualifiers. Maerad was unique in that,
     because of her particular triple identity, her Truename was gener-
     ally known but it could not be used against her. (*Naming Systems of
     Edil-Amarandh*, unpublished monograph by Cyril Atlee, 2002)

3   Lanorgil of Pellinor (N307). Lanorgil was the first great historian
     of the Bards.

4   For much of the information about the Pilanel I am indebted to Joan
     Corbett's essay "Pilanel Society" in *Genealogies of Light: Power in Edil-
     Amarandh* ed. Alannah Casagrande (Chicago: Sorensen Academic
     Publishers, 2000) and also to Jacqueline Allison's *The Annaren Scripts:
     History Rewritten* (Mexico: Querétaro University Press, 1998).

5   See *Pilanel Society* by Joan Corbett (ibid)

6   *Dhillarearën Rulers among the Pilanel*, Anarkin of Lirigon (N345)

7   *On the Howes of the Pilanel*, Belgar of Gent (N17)

8   Book 5, *Naraudh Lar-Chanë*, Maerad of Pellinor and Cadvan of
     Lirigon, Library of Busk (N1012)

9   The only possible exception is in the Suderain, whose civilization
     predated the Restoration by several millennia. There, as Camilla
     Johnson has argued in her paper "Idols of Light: Aspects of
     Religious Worship in the Suderain of Edil-Amarandh", delivered
     at the inaugural Conference of Edil-Amarandh Studies at the
     University of Querétaro, Mexico in November 2003, the Elidhu
     and the Light were often conflated as objects of worship or respect,
     and she has conclusively demonstrated that in Turbansk there was
     a Cult of the Light, with its own shrines and rituals and even gods.
     This tendency led, in the later years of the Restoration, to a certain
     distrust between the South and Annar.

10   Across Annar, the fealty to the Light and the Balance served
     as what we might recognize as an organized religion, and it is
     tempting, but I believe a little misleading, to see the Bards as the
     equivalent of priests, with the concept of the Light serving as a
     substitute for God. It was, more properly, a complex and evolv-
     ing system of ethics, grown over millennia from the days of Afinil
     and preserved through the Great Silence, to be reinstated during
     the Restoration. To a contemporary eye, many of the Bards' most
     important documents seem unsettlingly modern. The idea of
     canonical texts received straight from the Godhead would have
     been treated with ridicule by Bards, who were pragmatically
     historical in many of their studies. Their belief in prophecy, for
     example, was not connected to a belief in a God who foresaw
     everything, but to a certain set of theories about time: Bards
     believed that linear time was illusory, that the present was co-
     existent with all other times, and Seers were those Bards able to
     pierce the veil of the present and perceive its multiple realities. See
     Knowing the Light: Comparative Studies in Annaran Spiritual Practice,
     ed. Charles A. James (Oxford: Cipher Press, 2001) and also *The
     Ethics of Balance: Ecology and Morality in Annar* by Jennifer Atkins
     (Chicago: Sorensen Academic Publishers, 2003).

11   Tulkan of Lirion, a Bard of Afinil, wrote one of the most popular

lays, but it was only one of innumerable variants on this theme.
Tulkan's is particularly attractive, as it is written in the complex
metrical pattern known in Old Lironese as *inel-fardhalen*. It is
notoriously difficult to translate, as Old Lironese had many more
rhyming words than Annaren. Old Lironese was little used in
Lirigon after the Restoration, as most people spoke Annaren, but
Cadvan of Lirigon was a famous scholar and translator from this
archaic tongue and made the most widely quoted translation.
The song is worth quoting in full, for its insight into the nature of
Ardina as much as its own virtues, and here is my own translation
from the Annaren.

> When Arkan deemed an endless cold
> And greenwoods rotted bleak and sere
> The moon wept high above the world
> > To see its beauty dwindling:
> To earth fell down a single tear
> And there stepped forth a shining girl
> Like moonlight that through alabaster
> > Wells, its pallor kindling.

> Such beauty made all beauty dim
> And homage called from voiceless stone:
> Like whitest samite was her skin
> > Or seafoam softly glimmering:
> A star that lit the night alone
> She stepped the winter woods within,
> A pearl a-glisten in the gloam,
> > A moonbeam fleetly shimmering.

> Then wild amazement fastened on
> The Moonchild's heart, and far she ran,
> Through all the vales of Lirion

Her voice like bellnotes echoing:
And from the branches blossom sprang
In iron groves of leafmeal wan,
And Spring herself woke up and sang,
    The gentle Summer beckoning.

She passed into the mountain keeps
Where stormdogs guard the ravined walls,
A moonbeam piercing dismal deeps,
    Down jagged ridges clambering:
Until she found a crystal fall,
A river frozen in its leap,
And in its depths a marble hall
    Of lofty spires was trembling.

In wonderment she silent fell,
And stood before the wall of glass
Enraptured by the citadel,
    Its endless, sparkling mullions:
Like lilies caught in sudden frost
Which grow no more, but comely still,
Forlornly cast those towers of ice
    Their cold and lifeless brilliance.

She knew not that the hours passed
Nor noticed that the darkness fell;
And as she looked, she thought at last
    Her heart must break with heaviness:
She wept, though why she could not tell:
For love unborn, for beauty lost,
For all that lives and breathes and will
    Grow cold and lose its loveliness.

And in the icy halls a king
Woke from his spellbound sleep and saw
A vision of the banished spring,
    A form so fair and luminous
That from his frosted eyes the hoar
Ran down like tears and, marvelling,
He felt the chains of winter thaw
    And years of thraldom ruinous.

Ardina met his eyes, and through
Her moonlit veins a shudder ran
That kissed her skin with fiery dew,
    Its marble pallor chastening:
A doom it seemed to see this man
In whose dark eyes such ardour grew,
A grief stored up through summer's span
    From joy to winter hastening.

Between them stood the wall of ice
And round them barren winter waste,
But each saw in the other's face
    The light of springtime lingering:
Like thunder broke the charméd frost,
And freed at last to bitter bliss
Immortal maid and man embraced,
    Their light and shadow mingling.

So swore Ardina and Ardhor
That ever would the other cleave,
And heavy was the doom they bore
    In war and clamour perilous:
Through grief and death they passed alive
To meet on the immortal shores

> And still in starry glades their love
> Shines ever strong and sorrowless.

12 Book 2, *Naraudh Lar-Chanë*, Maerad of Pellinor and Cadvan of Lirigon, Library of Busk (N1012)

13 *The Elidhu in Afinil* by the Bard Menellin, Library of Norloch (A1505)

14 *The Enemies of the Light*, Piron of Il-Arunedh, Library of Thorold (N562)

15 *The Symbolism of the Treesong Runes*, by Professor Patrick Insole, Department of Ancient Languages, University of Leeds. Unpublished monograph, 2003.